LORD HAW-HAW

LORD HAW-HAW

The Full Story of William Joyce

J. A. Cole

faber and faber
LONDON · BOSTON

First published in 1964 by
Faber and Faber Limited
3 Queen Square, London WC1N 3AU

This new paperback edition first published in 1987

Printed in Great Britain by
Richard Clay Ltd, Bungay, Suffolk
All rights reserved

CONTENTS

Contents

FOREWORD

When this book was first published in 1964, the majority of readers had lived through the Second World War and could remember the German English-language radio broadcasts. Later generations may find it difficult to appreciate how startling it was for people to hear the enemy's voice in their homes. Although, during the crisis year before the war, both the British Broadcasting Corporation and the German radio organization, Reichsrundfunkgesellschaft, broadcast in each other's language, their bulletins sounded improvised, enjoyed no monopoly of news while foreign correspondents were working in London and Berlin, and aroused little more than a mild curiosity. When war was declared, however, a craving for news became intense.

On both sides during the war sound radio was the main form of amusement (cinema and theatre-going being complicated by the black-out, poor transport and raids) and the principal source of up-to-date news. The infant television services, not yet emerged from the novelty stage, were suspended, and radio, unchallenged, entertained and informed civilians at home, in factories and air raid shelters, and the fighting forces wherever they were. The war was fought to a background of radio noises. In Germany one of the sounds was the jamming of enemy broadcasts, but this interference was only partly effective. The British did not resort to jamming; in fact, in the early days of the war British newspapers published, alongside information about BBC programmes, the times of the enemy's news bulletins.

Listening to hostile broadcasts in Britain never, therefore, brought with it—as it did in Germany—the awful thrill of breaking the law and risking severe penalties. German broadcasts were openly discussed by everybody in Britain, frequently mentioned in Parliament, answered by the BBC in its domestic services, extensively written about in newsapers, and parodied by comedians.

Attempts were made, largely by newspapers, to persuade the public to laugh them off, and during the so-called Phoney War some of the German propaganda was so inept as to be funny. But a bizarre phenomenon occurred which worried the British authorities as hostilities developed. The existence of the German broadcasts, as distinct from their contents, preyed on an apprehensive public and occasioned the greatest wave of rumours that ever swept the country. The First World War had its share of rumours, of which the best remembered are the Angels of Mons, who reinforced the hard-pressed British Army, and the Czarist Russian reinforcements who landed in the north of England en route for the Western Front and were recognized as Russians by the snow on their boots. While these revealed dismay at British setbacks, they caused the Government no concern; indeed, if believed, they boosted morale. The rumours of the second war were quite different. However it may blur the picture of the steadfast and imperturbable British under threat it cannot be denied that the belief in alarming stories attributing omniscience to enemy broadcasters was a symptom of acute anxiety. The voices from Hamburg and Bremen acquired a collective personality, Lord Haw-Haw, who in the course of time became incarnated in the person of William Joyce.

Joyce now enjoyed the largest audience that an English-speaking Fascist has ever had, an achievement arrived at with a rapidity he could never have foreseen when he so optimistically founded his tiny National Socialist League in London. His definition of National Socialism is quoted in Chapter 7, from which it is clear that he was no serious political theorist—a type more at home in libraries than on platforms. In thought and style Joyce was an agitator; the term National Socialist meant whatever he said it meant, and he expressed himself in extravagant language unusual in British political controversy. With his characteristic manner he got under the nation's skin and he probably qualifies in Britain as the most hated man of the Second World War.

His trial was sensational because of the possibility that his unexpected defence would succeed, and the judge's ruling in his case extended the law of treason.

Even his execution did not appease British anger, and an extraordinary viciousness characterized much of the writing about him. As though to reassure themselves that he was not so alarming after all, some writers have tried to dismiss him as a social reject, a crook and a buffoon. A desire to wreak a literary revenge on Joyce was, I suppose, natural enough in the immediate post-war period, but what was written in anger soon came to look spiteful and even absurd.

Shortly before his death Joyce expressed the view that his life provided material for a book, and this is one of the few points at which his opinions and mine coincide. But although he hoped his biography would be written, he would not have expected someone who differed from him so fundamentally to do it. To people who were surprised that I did it, I have explained that my original interest was in rumour and the aggressive conviction with which it is retailed. The Reichsrundfunk staff were puzzled when they read in the British press what their speakers were reported as saying. They were to learn, as even uncontroversial broadcasters do, that what is spoken into the microphone can be mysteriously transformed as it is heard on the domestic receiving set. Joyce was the outstanding speaker in a team whose pronouncements sent listeners' thoughts rushing distractedly along dark tunnels in the psyche. It seemed to me remarkable that no one had researched such a fascinating aspect of the war. And so (aided by the odd kind of coincidence which so often pushed Joyce this way and that) I came upon the track of this tantalizing man, who was so unlike the stereotype which fear and prejudice had created.

Although my views on Joyce would probably have sent him into a temper-tantrum, he would, I think, have been gratified that his name has endured while so many once-prominent ones have faded. It is impossible to imagine the Second World War without him.

Chapter 1

THE MERRY JOYCES

The Joyces have imprinted their name on the map of Ireland—
an area north of Galway is marked Joyce's Country. I have seen
varying versions of how they became established there. That
favoured by William Joyce started with a Norman family named
Joyeux going to England with William the Conqueror. In the
twelfth century two descendants, brothers called Joyce, set out
under Earl Fitzgerald for Ireland. One got no farther than Wales;
the other went on to Ireland, arriving in 1172 and founding a
branch of the family styled the 'gentlemen Joyces', whom
William Joyce claimed as his ancestors. Descendants of the
Joyce who stayed in Wales migrated to Ireland in the reign of
Elizabeth I; these later arrivals were known as 'the tinkers'.

A modern standard work, *Irish Families*, by Edward Mac-
Lysaght, makes no reference to the gentlemen or the tinkers but
mentions the first Joyce of whom there is authentic record in
Ireland as Thomas de Jorse or Joyce, a Welshman who in 1283
married the daughter of O'Brien, Prince of Thomond, and went
with her to Galway. The Joyces, who were known for their exceptional stature, got on very well there, pushing out the
O'Flahertys, to whom they were at first tributary, and eventually
dominating the territory which still bears their name. They were
one of fourteen prominent families who proudly accepted the
opprobrious title of 'the tribes of Galway' applied to them by the
Cromwellian forces. They produced some distinguished men,
including three archbishops, three founders of the Dominican
College at Louvain, several mayors of Galway City, an historian,
a nineteenth-century poet-physician who worked in the United
States, an American revivalist preacher, and the author, James

Joyce. The description of the Joyce coat of arms is: 'Argent an eagle with two heads displayed gules, over all a fess ermine', the crest 'a demi-wolf argent ducally gorged or'; not everyone of the name is entitled to bear it.

Perhaps the eagle in the coat of arms commemorates the rôle played by eagles in two picturesque legends about the Joyces (whom he heard called the merry Joyces) related by the Reverend Caesar Otway in *A Tour in Connaught* published in 1839. Crusading against the Saracens, a Joyce was guided by an eagle to the buried treasure of a defeated Moorish king. Thus acquiring great wealth, he endowed churches and strengthened the Galway town wall. The other story tells how Margaret, the daughter of a John Joyce, became rich by being twice married, the first time to a Spanish merchant who left her a widow of means, and then to Oliver Oge Ffrench, a Galway trader and smuggler in a substantial way of business. She financed bridge-building. While she was watching her masons at work an eagle dropped a strange and beautiful single-stone ring at her feet.

Today the name Joyce is very much in evidence in and around their traditional territory; over four out of five of the Joyces in Ireland come from Galway or Mayo. A comment on the prevalence of the name locally led me into a misunderstanding with a hotel receptionist in Connemara. I had remarked that Joyce was a common name in that area. 'They're not common,' she said reprovingly. 'They're the famous Joyces.'

Michael Francis Joyce, the father of William, was born in Mayo in 1868. He was, of course, a British subject by birth. At the age of twenty he emigrated, like many young Irishmen, to the United States. On 22nd July 1892 he began the passport history of his branch of the Joyces by signing a formal declaration that it was 'his bona fide intention to become a citizen of the United States, and to renounce for ever all allegiance and fidelity to any and every Foreign Prince, Potentate, State and Sovereignty whatever, and particularly to the Queen of the United Kingdom of Great Britain and Ireland, whose subject he has heretofore been'. His naturalization was completed after he had sworn, on 25th October 1894, a petition repeating this renunciation and undertaking to support the constitution. A friend named John Duane certified that the petitioner had 'behaved himself as a man of good moral character, attached to the principles and Constitution of the United States and well disposed to the good order and happiness of the same'.

Michael Joyce had every reason to be well disposed to the United States. In the tradition of his fabulous forebears he had become a builder, and although no eagles had led him to buried treasure or dropped a ring at his feet, prosperity had come his way through a building boom.

He had been an American citizen for about ten years when, paying a visit home, he became engaged to Gertrude Emily Brooke of Shaw, Lancashire, who had been born at Crompton, Lancashire, in 1879. Her father, a doctor belonging to a Northern Irish Protestant family, and her mother did not wholly approve, because Michael Joyce was a Catholic. In 1905, accompanied by her brother Edgar, a solicitor, she went to the United States. She and Michael Joyce were married on May 2nd that year, according to the rites of the Roman Catholic Church, at All Saints Church, Madison Avenue and 129th Street, New York. Their first son was born, a United States national, at 1377 Herkimer Street, Brooklyn, on 24th April 1906. The mother wanted to call the child William Brooke Joyce, but the father objected and registered the birth in the name of William Joyce. At the christening at a Catholic church, however, Gertrude Joyce got her own way. Only the family and a small circle of friends knew the son's full name.

Later in the same year a schoolfriend of Gertrude Joyce arrived in the United States with her husband, Frank Holland, a civil engineer. They visited the Joyces at the end of the year and saw the eight-month-old baby, William. The two families exchanged visits regularly. On the advice of Michael Joyce, Frank Holland determined to become an American citizen when he had fulfilled the residence qualification.

William Joyce claimed to have memories of his life in New York up to the age of three. He certainly had an unusually good memory, but it is more probable that he heard his parents' recollections of how he had played with English, German and Danish-speaking cousins there. He also thought that he could remember refraining from uttering babyish monosyllables and from talking until he could put words together to form a coherent phrase.

In 1909 Michael Joyce, travelling on a United States passport, returned to Mayo. His wife, with her three-year-old son, followed him after a few weeks. The family never went back to America. Why Michael Joyce made this move it is useless now to speculate. Probably his reasons were simple enough. He had done well in business and accumulated capital which, although modest in New York, would be a fortune in Mayo and Connemara. Many people feel the pull of their birthplace, and nobody in the West of Ireland, where bureaucratic formalities were never held in high respect, would bother about his American citizenship.

At first he lived in Ballinrobe, County Mayo. Despite his wife's disapproval, he was for a while a publican. In 1913 he moved to Galway, where he acquired house property and became the land-lord of barracks occupied by the Royal Irish Constabulary. The family finally settled at 1 Rutledge Terrace, Rockbarton, Salthill. Still standing, this is a two-storey comfortable-looking house, with a tiny walled garden, in a pleasantly-secluded position just off the promenade.

The child was lively and enterprising. While on a visit to Shaw at the age of four he crept downstairs at night and ate some cheese and smoked the butt of a cigar. The resultant sickness gave him an aversion to cheese, but not to tobacco. He showed cunning, tricking an older cousin, a greedy bully, into eating salt by pre-tending to like it himself.

He was educated at Catholic schools, starting at a convent at the age of six and going on to the Jesuit-run St. Ignatius Loyola College where (as he was accustomed to recall) the staff and the boys were tough, Latin was supreme, and an excitable Latin master banged boys' heads on a radiator. William's best subjects were Latin, French and German. He was a gang-leader, com-bative, argumentative, impatient, and inclined to an excess of enthusiasm, as when, assisting at a service in the chapel, he swung the censer with such vigour that the glowing incense was scattered down the aisle.

While fighting another boy he suffered a broken nose. He had rather short arms, which put him at a disadvantage, but the handicap did not deter him from accepting a challenge. On this occasion a schoolfellow had called him an Orangeman—a stan-dard insult among Irish Catholic schoolboys. The Orange Society, an Irish Protestant organization 'to maintain the laws and peace of the country and the Protestant constitution', was formed in

1795 and called after William of Orange. Later known as the
Orange Order, it opposed Irish home rule. William did not report
his injury. As a consequence of the delay in treatment his nose
could never properly be put right and his voice acquired a nasal
tone.

Games were not a fetish, and his participation ended when,
early in his school career, he was sent off the rugby field—one is
tempted to see something prophetic in this—for not knowing
which side he was on. He was taught to sail by fishermen in
Galway Bay. That and skating seem to have been the limit of his
sporting achievements.

His mother kept the pledge required of the non-Catholic party
in a mixed marriage to bring up her children in the Catholic
faith, but (despite tension in the home over religion) she remained
a Protestant. William, who was devoted to her, was distressed at
school by his religious preceptor's dogmatic interpretation of the
maxim *Extra Ecclesiam, nulla salus* (No salvation outside the
Church). When he asked whether this meant that his mother was
damned unless she joined the Catholic Church, he was assured
that it did. Thereafter he grew critical, he declared that he rejected the Catholic doctrine regarding the Eucharist, and his
precocious disposition to theological controversy became apparent
to the Jesuits. He was summoned to an interview by the Bishop of
Galway; the Bishop made as little impression on William as
William on him.

The preceptor responsible for his leaving the Church thought
highly of the boy's ability, and made to his mother a typical
schoolmaster's prediction concerning the future of a bright but
awkward pupil: 'That boy will either do something very great in
the world, or he will finish on the end of a rope.'

In words which William Joyce wrote twenty years later there is
perhaps the hint of an apology for his obstreperousness. 'I went
to school in Ireland where the Jesuits, with whom I had differences, gave me the benefit of their splendid educational system.
However recalcitrant I may have proved in some matters, I have
good reason to be grateful to them for what they did for me.'
He had less reason to be grateful that his upbringing had implanted in him a feeling of guilt about sex.

In the political conflict the Joyce household was united. His
father and mother were fervent supporters of the British Govern-

ment against the Irish rebels. Michael Joyce's devotion to the Crown is difficult to reconcile with his earlier renunciation of his loyalty to the Queen and his failure to regain his British nationality. None the less, he was staunchly pro-British; the Galway County Inspector of Police described him as 'one of the most respectable, law-abiding and loyal men in this locality and one who has been consistently an advocate of the "pro-allied" cause since the beginning of the war'.

This tribute was written in answer to a letter from the Chief Constable of Lancashire who had asked why Gertrude Joyce (whom he called 'this alien') had not registered her departure from Shaw, where she had been with her husband, William and the second son, Francis, on family business following her father's death. Michael Joyce, who preceded her, had correctly notified his departure. Instructed to investigate, Sergeant Bernard Riley of the Royal Irish Constabulary had interviewed Michael, who thought that he had lost his United States citizenship through being absent for over two years without registering and who considered that his nationality was now British. When the County Inspector wrote his letter based on Sergeant Riley's report, he observed that 'there seems some doubt whether these people are aliens at all.'

No such doubt troubled the Chief Constable of Lancashire, who knew that nationality has nothing to do with where your heart is but depends on having your name in a register. Not bothering to argue, he wrote a polite but firm note. 'In view of the fact that Mr. Joyce was admitted to American nationality and has not been re-admitted to British nationality, I must treat his wife as an American subject. I should be much obliged if you would kindly cause Mrs. Joyce to be cautioned for the offence she has committed against the provisions of the Aliens Restriction Order.'

The caution was administered on 8th July 1917. Michael Joyce now learned, if he had been vague about it before, that he was not a British subject.

The rebels' fire-raising caused serious losses to Michael Joyce as a landlord, and he never received compensation. The spectacle of his father's burnt-out properties was bad enough for William Joyce to contemplate, but there were worse sights. In the twilight, walking along a familiar path, he came upon a dead police-

man, a neighbour, with a bullet hole in his head. He saw a Sinn
Feiner pursued by police, cornered and shot dead. The memory
of these two incidents haunted him all his life.

In 1920, the situation rapidly deteriorating, the British Government reinforced the Royal Irish Constabulary with two para-
military forces hastily recruited from ex-service men, the Black
and Tans (a name given them by the Irish after a famous breed
of hounds, because they wore part khaki service dress and part
police uniform) and the Auxiliary Division Royal Irish Constabulary (which enrolled ex-officers). Some of the Auxiliary
Division appeared in Galway, a major rebel centre, in August of
that year.

There is no need here to repeat or add to the judgements which
liberal opinion has passed on the behaviour of these supplementary police forces. The widely expressed condemnations would
not have been endorsed by the Joyce family, who naturally
welcomed the reinforcements. William Joyce at this time gained
his first experience of active participation in politics. In his brief
life political controversy had been carried on by means of guns,
grenades and drums of petrol. He was ten at the time of the
Easter rebellion and the tragic events which Irish writers have
been working over ever since were for him the pattern of everyday life. When the Auxiliaries arrived he himself was able to take
a part; he became an informer, or, as he himself put it, he 'served
with the irregular forces of the Crown in an Intelligence capacity,
against the Irish guerrillas'.

The term informer has a dubious ring; working 'in an Intelligence capacity' sounds much better, although in this case it
amounts to the same thing. William Joyce, with a tact which he
did not invariably display, chose the more respectable description when he later applied to join the Officers Training Corps, but
I cannot see that there was anything discreditable in providing
information for his own side. He had been brought up pro-
British, here were British forces of the swashbuckling type
likely to fire a child's imagination, and he served them in the only
way he was able. Although young, he could have been useful—or
at least no less useful than the general run of agents. The
qualifications for Intelligence are not easily definable and they
vary from job to job; in the kind of conflict then going on in
Ireland a boy could have been better than an adult at eaves-

dropping and trailing suspects. No doubt there was a certain amount of play-acting—he claimed to have been 'in charge of a squad of sub-agents'—but play-acting is not unknown in Intelligence operations on a higher level.

His services were not used for long. The truce came on 11th July 1921, recruiting for the Royal Irish Constabulary ceased on the same day, and the Black and Tans and Auxiliaries began withdrawing in October. On both sides the extremists felt that they had been betrayed.

Perhaps, now that so much time has passed since 'the troubles' and we have grown accustomed to the spectacle of nationalist movements securing their countries' independence from imperial governments, we can, whatever our views, understand the bitterness of those 'loyal' citizens who see the home government concluding agreements with the rebel leaders whom it has formerly imprisoned. They, who have stood for law, order and the established authority, become an embarrassment to the government which has abandoned them and objects of reproach by the progressive-minded for not perceiving sooner that the insurrectionaries had been right all the time and were bound to triumph. Sick of the long, squalid guerrilla struggle, the abdicating power no longer likes to be reminded of the existence of those who risked their lives and lost their property for a now outdated cause.

The Joyce family had remained obstinately loyal to the Crown, and so Michael found it expedient, their protectors having gone, to remove them to England. About fifteen years later, relating the story of their departure from Ireland, William told close acquaintances that he had left ahead of his family because his Intelligence activities were known to the Irish Republican Army, and that he had travelled on a British passport (which stated his birthplace as Galway) issued with the connivance of the then Foreign Secretary to ensure that he, a United States citizen, could enter England without formalities. No record of this document exists at the Passport Office and he never made a written claim to having owned it, so it is puzzling that he should have put this tale about at a time when he actually held a British passport, obtained in 1933 by the usual means, to which his right had not yet been challenged. Was he simply adding a sequel to the inflated account of his Intelligence work, or is there another explanation? By pretending to have had an earlier passport he

24

could have been supporting a claim he sometimes made to have visited Berlin in the 1920's. Or he might have been priming his friends with a story in case he were prosecuted for having obtained a passport illegally.

His landing in England on 8th December 1921, two days after the Anglo-Irish Treaty was signed, is no proof that he held a passport then, because all he would have needed was a boat ticket. An idealistic and passionately patriotic schoolboy, highly intelligent, fair-haired, blue-eyed, strongly built although not following his forebears in being of exceptional stature, an earnest rather than a merry Joyce, he came 'home' to dedicate himself, unfashionably, to King and Empire, convinced that only those sharing his experience knew the meaning of loyalty and understood that one surrender could lead to others.

Chapter 2

THE SCAR

Although not yet sixteen, William Joyce started to serve the Crown without delay. He enlisted at Worcester in the regular Army, giving his age as eighteen and explaining, when his birth certificate was demanded, that he had never had one as the authorities in Ireland were less meticulous about the registration of births than were those in England. Any allegation of anarchy in Irish administration was certain to be believed by the English, although acts requiring the registration of births had been in force in Ireland, as in England and Wales, since 1837.

The other recruits, he said later, found him a queer fish. They thought his patriotism very funny, and they were delighted to discover that by whistling the national anthem they could get him to leap out of his cot and stand to attention. After a while his sense of humour asserted itself, and nocturnal performances of 'God Save the King' failed to make him turn out, but he had had his first insight into the post-war mood of the British.

He soon developed rheumatic fever, through, he believed, wearing damp denims. In hospital his real age was discovered, and on recovery he was discharged. His Army service had lasted four months.

It is difficult to think of William Joyce acquiring that attitude of amused contempt for the military life, skill in dodging work, ability to spend long hours doing nothing but gaze out of a window on to an empty yard, which characterize the professional soldier in peacetime. As a non-commissioned officer he would have been unpopular for his unnatural willingness to undertake irksome duties and refusal to overdraw rations, and if he had applied for a commission he would have made selection boards nervous by his verbal facility. But for William the Army had not lost its attraction and he determined to become an officer.

By now his family had settled in Lancashire, and were living not as aliens but as British subjects, although Michael Joyce had done nothing to regain his nationality. William, however, was uneasy about his. He had procured a copy of the *University of London Officers Training Corps Handbook*, and in acknowledgement he wrote, on 9th August 1922, a letter, which has been much quoted, to the Officer Commanding the London University O.T.C. He opened by expressing his desire for a regular Army commission, mentioned his Intelligence service in Ireland (in the terms quoted in Chapter 1), and claimed a knowledge of the rudiments of musketry, bayonet fighting and squad drill. Then he tried to forestall trouble about his nationality.

He wrote: 'I must now mention a point which I hope will not give rise to difficulties. I was born in America, but of British parents. I left America when two years of age, have not returned since, and do not propose to return. I was informed, at the Brigade Headquarters of the district in which I was stationed in Ireland, that I possessed the same rights and privileges as I would if of natural British birth. I can obtain testimonials as to my loyalty to the Crown. I am in no way connected with the United States of America, against which, as against all other nations, I am prepared to draw the sword in British interests. As a young man of pure British descent, some of whose forefathers have held high positions in the British army, I have always been desirous of devoting what little capability and energy I may possess to the country which I love so dearly. I ask that you may inform me if the accident of my birth, to which I refer above, will affect my position.'

When reading this letter, the oldest available example of his prose style, one should remember that he was a sixteen-year-old schoolboy who had been brought up in a country where people are naturally voluble and not averse to picturesque and flamboyant phrases. It already reveals him as an orator. That cliché about drawing the sword, the modest reference to 'what little capability and energy I may possess', and his unashamed profession of love for the country may raise a smile when read, but they are phrases a platform speaker could use effectively. The way he followed up his claim to have worked in Intelligence by

27

converting the town where his parents lived to 'the district in which I was stationed in Ireland' was worthy of an experienced propagandist. His claim to be of pure British descent is interesting because of his later readiness to explain people's actions by their blood—when arrested after the Second World War he attributed his affection for Germany to German blood in his veins. By his reference to forefathers who had held high positions in the British Army he presumably meant the Brookes. The small inaccuracy about his age on leaving America (he was three and not two) probably reflected his father's vagueness.

By what it omits the letter demolishes his story that he had entered England from Ireland with a British passport. Surely his argument that he was British would have been strengthened by his production of that document. Instead he quoted an assurance given him at Brigade Headquarters, a curious place to issue a ruling on an individual's nationality.

London University O.T.C. replied in prosaic terms. Like the Chief Constable of Lancashire, the officials needed papers properly completed, so they merely sent him an enrolment form to fill up after he had matriculated.

He passed the London Matriculation examination later in the same year and registered as a student at Battersea Polytechnic. On October 21st he returned the O.T.C. enrolment form to London University. He entered his place of birth as New York, his permanent address as 10 Longbeach Road, London, S.W.11, his previous military service as 'Worcestershire (four months)' and stated his preference for the infantry unit. Then the adjutant of the O.T.C. wrote to Michael Joyce in Oldham: 'Your son William Joyce has seen me with a view to joining the University of London O.T.C., and has also spoken of his desiring to register as a candidate for a Commission in the Regular Army. It appears, however, that he is in doubt as to whether he is a "British subject of pure European descent". From what he tells me I think he comes within this definition, as he says you were never naturalized as an American. Perhaps therefore you would confirm this point, when I shall be able to proceed with his enrolment and registration.'

Michael Joyce, who lacked the colourful epistolary style of his son, replied on October 26th: 'Your letter of 23rd October received. Would have replied sooner, but have been away from

The Scar

home. With regard to my son William. He was born in America, I was born in Ireland, his mother was born in England. We are all British and not American citizens.'

The University O.T.C. authorities were satisfied with this equivocal letter, which ignored the question the adjutant had asked. William Joyce was enrolled in the O.T.C.

He passed from Battersea Polytechnic to Birkbeck College (a college of London University) in September 1923. In him the College O.T.C. gained an ardent member and an earnest propagandist for its object, which was, as he wrote, 'to enable educated and intelligent men to discharge, in case of need, their military debts to the State, and in a way more useful and congenial than service in the ranks would permit'. His description of the benefits was quaintly pre-1914: 'The bodily health is improved, as the action of the mind is quickened, by a graduated course of military education, calculated to develop the powers both of self-control and the command of others.' But even when he was being persuasive, he could not resist taking up a dogmatic and aggressive attitude. His appeal to possible recruits was prefaced: 'To many of the ultra-democratic minds of today militarism seems incompatible with the worship of the fetish known as Progress.'

While following the intermediate B.A. course in Latin, French, English and History (he passed in all subjects at the examination in June 1924) he became politically active. On 6th December 1923, at Battersea, he joined a group formed that year by Miss R. L. Linton-Orman, a member of a distinguished military family, who was alarmed by the internationalism and what she thought the class-war tendencies of the Labour Party. Registered in 1924 under the style of British Fascisti Limited, her association was to constitute a body of patriotic citizens, distinguished by a black handkerchief in the breast pocket, who would resist revolution. Local units, including some formed of women, were to deal with 'Bolshevik activities' in their own districts, and if they failed to suppress the Russian-type soldiers' and peasants' councils which they appeared to visualize emerging in Essex villages, there were plans for national mobilization. The older members were people in comfortable circumstances who feared that their property and way of life were menaced, and the younger men were the plus-fours wearing blacklegs who used to intervene ineffectually in strikes. No one could have thought the

Fascisti anti-capitalist and, whatever their private views, they were not officially anti-Semitic, but they appealed to Joyce because of their strong-arm action against the Left at the rowdy political meetings then common.

On the evening of 22nd October 1924, William Joyce, in charge of 'I squad' of the British Fascisti, stationed his men inside the Lambeth Baths hall in South-East London in preparation for an election meeting in support of the Unionist Parliamentary candidate for Lambeth North, Jack Lazarus. A senior official of the Fascisti had warned Joyce that 'the Reds' were going to demonstrate, so the squad was expecting violence. The candidate must have known the kind of meeting he was going to have when he saw those strange allies waiting to protect him from Jewish Communists.

The anticipated fracas developed and turned out to be vicious. According to Joyce's account, a Jewish Communist jumped on his back and tried to cut his throat with a razor. The razor missed his throat because he was wearing a thick woollen scarf, but he was slashed across the right cheek from the corner of his mouth to behind his ear. He did not realize what had happened until the crowd drew back in horror. Someone handed him what he later described as 'a filthy handkerchief' to staunch the wound, and he walked to a police station, where he collapsed. With another casualty, a man who had been hit on the head with a bottle, he was taken to Lambeth Infirmary. The name of William Joyce made its first appearance in the newspapers next day. According to one London evening paper, which published a picture of him bandaged in a hospital bed, there had been 'a scene of mild disorder' and Joyce was not on the danger list; another reported 'wild scenes by hooligans' and described his condition as critical.

His assailant was not identified, and there is no proof that the man was a Jew or that he intended to cut Joyce's throat. In razor-carrying circles face-slashing is a more frequent form of assault than throat cutting. If the man had meant to murder Joyce, he was running an unnecessary risk in attempting to do so in a crowded hall. Probably he was simply a thug, attracted to the meeting by the certainty of a fight. Whatever his intention, Joyce was left with a terrible scar to add to that other memento of battle, his broken nose.

The month when Joyce received his wound saw a split in the

The Scar

British Fascisti over how much violence was permissible. The president, a retired brigadier-general, and his solid-looking associates condoned scuffles when the Fascisti could pretend to be maintaining public order, but they looked askance at militants who advocated an offensive policy involving illegalities. The more aggressive members seceded to form the National Fascisti, whose aims were to keep Britain racially pure, repress all subversion except their own, and consolidate the Empire economically. It was not their programme but their actions which gave them notoriety, one of their much-publicized exploits being to drive away a van loaded with copies of the *Daily Herald*, which they chose to regard as a revolutionary paper. Joyce did not join this break-away (those who did were not his sort), but he attempted on his own to reform the British Fascisti by drafting regulations for a proposed disciplinary court; so that an accused could not get off, he included the clause: 'The court shall have the power to define an offence.' When on trial for his life he was to recall, with grim amusement, this attempt at law-making to the disadvantage of the defendant.

At Birkbeck College he was president of the Conservative Society and a frequent speaker in the College Parliament, which he addressed fluently in loud tones and an overbearingly dogmatic manner. Members commented on his soapbox style. He once brought a Hyde Park orator of strong nationalist views to speak at the College. His contemporaries did not notice that Joyce was anti-Semitic but he was acutely race-conscious, seeing the Conservatives (to quote his own words) as 'the upholders of Anglo-Saxon tradition and supremacy'.

Habitually he wore that uniform of illegal armies, a dirty trench coat with the belt pulled tight, but he seized every opportunity to appear in khaki. The first time he attended Miss Marjorie Daunt's English class, he was wearing his O.T.C. uniform and carrying a rifle. He sat alone in the front row, with his rifle across his knees, and stared at her. The scar was new and vivid, and occasionally that side of his face twitched. She thought: 'If he's as mad as he looks he may well stand up and shoot me.' After the lecture she told him that if he must bring a gun into the room he was to place it in the corner.

Joyce's English essays were remarkable for their purple passages. Warned that if he hoped to pass his examinations he would have to learn to write reasonably, he took the advice very well and modified his style so that it became unexceptionable, but this discipline had no effect on his speech and his other writings. His vocabulary and outlook were revealed in some 'Verses to an Impolite Reformer' written in the style of Pope, which he contributed to the College magazine, *The Loadstone*, in the spring term of 1927, as an attack on an Irish student's article on modern writers.

> *. . . that impious reptile Shaw,*
> *And Arlen, Pandar, 'gainst all virtue soured,*
> *And sickly, putrid, maggot-eaten Coward.*
> *Away with livid plays of modern sex,*
> *Eradicate, destroy, efface 'complex'!*
> *In days when martial valour was appraised,*
> *They loved a duel or a standard raised;*
> *But now Hypocrisy and Humane Cant*
> *Transform the soldier's honest blows to rant.*

The Irish student reacted sharply to a jibe in the verses at the Emerald Isle—'Mr. Joyce has been unable to restrain himself from gratuitous rudeness concerning a nation the shoes of whose lowliest peasant he is unworthy to unlace'. Another student protested that 'the proper place for such ill-bred and unprovoked effusions is the editorial wastepaper basket,' and the writer of an article described the poem as 'a remarkable farrago of nonsense and abuse'. Nobody wrote in Joyce's defence.

The over-enthusiastic boy who spilt the ashes in the chapel aisle had not changed. When the English class put on one of the lesser-known sixteenth-century plays, Joyce was cast in the character of a traveller armed with a stick who had to beat off two footpads. In rehearsing the fight Joyce grew so excited that he laid about him regardless of his fellow actors' safety. One of the footpads lost a tooth and the other was knocked off the stage. Both complained that Joyce's behaviour was impossible and demanded his removal from the cast. In the Birkbeck Players' performance of Jonson's *The Alchemist* Joyce was suitably typecast as Kestrel, and *The Loadstone* critic commented: 'We shall not easily forget the very beardless pink cheeks of the "angry boy".'

Miss Linton-Orman's fears had not been justified. No village soviets appeared, not even in 1926 during the General Strike, and with no revolution in sight members forsook the British Fascisti, the president resigned and subscriptions fell. The organization had permitted Joyce to reconstruct the pattern of political controversy as he knew it, with the subversive Jews substituted for the rebellious Irish; he had even become an informer, passing information about Communists to a British Intelligence officer; but he now saw that the Fascisti were declining. At this time he was very busy. Having passed in his subsidiary subject, History, in 1926, he was working hard for his Finals while earning money by part-time tutoring. He was, too, planning to marry an attractive girl, Hazel Kathleen Barr, as soon as he came of age.

They were married a week after his twenty-first birthday. Neither party belonging to a church, the ceremony took place at Chelsea Register Office.

After his marriage Joyce became, for a while, more sociable and less belligerent. He and his wife invited some of the Birkbeck staff and students to tea, he was a pleasant host, and the visitors' impression was that he was much happier. They felt sorry about his scar, although Joyce did not seem to mind it, because it both altered his otherwise boyish appearance and, when the right side of his face twitched, gave his voice a momentarily menacing note.

Joyce obtained First Class Honours in English at the degree examination in June 1927. Responding to Miss Daunt's advice to do some research, he began with a short note on vowels which was published in volume IV (1928) of *The Review of English Studies* under the heading 'A Note on the Mid Back Slack Unrounded Vowel [a] in the English of Today' and dealt with 'the value of the sound known vulgarly as "long a" in the speech of the moment'. By now Joyce seems to have dissociated himself from his Irish upbringing. 'As a Northerner', he wrote, 'I am keenly sensitive to the difference between the Low Front Slack [æ] of Received Standard and the corresponding sound, as in "hat" heard in the North.' A later contributor commented: 'Mr. William Joyce raises a problem of great interest in English phonetics.'

At that time Miss Daunt was working on London English before 1425. In the course of her research she had seen documents from all over the country which were no use for her purpose, so she put Joyce on to look at the language of the Ancient

Petitions in the Record Office, with a view to taking an M.A. degree. Joyce discovered that wherever the petition came from, the main body of it was in London language and only odd words were local; this showed a fact of some interest to scholars—the spread of respect for London English through law. Either the local notaries had learned the formulae, or the petitions had been sent to London and the documents written there. The material, however, was not nearly enough for an M.A. thesis. As his tutor, Miss Daunt intended to suggest widening the field, but Joyce apparently lost interest and drifted away.

Despite his successful career there, he seems to have wanted to break with Birkbeck. On leaving he had planned to become a secondary school teacher; with the recommendation he could have had from the College, if he had asked for it, he would have found a position without difficulty. Yet he never asked for the College's support, and he appeared at interviews in his old trench coat. Ideas of another kind of career were forming in his mind. His anti-Semitic fantasies were developing too. To explain his failure to proceed with his research, he made the groundless allegation that his material had been appropriated by 'a Jewish woman tutor'. The only tutor to whom this charge could apply was the one who had given him much help and encouragement, and to whose sympathy and kindness he had responded by inviting her several times to his home. She was not Jewish, as he must have known. He had already adopted the practice, which he later used so widely, of making people honorary Jews when it suited his argument to do so. From now on his political development was to consist broadly of the accumulation of what he considered evidence against Jewry and the sharpening of his polemical weapons to combat the chosen enemy.

On 30th March 1928 he applied to be considered for the Foreign Office. The normal rule was that candidates should be born 'within the United Kingdom or one of the self-governing Dominions', but this could be waived by permission of the Foreign Secretary, and he was allowed to proceed with his application. Applicants were then required to appear before a Board of Selection at the Office of the Civil Service Commission, which decided whether to recommend that they be permitted to take an examination. Joyce was one of a batch interviewed by the Board on May 1st and 2nd. He was rejected and told of the result in a letter dated May 4th. Following a long-standing policy, the Civil Service gave no explanation of why Joyce had not been recommended, and there is no record of the Board's grounds. If the Board decided that he was not the right type, even the strongest critics of their selection methods could not dispute their conclusion on this occasion.

This episode, like the story of the special passport, was incorporated by Joyce into a fantasy which he later related with every appearance of telling the truth. In his version he took the examination and passed it brilliantly, only to be told at a subsequent interview that Foreign Office salaries were so low that officials could not fulfil their duties and live as they were expected to if they had no private means. As in his writings, Joyce is here revealed as a stranger to English life; his England belonged to the nineteenth century, or at the latest to the period before 1919, and he never seems to have revised the view of it he formed in distant Galway. If the Board had given him a reason for his rejection, his lack of a private income would not, in 1928, have been the one advanced.

At about the time he applied to the Foreign Office he decided to give the Conservative Party a chance of being reformed. Marriage might seem to have inclined him to orthodoxy, but he had his own ideas of Conservative policy and he tried to introduce what he called 'the doctrine of true Nationalism'. His efforts, he confessed, 'met with the ignominious failure that they deserved', by which he meant that he had been misguided to waste his time on the Tories. Already he was a man with a mission. Had he been a calculating careerist he would have conformed and used his considerable powers of oratory to flatter the membership and the leadership. But his message was urgent, and when, after two years of promoting his policy, he saw no sign that the Conservative Party would alter its course at the bidding of a twenty-two-year-old man, he abandoned it. Even then his type of nationalism (which amounted to Sinn Fein for Britain) would have been found extreme by most Conservatives, and he was putting an increasing barrier between himself and other politicians by his developing anti-Semitism. It may help to make his later utterances intelligible if I remind the reader that anti-Semites are not simply people who dislike Jews for their faces, trading practices, ritual slaughtering technique, or other characteristics, real or imaginary. Although aversion to Jews is exploited in anti-Semitic propaganda, anti-Semites do not merely agitate against Jews as undesirable citizens, but hold that they are engaged in a conspiracy of world domination, in which some of them operate as Wall Street financiers, others as Communists, and yet others (whose purpose is to disarm the victim races by destroying their national cultures) as economists, historians, psycho-analysts, composers of contemporary music and as non-representational artists. Substitute dollar imperialists for Jews as the enemy and the resemblance to the Communist mentality is close. He could as a Communist speaker have been equally facile.

By now, although still attracted to the military life and having Certificate A from the O.T.C., Joyce had given up the idea of an Army career. In 1928 there seemed little future in the armed forces and he could not, as a soldier, have followed his destiny. What he needed now was an instrument. When Lord Rothermere's United Empire Party passed briefly across the political scene he thought it 'an interesting trend', but he was cautious, and his hesitation lasted until the United Empire Party expired. British Fascists Ltd. ('Fascisti' had been dropped as 'foreign') was near its end. He was not attracted by a rival movement, the Imperial Fascist League, a self-styled élite of defenders of racial purity; he thought the founder, Arnold Leese, was mad. Soon he was closely observing that political phenomenon, Oswald Mosley.

Chapter 3

THE FATAL PASSPORT

Born ten years before Joyce, educated at Winchester and Sand-hurst, Oswald Mosley served in the Army and the Royal Flying Corps in the First World War before entering politics. With his wealth, name, good looks and intelligence he was quickly off the mark, being elected, when only twenty-two, to Parliament as a Coalition-Unionist (a Conservative supporter of Lloyd George, the Prime Minister). Mosley, like Joyce, was a man with a mission but he discovered, as did Joyce (starting a long way lower down), that an established party does not capitulate to young men, how-ever gifted. Ill at ease as a Coalition member, objecting strongly to the employment of the Black and Tans in Ireland, he crossed the floor of the House, sat as an Independent, and became a nationally-known political personality by winning his own con-stituency in the 1922 election against Conservative opposition. A Socialist trend became perceptible in his speeches; his first wife, formerly Lady Cynthia Curzon, held Socialist views.

Dazzled and flattered, adoring titles and riches, the Labour Party welcomed him, not reflecting that a man with a mind of his own would prove even more uncomfortable to Labour leaders than he had to Conservatives. Eighty constituency Labour Parties (according to A. K. Chesterton in *Oswald Mosley: Portrait of a Leader*) competed for him as their candidate. He rose rapidly; the apprenticeship which Labour demanded of its proletarian supporters was not required of him. He won a place on the Party Executive and in 1929, when Ramsay MacDonald formed his second Labour Government, he was given the sinecure of Chan-cellor of the Duchy of Lancaster so that he could devote himself to assisting J. H. Thomas, the Lord Privy Seal, in tackling un-employment. 'I'm afraid I never had any use for Thomas,'

Mosley said later, a remark which arouses a certain sympathy. Energetic, advancing novel-sounding ideas, Mosley poured out memoranda without moving his bewildered minister, the squabbling Government or the aloof Treasury. The Cabinet, that pathetic repository of Socialist hopes, rejected his draft emergency programme written (with advice from J. M. Keynes, the economist) in collaboration with his Labour colleagues, George Lansbury and Tom Johnston. Resigning in disgust from the Government, he placed his memorandum before the Labour Party annual conference, a gathering ill-adapted to rational consideration of anything; wildly applauded though he was for his advocacy of it, the vote went against him. Still inside the Labour Party, he formed a Mosley Group.

Then he created his own New Party. The name was almost enough to kill it. Its proscription by the Labour Party frightened off most of his remaining Labour following; internal dissensions quickly weakened it; and some adherents became understandably nervous of the muscular youth club members who, acting as Mosley's bodyguard, glared challengingly at audiences. Before it could set up proper constituency organizations the 1931 ('bankers' ramp') general election was held, almost in conditions of panic, the Labour Party suffered an ignominious defeat, and Mosley and his twenty-three New Party candidates received such insignificant support that he sought another approach.

Beyond denouncing the 'Old Gangs', propounding economic nationalism and proposing to clip the functions of Parliament, Mosley had made no imperative appeal to Joyce. Busy as a whole-time tutor at the Victoria Tutorial College, Joyce had become a Licentiate of the College of Preceptors and, his studies for this examination having aroused his interest in educational psychology, he was thinking of taking a Ph.D. He called on the secretary at Birkbeck, his old college, where Dr. C. E. M. Joad was then head of the Philosophy and Psychology Department and enjoying great eminence.

About this interview he related a characteristic anecdote. The secretary rejected him, he said, with the remark: 'No, Joyce! Anything but that! We can't take the responsibility of having Joad and you in the same department.' The secretary, who had no authority to refuse a student admission, was merely remarking jocularly on the difference between Joad's and Joyce's political opinions, but Joyce chose to assume that Joad had to be protected from a rival philosopher.

He was accepted at King's College, where he worked part-time under Professor Aveling, for whom he acquired a profound respect.

Another of Joyce's stories dates from this period. His Intelligence contact, he said, sounded him on whether he would go to Germany as a British agent, become naturalized there and join the Nazi Party. That the Intelligence service, with its not very ample resources at that time, was preparing to plant a long-term agent in a party many people thought had no chance of power, seems unlikely; it is improbable, too, that an Intelligence officer studying Communist activities in London would also be recruiting an agent to penetrate a political party abroad or, if he were putting out a feeler for another department, that he would reveal the whole plan in advance. The Intelligence officer, who played a part in Joyce's fateful decision in 1939, cannot be called to say whether the story has any basis.

Joyce was now without any political attachment and uncertain where to turn. The romantic marriage was turning out badly, partly because of his unpredictable moods. He did not see himself settling down to teaching and bringing up his two daughters, when it was his mission to fire the British with a sense of their destiny. Mosley was to provide him with the platform he needed.

In January 1932 Mosley visited Mussolini in Rome. The Italian Fascists, ten years in office, were a possible model for a politician disillusioned by democracy and not attracted to Moscow. Joyce read the news of this trip with interest but he thought that all Mosley could usefully study in Italy was the way to seize power; what the Italians had done in office was not to be copied, as they had failed to introduce the corporate state and they seemed blind to the Jewish menace. Nothing more was to be expected of Wops, Joyce supposed. A rising politician named Hitler was more to his taste.

But at this time Mosley was Joyce's only hope. Nobody else in England seemed capable of welding the cranky little Fascist groups into a movement. Mosley's first step was unsuccessful; his invitation to like-minded organizations to amalgamate in the New Party under his leadership was rejected by all of them (Miss Linton-Orman could never have brought herself to support an ex-Labour Member of Parliament), but when Mosley dropped the New Party and, on 1st October 1932, founded the British Union of Fascists, the defections from the other bodies were numerous and British Fascists Ltd. went out of business altogether, being compulsorily wound up on a petition by the guarantor of its overdraft.

Still Joyce did not rush. He held back until a friend reported favourably on the new organization. All the top jobs were filled by the time he joined, but not by stuffy Tories and he knew that the way up would be less obstructed.

To most Fascist members the Leader and the public attitudes he struck were probably more important than a programme, but to appeal to an electorate accustomed to political programmes there had to be a statement of aims, which Mosley supplied in *The Greater Britain* and several other publications. He wrote in the knowledge that he was free of conferences that could turn his statement down, yet as an experienced politician he was more aware of the British public than was Joyce, who scorned persuasion and for whom *The Greater Britain* was only a pale sketch on to which he was going to splash some stronger colours.

It was, for the most part, a reasonably presented case intended to reassure the nervous. 'Fascism, as we understand it, is not a creed of personal Dictatorship in the Continental manner,' Mosley declared. Nor would it be oppressive. He did not share, he made plain, that attachment to regulations which had kept wartime restrictions in force. *'The plain fact is that the country is hag-ridden.'*

In the now familiar manner of totalitarian parties he adopted the pose that their use of violence, when it occurs, is made inevitable by the behaviour of opponents. 'If the situation of violence is to be averted, the Old Gang Government must be overthrown and effective measures must be adopted before the situation has gone too far. The enemy today is the Old Gang of parliamentarianism. The enemy of tomorrow, if their rule persists much longer, will be the Communist Party. *The Old Gangs are the architects of disaster, the Communists only its executors.* Not until the Old Gangs have muddled us to catastrophe can Communists really operate; so, in the first place, the enemy is the Old Gang, and the object is the overthrow of their power. To achieve this by constitutional means will entail at a later stage a bid for parliamentary power.' But if the situation rapidly degenerated before parliamentary power had been attained, 'other and sterner measures must be adopted for the saving of the State in a situation approaching anarchy. Such a situation will be none of our seeking. In no case shall we resort to violence against the forces of the Crown; but only against the forces of anarchy if, and when, the machinery of state has been allowed to drift into powerlessness.'

Mosley declined to dogmatize about the future but he went so far as to envisage the reconstitution of Britain as a corporate state, with the electorate represented primarily on an occupational instead of a residential basis and all forms of business activity, including finance, the economic development of the Empire, and the operations of employers' and workers' organizations becoming part of the state machinery.

There was some oratory. 'The essence of Fascism is the power of adaptation to fresh facts. Above all, it is a realist creed. It has no use for immortal principles in relation to the facts of bread-and-butter; and it despises the windy rhetoric which ascribes importance to mere formula. The steel creed of an iron age, it cuts through the verbiage of illusion to the achievement of a new reality.' He took his revenge for past sufferings in a contemptuous reference to 'organizations of old women, tea-fights and committees'.

Beyond a fleeting mention of the Rothschilds in the section on finance, there was no reference to Jews. Deploring this omission, Joyce determined to push British Fascism towards anti-Semitism.

In the expectation—finally unrealized—of accompanying the Leader to visit Hitler, Joyce acquired a British passport by making a false statement about his place of birth. Knowing that he was not a British subject, he disregarded the notice: 'Applicants, and persons recommending them, are warned that should any of the statements contained in their respective declarations prove to be untrue, the consequences to them may be serious,' and on 4th July 1933 signed this declaration: 'I, the Undersigned, William Joyce, at present residing at 41 Farquhar Road, S.E. 19, London, hereby declare that I am a British subject by birth, having been born at Rutledge Terrace, Galway, Ireland, on the 24th day of April, 1906, and not having lost the status of British subject thus acquired, I hereby apply for a passport for travelling to Belgium,

France, Germany, Switzerland, Italy, Austria for the purpose of holiday touring.' The formula, 'holiday touring', is a convenient one, and no doubt Joyce, looking forward to the five years of its validity, hoped to spend holidays in some of the countries he had named; at that time he did not need to consider its implication that the holder of the passport intends to be only temporarily absent from Britain.

His photograph accompanying the application showed a thin face with the scar very perceptible (he mentioned it in the space for 'Visible distinguishing marks or peculiarities'), unusually prominent ears, and a clumsily-knotted tie. He overstated his height as 5 feet 6½ inches and gave his occupation as 'Private Tutor'.

A birth certificate is not required of applicants for British passports; they are simply warned about the consequences of an untrue statement. All that is needed is for the declaration to be verified by a person in one of a number of categories; in Joyce's case a bank official countersigned the form.

From the Passport Office he received passport Number 125943 dated 5th July 1933 and bearing inside the front cover words which were to acquire a terrible significance: 'We' (the Foreign Secretary) 'request and require in the name of His Majesty all those whom it may concern to allow the bearer to pass freely without let or hindrance, and to afford him every assistance and protection of which he may stand in need.'

The application form and passport were packed with danger to Joyce, yet, though sensitive to premonitions, he had no awareness of having signed his own death sentence. He does, however, seem to have dwelt occasionally on his possession of the wrong passport and to have tried to justify his action. Before the war, in a private conversation, Joyce said that he had had to state his birthplace as Galway because the special passport given him in 1921 did so. But by his own action he refuted his claim to have had that passport in 1921. In the declaration he signed in 1933 he left in the clause: 'I declare that I have not previously been granted any Passport whatever, and that I have made no other application for a Passport' and he deleted the one for use by applicants returning an expired passport.

Suppose, however, that he had, by an exceptional arrangement, really received a British passport on leaving Galway although the

42

Foreign Office knew that he was a United States national. He would then have been debarred from making his application, in the form he did, in 1933, because the Foreign Office would have had a record of his nationality and would have had to decide whether to give him another special document or recommend that he register as an alien and apply for British naturalization.

I dwell on this mystery because at his trial, although no mention was made of a previous passport, there was a disposition to suppose that he may have declared himself British in the belief that he was. In fact, he consciously made a false statement, and no Foreign Secretary had put him in the position of having to do so. It was his father who, by insisting that he himself, his wife and his oldest son were British, set the son on the wrong track. In a futile gesture, Michael Joyce burnt his naturalization certificate; the only result was to give the defence at his son's trial a little more trouble. The longer William went on the harder it was to turn back. He went through the O.T.C. and the University as British, he claimed a Parliamentary vote and he engaged in political activities which, although legal, were potentially subversive. If his nationality had been discovered, he could have been expelled from Britain, a thought which must have been humiliating and painful. Yet he had to have a passport to leave and re-enter the country; if he wanted a British one, he had either to confess or make a false statement. He chose what may have seemed then a negligible risk. The chances are that if he had simply used his passport for holiday touring he would have escaped detection, at least until the war.

Unwittingly he had embarked on a course which was to raise an important legal question. As an alien holding a British passport what, if any, were his obligations to the British Crown while he was outside the realm?

The British Union of Fascists went further than the British Fascisti had done in providing Joyce with a familiar milieu. It created a para-military headquarters in Chelsea. The membership was mixed, ranging from scholarly idealists and eccentrics to the types Joyce would have known in the Black and Tans and the Auxiliaries, whose political outlook allowed of no ideological doubts or hesitations, who were convinced of their own natural supremacy, and who believed (as they demonstrated on occasion) that the arguments their opponents best understood were twisted arms and blows. In the yard stood military-looking tenders, ready to carry strong-arm squads to skirmishes and orators to their pitches. They could not, it was true, roar through the streets firing guns, as their prototypes had done in Ireland; the incendiarism and the ambushes were missing, and no one needed to view such sights as the spattered brains which haunted William Joyce; but the Fascists' demeanour was sufficiently warlike to create a stir among Saturday-afternoon shopping crowds. There was a similar atmosphere of an Intelligence war—the rumours brought in by informers, the fear of penetration agents.

Self-confident, willing to face any kind of meeting, Joyce rapidly distinguished himself from the toughs who were fit only for scuffles with the 'Reds', or with those whom they undiscriminatingly chose to regard as Reds. Competent speakers are rare in any party; Joyce's personality, vigour and wit were as welcome in a new movement as they would have been unwelcome in an established one. Soon, from talking at street corners, he graduated to deputizing at meetings for the Leader; to be a successful understudy to such a star performer was a severe test for a comparatively inexperienced orator, but he passed it triumphantly when, Mosley being ill with phlebitis, he addressed a rally at Streatham on 20th November 1933, and six days later faced an audience of over five thousand at Liverpool Stadium.

He rapidly became such a figure in the organization that, disregarding the well-meant warning of one Fascist official against adopting such a hazardous career, he resigned from the Victoria Tutorial College and abandoned his studies at London University to become West London Area Administrative Officer. Within a year of joining he was the Propaganda Director at the, for those days, respectable salary of £300 a year.

In this post he did not spare himself. A. K. Chesterton wrote of him: 'William Joyce, brilliant writer, speaker, and exponent of policy, has addressed hundreds of meetings, always at his best, always revealing the iron spirit of Fascism in his refusal to be intimidated by violent opposition.'

Here, as recorded in the preface to a pamphlet by Joyce, is the impression he made on John Beckett, the former Labour Member of Parliament who had acquired notoriety by attempting to remove the mace during a stormy sitting at the House of Commons.

The Fatal Passport

'I first met him in 1933 at a great and crowded meeting in Paddington Baths. I had left political life in disgust some years previously, and as I was much impressed with the Fascist creed a friend had been urging me to join the Mosley organisation. I asked who else they had to lead beside Mosley, and was taken to Joyce's meeting as an answer to this query. I have heard all those men who are claimed amongst our greatest speakers. Within ten minutes of this 28 year old youngster taking the platform, I knew that here was one of the dozen finest orators in the country. Snowden's close reasoning and unerring instinct for words were allied with Maxton's humour and Churchill's daring. That great audience assembled to hear a speaker quite unknown in the political world and the enthusiasm created was an eye-opener to me, and would have been to most of the Westminster hacks with whom I had previously associated public influence.'

A different kind of witness is Cecil Roberts, who heard Joyce at a political dinner at the Park Lane Hotel, London. Roberts was writing after the war, and thus in the knowledge of Joyce's later career, but even allowing that his recollection may have been coloured, how many speakers are there whom one remembers for months, let alone years? This vivid portrait of Joyce in action appears in *And so to America*. 'After dinner we adjourned to the ballroom in which a member of the British Fascist hierarchy was to make an address, in the unavoidable absence of Sir Oswald Mosley. I did not catch the name of the speaker, a person utterly unknown to most of us, I think. Thin, pale, intense, he had not been speaking many minutes before we were electrified by this man. I have been a connoisseur of speech-making for a quarter of a century, but never before, in any country, had I met a personality so terrifying in its dynamic force, so vituperative, so vitriolic. The words poured from him in a corrosive spate. He ridiculed our political system, he scarified our leading politicians, seizing upon their vulnerable points with a destructive analysis that left them bereft of merit or morality. We listened in a kind of frozen hypnotism to this cold, stabbing voice. There was a gleam of a Marat in his eyes, and his eloquence took on a Satanic ring when he invoked the rising wrath of his colleagues against the festering scum that by cowardice and sloth had reduced the British Empire to a moribund thing, in peril of annihilation.

'When the speaker finished, his white face luminous with hate,

45

the chairman announced that questions might be asked. But no questions were asked. The audience sat paralysed by that flood of vituperation. I felt as if I had seen something unclean, so fearful in its cold frenzy that one blanched, asphyxiated in so nauseous an atmosphere. . . .'

Joyce's after-dinner speech was part of a campaign to get at influential people. Robert Forgan, the Deputy Leader, had already helped to found, in 1934, the January Club to appeal to intellectuals. Members were interested in Fascism but they were not required to be supporters and a respectable appearance was given to the organization by the appointment of Sir John C. Squire, the editor of the *London Mercury*, as chairman. Joyce was a member and on several occasions a speaker. He cultivated well-to-do persons who might contribute to the British Union's funds. These included a north country department store proprietor, an eccentric country squire, and a stockbroker named Alec Scrimgeour. He also made attempts to stimulate interest at Oxford and Cambridge. Groups were formed, in the way that undergraduates adopt new enthusiasms, but their activities were sporadic, and the Fascist appeal to youth evoked little response.

No small part in publicizing the British Union of Fascists was played by sections of the press. The support of Lady Houston and her *Saturday Review* was of brief duration because of the movement's undiplomatic treatment of her; but her paper had little circulation. Nor did the help of the *English Review* mean much. The great newspaper-reading public learned about British Fascism from the Rothermere press. The Labour Party, twice in office, had never been presented to so many readers in such terms of encouragement. Many Fascists, however, looked askance at Lord Rothermere as an ally. 'He imagined, it seems,' wrote A. K. Chesterton, 'that Mosley was a Right-Wing Tory, instead of a Fascist revolutionary, and that his movement existed to bolster up big business in Britain. Incalculable harm was done by this intervention, and the large influx of recruits which resulted proved almost useless to a man.' The approval of this newspaper group was withdrawn in mid-1934 when Lord Rothermere perceived the movement's growing anti-Semitism. Advocacy of Fascism became increasingly difficult for newspapers as the personality of Hitler began to make its impact, readers realized that violence was becoming a normal feature of political meetings, and Jewish firms threatened to withdraw their advertising.

The public was jolted into consciousness of what was going on by the statements made by many well-known people who attended a Fascist rally at Olympia, in London, on 7th June 1934. Nothing like this meeting had previously been witnessed by such a large audience—fifteen thousand tickets had been distributed. Mosley, spotlighted, stood in isolation on the stage, his voice enormously amplified. At any interruption searchlights focused on the interrupter, Sir Oswald paused, the Blackshirts round the hall roared in chorus: 'We want Mosley!' and the nearest squad advanced on the heckler and violently ejected him or her and anyone else who protested at such treatment. Victims dragged out of public view were so brutally handled that some became unconscious and many had to be treated in hospital.

Public men who were far from having sympathy with the supposed 'Reds' were outraged. One Conservative member of Parliament called it a 'deeply shocking scene', accused the Blackshirts of behaving 'like bullies and cads', and after referring to the 'decent and orderly political life' in his and other constituencies, deplored the introduction into England of 'this vile bitterness, copied from foreign lands'. Other Members of Parliament, and well-known writers, clergymen and doctors expressed themselves in similar forthright terms.

British Fascists, like those on the Continent, never admitted that this association of political meetings with vicious brawls was part of a campaign to destroy democratic procedures. It was essential to their purpose to appear as guardians of law and order suppressing Red anarchy. Not long after the Olympia meeting Joyce unsuccessfully attempted, at Bow Street, to prosecute the *Daily Worker* for incitement to violence.

Mosley's illness had given Joyce the chance to appear as chief speaker at larger meetings than a young and unknown politician could have drawn, and he deliberately used his opportunities to try to run away with Sir Oswald and the British Union. Goebbels not Mussolini was his model, and a German Nazi audience would have felt at home listening to him; in policy he marched several steps ahead of the Leader. He was marching, physically, beside him when a fracas occurred at Worthing resulting in their appearance, with two other Fascists, in the dock at Lewes

Assizes in December 1934 on a charge of riotous assembly. Having held a meeting at Worthing Pavilion, the Fascists had marched through the streets and fighting had broken out. Witnesses' accounts were confused and no allegations were specifically made against Joyce. For the defence Sir Patrick Hastings (a former Labour M.P.) submitted that there was no case to answer and the defendants were discharged. The pre-war Fascists had no reason to complain of their treatment by British courts.

These were good days for Joyce. He made speeches, gave policy lectures to recruits, ran speakers' classes and wrote for Fascist papers. Divisions had not yet widened in the movement, all was new and exciting, and—although he thought him still too cautious—he was proud to be so close to the man who was going to shape Britain's future.

'We know that England is crying for a leader,' he told a Brighton audience in 1934, 'and that leader has emerged in the person of the greatest Englishman I have ever known, Sir Oswald Mosley.'

Chapter 4

'WHENCE CAME YOU?'

Propounding the steel creed of an iron age, Sir Oswald made an exhilarating impression on a young woman who had come to his meeting in Carlisle out of curiosity. He talked as though he meant what he said, his hair sometimes getting quite dishevelled and his voice hoarse as he did so. Fascist orators had broken the convention of moderation and courtesy towards political opponents, and the young, to whom politeness tends to sound like hypocrisy, found it releasing to hear a man speak of his opponents as though he thought them evil. The immediacy of his message was reinforced by the presence of the jaw-jutting Blackshirts, who looked prepared to take over the town hall at a word of command.

Margaret Cairns White, pretty, vivacious, and only twenty-two, daughter of a Lancashire textile warehouse manager of Irish descent and a mother whose maiden name was Bardo (the family tradition was that she had an Italian ancestor called di Bardi, one of whose grandsons had served as a captain under Nelson), was then a secretary employed by Morton Sundour Fabrics. Hers was not one of those politically stable Labour, trade union and Co-op Lancashire families, but that socially aspiring kind to which the Fascist mixture of respectability and revolution is peculiarly palatable. She had gone political window-shopping, even having a look at the Communists and being put off by some of their sleazy, alien types, but had come upon nothing so smart and invigorating as Sir Oswald. Personal ambition had little or nothing to do with her search for a party; her pay was fair at a time when people counted themselves fortunate to have work at all, she was a good dancer and never lacked boy-friends; she went to church (high Anglican); in fact, she was not embittered or frustrated but a normal, good-natured, intelligent girl who saw depression and wasted lives around her and wondered that the human race did not manage things better.

In her own phrase, Sir Oswald 'put into words all I had been trying to think'. Elated, she signed an application form for membership of the British Union of Fascists. After that nothing happened until she had a chance street encounter with a black-shirted girl Fascist and through her came to know others who were also waiting for headquarters to perform the mundane business of registering their names. Political parties clamouring to be allowed to run the country seldom demonstrate their administrative capacity in their own offices. Ultimately a small branch was formed and visited by an official from London looking for likely speakers. Margaret White, clear-sighted about her own capacities, was reluctant, but she was better than the others and she found herself taking the platform with an unintended frequency, going through the crushing experiences essential to a party worker's training (she candidly admitted having been completely floored by a Communist interrupter), and on one alarming occasion standing up valiantly to gentlemanly heckling by Sir Edward Spears, the local Conservative Member of Parliament.

Brushes with opponents determined her to improve, and on a holiday in London her first call was at the British Union headquarters for speakers' notes. Two debutantes were staffing the reception desk when she arrived and, in the penetrating tones of their kind, tossing about the name of Major Yeats-Brown. This classy barrier surmounted, she met Lady Mosley, Sir Oswald's mother, made the acquaintance of John Beckett, acquired a lot of printed matter and returned to Manchester with renewed faith.

Shortly afterwards, her political affiliation having become known in the firm, she was invited to debate with the son of the head of Morton Sundour Fabrics. An invitation of this kind could not be accepted, under British Union rules, without headquarters' permission, so she applied as a formality, only to receive a curt refusal signed by the Propaganda Director, William Joyce, whose photograph she had seen in *Fascist Week*. Affronted, she and her fellow members began that game, so popular with the branches of political parties, of writing acrimonious letters to head office. In the course of this correspondence they suggested that Joyce should address them.

Inside the Fascist movement his name now had considerable pulling power, and his programme was too full for him to agree. Learning that he was booked to speak in Dumfries on 7th February 1935, they hired a bus and went to hear him.

They arrived late in Dumfries, and Margaret was further delayed by a conversation outside the hall with the local Fascist propaganda officer. When she entered the meeting Joyce was already speaking.

Quietly she closed the door behind her, surveyed the nearest rows to find the most conveniently placed empty seat, and tiptoed forward.

Abruptly the black-uniformed orator interrupted his speech. She saw that he was looking at her, not angrily, as a speaker might at a latecomer who disturbed his train of thought, but steadily, as though he had forgotten the meeting. They might have been alone and he waiting for her. She had entered with no sense of foreboding and with no concern beyond that of not making a noise. Now two blue eyes were staring fixedly at her. Involuntarily she stopped. The silence became painful. Heads turned in her direction. With embarrassment rising to fury, she stared back resentfully at the man who had written her the curt letter and who was now making her the centre of attention. She forced herself to move towards the chair she intended to occupy. The silence continued, broken only by coughs and shuffling feet while Joyce regarded her thoughtfully. Feeling foolish and mystified, she sat down, and again looked into his eyes. He seemed to be waiting until she was settled.

Suddenly this curious episode was ended. He ceased to look at her, tilted his chin and began to talk as though there had been no interval. Heads swung towards him. Her cheeks burning, she sat looking straight ahead.

From his correspondence she had expected the Propaganda Director of the British Union of Fascists to be aggressive, but she had in no way been prepared for what she now saw and heard—a man charged with energy, dominating the audience so that everyone else there seemed subordinate to him and only half alive, raking the rows of listeners with his oratory, stirring them with his fierce scorn, suddenly arousing a burst of nervous laughter with his vicious wit.

People who saw Joyce over ten years later, ill-fed, recovering from wounds, escorted by taller than average men, described him as small, puny and insignificant, the little man whose sense of his physical deficiencies had driven him to a monstrous self-assertion and exhibitionism. The legend of his smallness has now become firmly established, and his size diminishes each time the recollection of him is revived. 'Was This Dwarf Really Lord Haw-Haw?' asked the *Evening Standard* in a headline on 8th December 1959, accompanying the question with a picture of a man who would have been brusquely refused a card by a dwarfs' union. On that February night in 1935 he did not strike Margaret White as small and frail. Nor, to her, did his pronunciation sound odd, except perhaps that there was a slight American intonation in the way he pronounced the word 'well' when pausing to think. North-country audiences are quick to resent what they think is affectation; they even tend to deride any accent differing from theirs. No one in those days rocked with laughter at the sound of his voice, as later they roared at the comedians who purported to be impersonating him.

The meeting adjourned for an interval before question time. The occupants of the platform moved to an ante-room and, by a prior arrangement, the local and visiting officials, including Margaret, joined them there. She scanned the faces for anyone she knew, hoping—after her recent unwelcome prominence—to remain anonymous in the crowd.

Joyce appeared and stood, shoulders squared, hands by his side, heels together, in the doorway. The Fascist officials turned to stare at him. Expressionless he slowly looked round the room. Margaret tried to avoid his glance, but too late. He strode forward and halted, facing her. She was tall for a woman and he was shorter than she was. The terrible scar on the right side of his face was emphasized by the lights; it aroused curiosity but not distaste. His shoulders gave the impression of strength. Margaret was aware that the people standing round were watching them. Self-possessed and unsmiling, Joyce spoke.

'Whence came you?'

The odd, archaic formulation of the question caused her to suppose it to be a quotation.

She told him her name. He did not recognize it until she reminded him of their correspondence.

'From your letters I thought you must be at least fifty!' he exclaimed. 'I imagined you as wearing glasses and carrying a tightly-rolled umbrella.'

She laughed uneasily. Then he began to speak, first about their exchange of letters, and about the reasons he had taken the line he had. He talked as fluently as he had on the platform, and under the influence of his friendly manner she lost her resentment over his staring at her when she entered the hall. The people standing round resumed their talk, leaving them in that kind of privacy which is possible in a crowd. By the time the short interval was over he and she had agreed that the future correspondence between the Carlisle branch and head office would be more harmonious.

Both publicly and privately Joyce readily expressed his views on anything, and he had the typical politician's propensity to plunge into highly specialized subjects. He had opinions on cancer research, to which he was apparently convinced he could make a contribution; he sometimes talked in scientific-sounding jargon, giving the impression that his study of science had been much more advanced than it actually was; he had even written and despatched to Dr. Goebbels, the German Propaganda Minister, a *Draft Scheme for a Scientifically Managed Currency as Adapted to the Needs of the Third Reich*, evidently believing that his layman's knowledge of economics and lack of experience as a banker had put him ahead of Germany's financial wizard, Dr. Schacht.

With the unshakable confidence of the man who had read a book he combined a phenomenal memory for facts and quotations, unusual fluency, mental adroitness, a lack of inhibitions about extravagant language and scandalous allegations, a malicious wit and a capacity for public anger. Answering questions that night he displayed all these qualities, and the meeting ended in an atmosphere that would have gratified any orator.

Going home in the bus the Carlisle Fascists felt that this was what they had joined the movement for. Their ardour, recently flagging a little because of their off-hand treatment by head office, had been revived and they were now in the same euphoric state as they had been when they signed their application forms after hearing the Leader. The man sitting next to Margaret had already decided to drive the following evening to Kirkcudbright, the next stage in Joyce's speaking tour, and he invited Margaret to accompany him. After she had accepted she remembered that she had already taken time off from the office that day. The following morning she went to work determined that nothing would stop her getting away early again.

Margaret and her companion were already seated when Joyce appeared on the platform at Kirkcudbright. If he noticed her in the audience he gave no sign. Despite his heavy programme he showed no weariness, his performance was as dynamic as on the previous evening, and during the interval he was surrounded by the admiring and the curious, all anxious to become acquainted with this political prodigy.

The two Carlisle members joined the local officials. Joyce firmly detached himself from a group of men and drew Margaret aside. Their conversation that evening was brief, but it included a suggestion that she should call on him at the London headquarters.

Her visit later that year turned out to be rather depressing. She first encountered John Beckett, who asked her to a party. She had expected that Joyce would be there but he had not been invited, and she sensed that there was discord in the higher reaches of the movement. Enthusiastic and inexperienced, she was shocked to learn that the British Union was less united than it appeared from a distance.

When she met Joyce, he was in the company of a girl whom he introduced as his daughter. Father and daughter seemed to be very attached to one another. Joyce expressed pleasure at her visit, but his manner was that of a man who has a lot on his mind, and she returned to Carlisle wondering why he had been so anxious to make her acquaintance and to have her meet him in London.

She did not dwell on the episode. Whatever strains there might be in London, the Carlisle branch was going well and absorbing a good deal of her spare time. Very tentatively she was wondering whether to get married. A young man had asked her to marry him and an older man, a doctor, seemed likely to do so at any time.

Chapter 5

SPILT CHAMPAGNE

Joyce's temperament was unsuited to the rôle of the father of a family, or the husband of a woman who wanted a stable home life. Despite his anxiety to marry as soon as he came of age, he was not interested in settling down. The haunting childhood recollections of disunity and ugly violence, his feelings of guilt, his apparent inability to make concessions for the sake of harmony, his sense of an as yet undefined mission—all this turmoil within him found expression in moods which swung irrationally from kindness to rage. When the marriage broke up each party had complaints about the behaviour of the other; what was clear was that the break was irreparable. His wife Hazel left him for another man, with his agreement taking the children with her. Some time later he started divorce proceedings.

When Margaret White called on him she did not know that she had intruded on the parting of Joyce from one of his daughters. Their mutual affection was heightened by the imminence of their farewell.

Left alone, Joyce moved into a flat with the man who had become his closest friend, a fellow British Union member named John Angus Macnab. The two found each other's company congenial and respected each other's intellect. Macnab never wavered in his regard for and his loyalty to Joyce. No one else today can give such an eloquent and intimate picture. With his permission I quote from his recollections.

'He kept no files, diaries or notes of any kind, but he could recall the date, place and circumstances of remote events and meetings with people. He never forgot a face or a name, and could give a full account, unhesitatingly, of almost anything that had ever happened to him. At intervals of years he would repeat the same account without the least variation. He could quote—always exactly—any poem he had ever read with attention, and even notable pieces of prose. As a Latin scholar his technical qualifications were inferior to my own; yet he was the one who could quote Virgil or Horace, etc., freely and always to the point, not I. He possessed no Latin books; but I have *The Oxford Companion to Classical Literature* which he gave me as a Christmas (I beg pardon, he called it "Christtide" in the dedication! "No Popery!") present in 1937, inscribed with the following on the flyleaf: ". . . *Bacchum in remotis carmina rupibus Vidi docentem*. . . . In memory of some speakers' schools." (This is a quotation from an Ode of Horace, goodness knows how many years since he had ever read it, but the appropriateness is delightful: "I have seen Bacchus teaching poetry amid remote crags"; when he and I were the joint conductors of speakers' schools we did ourselves fairly well in the matter of drinks at times.)'

Macnab was impressed with Joyce's versatility and his wide interests. Besides his knowledge of German he spoke French fairly well and he had some Italian. He was not only gifted in mathematics but he had a flair for teaching it, and he read widely in history, philosophy, theology, psychology, theoretical physics and chemistry, economics, law, medicine, anatomy and physiology. When in 1936 he broke his collarbone while skating he applied his knowledge of anatomy to set it himself and kept it in position by proper strapping.

He played the piano by ear. German operatic music, especially Wagner's, pleased him but he could neither sing nor dance. The cinema he disliked and he was uninterested in the theatre. Although able to ride a bicycle, he looked alarmingly unsafe while doing so. He never learned to drive a car, and his inability to cope with machinery was such that he could not properly tune a radio set. Macnab dismisses any idea that he could ride—'he would have been fatal on a horse'. Chess alone among games attracted him. Playing with him, Macnab observed an unexpected characteristic.

'At chess he was strange. With his extraordinary speed of brain and his mathematical bent, he should have been first-class. He seemed to play soundly, never making a crass blunder as even good players do at times; yet he almost always lost to me who am a very indifferent player by club standards. The reason was his complete lack of aggressiveness. Occasionally he won a game from me when he had the black pieces, if I launched an unsound "blitzkrieg" attack and gambled wildly; but he never, absolutely never won with the white pieces, because he would always go on the defensive with the very first moves. In this respect he showed a curiously defeatist mentality. To beat him all one had to do was to avoid making any "howlers" and to go on pressing home the attack; he would merely defend, and never make a counter-attack. I find this perhaps the strangest thing in his whole mentality, for most people would describe him as somewhat "aggressive" in outlook—especially on the platform.'

Macnab was present when, in 1934, Mrs. Doris Chesterton (the wife of A. K. Chesterton) looked at Joyce's palm with the intention of reading it, and then declined to say anything. Recording this incident, Macnab wrote: 'I, too, had a good look at it, but I failed to see what she saw. I only remember that his head line, though beautifully clear and sharp and in other respects excellent, was extremely short, and I think the life-line was short also. The hand lines were few and simple, not a network of complicated interferences.'

In public Joyce concealed that other side of his character, the defensiveness and defeatism. He carried a stick and even his dress—uniform and trench coat—was aggressive. In 1935 he lost his luggage, including his evening clothes, and he never bothered to replenish his wardrobe completely. As the Carlisle branch knew, he was forceful not only at public meetings but within the Fascist movement. His classes, held jointly with Macnab, encouraged and inspired even those with no natural inclination to platform speaking. At every opportunity he pushed his views of what British Fascism ought to be; although opposed to merely imitating foreign movements, he strongly held that the model should be Hitler instead of Mussolini, and he introduced the term National Socialism with great frequency into his speeches and writings. Early in 1936 the British Union of Fascists renamed itself the British Union of Fascists and National Socialists, a clumsy title abbreviated in everyday use to the British Union. Not all the leading members favoured the alteration, but Joyce, who had pressed hard for the addition, plugged a slogan he had devised: 'If you love your country you are National. If you love her people you are Socialist. Be a National Socialist.'

Spilt Champagne

Joyce did his share of fund-raising but was careful, so he said, not to accept money from sources which might pollute what he considered the pure Fascist doctrine. To illustrate his determination that the British Union should pursue an unambiguous anti-Semitic policy, he related how in the summer of 1934 he had rejected an offer from a Jewish business man prominent in the tobacco trade of £300,000 for the British Fascist movement on condition that it should not be anti-Semitic. Without even consulting the Leader he replied 'with an impolite message'.

This sounds like another of Joyce's ego-inflating stories. Surely a potential contributor of such a substantial amount, which (accepting Beckett's estimate that Fascist propaganda was costing £3,000 a week) could have kept the organization going for nearly two years, would have gone straight to the Leader, who was footing most of the bills out of his private fortune, and who alone was ultimately responsible for policy. What would have been the purpose of approaching one of Mosley's staff, whose answer could not have been binding on the British Union?

Joyce left no estimate of how much money he himself raised for the British Union from the wealthy whose acquaintance he cultivated. The most regular contributor among his recruits was Alec Scrimgeour, at whose farm on the coast near Chichester Joyce spent occasional week-ends; his friendship with this supporter and his sister, Miss Ethel Scrimgeour, grew into genuine affection, although both were much older than Joyce. Their admiration of the young Blackshirt, which they did not conceal from other visitors, seems to have aroused jealousy among fellow-Fascists, who voiced suspicions that Joyce was not paying into the funds the whole of this couple's donations. From the evidence of Joyce's character it is most improbable that he would have been financially dishonest; and if he had been, the Leader could have taken disciplinary action.

His week-ends at Scrimgeour's farm, or at Ethel Scrimgeour's cottage at Pigeon Hill, Midhurst, in Sussex, were later to become part of the most pleasant of Joyce's recollections. Apart from the hospitality, he liked wooded country—he took great pleasure in contemplating trees—and he was sentimental about English rural scenes and country pubs. Scrimgeour was paralysed, and his house was run by servants from a cripples' home managed by his sister. The guests arrived for lunch, were left to themselves during the afternoon, and then assembled for supper (with champagne) and talk (with brandy). Scrimgeour withdrew early and went to bed by lift.

Sometimes the visitors sought to enliven the quiet of this Sussex farm and after the drinks generously served before and during lunch they were inclined to schoolboyish larks. One afternoon they competed in trying to catch and ride, without saddle and bridle, the fat, bad-tempered pony kept to draw a trap. On this occasion Joyce performed a feat which might have caused Macnab to modify slightly his view of his friend's horsemanship; he succeeded in scrambling on to the pony and staying on while it unwillingly trotted round the field.

In view of Joyce's later activities it is pertinent to ask whether he knew any Germans at this time. The answer seems to be that, considering his admiration for the Third Reich, he was acquainted with remarkably few. Occasionally he met Germans at parties and meetings, but he appears to have become particularly friendly with only one, Christian Bauer, a young man who spoke good English and cultivated an English appearance. Officially Bauer represented Goebbels's paper, *Der Angriff*, but he confided to Joyce that he was actually head of the Propaganda Minister's personal Intelligence service. That a journalist on a Nazi paper was primarily an agent was highly probable and, discretion not being a trait for which Germans are remarkable, there was nothing strange in his confessing his real function to Joyce. He might, of course, have had Joyce in mind as a potential sub-agent. Joyce accepted unquestioningly Bauer's claim to be on close terms with Goebbels. On Bauer's return to Germany he asked Joyce to keep in touch with him.

Another German whose acquaintance Joyce made was the bearer of a famous name, von Bülow, who married an American woman. He deserves mention here only because Joyce saw him again at a crucial period. Joyce might have met a young German whom he was to encounter later but, although they were once at the same party, they were not introduced. The man was Dr. Erich Hetzler, then on the personal staff of von Ribbentrop, the Foreign Minister.

As he was probably the most ardent pro-Nazi in Britain, I find it odd that Joyce did not go to Germany to study National Socialism in practice. It is true that he was helping to keep two daughters; none the less, fares were cheap then and a man so dedicated to a cause would surely have raised the money if he had really wanted to see how Nazism worked. The explanation, I think, is that he was not interested in the practical results of applying the idea. For him the idea was all-important; using it as a base, he attacked almost everybody—opponents because they disliked National Socialism and supporters because in his view they were not genuine National Socialists. The true doctrine was his alone.

Whatever subject Joyce discussed—poverty, housing, rents, wages, hire purchase contracts, the squeezing out of small shop-keepers by multiple stores, the plight of farmers, the importation of cheap foreign-made goods, the investment of British money abroad, the City, the indifference of the British to their imperial heritage, the need of Anglo-German agreement—was related, before he closed, to his central thesis, the two-pronged Jewish advance, by means of capitalism and Communism, towards world domination. Like any Labour speaker, he quoted newspaper stories about evicted tenants whose furniture was thrown on the pavement, and widows whose sewing-machines were grabbed by bailiffs because they could not maintain exorbitant hire purchase payments. He produced the results of his researches at the Registry of Limited Companies, pronouncing with an exaggerated foreign accent the alien names of directors and shareholders of reputedly British enterprises. He condemned aristocratic decadence and immorality like a nineteenth-century Radical agitator or the editor of a twentieth-century popular Sunday paper. For him diplomats were fops and dandies; noblemen's sons squandered their inheritances in night clubs drinking champagne with actresses and fell into Jewish money-lenders' clutches; Mayfair was a word redolent of expensive and unspeakable indulgences. He might have been a right-wing Tory when he spoke contemptuously of the leaders of the Indian independence movement. Urging that Britain must cultivate Hitler's friendship, and thus acquire as an ally against the Communist threat the most powerful nation on the Continent, he was both the realistic military commentator and the impassioned evangelist.

With their mixture of humanitarianism, revolutionary agitation, outmoded prudery, patriotism, xenophobia, slander of the powerful and respected, and academic-sounding analyses of political and economic trends, his fluent, dramatic speeches might have been justly compared with those of Dr. Josef Goebbels, and Joyce would have been proud of the comparison. Unlike a vote-canvassing politician, he did not flatter his audiences; he scolded, threatened and warned, and his appeal was for hard work, discipline and national purification. He aroused sympathetic anger in those who agreed with him; disquiet and sometimes rage in those who did not. Some who were alarmed by the revolutionary aspects of Joyce's thesis were reassured by his fervent expressions of loyalty to the Crown and the singing of the National Anthem at the end of his meetings. Joyce never shared the view (often advanced at that time) that the monarchy was a safeguard against Fascism.

The growth of Mosley's movement enabled Margaret White in February 1936 to leave her commercial job for full-time work at the Manchester branch. She found her new post more exciting and satisfying and that was enough for the moment. When she thought of the future she saw herself as getting married. Her doctor suitor was still available, and if she did not marry him there were young men who were interested.

When a fellow member who owned a sports car planned to drive to a meeting at Leeds, and offered her the other seat, she accepted without any intention of deepening her acquaintance with Joyce. From the platform Joyce gave no indication that he had noticed her, but during the usual interval gathering he discreetly contrived to invite her to see him in London before attending a Fascist rally at the Albert Hall.

On the way back to Manchester that night fog closed in on the small open car, road signs and turnings were blotted out, the driver was forced to reduce his speed to walking pace, and after long concentration on not running off the road, to confess himself lost. By the time they crawled out of the murk they were far off their route on the Yorkshire moors, weary and cold, with hours of driving before them.

A few days later Margaret fell ill with pleurisy, and feared that she would not be well enough to travel to London. When the time arrived she was doubtful whether to go, but she made the effort. The doctor who wanted to marry her was to be in London on the same day and they had arranged to lunch together. In the train she felt so weak that she regretted not staying in bed.

Common sense told her to cut her visit short, miss the rally and go home.

But having reached London she went to the British Union offices and there met John Macnab from whom she learned that Joyce was suing his wife for divorce—a piece of information she received without feeling that it had personal significance for her.

Stronger after a night's rest, but still with a convalescent's apathy, she revisited the headquarters, this time to fulfil her promise to see Joyce before the rally. John Beckett welcomed her with the announcement that they were to meet Joyce (the two men were now on good terms) in a Tothill Street bar.

Joyce was voluble, entertaining and kind. It was an amusing little interlude and she enjoyed herself. He did not want her to go.

'You know, we've never had a meal together,' he said to her. 'Not that it's essential, but let's have lunch.'

She refused because of her engagement, but Joyce was determined to talk to her again that day. A titled and rich aunt of a British Union member was giving a party that evening at her house in Mayfair, he said, immediately after the rally. He would see that she was invited.

The Albert Hall meeting followed what had now become a pattern. Police stood outside in force, opposition groups surged about chanting: 'Red front, red front, red front, united front,' and singing the 'Internationale', and Fascist stewards checking tickets at the door failed to prevent hecklers gaining entry. A bunch of young women—assumed by the Fascists to be Jewish—waved a banner and were ejected. Afterwards the Blackshirts paraded outside to defy the undisciplined Reds.

Arriving at the mansion while the more active members were still tramping the streets, Margaret was shown in by a footman. Except for John Macnab's sister, cut off from approach by a circle of young men, she knew no one there. Another manservant, with a non-committal expression, brought her a glass of whisky. She was sitting alone, sipping it and cautiously taking in the plush surroundings, when to her relief Joyce appeared with the hostess's nephew, a young man who before long was to abandon Fascism, marry a Jewess, and go to the United States.

In his deliberate, stage-hussar manner, Joyce approached Margaret, touched her arm, and drew her out of earshot of the others.

Spilt Champagne

'What are you drinking?' he asked, looking disparagingly at her glass.

'Whisky.'

'Nonsense!' He was in an exalted mood. He took her glass away, beckoned grandly, and ordered two glasses of champagne.

The young men round Miss Macnab were talking and laughing. The other guests were absorbed in conversation. When the champagne glasses were in their hands, Joyce remarked quietly that he was glad to see her again, adding immediately: 'No doubt you've heard about my private affairs.'

Margaret nodded, her attention still partly on the other guests.

'When they're settled I hope we can see each other more often.'

Had she felt stronger and less distracted by the surroundings, she might have been alerted by this sentence. As she took a sip it seemed little more than an ordinary pleasantry. No doubt they would meet from time to time. Joyce was, in fact, due to address a meeting in Manchester on the following evening. She would be there and they could talk again. She smiled in agreement. Nothing had prepared her for what he said next.

'In fact, I wondered whether you would consider marrying me.'

Spoken in an undertone, the words reached her against the accompaniment of many voices, and she felt their impact before she realized their meaning. Suddenly she was near to collapse, unable to think and not knowing what she wanted to say. This stranger who had put the question, with whom she had never been alone, was watching her fixedly.

In difficult situations she was liable to escape into flippancy. As though detached, she heard herself answering.

'Well, we can try. We can always undo it if we don't like it.'

Joyce was standing in his characteristic attitude, heels together, shoulders squared, head tilted slightly upwards, giving the solemn occasion its full value. Formally he raised his glass, waiting while she summoned her faculties to pierce the unreality of this scene. She advanced her glass towards his.

At the moment when the glasses clinked, Joyce's wrist gave a sharp jerk. Champagne splashed over her hand.

Behind his pose of polite formality he had been controlling his anxiety, and just for a second his nerves had betrayed him. His hand was firm again as, looking steadily at each other, they drank.

Suddenly Joyce exuberantly seized Margaret's hand, strode towards the hostess, her nephew, Macnab and Beckett, and—the King's Proctor temporarily forgotten—proudly announced the engagement. A confusion of congratulations and toasts followed, and smiling strangers milled round the bewildered young woman.

Faint, puzzled yet elated, as the Manchester train that night rocked through the darkness, she tried hopelessly to review the astonishing events of the evening. The next day she spent with her secret, confiding in nobody, worrying about what to tell the doctor who had lunched with her only the day before, and wondering whether Joyce was regretting his impetuosity.

Sitting among the audience she stared at the man who focused everybody's attention and tried to grasp that she was going to marry him. Whatever Joyce's private concerns, his platform behaviour was consistent, and he made a typical speech. Doubtfully she joined the official group afterwards. Joyce skilfully eluded his admirers and at once made it plain to her, by propounding plans of when and how they could meet, that his proposal was serious. In the meantime, however, he had realized the wisdom of discretion until his divorce went through, and he urged her not to tell anybody yet except a friend at the Manchester branch.

This confidant, a Fascist of the scholarly type, said: 'Well, I do hope you'll be happy, but it may be uncomfortable being married to a genius. And William is a genius, you know!'

Chapter 6

QUIET WEDDING

Occasional meetings and letters, even during the few months before the decree was made absolute, strained Joyce's patience. Overriding Margaret's objections to leaving her home and job, he insisted that she must move to London, finding an unwitting ally in the doctor who had treated her for pleurisy and who opposed her spending another winter in Manchester.

She took a bed-sitting room in the house in Bramerton Street, Chelsea, where Joyce and Macnab lived. There she was a virtual prisoner for fear that if she went about with Joyce there might be talk and the King's Proctor would intervene. In the house her presence was accepted; the landlady and the other tenants minded their own business. Whenever possible Joyce spent his evenings at home, and his two companions felt they could have no better entertainment than his conversation. After two months, Joyce finding the cost of the extra accommodation too much, the three moved to a furnished flat in Fawcett Street, which runs parallel to Fulham Road.

Through the two men's talk Margaret experienced vicariously the life at Fascist headquarters. The main excitement was the Abdication, when the British Union campaigned for King Edward VIII, and hopes were seriously entertained by Fascists that he would ask Sir Oswald Mosley to form a government. A monarchist and an ardent admirer of Edward, Joyce fiercely advocated the King's cause, hitting out in *Action* at all his favourite targets including, of course, 'the parasites of Mayfair'.

On 1st January 1937 the new Public Order Bill came into force, banning the wearing of political uniforms on public occasions, prohibiting stewards at open-air meetings, giving the police powers to forbid processions likely to lead to a breach of the peace, and tightening up the law about insulting words. It applied impartially to all political organizations but it hit primarily—as intended—the Fascists, depriving them of the attraction of the uniform and of the official look which their stewards and the Leader's bodyguard acquired by wearing it. Joyce, however, in his trench coat and muffler, contrived to give the impression of still being in uniform.

The British Union was now preparing to put up some hundred parliamentary candidates, and as a trial run it contested London County Council seats in Shoreditch, North-East Bethnal Green and Limehouse, all Labour strongholds. The war intervening, no general election was held until 1945, so Fascism's national electoral strength was never tested.

At Shoreditch two retiring Labour councillors were opposed by Joyce and another British Union nominee, J. A. Bailey, a local resident employed in the furniture trade. The other challengers were two Municipal Progressive (Conservative) candidates and a man calling himself Independent Labour.

The nomination papers did not require a candidate's nationality to be stated. The Fascists had no chance of election, and Joyce therefore incurred no risk of the substantial fine to which he would have been liable had he taken his seat on the London County Council and then been revealed as an alien.

Obsessed by the election campaign, in planning his second marriage he gave no thought to a honeymoon or, indeed, to celebrations at all. He was concerned, however, to marry at the first possible moment. Five days after his decree was made absolute he was married again.

The ceremony took place at Kensington Register Office on 13th February 1937. Then thirty, he was five years older than his bride. Something came over Joyce where forms were concerned, and he caused to be entered on the marriage certificate the description of himself as 'University tutor (retired)'. He gave his father's status as 'of independent means'. The witnesses were Mrs. Hastings Bonora, a British Union member, and John Macnab. The Joyce family appeared and a few fellow-Fascists attended. Margaret's parents (who had become nominal members of the British Union) were absent, her mother being ill. It was just as well they were not there because they thought, rightly, that materially their daughter could have done better.

A gift of money arrived from the Scrimgeours. Mrs. Bonora gave a brief cocktail party. Another friend provided a wedding cake at his flat. Then the newly-married couple returned to Fawcett Street for a snack before leaving to canvass the Shoreditch electors. Joyce warned his wife that he might lose support if voters learned of his divorce. He hoped that people who knew him only slightly might not realize that Margaret was his second wife, and he prepared her for the possibility.

'If anyone comes up to you and says: "Good-day, Mrs. Joyce, and how are your dear children?", for God's sake keep your head!'

The campaign had not yet warmed up. They had the usual experiences of slammed doors as soon as they uttered the word 'election', and of gossiping voters who wasted their time. Most residents regarded a Labour victory as a foregone conclusion, and said so. With aching feet the Joyces limped to a Fascist meeting and hobbled from there to another party given for them by friends.

Local issues were overshadowed during the campaign; it might have been a parliamentary election from the national press coverage and the excitement and bitterness unprecedented in a municipal contest. More than half Joyce's election address was devoted to attacking the Jews and he intensively canvassed non-Jewish shopkeepers and stallholders; he conceded nothing to the view of those Fascists who thought that the British Union should go easy on anti-Semitism. Ceaselessly active, he even did his own bill-posting, which involved him in a scene with the Labour woman candidate. Detecting Joyce pasting a Fascist poster on her wall, her horrified grandson shouted to his grandparents to come out and stop this defilement, whereupon Joyce, she alleged, emptied his pastepot over the child's head.

Margaret had little time to reflect on her husband's disclosure, made shortly after their marriage, that he was an American national and that she had now lost her British nationality without gaining United States citizenship. The idea occurred to her that, her father being of Irish descent, she might try to claim Irish nationality. She would have had no title to it, but the thought took root that she and Joyce would be safer in the Irish Free State. The danger was undefined, but she suspected that her husband was also aware of a menace. He owned, she was disturbed to discover, an unlicensed pistol. Although he did not carry it, or keep it loaded, it was in the flat, and she did not come from a home where a firearm was part of the household equipment.

By the end of the election they were weary but satisfied that they had done all they could. They had, in fact, scored much better than their opponents had predicted. The two Labour candidates, with over 11,000 votes each, received the expected large majority. The Municipal Progressives polled over 3,000 votes each. The shock for the two established parties came when the Fascist vote was announced. Joyce had 2,564 votes and Bailey 2,492.

The candidates and their supporters assembled to hear the returning officer declare the result. After the cheers and counter-cheers the usual post-election speeches were made. The re-elected candidates and the defeated ones (including the Independent Labour man, who had managed to persuade only 395 electors to support him) were prepared to observe the routine courtesies. Had Joyce done what was expected of him he would have congratulated his successful opponents, acknowledged (whether he meant it or not) that the fight had been fair, and thanked his supporters while conceding, with a good grace, that the electors had expressed their will.

Instead, he created a painful scene when his turn came to speak. Feeling proprietary and gratified that he had done so well, his wife waited beside him, expecting that he would be more than adequate to the occasion. Joyce, his expression grim, stood rigidly with his hands to his sides. In his most truculent manner he shouted that it had been a thoroughly dirty fight. Then he suddenly turned and strode from the platform followed, after a few seconds, by the subdued Bailey. The audience of election helpers and other political workers gasped and stared after him.

Shocked, embarrassed, and left standing alone, Margaret hurried after the two retreating Fascists. When she caught up with her husband she tried to tell him that his demonstration had achieved nothing except make him look a bad loser, but coherent conversation was impossible until he had calmed down a little. To her protest that his behaviour had not only been tactless but bad propaganda, he argued with stubborn logic that it was ridiculous for everyone to pretend to be good sports, to shake hands and pat backs, when he had called his two opponents everything possible within the law, they had riposted, and each side had thought itself justified.

Joyce saw himself as upholding standards of absolute honesty. When you thought someone was wrong, he asserted, it was dishonest to treat him as though he might be right. For a man of his views he had, of course, put himself in an impossible position by participating, as a candidate, in a democratic process his doctrine rejected. But even in social life he could not make such a small concession as to talk to people he found uninteresting. 'Why should I,' he would ask, 'when I know exactly what they're going to say?' Nor did he see why he should listen to Jewish music so, regardless of who was present, he would turn off a radio set if it was playing what he took to be jazz.

Despite the unexpected size of the Fascist vote in Shoreditch, the outlook for British Fascism was deteriorating. The Italian onslaught on Abyssinia, the Spanish Civil War, and Hitler's speeches and actions, welcomed by Joyce as proofs of Fascist vigour, were outraging British liberal opinion. Inside Britain, what popular press support there had been for the Fascists had fallen away, to the relief of the more doctrinaire British Union members but to the detriment of the dissemination of Fascist propaganda. Afraid of disturbances, the proprietors of halls were showing reluctance to let their premises for British Union meetings. Inevitably, within the Fascist movement there were disagreements about policy, as well as the customary tensions in any political body between militants and persuaders, administrators and propagandists.

Mosley was no longer Joyce's nominee as the greatest Englishman; addicted to inventing insulting nicknames, Joyce privately referred to the Leader as 'the Bleeder'. He thought that Sir Oswald still had reservations about anti-Semitism and was keeping his franker Propaganda Director in the background; he adapted a favourite quotation from Pope: 'Bear, like the Turk, no brother near the throne,' to apply to the Leader: 'He, like the Turk, bore no rival near the throne.' Beckett, editor of *Action* and *The Blackshirt*, was also severely critical of Mosley and of the headquarters staff. Even the large expenditure, he wrote later in his preface to Joyce's pamphlet, had 'failed to gain support for heel-clicking and petty militarism' and he revealed that for nearly four years he had found himself 'in growing alliance with Joyce against the petty malicious intrigue with which the organization is riddled'.

What precipitated a crisis was not the external difficulties and the internal dissensions, however, but the heavy cost which was not balanced by a sufficiently large income. The British Union was, for a party with no prospect of power, carrying an inflated staff. When the blow fell it was unexpectedly severe. The Leader briefly addressed his assembled employees and read out a list of dismissals. By the time he had finished reading, the paid staff had been reduced by four-fifths. Among those to go were Joyce and Beckett.

Married little more than a month, Margaret faced the fact that her husband was unemployed. She made the gesture of writing a formal letter of resignation, to which the British Union sent her a polite acknowledgement regretting her decision. Macnab, the editor of *Fascist Quarterly*, was unemployed too, he having resigned as a protest against Joyce's dismissal.

In urgent domestic conferences Joyce flatly refused to get a job. If he had to work purely for money, he declared, he would do so only part-time. His main energies were to be devoted to politics.

They moved to a flat more suitable for taking pupils and the firm of Macnab & Joyce, Private Tutors, now came into being. The principals, John Angus Macnab, B.A. (Oxon.), and William Joyce, B.A. (Lond.), L.C.P., issued from 83 Onslow Gardens, South Kensington, London, S.W.7, a prospectus written in a severe and no-nonsense style offering expert private tuition for university entrance and professional preliminary examinations and to persons not proceeding to academic qualifications who proposed to 'undertake courses of study pertinent to their particular and personal needs. Thus, for example, the firm is prepared to give intensive instruction in the English language to foreigners of suitable character who are staying in England for the purpose of acquiring a knowledge of our speech and customs.' Parents and guardians were promised 'a regular report of scrupulous accuracy' on the work of each student.

As Margaret saw it, two capable teachers could expect to make a reasonable living, and she looked forward to managing the household for the partners. Then Joyce infuriated her by telling the agents, on whom the firm was in part relying for a supply of

students, that no coloured or Jewish clients would be accepted.
'What's wrong with that?' Joyce demanded.

'Apart from any other consideration,' she retorted, 'it's tactless.'

Joyce argued volubly to justify the refusal to admit coloured students. Their mentality was so different, he said, that unless they took individual tuition, which most of them did not want to do, a small-scale crammer had difficulty in fitting them into his classes. Besides, the type of young man they were trying to attract would come from parents who might object to their son attending lessons with coloured youths. His objection to Jews, he thought, required no justification.

Vainly Margaret contended that no tutor need accept students he felt he could not teach. The time to decline was when would-be students presented themselves. There was no need for preliminary statements which would antagonize people. She added a few practical remarks about the financial situation which she, as his wife, now found herself in.

'You're proposing that we should be deceitful!' he stormed. 'That comes from your Italian blood! We must make our position clear!'

Some 'foreign students of suitable character' appeared, including a few German army officers working with the Military Attaché at the German Embassy. Joyce entered with zest into drilling them in the English language. One of his devices to impart interest to his lessons was to pretend that he was a British prisoner-of-war being interrogated by them.

But Margaret's fears were well-founded. Not enough acceptable students applied. The mother of one who had already enrolled withdrew him and sent a strongly-worded letter accusing the tutors of being pro-Hitler.

Joyce was unperturbed. The sole amenities he needed were books, cigarettes, alcohol and agreeable companions. He was not interested in dressing well, getting a home together or living in a good district; all he noticed about a flat was whether there were trees in the neighbourhood. His thoughts were not on such bourgeois pretensions but on plans for a political organization in which he could be his uninhibited self.

Only Margaret worried. One day the landlord's wife found her in tears about the lack of money.

Chapter 7

STEER STRAIGHT

With Beckett, Macnab and a few others Joyce founded the National Socialist League. The title was chosen because it did not, like the name Fascist, sound alien, and it described the founders' aims. As he had always had good meetings in the area round Victoria Station, Joyce set up the headquarters at 190 Vauxhall Bridge Road. He designed a membership badge in the form of a steering wheel with the words 'Steer Straight' underneath, and eagerly set about producing a 71-page booklet, *National Socialism Now*, to be sold for a shilling at meetings as a statement by 'the only 100% British organization working with British people and British funds for the rebuilding of Britain in the modern way'.

Beckett, in a foreword, introduced him. 'The author is, for politics, a very young man. Now only 31, he will, in coming years, exercise a very great influence upon the life and thought of our people. He himself prefers the spoken word to the written, and his name is already known as a fine and compelling speaker throughout the country. An Honours graduate of London University, he has served in the Army as a private soldier and acquired a varied experience of many different kinds of social life.'

The reference to Joyce's army service rather over-emphasized a minor episode in his career, but as the National Socialist League was out to 'seek its support amongst the hundreds of thousands of the common people', service in the ranks was more telling than experience in the Officers Training Corps.

The National Socialist League, Beckett emphasized, was to be very different from the British Union. 'Arguments about leadership before there is anything to lead are stupid. When the people decide that "these things shall be," they will not fail to find their leaders.' After outlining the aim of setting up district National Socialist Leagues to be loosely knitted nationally, and explaining how elected county leaders would select the national leadership, Beckett assured readers that 'Joyce and I then do not set up as people to be saluted and "hailed" on every possible, and impossible, occasion. We merely come forward as the instruments of a great policy, and we conceive our task to be the building of the framework upon which a mighty national edifice may rest. What will happen to us when National-Socialism attracts the thousands of brilliant young men and women whom it must attract, is a matter of great indifference. We do not make National-Socialism contingent upon accepting us. That is an impertinence of which we have seen too much.'

Now Joyce, making his own statement unhampered by other people's ideas of expediency, began with the provocative gesture of a tribute to Hitler, while emphasizing that his own movement was British. National Socialism, he wrote, 'no matter who may use the term or feel the spirit first, must arise from soil and people or not at all. It springs from no temporary grievance, but from the revolutionary yearning of the people to cast off the chains of gross, sordid, democratic materialism without having to put on the shackles of Marxian Materialism, which would be identical with the chains cast off.

'The matter touches our own British people, who cannot be debarred from sharing in a spirit of revolt which is confined to no one nation. Therefore, in true respect for the German Leader's gallant achievement against international Jewish finance and its other self—international Jewish Communism, I would gladly say, "Heil Hitler!" and at once part company with him, realizing what a pitiable insult it is to such a great man to try to flatter him with an imitation which he has always disdained. His way is for Germany, ours is for Britain; let us tread our paths with mutual respect, which is rarely increased by borrowing.'

Joyce went on to explain his National Socialism. 'Nationalism stands for the nation and Socialism for the people. Unless the people be identical with the nation, all politics and all statecraft are a waste of time. People without a nation are a helpless flock or, like the Jews, a perpetual nuisance; a nation without people is an abstract nothing or a historical ghost.'

His programme required the abolition of Parliament as

73

constituted because it had failed to manage the economic affairs
of the nation and its replacement by a syndicalist-type assembly.
'It is now clear that the National Socialist has no apology to make
for his decision to end the Parliamentary farce. Constitutionally,
and in perfect loyalty to the Crown as the symbol of Britain's
continuous majesty, the National Socialist proposes to make
such changes in the system of Government as are necessary to
produce the required changes in our system of living.' Each
occupation was to have its guild, and the guilds were to elect the
House of Commons. Membership of a trade union was to be compulsory for each worker registered in his guild, and the unions,
no longer having to fight on their members' behalf, would act for
them within the guild structure. The House of Lords would be
reconstituted, 'giving representation to all those aspects of the
National life which cannot be classed as economic. . . . Imperial
and foreign affairs, the Services, the Universities, and the various
Christian religious denominations, art, science, general culture
are all subjects which should come within the scope of an en-
lightened and hygienic Second Chamber.'

Similar proposals to his for raising purchasing power, reducing
working hours and developing Empire markets appeared in
numerous pamphlets in those days by people who were not
Fascists, but Joyce could not advocate even prosaic measures
without dropping into his characteristic style. 'Our bourgeois
merchants and internationalist political pandars must learn,
somehow or other, that when tremendous markets can be created
here, it is derogatory to the national prestige to send simpering
amateur ambassadors abroad in the hope that by adopting fancy
dress or some other peculiarity they may persuade the foreigner
to cause unemployment in his country merely to produce employment in ours. If the idea is to persuade the foreigner to buy from
us what he does not want it is to be feared that God will not help
us. Champagne may bubble and rose petals bestrew the footwear
of some itinerant scion of declining nobility, but no benefit will
accrue to us.'

On the dissolution of the Empire he was no less colourful.
'Nothing more shameful has ever been known in the history of
Empires than that we who have given three centuries of work,
blood, and ability to create what is good in India should have had
the results of our work filched from us by Tory politicians who

have yielded to the noisy fakirs and the chattering babus because behind these ludicrous creatures there stands the power of international Jewish finance which grinds down and exploits day by day, the poor sweated Indian worker in the cotton mills of Bombay, Ahmenabad, and other places too numerous to mention, not to benefit India or Lancashire, but to turn the sweat of slaves into filthy lucre.'

The fanatical orator's scream could be heard when he denounced the supporters of disarmament—'the political crimps of Judah and moral anarchy, who wanted no army at all until there occurred to them the thrice scaly thought of getting Englishmen to fight a war to make Germany safe for Jewry. For years the crimps aforesaid, dribbling old prelates, verminous Bloomsburgians, myopic printers' hacks, and every sort of meddlesome old woman, male and otherwise, joined in neurotic crusades of Pacifism, designed, of course, to weaken the Empire. Now, however, these curious doves have moulted and dropped their olive-branches. They all want war, because certain regenerated nations seem more dangerous to Jewish international finance than does Britain.'

He wrote as he talked, too impatient to read over his sentences and to ask himself if the reader would know what he meant. Such a sentence as 'Mayfair night clubs and Left Book Clubs provide unearned and unprofitable recreation for many spoilt darlings who can show no moral claim to the wealth that they hold' may raise a laugh when shouted at a street corner but, seeing it in print, the reader pauses to wonder what it means.

But obscure though he was in places, his main message was stated unequivocally—he wanted a pact with Hitler and discrimination against Jews. 'Britain and Germany, particularly with the assistance of Italy, can form against Bolshevism and international finance, twin Jewish manifestations, a bulwark much too strong to invite attack.' What followed could well have been taken from any contemporary Nazi paper. 'From the days of the Revolution Russia has been financed by great New York banking firms; she has been armed by their money; and she is being used by them as the last but most powerful weapon in the armoury of internationalism . . . International Finance is controlled by great Jewish moneylenders and Communism is being propagated by Jewish agitators who are at one fundamentally

with the powerful capitalists of their race in desiring an international world order, which would, of course, give universal
sovereignty to the only international race in existence.'

Jews, whether Jewish by religion or not, were to be treated as
aliens. 'The right attitude for Britain to adopt is not to persecute,
not necessarily to hate, but simply and frankly to recognize them
as a foreign people to be considered like any other foreign people,
and to be placed on an appropriate territorial basis, with such
exceptions as the state would make in the case of any well-
disposed foreigner whose presence could harm nobody and
benefit some. Naturally, the first right of all employment in
Britain belongs to the British people.'

The familiar Joyce of the wartime German radio had already
appeared—speaking English but oddly alien in manner, employing extravagant figures of speech which obscured rather than
emphasized his message, upholding traditions and denouncing
traditionalists, plugging that thesis of the Wall Street-Moscow
conspiracy.

The thousands of brilliant young men and women whom
Beckett had foreseen rallying to the National Socialist League
remained indifferent to its appeal. How small the League's
operations were can be judged from one of its meetings in
Denison Hall, when the expenditure was about £2 and the
organizers were delighted that the collection raised £3 15s.
Without the Scrimgeours' support the organization would probably have never got started. The membership scarcely spread
beyond the friends and acquaintances of the founders and a few
eccentrics. One adherent, whose support was unwelcome,
claimed to be the King of Poland. Less remarkable, but an
occasional embarrassment, was a boisterous Irishman, who per-
sisted in working for the League. Late one evening, when drunk,
this follower decided to pay a social call on the Joyces and
Macnab. Refused admission, he shouted so loudly that their
landlord and his wife were disturbed and Joyce had to threaten
to send for the police.

Joyce and his wife lived economically. Miss Scrimgeour entertained them for week-ends now and again at Pigeon Hill. On
Sundays, when the City of London was deserted, Joyce liked to
walk through the silent streets. Their only trip abroad was a one-
day no-passport excursion to Boulogne. Sometimes they were

invited to spend an evening with friends or they gave small parties themselves. Then Joyce could be amusing, so long as he dominated the talk. He had the reformer's scorn for what did not interest him, and he was quick to change the subject when conversation drifted to topics he considered unimportant. People who met him when he was feeling unsociable thought him excessively vain. Margaret Joyce denies a story, which has gained some currency, that he concluded every party by making his guests stand and sing the National Anthem. The legend may have had its origin in an occasion when, after a good deal had been drunk, Joyce and his guests sang the kind of songs which people do in such circumstances, and they ended with a riotous version of 'God Save the King'.

During the international tension preceding the Munich agreement in 1938 Joyce saw that in being pro-Hitler and pro-British Empire he might soon be placed in a quandary. If hostilities broke out between Britain and Germany he could not, he said to Macnab, support a war engineered by corrupt politicians at the bidding of international finance for the express purpose of destroying National Socialism. Yet evasion of national service was for him unthinkable, it would be 'utterly abhorrent' to him to sabotage the national defence in any way, and conscientious objectors he regarded as 'lower than the amoeba'.

With his wife and Macnab he made a provisional plan. If war seemed unavoidable, Macnab was to go with Margaret and their luggage to Dublin. Joyce would stay in England to wind up their affairs and join them at the last moment. What they were to do after that was undecided. He speculated on the possibility of getting from Ireland to Germany and there volunteering in the defence of the Reich against Russia. Macnab and Margaret were to stay in Ireland.

In pursuance of this project Joyce renewed his passport for one year, it having expired by more than two months. To obtain it he again declared that he was a British subject by birth and that he had not lost his British nationality. Margaret procured a passport, making no mention of her marriage to an alien; passports were not required by travellers between England and Ireland but Joyce thought it well for her to have an identification document. As the crisis developed Macnab booked two passages to Ireland.

The British Fascists' tactic at this time, like that of the

Communists in their post-war 'peace' campaigns, was to expound a sentiment calculated to make a popular common-sense appeal and thus obscure the military aggression being practised by the state they supported. What happened abroad, the Fascists urged, was no concern of the British. 'Mind Britain's Business', the slogan of the Mosley organization, could be seen everywhere chalked on walls and roadways. Joyce could mount nothing on the scale of the British Union. He preached non-involvement at his small open-air meetings, associated with people whose main concern was not to promote Fascism but to avoid war, and in pursuit of this policy joined in founding, with the then Viscount Lymington as president and himself as vice-president, the British Council against European Commitments, a body which made scarcely any public impact.

From day to day his wife and Macnab postponed their departure until the Munich agreement caused them to cancel their arrangement. Their immediate object achieved, the British Council against European Commitments hesitated about going on with a planned meeting, but as they had booked Caxton Hall they decided to assemble there although they feared nobody would attend. Public relief, however, resulted in a full meeting, and gave the promoters the agreeable feeling of being influential.

To celebrate the end of the crisis Joyce spent a brief holiday with his wife at Ryde in the Isle of Wight. While there he experienced a premonition that he was being prepared to play a rôle in a great event, and under the impact of this experience he talked rapidly and excitedly all night.

On his return trouble awaited him, culminating in a split in his tiny organization. Beckett, despite his admiration for Joyce, had different ideas about running the League, and the two men got on one another's nerves. In October Beckett left Joyce for the British People's Party, yet another society with a policy of getting along with Hitler and keeping Britain for the British. The defection was a relief to Joyce, who wanted no dissenters round him. A less dedicated man would have felt himself drifting into defeat, because he earned only a modest income from his students and the League had got into debt. But he liked giving lessons, he enjoyed his independence, and he found it fun to run a bar, selling ale, bitter and three types of Cyprus sherry at a small profit to the funds—he had moved into cheaper headquarters and registered the new office as a club so that it could sell drink. At home he was good-tempered and Margaret had adjusted herself to what she would earlier have thought a precarious existence. 'We ourselves were extraordinarily happy,' she wrote of this time. If events had permitted it Joyce might have led this life for years, reading every week the *Observer*, the *News of the World* and the *Jewish Chronicle* for material and ideas, shouting down traffic and hecklers at street corners and market places, mellowing perhaps into an untidy, hoarse-voiced, tolerated oddity. Praise of Hitler, however, went down badly with London audiences, meetings got rough, and on two occasions Joyce appeared in court.

In November 1938 he was charged with assault. According to the evidence, having been asked by the police to close his meeting at half-past nine, Joyce punctually complied by leading the singing of the National Anthem. An associate was arrested for obstruction and, moving towards him, Joyce was intercepted by a man to whom he gave what he called 'a tap on the head' with his stick. Medical evidence was to the effect that only a slight cut had been inflicted, and the case against Joyce was dismissed.

The second prosecution, in the following May, was also a minor affair, but it worried Joyce so much that, with friends' help, he engaged counsel. The hearing brought out a squalid story of a street-corner meeting, with Joyce and about five supporters being subjected by fifteen or twenty people to what he termed 'shouting of an abusive nature' and the singing of the 'Internationale'. A heckler had said that if the speaker thought Germany such an agreeable place it was a pity he did not go there instead of trying to bring to this country a system it did not want. Joyce was alleged to have struck the interrupter in the face. Later Joyce suspected that the aggrieved man was a police *agent provocateur*.

If the police really were trying to get a conviction against Joyce they stage-managed the incident badly. Evidence about the scuffle was conflicting. Joyce denied that he had heard the suggestion that he should go to Germany and maintained that he had done no more than push the man in the left side with his right fist while trying to make his way through the crowd. Asked by his counsel: 'Had you any desire to provoke any disorder?' he virtuously replied: 'Far from it.' The magistrate thought there was nothing to justify a conviction and dismissed the case.

Steer Straight

Joyce was too hardened an agitator to be bothered about a mere fracas followed by an appearance in court. This case was for him an indication of mounting danger. Once convicted he would have a police record, and there would be charges whenever a meeting got out of hand. A reputation as a nuisance might cause his origin to be investigated, and he could have been deported. But to become inconspicuous and find himself a regular job still did not occur to him. Now it was plain that Hitler's annexation plans had not finished with his action against Czechoslovakia in March, public hostility to pro-Nazi speakers had sharpened, but Joyce continued to steer straight as before. His opportunities of publicity were small but he made the most of them. The National Socialist League had a tiny offshoot called the Carlyle Club (the name was chosen by him because he admired Carlyle, his first home with his new wife was just round the corner from Carlyle's house, and it sounded more club-like than political), and he never missed its weekly politico-social meetings. He belonged to Captain Ramsay's Right Club, another organization where he thought he could spread his doctrine among the influential. A fellow-member was Anna Wolkoff, the daughter of an admiral in the Imperial Russian Navy, whose admiration of him was to bring her a prison sentence during the war.

At home he made no direct reference to his worry, although he talked a great deal about the international situation. By midsummer so few students remained that the partnership of Joyce and Macnab, Private Tutors, no longer justified its existence. As they could not afford the rent of their flat in South Kensington, Macnab moved to a room in Pimlico and the Joyces to a basement in Earls Court.

The night after their removal Joyce was attacked with forebodings of disaster. He talked wildly, shook off attempts to calm him, shouted, and finally, in a terrifying outburst of temper, raved at his bewildered wife.

Next morning he was tranquil. She expected him to say something about the previous night, but he acted as though nothing unusual had occurred. He was even cheerful and kind, and this mood lasted. For a few weeks they were happy living in what they called their 'dolls' house'.

Anxiously he tried to interpret the conflicting signs. The

domestic German radio, to which he regularly listened, was reassuring, but the feeling in London was that 1939 might be the last peaceful summer for years. British Union members were chalking 'Mosley and Peace' on walls.

One supporter of his, Mrs. Frances Dorothy Eckersley, was unperturbed. She took leave of him, announcing that she was to spend a holiday first in Hungary and then in Germany, where her son by her first marriage was at school. Casually she mentioned that she expected to be staying in Berlin at the Hotel Continental about the end of August.

Macnab, also planning a holiday in Berlin, argued that as the Sudetenland and Czech crises had passed and Memel been incorporated in the Reich, war was unlikely to start over Danzig.

Joyce desperately hoped that his friends were right, but the vital question plagued him. Southern Ireland or Germany? As though not wanting to face the decision, he postponed the renewal of his now-expired passport. He still did not know how he would answer if the emergency arose.

Chapter 8

LET FATE DECIDE

During their last talk before Macnab left for Berlin, Joyce asked him if he knew anyone there, and on learning that he did not, wrote him a note of introduction to Christian Bauer. Macnab had risen to go when Joyce detained him, as though a thought had crossed his mind. Then he said: 'John, if you are willing, I want you to do something for me after you have got to know Christian. I want him to find out whether, in the event of my leaving England and going to Germany for good, Goebbels is able and willing to arrange for my immediate naturalization as a German citizen, together of course with Margaret if she accompanies me.'

Joyce was taking for granted that young Bauer's relations with Goebbels were as close as he had claimed. Whether the name of William Joyce meant anything to the German Propaganda Minister he did not know, but he thought that Bauer would have mentioned their acquaintanceship to his chief, and he hoped that Goebbels remembered his *Draft Scheme for a Scientifically Managed Currency as Adapted to the Needs of the Third Reich.* Joyce had even persuaded himself that his financial advice had had an influence on German monetary policy.

His wife was never told of this request to Macnab, and at this stage she was the one pressing for a decision in favour of Berlin instead of Dublin. After much thought she had concluded that, in view of their political beliefs, it would be logical and honest to go to Germany and, as she put it, 'let fate decide the rest'. In their renewed discussions on this choice, Joyce seemed indifferent, like a despondent punter pricking his racecard with a pin.

In Berlin Macnab found Bauer occupying an office suite on the first floor of the expensive Adlon Hotel and he assumed, reasonably enough, that no further evidence was required of the German's status. His claim to represent *Der Angriff* was also substantiated; in Macnab's presence he telephoned the paper on what seemed to be a private line.

Bauer read Joyce's letter, greeted Macnab warmly, assured him that no one there was infected by London's tension, and proposed another meeting.

During their second talk Macnab put Joyce's question, and in doing so asked Bauer to include him as a hypothetical candidate for German nationality. Bauer, just off to Hamburg for three days, promised to reply on his return.

When they met again Bauer said that he had seen Dr. Goebbels, in whose name he could assure William Joyce that immediate naturalization would be available for him in Germany, and for his wife if she accompanied him.

'Does that go for me too?' Macnab asked.

'Yes,' answered Bauer, 'provided you are vouched for by William, and as you clearly would be, the same facilities are open to you.'

Macnab left Berlin on August 21st. That evening the German Government made the startling announcement that Germany and the Soviet Union had concluded a non-aggression pact and that the Foreign Minister, von Ribbentrop, was to sign the agreement in Moscow on Wednesday, August 23rd.

The British public received the news the following morning with dismay. For once Joyce was in tune with their mood, although for different reasons. In his tiny basement dwelling he brooded over the papers, numbed by this wholly unexpected blow. He had enraged hostile street-corner groups and aroused Fascist cheers by maintaining that Hitler was the farseeing statesman who had recognized the Jewish-Bolshevik menace. He could have seized this chance to reject the Führer as a National Socialist who had failed to steer straight; then Dublin not Berlin would have been the obvious choice. But he proved as agile as his opposite numbers in the British Communist Party, who had also reeled under the shock. Reassessing the situation, he talked to his wife. A section of German opinion, he reflected, had for military reasons always wanted a pact with the Soviet Union, and as Hitler had been rebuffed by the Western powers in his search for allies against the Communist menace, he had had to take this step to safeguard the fatherland. But explaining the pact did not remove the fear that war had been brought nearer. With volunteers filling sandbags and digging trenches in parks, air raid warnings and a black-out being rehearsed, the time for a decision was running short.

When Macnab called, Joyce was anxious and depressed. Bauer's assurance of immediate naturalization if he went to Germany seemed to give him some relief, but he did not discuss it. His thoughts were occupied with the recall of both Houses of Parliament for the coming Thursday to pass all stages of the Emergency Powers (Defence) Act, a comprehensive measure giving the Government exceptional powers in the event of war. Joyce was concerned with the section providing for the detention of security suspects. He had reason to believe, he said, giving the impression that he had information from an authoritative source, that Parliament would modify some of the more stringent provisions, but he was none the less apprehensive that he himself would be arrested immediately the Act came into force.

But still he took no action, not even the precautionary one of completing a form to renew his passport. The year's extension, made in the previous September, had been valid only until 1st July 1939. He and his wife had another of several sleepless nights. Repeatedly he asked whether she still thought they ought to leave for Germany, pointing out that they could more easily go to Ireland. It seemed that he wanted to be argued out of going to Berlin.

On Wednesday von Ribbentrop, in jubilant Moscow, signed the non-aggression pact. Britain had been outmanœuvred by this diplomatic coup, and the Communists had given the Nazis the green light for further aggression. Joyce did nothing but read the papers and sit about smoking. If he was to leave the country he needed a valid passport, and still he did not take the simple action necessary.

It was not until the Thursday, when Members of Parliament were already making their way to the House, a few hours before the Emergency Powers Act was to be approved by them, that Joyce reluctantly sat down to fill up the application form.

If he had a belated presentiment now it was too indistinct to tell him that he was tightening the rope he had put round his neck in 1933 by signing his first passport application. Since then

the authorities had sharpened the warning about the consequences of false statements, but they had not suggested that in-
fringement might constitute a capital offence. For the third time
he wrongly affirmed: 'I, the Undersigned, William Joyce, at
present residing at 38a Eardley Crescent, S.W.5, London, hereby
make application for the renewal of British passport No. 125943
issued to me at London on the 6th July, 1933, for a further
period of one year. I declare that I am a British subject by birth
and I have not lost that national status, and that the whole of the
particulars given by me in respect of this application are true.'

Why did Joyce renew his passport on this and the previous
occasion for one year? The regulations on the form appear to
imply that a year is the minimum period by stating that 'Foreign
Office passports may be renewed for any consecutive period of
one to five years from the date of expiry'. It seems that, needing a
document to leave the country, and expecting (in the event of
going to Germany) to acquire German naturalization at once, he
asked for what he incorrectly thought was the shortest possible
period. If his passport had expired within, say, a fortnight from
the time of his landing in Germany, his fate would have been
different, but no one then (had the need arisen) could have
advised him with certainty about the full implications of holding
a valid British passport while working for the enemy.

On that day, August 24th, one of his few remaining students
was due for coaching, so Margaret took the form and his passport
to the Passport Office. The renewal was made from the last expiry
date, prolonging the passport's validity until 1st July 1940. With
their two passports in order, she went to the German Consulate,
which was full of apprehensive German and Austrian domestic
servants. The visa official, smilingly reassuring, asked whether
the Joyces were going on holiday. She answered 'Yes', although
feeling very much unlike a tourist with happy expectations. They
were wise not to let war scares change their plans, he said. Hand-
ing back the passports, he wished her a good journey.

In the evening the exhausting debate was resumed. No precautionary preparations to go to Dublin had been made as in
1938, but now, with Bauer's assurance, the fear of internment in
Germany as an enemy alien, and the consequent separation from
his wife, was removed, and Joyce said less about the advantages
of Ireland. Ignorant of the message from Berlin, Margaret

thought her arguments were convincing him, but whenever he seemed about to decide finally his misgivings returned.

At about midnight the telephone rang. Startled, they looked at each other. Joyce, his expression strained, lifted the receiver, announced himself, listened for a few seconds and replaced it.

The actual text of the curt message Joyce never revealed. The call came from the Intelligence officer to whom he had reported on Communist activities and who had (or so he said) sounded him on his willingness to go to Germany as an agent. Its purport was that the clause covering the detention of security suspects in the Emergency Powers (Defence) Act had not been modified, that it could, or would, apply to him, but that the machinery for detaining suspects would not operate before Saturday, August 26th. In other words, if Joyce wanted to get away, he had less than two days.

The dramatic tip-off—a final reward for Joyce's services—merely confirmed his long-held belief that he would be classed as a security risk; its value lay in the hint that he still had time to escape.

'We must now make a final decision,' Joyce said despondently. But that was what he could not do, and he spent the night in repetitive, anxious talk. His wife was puzzled by his anguish, because she did not know that they were trying to answer different questions. For her the problem was what they would need with them, and where to deposit their furniture and books, while they were abroad during a probably brief crisis. Berlin sounded to her more interesting than Dublin. What occupied him was the momentous step of settling permanently in Germany. The coming of morning forced them to end the debate. By breakfast time it was assumed that they had chosen Berlin.

Her first task, Margaret decided, was to see Miss Scrimgeour, who had no telephone, explain their intentions, and ask her to store their property. While she was preparing to leave Joyce took his pistol from the tin box where it lay wrapped in a cloth, suggesting that she should dispose of it in a lonely place. She journeyed to Pigeon Hill conscious of the heavy bulk of the weapon in her bag.

Poor Miss Scrimgeour, unused to emergencies, first looked startled at this unexpected visit but then grew bewildered on hearing Margaret's story, as she had not kept abreast of events,

could not believe in the imminence of war, knew nothing about
the new Defence Regulations, and was unable to comprehend
why the Joyces were launching themselves into a highly uncertain
future. Exhausted by battling with her incomprehension, Margaret dropped the subject of storage space, took a melancholy
farewell, and walked slowly along the lonely familiar road. Under
a tree with spreading roots she buried the pistol in soft soil.

While she was gone Joyce withdrew from the bank all the
money from his and his wife's accounts, the sum including the
National Socialist League funds, which were in a sounder state
than usual as the money collected to finance Joyce's legal defence
had not all been expended.

That evening the small group of friends constituting the membership of the National Socialist League and the Carlyle Club
assembled. Joyce announced that the two organizations' activities
must be suspended as in the existing situation they could serve
no useful purpose and might even do harm. Giving no explanation, he said that he was going away for a time and he named
Macnab as his deputy. The members, who seem to have been
remarkably incurious, agreed that he should take the funds with
him.

Although he had brought Bauer's message, Macnab was taken
aback by Joyce's farewells. The two friends went together to
Joyce's basement flat, where Margaret, helped by Joyce's sister and one of his brothers, was packing, watched by the rest
of the excited Joyce family, who were drinking whisky and
advising on what should be taken and what left.

Facing Macnab, Joyce said: 'Margaret and I are making a little
trip to Deutschland in the morning.'

'Oh, William!' Macnab exclaimed. 'Why didn't you tell me
before? It's ten o'clock now. How can I get my stuff packed and
my passport visaed and my money arranged for? Where you go I
go—you know that! And Bauer told me it's all arranged for me
too.'

'No, John,' Joyce answered, 'this trip is not for you. Believe
me, I know your loyalty to me, and your feelings. But it isn't fair
to you, and you're engaged to be married. I wouldn't have asked
you to come, and that's why I've delayed telling you until now.'
After explaining that the Defence Regulations would operate
from the following day, Joyce added: 'If I waited another day I

fear it would be jail for yours truly and starvation for Margaret.'

Joyce and Macnab then destroyed the League's and the Club's papers, keeping only the card index of members, which Macnab later hid. They discussed the final liquidation of their partnership and the disposal of the furniture and other property.

With the preparations nearing completion Joyce, suddenly practical, suggested to his wife that they should take all their clothes. Margaret agreed, and among other things she packed a good costume given her by an aunt in 1936. If they had known Germany they would have included a large supply of soap, but they took enough only for a holiday. The weight was becoming unmanageable. Twice Margaret (ignorant of the part attributed to eagles in the family history) removed a heavy bronze eagle from Joyce's suitcase.

While the party was finishing the whisky, Macnab asked Joyce what they would do if there were no war. Joyce's reply (inaudible to his wife, presumably because of the noise) was to the effect that they would return for a few days to visit their parents and wind up their affairs, but that they would make Germany their home. As Macnab recalls the conversation, Joyce made such statements as: 'I am going to Germany for good, to become a German national and to throw in my lot with Germany for good or ill,' and 'In any event, my life in England is over.'

In the early morning, left to themselves, Joyce and his wife lay down sleeplessly for an hour, talking incessantly, and then rose, hot-eyed and weary.

Suggestions have been made that Joyce slipped secretly out of the country, and that he found a port where there was slackness or even collusion. He could, in fact, scarcely have left more publicly. His luggage was plainly labelled 'Berlin'. On the morning of 26th August 1939 he and his wife, accompanied by Macnab, went to Victoria Station. Joyce bought single tickets to Berlin from a busy clerk who scarcely looked up. The station seethed with British returning from the Continent and foreigners returning to it. The porter who carried their cases exclaimed on seeing the labels: 'What! Berlin! That's a funny place to be going to!'

Their luggage in the train, they stood on the platform talking to Macnab (they promised to send him a postcard) and looking out for the Joyce family. When the other Joyces appeared the two brothers, on their way to work, had to say good-bye briefly and leave, one for a government office and the other for a technical department in the British Broadcasting Corporation. Joyce's mother gave Margaret a Brussels lace collar inherited from her own mother. Uneasy, repetitive conversation filled the time until whistles blew, doors slammed, and last farewells were hastily taken.

After waving from a window, Joyce and his wife sat down and could find little to say. Despite her resolution, Margaret was miserable at leaving England and afraid of sea-sickness.

At Dover they nervously shuffled in a queue towards a man who glanced at the passport photographs and at their faces. For a breath-catching moment they both thought he hesitated, and then they had their passports back and—a private tutor and his wife with valid travel documents—they were boarding the ship. Even if Joyce had been notorious nobody would have had authority to detain him.

Many of the homeward-bound foreigners sobbed as the ship cast off. Standing at the rail staring towards the land, Joyce showed no emotion. What his thoughts were he never confided to anyone but he had, perhaps in one of his precognitive flashes, anticipated this departure in a curious (and in the context irrelevant) passage in his *National Socialism Now*, written in 1937 when he was planning his League and Beckett was predicting for him an influential future.

'For all of us British people,' Joyce had written, 'there is a land in which we have played our part, great or humble, in the drama of life, a land where we have had our happy days, as well as the sad. We generally forget the spring morning, with the splendid sun sparkling on the dew in the green fields, the white lanes with their smiling hedges in summer, the rich tint of the leaves in the declining autumn afternoon, the first nip of winter, the English Christmas with our nearest and dearest, the mists on the fens, the gigantic bustle of our great cities, the fire-breathing giants of the night in the Black Country or by South Shields, the long, snaky monsters that bring happiness, sorrow, hope or anxiety into Euston or King's Cross, the ocean battering away at the rocks of Devon, the Cockney, with his Shoreditch barrow, making fun of every moment in his struggling little life, the broad Mersey restively bringing the challenge of the sea into the heart of Liverpool, the godly majesty of the Highlands, the serene power in the mountains of North Wales, even the rain blending so strangely with the romance of our early days, when, as children we played in it—all these things are most often out of our minds; but if it ever happens to us to see the chalk cliffs receding for the last time as the water widens between us and our homeland, then the memories will come in a choking flood, and we shall know our land when it is too late.'

What Joyce had meant by this Kitsch is puzzling. In writing of people and scenes he produced only clichés and if his thoughts were then on Britain and the British, there is no reason to think that he understood them any better at his departure than he had on his arrival from Ireland. If by 'we' he had implied that his fellow Fascists would leave England in substantial numbers in a crisis he had been wrong; his own supporters and Mosley's nine thousand adherents had stayed behind and he was proceeding towards Berlin as a one-man reinforcement for the Third Reich.

The sea was calm, Margaret's fears of sea-sickness abated, and she and her husband went below for a meal, during which he said nothing until she inquired what he was thinking about.

'Suppose the war breaks out before we land,' he responded, 'or while we're still in Belgium.'

Asked what they would do then, he confessed that he had no idea. He went on deck alone, leaving his wife in the saloon, and he did not reappear until the roofs of Ostend came into view.

The passengers, apparently feeling no sense of urgency, were painfully slow in disembarking, and the Joyces seized every opportunity of a gap in the crowd to push forward. Hurriedly, the passport control and the customs behind them, they walked towards the long, high, alien train, anxiously searching for the through coach to Berlin. Climbing in quickly they stowed their luggage and sat down, expecting the train to leave. Inexperienced travellers as they were, they did not know that this train, made up of coaches for numerous destinations, waited for more contingents of passengers. Others, who had tipped porters to rush them and their luggage into it, looked out of the windows at goods trucks and an occasional blue-overalled railwayman, or they paced the corridors. A few were reckless enough to get out and stroll about.

Sitting tensely in the seemingly forgotten train the Joyces pictured ahead a continent in the fever of mobilization, trains packed with troops, services stopped at the frontiers. Even when the train moved and they settled back in their seats, their relief was short-lived, because instead of gathering speed and thundering across the flat landscape it crawled, stopped at insignificant stations and between stations while hoarse argumentative voices penetrated from outside, and then jolted forward with such clanking that they thought the coaches were being disconnected. Belgium, seen from the railway, depressed them, although the sun was still shining.

Now they felt painfully thirsty. Joyce vainly walked the length of the train, seeking a dining car or at least someone hawking drinks. The passengers in the compartments he passed looked asleep.

Dusk fell, and nothing could be seen through the windows. They no longer peered out when the train stopped, or wondered what the arguments were about, but sat resignedly waiting.

Passengers stirred, brisk footsteps sounded along the corridor, and a uniformed man put his head into the compartment and said something quickly. They were at the frontier.

On the German side a portrait of Hitler hung on the passport office wall. The official was cheerfully courteous, like his London colleague he showed no astonishment that British subjects were travelling to Germany, and he wished the couple a happy holiday as he returned their passports.

Their thirst made sleep impossible. At one station Joyce pushed the window down, saw below a man with a trolley, and made his first purchase in Germany—two bottles of beer. Later he bought from a train attendant two neat white paper bags containing—an unpromising introduction to the Third Reich—slices of stale white unbuttered bread and salami.

For a while, the other passengers having left, they lay on the seats, sleeping uneasily. Both awoke, their thirst revived by the salami, to see flickering light reflected on the ceiling from the flames of furnaces—a reassuring sight indicating, they thought, that the war was not expected to start that night. They dozed again, sat up with no idea of where they were, thankfully bought hot coffee from a man who appeared at the door of their compartment, and then moodily stared at the sand and fir trees of Mark Brandenburg. Although now assured of reaching their destination, their spirits drooped at the sight of shabby backs of buildings on the Berlin outskirts. Glimpses of shopping streets, office blocks, the Siegessäule and the Tiergarten were more heartening. At the Friedrichstrasse terminus they expected a throng of porters, but, seeing passengers carrying their own luggage, they climbed stiffly from the train, dragging their cases after them. A long wait ensued before a porter arrived. They followed him, to emerge not as they had expected in the centre of a busy metropolis but in tranquil Sunday-morning Berlin. An elderly, cigar-smoking street sweeper pushed a wide broom along the gutter. A solitary taxi stood by the kerb.

As he surveyed this placid scene Joyce supported his story of a previous visit by remarking that the place seemed to have changed. The porter put their luggage in the taxi, which took them to a small hotel, recommended by Macnab, in what was then Saarlandstrasse.

The hotel, too, was hushed and the yawning receptionist unmoved by British visitors. The bedroom was oppressively full of huge pieces of furniture, but it was clean and smelt fresh. After washing and changing they went downstairs to a nearly empty dining-room, ate breakfast in silence and, only slightly revived, returned to their room, feeling that their rush to Berlin had been ridiculous.

Joyce was nettled by the city's indifference. As though there was not a minute to be lost, he opened his notebook and lifted the telephone receiver.

Chapter 9

THE DRINK WAS GOOD

Joyce asked in German for Christian Bauer's number, gasped with impatience while waiting, sat down, and at last, nodding reassuringly to his wife, said in English: 'This is William. Margaret is with me. We have left England.'

Seconds elapsed before Bauer spoke. Joyce urgently related why they had come to Germany. Margaret saw his expression change.

Another pause followed. Joyce frowned in puzzlement. 'I see. . . . Yes. . . . Yes,' he murmured despondently. He replaced the receiver.

Anxiously Margaret asked whether everything was all right.

'He seemed rather surprised,' Joyce answered, adding that Bauer could not meet them until the evening.

Neither commented. They had expected that Goebbels's adviser would want to see them within an hour, yet he was treating them as visitors whose time was unimportant.

With no other plans they could only go sight-seeing in the peaceful, sunlit streets. Some of the men, promenading with families and dogs, wore uniform but their figures were unmilitary. No troops and tanks appeared.

Joyce bought a Sunday paper at a kiosk and glanced at the headlines. They gave him a shock. News of military movements would not have surprised him; he had not thought of the inevitably uncomfortable civilian regulations. Food ration cards were being issued that day, and hotels and restaurants were not exempted. Readers were told that the system was merely being tried out. He repeated this assurance to his wife when he translated the statement—the first but not the last time in Germany that he was to present the situation in the most favourable terms

93

—so as not to mar her enjoyment of the walk. They sauntered through the Wilhelmplatz, past the Reichskanzlei (where a crowd stared at the balcony, the scene of Hitler's dramatic public appearances), and along Unter den Linden, pleasant as it then was, back to the Saarlandstrasse. Lunch at a small restaurant was very cheap and ample, seeming to confirm that rationing was only being rehearsed.

They dawdled, killing time, before returning to the hotel, where, instead of resting as they had intended, they nervously awaited their meeting with Bauer.

The young man and his fiancée arrived by car. The Joyces, grown cautious, suspected a reserve in his welcome, but they cheered up when he drove to a restaurant in Savignyplatz, selected a table in the garden, and ordered a meal and wine. Perhaps Bauer was less at ease than he had been in London, and he was obviously keeping the talk away from the reason the Joyces were there, but they reflected that he was, after all, giving his fiancée an evening out, and he would not want to start a conversation which excluded her. Over coffee, however, Bauer broached the awkward subject.

'What do you think of doing now that you are in Germany?'

'I don't know,' Joyce answered, feeling that this was an unpromising beginning. 'What do you think?'

'Oh,' Bauer said lightly, 'there'll be something for you to do, I expect.' Before Joyce could speak again, Bauer added: 'As long as there is no war.'

This afterthought momentarily stunned Joyce. Very quietly he asked: 'And if there is a war?'

Plainly embarrassed, Bauer replied: 'Then you will both be interned.'

'Together?' Joyce rapped out the word.

'Good heavens, no!' the young man exclaimed.

The Joyces exchanged glances. Margaret felt sick. Joyce flushed and seemed about to speak, but the questions he might have put to Bauer had they been alone remained unuttered and he suppressed his anger.

It became apparent that Bauer was not the important person he had represented himself to be. No doubt, a few weeks earlier, he had felt it safe to make an expansive gesture; officials of all grades had been ignorant of the feeling abroad about Hitler's actions; like the rest of the population, they were unaware that a crisis was near. Whatever his position in the Propaganda Ministry, whatever he might be doing in that suite in the Adlon Hotel, he did not have the ear of ministers and he could do nothing to protect two aliens who had arrived for no obviously good reason. He was not even important enough to be given a special petrol allowance; the previous week, when temporary restrictions had been imposed, he had been unable (as had transpired in the conversation) to run his car.

Through the screen of Bauer's good manners Joyce could discern irritation at having been taken literally and disapproval of the foreigners' irresponsibility. But for all Bauer's deficiencies he was the Joyces' only German contact and it seemed likely that they would need his aid, however limited. If war were averted he might find Joyce work; if he did not, their money would soon run out.

Now Joyce and his wife would have liked to return to their room to talk, but Bauer, relieved that recriminations had been avoided, insisted on driving them to see the floodlighting. Berlin at night, the streets thronged with people whose animated faces were illumined by brilliant lights, the crowded restaurants—the scene would have been exciting and picturesque had they been on holiday, but for the Joyces it emphasized their loneliness.

When Bauer delivered them to their hotel they managed to smile and thank him for the entertainment. Joyce promised to telephone him in the morning, so that they parted with protestations of continuing friendship.

The moment they entered their room Margaret's control broke and she wept helplessly. Joyce, knowing that in coming to Germany he had relied on an undertaking which the Propaganda Minister had never given, realizing that his flight from London to escape detention was likely to result in his internment in Germany as an enemy alien, tried to comfort her by declaring that rather than risk separation in Berlin he would take her back. Exhausted, they went to bed and slept soundly.

On Monday morning the dining-room, so quiet the day before, was crowded with uniformed men. Newcomers stood to attention at the door and barked: 'Heil Hitler!' at which everyone else, although remaining seated, gave the Nazi salute of the raised arm. A stickler for military formality, Joyce found it improper to salute while seated, so he rose every time anyone arrived and responded with a vigorous salute. Margaret did not get up, being embarrassed by the silliness of this greeting. Joyce soon found, as he had in the British Army, that life was going to be unbearable if he paraded his loyalty without regard for circumstances. There were so many entrants and so many shouts of Heil that he had to choose between saluting and eating his breakfast. Soon, like the rest, he was flipping his right hand while seated and getting on with the meal.

When they were back in their room Joyce telephoned Bauer. A feminine voice answered. He asked in English for Bauer, repeating the request in German. Bauer's fiancée was speaking and Joyce had difficulty in understanding her. Bauer was not there, he gathered, but he could not follow her explanation of what had happened. He had to ask her to start again and he listened intently, puzzling out the sentences. When he replaced the receiver Margaret sensed that he had suffered another shock.

'Christian got his calling-up papers this morning and he's already left the house. That was his fiancée and she seems upset.'

Joyce sank on to the bed, lit a cigarette and, avoiding his wife's eyes, gloomily reviewed their situation. Here was the final proof, he said, that Bauer was a person of little importance. High-grade staff were not among the first to be called up. Probably they had seen the end of Bauer. If he had intervened on their behalf his efforts would doubtless have been ineffectual, so perhaps the loss was not a great one. But now they were quite on their own and they would have to think out afresh what to do.

It was August 28th, their second day in Berlin, and too early to admit failure, but they were bereft of ideas. A chambermaid opened the door and closed it. Her vacuum cleaner started in the next room. All they could do was to go out again as though they were on holiday.

Seeing an exchange office, Joyce grew nervous that sterling might at any moment become unchangeable, so he went in and—congratulating himself on his foresight—converted the rest of their money into Reichsmarks. Then they sent postcards to their families, to Miss Scrimgeour, and (partly in Latin) to Macnab.

Margaret suggested that, as they had not brought much soap with them, they ought to buy some. The flat refusal of the assistant in the first shop they entered puzzled them. Joyce thought the man could not have understood his request, and he asked whether there was really no soap in the shop. The assistant admitted that a quantity was in stock, but insisted that he could not part with any until the rationing regulations became available.

They had not thought of a soap shortage. Even more than the announcement about food supplies, this discovery revealed the difficulties ahead for foreigners. A minor panic assailed them; they had to procure soap and what had been a leisurely walk now became a rush from shop to shop. After several refusals they felt triumphant when an easy-going salesman, learning that as visitors they were afraid of not receiving a ration, sold them a tablet.

After this success they agreed to stop worrying about soap for the time being and they strolled on, avoiding depressing subjects by chatting about friends. Where was Mrs. Eckersley, Joyce wondered. After leaving Hungary she had intended to go to Berlin about the end of August, so she was probably there now. In their loneliness this thought was extraordinarily encouraging. But what chance had they of finding her? Joyce's good memory did not fail him. He thought he recalled the name Continental. Was there a hotel in Berlin called the Continental? A directory in the next telephone kiosk answered that question.

Glad to have an aim, they decided to lunch at the Hotel Continental and to inquire whether Mrs. Eckersley was staying there. Entering from the bright sunlight, they had to stand for a few moments to accustom themselves to the cool dimness of the Continental's restaurant. They were about to select a table commanding a view of the door when they noticed that the room was small and led to another. Passing through this, they went into a third room.

At a table were Mrs. Eckersley and her son James. The Joyces could hardly believe their luck. Something had, at last, gone right. Mrs. Eckersley looked up, pushed back her chair and rose to her feet with an exclamation of delighted surprise.

Over lunch they all cheered each other up considerably. Afterwards Joyce and his wife had the impression that Mrs. Eckersley had congratulated them on having left England, declared her intention of staying in Germany if there were a war, and dismissed the risk of internment. Mrs. Eckersley felt that it was the

Joyces who had been confident and helped her to resolve her doubts about staying.

Whichever party was the more optimistic, it was Mrs. Eckersley who offered practical assistance. When Joyce told her that he must soon earn money, she said that she had a good friend in Berlin, a Fräulein Dr. Schirmer, whose brother was a very important man in the Foreign Office, so influential as to be able to shield anyone he wanted to and, no doubt, put a protégé in the way of a job. She would introduce them if they would come to Fräulein Schirmer's tea party that afternoon.

To enter a private house was a peculiar pleasure to Joyce and his wife after their aimless pavement-tramping. They had feared that Fräulein Schirmer's brother would not appear, but he came and was very affable. While Margaret talked to her hostess and Mrs. Eckersley, he sat with Joyce on the other side of the room and listened to his story. After his experience with Bauer Joyce had been wary of assuming that this official was quite so important as Mrs. Eckersley had thought him to be, and in this he was justified. Herr Dr. Schirmer denied that he could shield any alien but he thought he might do something about providing work, and he promised that Joyce would hear from him.

No longer quite alone, having acquaintances they could ring up or call on, being told that employment was not out of the question, the Joyces returned to their hotel in a better state of mind. They spent a restful night, but their relative tranquillity was shattered again the next morning.

Until then there had been the threat of war but no certainty. The morning papers now reported that on the previous evening the British Ambassador had handed a note to the Führer expressing the British Government's determination to fulfil its obligations to Poland. On reading this news, Joyce's resolution wavered. With war imminent they were unknown aliens in Berlin, desperate enough to be elated at a stranger's offer of help in finding work, likely to spend years in internment. This time he did not argue at length. The adventure was over, and they had no alternative but to return to London as holidaymakers rushing home while there was still time. As soon as the decision was made their minds were at rest, they enjoyed their breakfast, and immediately afterwards set out for a travel office in Unter den Linden, intending to buy tickets, learn the time of a train, and fetch their luggage from the hotel. On the way Margaret consciously stored up memories of the Berlin which would soon be behind her.

In the travel office Joyce ordered two tickets to London. The assistant asked them to wait a moment, extracted a leaflet from a clip of papers, ran his pencil down the paragraphs, stopped at one and studied it.

'How are you going to pay?' he inquired.

Producing a bundle of German notes, Joyce replied: 'In Reichsmark.'

The assistant re-read the paragraph and slowly shook his head.

'I am sorry,' he said. 'We are not allowed to accept German currency for a journey outside Germany.'

Mechanically Joyce put the money back in his pocket, while continuing to stare at the clerk. His usually quick brain took several seconds to grasp the magnitude of his mistake twenty-four hours earlier in changing his British money for marks.

The man behind the counter, seeing the caller's stunned expression, offered two tickets to the frontier, where they could cross out of Germany. It was a practicable suggestion but Joyce, numbed, could think only of the difficulties of being stranded, in the midst of confusion, on the Continent. In Berlin aliens were more likely, he thought, to be dealt with in an orderly manner.

All the clerk could now advise was an appeal to the British Embassy. Joyce despondently expressed his thanks, said to his wife that they would go there at once, and strode from the building, furiously angry with himself and seized with the urgency of starting for London. Margaret forgot, as she hurried beside him, that she had been taking a slow, conscious farewell of Berlin. Sweating and breathless, they rushed into the Embassy.

Packing cases encumbered the entrance hall. Hearing their footsteps, a very old German porter emerged. Tensely Joyce explained their plight. To the old man this was just another incident in a harassing week and, after listening with an air of much-tried patience, he told them to wait and then disappeared behind the crates. With the valuable minutes ebbing away, the Joyces viewed the sad spectacle of the littered hall.

Rapid footsteps brought a busy-looking official who raised his eyebrows on learning that they were British subjects trying to get home. Obviously shocked at their stupidity in delaying their departure, he told them that they had come to the wrong office and they would have to go to the Consulate in Tiergartenstrasse.

Embarrassed at not having known this and fearing that his further mistake had lost them their last chance of escaping, Joyce dashed in a frenzy through the baking streets, taking a longer route than necessary because he was unsure of the way. To their relief no luggage was visible at the Consulate. A receptionist calmly greeted the panting visitors, listened to Joyce's barely coherent explanation, telephoned, and said that someone would see them.

The young man who soon appeared was cool and unhurried. His well-barbered look, unwrinkled collar, carefully-arranged tie and good suit made them acutely aware that they were dusty, hot and shaking. He was the type whom Joyce the agitator had portrayed walking on rose petals. Politely he inclined his head while listening non-committally to Joyce's recital. A shadow of distaste crossed his features as he heard how they had rushed about Berlin in an endeavour to get away.

Dismissing them, he said that there was nothing he could do to help and they should go to the Consulate at Cologne.

They found themselves thanking him more effusively than they intended and then they fled from the building, back to the comparatively familiar surroundings of Friedrichstrasse, near their room and their few possessions. They did not slacken their pace until they were almost at their hotel when, exhausted, they stopped before the open door of a small Bierstube and looked into a dark, cool room furnished with plain wooden chairs and tables and empty of customers.

In the dimness Joyce glanced across the table at his wife's pale face and trembling hands. He ordered beer and vodkas. The beer was nearly gone before he spoke.

'What do you want to do, darling? I'll do anything you want. Do you want to go to Cologne?'

She stared into her glass of vodka, trying to think. The hot train back to Cologne . . . then more streets, another office and more shoulder-shrugging. He waited patiently for her answer.

'Oh, let's stop messing about and just stay here. They'll be just as unhelpful in Cologne.' She paused before adding a characteristically flippant remark. 'There's at least good drink here.'

Joyce ordered two more vodkas.

Chapter 10

JOB-HUNTING IN BERLIN

On Wednesday, August 30th, while Sir Oswald Mosley was addressing a Fascist anti-war demonstration in London, Joyce and his wife, faced with having to make their money stretch indefinitely, were looking for a cheap furnished lodging in Berlin. With agencies' lists, and a street map to make them independent of taxis, they set out to view their first selection, a vacant room in Karlstrasse.

A nauseating smell pervaded the surrounding slum. They entered a courtyard and groped their way in darkness up echoing stairs. A flabby, dirty woman, the landlady, whose name they could not pronounce, looked dubious on learning that they were aliens.

'I suppose you can have the room,' she said surlily, 'but I didn't want any more foreigners. The Pole who lived here was fetched by the police.'

She flung open a door and followed them into a scene of hideous squalor. Extricating themselves was difficult, but they managed to smile and bow their way out and to restrain an impulse to run down the stairs and beyond the range of eyes they sensed peeping at them through cracks in the doors.

After this experience they were more cautious, entering only houses which looked respectable from outside. Some rooms they saw were tidy, clean and cheap, but these had always just been let. The owners, they suspected, were nervous of taking foreigners, yet they encountered no hostility.

The morning was without result. For a meal they went by chance to Aschingers, and thus made the useful discovery of this chain of cheap restaurants. All that afternoon they walked, not yet daring to trust themselves to the unfamiliar public transport system. When, dejectedly, they returned to their hotel in the evening, they seemed to have been away a long time. Fantasies that the war danger had passed and they were boarding the train for London passed through Margaret's brain.

As he collected the room key Joyce, to his surprise, was handed an envelope. It contained a note from Dr. Schirmer with a number which Joyce was to telephone on the following day. The hopes this message aroused lightened the evening, and he made the call early next morning. Immediately he announced himself a secretary's voice dictated an address and asked him to present himself there in the afternoon.

Before this appointment they still had time to visit more of the lodgings on their lists. Fearing that their search would last for days, they were incredulous when shown into a large room containing huge twin beds and a monumental tiled stove and told, by the pleasant-looking owner and his wife, that the room was available and that foreigners were welcome.

The landlord, detaining them while he genially reviewed the news, assured them that this Polish business would not last long. His two small children gazed fascinatedly at Margaret, because they could not understand her speech. Asked about England's attitude, Joyce was placatory, for he hesitated to spoil the atmosphere of innocent confidence. His replies pleased the couple so much that they repeated their expressions of welcome while showing their new tenants out.

At last Berlin was exhibiting signs of excitement. Crowds stood before radio shops and squeezed into restaurants to listen to a broadcast by Hitler. Joyce could make little of the hoarse screaming, distorted as it was by the loudspeakers, and they walked on to their hotel, temporarily occupied more with thoughts of their new accommodation and Joyce's appointment than with the crisis.

The address Joyce had been given was of a villa occupied by a Foreign Office department. Several callers went straight to a large room where they sat down at tables, and on inquiring what to do Joyce was told to join them. The others obviously knew each other and were familiar with the place and the procedure. Soon everyone was given writing paper and a few sheets of the text of Hitler's recently-delivered oration. With dismay Joyce realized that he was not to be interviewed for a job. All these people were translators living on occasional commissions whose present task was to produce an English version of the speech.

However, this was at least a chance to earn money, so Joyce applied himself to the Führer's tortuous sentences, determined to produce a good translation in the shortest time. It was not difficult to outstrip the others in speed. Glancing round after completing two sheets, he was elated to see his neighbours still labouring slowly on their first page. When he had finished his allocation he handed his work in and was paid in cash. No one left with him; his fellow translators looked as though they were settled for the afternoon.

Back at the hotel he broke the news to Margaret that he had no regular employment in sight. But he had earned his first money in Germany, got his name on a list of part-time translators, and reduced his expenses. They slept well and rose early to pack.

Descending to the breakfast-room they could already hear martial music played at full volume on the radio. Among the hotel guests the usual saluting was going on, perhaps a shade more briskly than before, but barks of 'Heil Hitler!' by unamplified voices were barely audible.

As they took their places a trumpet fanfare sounded, prefacing a special announcement, and everyone sat listening expectantly to hear only an urgent voice giving a warning that an important statement would be made later. The programme was resumed, and was interrupted after a short interval by another fanfare and a repeated warning.

It became unbearable, the way their attention was held until the first words of the increasingly familiar formula told them that they must wait longer and they were left expecting the programme to fade out again for the fanfare. Anxious though they were to settle in their new lodging, the Joyces felt they could not leave the hotel. Nervously remaining within earshot of the radio set they hung about until a longer pause followed the trumpets, guests emerged from corridors and bedrooms, and at last, to a population made tense by the prolonged build-up, the statement was read that 'on the order of the Führer and the High Command' the armed forces had 'taken over the active protection of the Reich'. In fulfilment of this order 'to put a stop to Polish violence', early that morning German troops had crossed the

German-Polish frontier and counter-attacked. At the same time, aircraft had taken off to attack military targets in Poland and the Navy had assumed the defence of the Baltic.

Thus the war was presented as a punitive expedition against the aggressive Poles. As such it could surely not last very long. That was substantially what the excited guests were telling one another as the Joyces moved out of the hotel and it was what their amiable landlord was repeating when they arrived at their room. The police took the same view when Joyce went to register. At the sight of the two British passports smiling policemen gathered round, they protested affably when Joyce tried to tell them that there was a serious possibility that Britain would enter the war, and they shook hands with him as he left.

On his way back to the lodging, Joyce vainly endeavoured to buy a British newspaper.

That night the black-out was no practice and the streets were so dark that after a drink in a bar Joyce, who was night-blind, had to be piloted home by Margaret. She noted that the bar could be identified by a gleam from an ill-fitting curtain.

Next day Joyce did nothing but read the Berlin papers and try to follow the news—which Margaret anxiously waited for him to interpret—on his landlord's radio set. As hours passed what little hope they had that war might be averted vanished. Gloomily they went out in the evening and, guided by the chink of light, found the bar.

In *Twilight over England* (discussed in Chapter 15) Joyce wrote this account of how they heard the news on September 3rd.

'At twenty minutes past twelve Central European time, my landlady rushed into my room and told me: "Jetzt ist es Krieg mit England!" (It's war now, with England!) Her husband at once came in and shook hands with my wife and myself, saying: "Whatever happens, we remain friends." We had known these simple people only since the previous day: they had no proof that I too was not an enemy: but their action was typical of the whole attitude of the German people.

'At about three in the afternoon, the first newspapers announcing England's declaration of war were on the streets. They were given away free. Under the bridge outside the Friedrichstrasse Station, we all scrambled for papers. There was no sign of anger or hatred: people looked at each other as if the incredible had happened. We went to tea with some friends whose name is famous in German history. They too felt no emotion except surprise and regret. We talked of England: and my host was so inspiring in his eloquence on the subject of what England might have achieved in friendship with Germany that, as I looked out on the twilight enshrouding the Kurfürstendamm, I could think of nothing to say but Marlowe's famous lines:

> *Cut is the branch that might have grown full strait*
> *And burned is Apollo's laurel bough!'*

The friends were von Bülow and his American wife, who had hastily returned from London to Berlin.

During stress Joyce's practice was to express his feelings by a quotation. He had regarded Hitler as inspired, but that afternoon he was depressed by forebodings. Although not doubting the rightness of the Nazi cause, he thought that he detected defeatism among the Germans from the start. He was worried, too, about his probable treatment. Despite his sweeping statement, for which he could have had no adequate evidence, that the attitude of the landlord and his wife was typical of the whole German people, he disbelieved von Bülow's assertion that he would encounter no hostility.

Each conscious that the other was unhappy, Joyce and his wife were walking that evening in the Tiergarten when the calm was broken by a sound, still unfamiliar, which they supposed must be an air raid siren. They stopped, expecting that hostilities were opening with a massive air raid, and they wondered whether they were breaking a regulation by not being in a shelter. The faint hum of a distant aircraft engine imposed itself on the noise of far-off traffic, and two explosions reverberated across the city. It was a false alarm, and what had caused the bangs they never discovered, but they felt that the war had been given its starting signal.

The next day, in London, Macnab was visited by a police officer and a constable, who searched his room before asking when he had last seen Joyce. He told them of his friend's departure—Joyce had not asked that it should be kept secret—and he produced the postcard and obligingly translated the Latin passage. Thus the day after the war started the police knew where Joyce was.

No news from home had reached the couple, and now they could not hope for any. Although they had a few acquaintances in the city, they felt lonely, helpless and homesick. Food rationing made shopping too complicated for them and they relied on their landlady who, through the good offices of the Nazi Blockleiter (the lowest level of Party official, responsible for supervising one block of flats or a group of dwellings), procured and used their ration cards. Whenever she returned with her purchases they counted their remaining money.

They were drawing steadily on their small capital. Anxious to earn any sum, however small, Joyce learned with indignation that he had been reducing his translation fees by working so fast, because payment was made by the hour and not by the page. The slowness of the other translators was now explained, and by dawdling like them he managed to get a little more money, but even so he saw that there was no chance of a living from this work.

But Dr. Schirmer had not forgotten him. Joyce was summoned to the Foreign Office and interviewed by an official who had been persuaded that this unknown alien was a likely recruit for the service. The official was polite but evasive and obviously suspicious. Joyce froze under this treatment, said little, and received with a slight bow and an expressionless face the statement that there was no suitable vacancy in that department.

Home again, he tried vainly to conceal his hopelessness from his wife who, frightened to go out in case someone spoke to her and revealed her ignorance of German, stayed miserably at home with nothing to do except keep one room in order. Without even anything to read, Margaret had no distractions except visits by the landlady, who brought in meals and clearly enunciated a few words in German in an endeavour to teach her useful phrases. Through the language barrier Margaret perceived that this kind-hearted woman was less confident about the future than she had at first seemed and was by no means a wholehearted supporter of the Führer. When a young brown-shirted man called to ask why her son was not attending Hitler Jugend meetings, she brusquely dismissed him.

Although Joyce was discouraged by his interview, Dr. Schirmer was not and he arranged appointments with other officials, all of whom behaved rather like the first and made it plain that there was no place for Joyce in the Foreign Office.

Joyce himself was unhelpful in the interviews as he had no clear idea of what kind of work he was seeking; vaguely he thought that there might be a department of advisers on British affairs where he could make himself useful. He did not know that the German Foreign Office had a rich assortment of self-styled experts on England; any civil servant who had so much as spent a fortnight in London was clamouring to be allowed to set up his own department, and the intrusion of an apparently genuine Englishman would have been highly unwelcome to these. Joyce was made to realize acutely that he was a foreigner, unknown to any person of consequence and with no qualifications for which there was any demand. A bad head cold added to his misery.

The last man he saw in the Foreign Office employed the bureaucrat's trick of professing to think that there would be a better chance for Joyce somewhere outside, and recommended him to see Dr. Erich Hetzler, who sat in the private office of von Ribbentrop, the Foreign Minister. Although this office dealt with foreign affairs, it was not part of the Foreign Office.

Hetzler, a Doctor of Economics of Munich University and a tall, well-built, determined-looking man, was an admirer of English ways of thought, two terms at the London School of Economics having impressed him with the pragmatic approach of British economists to their subject. During the slump of the early 1930's his father's business had gone bankrupt, he had been unable to find a job in industry, and he had joined the Nazi Party. His professor in Munich recommended him, as having a good knowledge of English, for employment in von Ribbentrop's office. He was sent with other envoys to England, at the time of the funeral of King George V, to help report on probable British reactions to a German reoccupation of the Rhineland. While in London he met public personalities, such as Labour leaders, with whom German diplomats had no official contact. Thus he had a sounder claim to know something of British affairs than had many of his contemporaries. When a secretary told him that an Englishman was asking to see him he stopped what he was doing to receive the visitor at once.

The girl returned leading Joyce, who stood in the doorway head erect, hands to his sides, and heels together. He inclined his head in acknowledgement of Hetzler's greeting and, speaking English, gave his name. Moving forward with military stiffness, he sat down at Hetzler's invitation. These un-English manners temporarily mystified Hetzler, and he studied with curiosity his caller's scar and neat rather than smart turnout.

At first Joyce was uneasy; he expected nothing of this interview and was prepared for another polite dismissal. Hetzler had to question him to start him talking. Joyce announced, rather coolly, that he was British and a National Socialist. Then he qualified this statement by adding that a National Socialist in Britain was not the same as one in Germany.

Apart from a few in England, the only British Fascists Hetzler had met were those who attended a Nazi rally at Nuremberg where he had acted as Hitler's interpreter, and he had thought these 'cheap and anxious to please'. Joyce struck him as straightforward, independent and likeable. At last, sensing sympathy, Joyce began to talk more freely, looking straight at Hetzler.

As an anti-Semite, Joyce explained, he supported Hitler's policy towards the Jews, and in a war against them he was on the side of the anti-Semites. Accordingly, fearing that a war was inevitable, he had left England for Germany. When he came to talk of his experience in Berlin he grew indignant. He would have supposed, he said, that the German Foreign Office could have offered employment to a sympathizer who knew Britain and the British mentality.

'What sort of employment?' Hetzler asked.

Joyce was still vague about what he might do, and he answered: 'Any suitable work.'

Unlike others who had seen Joyce, Hetzler was not suspicious and no thought crossed his mind that the visitor might have been planted by the British. He accepted that Joyce was what he claimed to be. But what could he do for him? Obviously the Foreign Office was not going to take this unsponsored alien. There was no possibility, either, of his being employed in von Ribbentrop's office. If he were to help Joyce he had to do it now, as he himself had volunteered for service in an anti-aircraft unit with which he had trained, and he did not know how much longer he would be sitting at his desk. Where, apart from the Foreign Office, would a knowledge of English be useful? Possibly in the radio external service where the English-speaking department was being enlarged.

'Have you ever thought of working for the radio?' he inquired.

Joyce replied that he had not. The question warned him that he was again being referred to another organization, but he felt that Hetzler was genuinely trying to help him and not simply getting rid of him. He listened, but without hope, while Hetzler telephoned a Walter Kamm in Reichsrundfunk (the German radio corporation) and asked him to see an Englishman named Joyce.

Chapter 11

THE BIRTH OF LORD HAW-HAW

'Germany calling, Germany calling, Germany calling! Here are the Reichssender Hamburg, station Bremen. . . .' The details of the stations varied according to the transmitters available to Reichsrundfunk's English-speaking service. The announcers tended to stress the first syllable in 'Germany' in a way that sounded unfamiliar and sinisterly-funny to English ears. The pronunciation was widely mimicked as 'Jairmany'—a poor imitation which became part of the myth about these broadcasts.

British people having grown accustomed to the idea that war would open with an enemy attempt at a knock-out blow, they were nonplussed when, with a stringently-enforced blackout and children evacuated from what were thought to be the more vulnerable areas, a strange calm settled over the country. There were reports of sunken ships and some air activity, but the nights were undisturbed by raiders and the armies facing each other in France had not fired a shot. The official-sounding bulletins became monotonously repetitive. Somewhere, millions of people thought, there must be news, so they turned the dials of their radio sets for news in English from any source—Hamburg, Paris, Rome, Madrid, Moscow or Radio Athlone. As the voice of the enemy, the German radio enjoyed an advantage over its competitors.

The headquarters of Reichsrundfunk were at the Rundfunk-haus, Masurenallee, in the Charlottenburg district of Berlin. The news in English was read live in the studios there and the commentaries, except in emergencies, were recorded, the programmes being sent by post office land line to transmitters at Hamburg, Bremen, Cologne and Zeesen, according to their availability. The German home programmes were interrupted by an announcement that the station was now going to transmit news in English. Germans also suspected that they were being starved of news, and those who could understand English listened in the hope of picking up items not released for home consumption. In some schools children listened as part of their English lessons, so that their accents would be improved.

The service for Britain was only one of several. Early in the war Reichsrundfunk was operating other English services to North America and the Far East and putting out programmes in French, Polish, Italian, Spanish, Portuguese and Afrikaans. Policy was decided by Dr. Josef Goebbels's Propaganda Ministry in liaison with the Foreign Office, the fighting services and other government departments. The general line early in September 1939 was to present the war as a struggle between idealistic youth and corrupt age. 'The young nations of Germany and Russia will bring a new dawn to Europe,' Deutschlandsender was telling its home audience on September 5th, while programmes in English to the United States and the Far East were ending with the slogan: 'Germany is fighting for the restoration of an injustice. Others are fighting for its preservation.'

The head of the overseas short wave services, Walter Kamm, was at this time also looking after the European foreign departments. He had assembled a small Anglo-German team of newsreaders and commentators, the senior being Norman Baillie-Stewart, a former subaltern in the Seaforth Highlanders who, much publicized by the British press as 'the officer in the Tower', had been sentenced by a court martial in 1933 to five years' imprisonment for offences under the Official Secrets Act; released in 1937, he was known to have gone to the Continent. Nobody in Britain knew the identities of the English-speaking radio contributors; when names were mentioned they were false, Baillie-Stewart being called Manfred von Krause.

Listening on September 6th the British Broadcasting Corporation's monitors made a note that one of the Reichsrundfunk speakers spoke such good English that it was obviously his mother tongue. Next day they added another comment, this time on Baillie-Stewart's style: 'In all references to England the announcer's intonation was extremely sarcastic.'

By the second week of the war the small English-speaking department was putting out nine bulletins daily and Kamm badly needed more voices, especially native English ones. Hetzler's telephone call came opportunely.

Desperate though he was for a job, Joyce was reserved and dignified when interviewed by Kamm and he made no attempt to sell himself. He stated who he was and why he had come to Germany, leaving it to Kamm to make suggestions. When Kamm asked whether he would care to work as a news-reader, Joyce merely said that he was willing to try. The proposal that he should have an immediate voice test alarmed him, because his cold was still troublesome. Kamm was in no mood to wait, however, and he had Joyce escorted to a studio.

Joyce had never been in a broadcasting studio and his only microphone experience had been at public meetings of the British Union. Reading to an unresponsive microphone was disconcerting to an orator used to facing an excited audience, and he was nervous. Speaking from a parched throat, he enunciated each word carefully, as had been his custom when teaching his students, and he took longer than the specified time to finish the script. He realized that he had done badly and he knew what the producers' decision would be.

Radio producers tend to think that all broadcasters should sound alike; even making allowances for his cold, Joyce was not at all their idea of a news-reader. As they listened to him in the control room they agreed to reject him.

Joyce's destiny was now in the balance. If turned down as a radio voice he might still have been given work reading and clipping the British papers, building up a library of press cuttings, perhaps translating talks for other people to read. In this capacity he would have remained obscure, the name of William Joyce would have meant nothing to the British public, and if caught after the war he would have appeared in the dock on a lesser charge than high treason.

But a radio engineer now intervened and settled his fate. He broke into the producers' conversation to insist emphatically that the voice had possibilities. Conscious of the dearth of English speakers, the producers hesitated. Joyce sat awaiting their verdict, wondering what they could be talking about next door.

There seemed no point in asking the candidate to go through the test piece again so they decided, without much enthusiasm, to let Joyce read an actual bulletin later in the day and see how he got on.

The day was 11th September 1939. Nobody now recalls the time of Joyce's first broadcast or the words he read. The general theme of the external services that day was British hypocrisy, British colonialism, Britain's alleged attempts to involve neutral countries in the war, and the inefficiency of the British blockade of Germany. At 1555 Zeesen, in English, after a reference to the Franco-British alliance, produced that familiar gibe that 'England will fight to the last Frenchman'. To Poland Deutschland-sender was saying in Polish: 'Britain is always ready to fight with other people's soldiers and has already fought to the last Polish soldier.' Zeesen then appealed in Arabic: 'Arabs! Now is the time to fight for your independence. The souls of those Arabs who have been killed by British hands call you up to fight and get rid of hypocritical Britain.' At 1730 a broadcast in English from Hamburg, Cologne and Zeesen reported concern in Bucharest at Britain's efforts to bring Turkey into the war, and the Scandinavian refusal to be bullied by Britain into withholding food supplies from Germany. There seems to have been a shortage of hard news on that day.

Joyce did better than the producers had anticipated. They agreed that their engineer colleague might be right. Joyce was told that he could stay on and if found satisfactory he would be given a contract. Then he was introduced to some of the broadcasters with whom he would be working.

Baillie-Stewart and he, coming face to face for the first time, promptly took a dislike to each other. According to Joyce, Baillie-Stewart greeted him with: 'I suppose you've come to take our jobs away.'

Why, after Joyce's indifferent first performance as a newsreader, Baillie-Stewart should fear his competition I cannot imagine. The remark, if made, would have implied that Joyce was better than everyone else on the staff, and the anecdote probably reveals Joyce's determination to make himself so.

Joyce, the man who had railed at the British for their lack of patriotism, had broadcast for the enemy against Britain. The occasion was a turning point in his life. Now should have followed one of his all-night talking sessions, but he was concerned only to have employment and earn money to save himself and his wife from internment or destitution. After his first broadcast, when he told his wife of the day's events, they pooled and counted their cash. They had twenty marks left. What they would have done had he not got a job that week they had no idea.

Only four days later Captain Plugge, the Conservative Member of Parliament for Chatham, asked the Home Secretary if he would take steps to make it known to English men and women who, being still British subjects in enemy countries, agreed to be employed as announcers of anti-British propaganda in English from enemy broadcasting stations, that they thereby rendered themselves liable to prosecution in England for treason. Joyce did not learn of the question and the answer ('Any British subject who undertakes work of the kind described must be well aware that his conduct may lead to his having to meet charges of the gravest character hereafter') but he needed no such reminder. He was fatalistic about what would happen to him if the British caught him.

Just after Joyce had started his radio work, and before he had signed a contract, a disturbing incident occurred. He was on night shift when Margaret was roused in the early morning by the landlady, who conveyed to her that a policeman was there to arrest Joyce. Margaret did not know that the German Government had ordered the arrest of all adult British males living in Germany. The policeman, peeping into the room and seeing that the Englishwoman was alone, questioned the landlady. On learning where Joyce was, he politely said he would come again later.

Now it seemed to Margaret that what they had tried to avoid was bound to happen. Her husband would be interned and their worst fear, that they would be parted in a strange country, would come true. Distracted, she counted the minutes to his return.

Joyce reacted promptly when he heard of his danger. He rushed out to a public telephone box and called first the police, to tell them that he was at home, and then Hetzler, who promised to take action.

A morning of apprehension followed but as the day wore on and the policeman did not reappear, they gained confidence. Joyce's new employers, alerted by Hetzler, had intervened to secure their news-reader's exemption from the general arrest order.

Captain Plugge's question was evidence of the great interest now being taken in Britain in the enemy's broadcasts. Newspapers were commenting on them daily. In the *Daily Express* of September 14th Jonah Barrington (a pseudonym), who was running a feature based on the monitoring of enemy broadcasts, made this observation.

'A gent I'd like to meet is moaning periodically from Zeesen. He speaks English of the haw-haw, damit-get-out-of-my-way variety, and his strong suit is gentlemanly indignation.'

The word 'haw-haw', soon to be repeated nightly by millions of radio listeners, had appeared in print for the first time as a description of the officer-and-gentleman voice of Reichsrundfunk's English-language commentator Norman Baillie-Stewart. It had not yet been prefixed by 'Lord' to form the best-known nickname of the Second World War. 'This name occurred to me while scratching the neck of a browsing cow in a lonely Sussex field, outside a secret receiving station where I was working at the beginning of the war,' Mr. Barrington later revealed in the *Sunday Chronicle*. He was quick to get it into print.

On September 18th the *Daily Express* announced: 'Jonah Barrington, listening at the *Daily Express* short wave station in Surrey to the war on the radio, introduces "Lord Haw-Haw".'

Barrington had already commented on a woman speaker whom he had named Winnie of Warsaw. Now he detected a similarity between her scripts and those of the speaker from Zeesen.

'Winnie of Warsaw (who really works for the Nazi station at Breslau) has a follower—Lord Haw-Haw of Zeesen.

'From his accent and personality I imagine him with a receding chin, a questing nose, thin, yellow hair brushed back, a monocle, a vacant eye, a gardenia in his button-hole. Rather like P. G. Wodehouse's Bertie Wooster.'

Lower down the column, however, appeared a paragraph which damaged the Bertie Wooster picture.

'Lord Haw-Haw, hard though he tries to be blue-blooded and British, trips up occasionally. "Sir Winston Churchill," he said recently, and then: "Ach, nein! I mean Mr. Winston Churchill."'

Who could this speaker have been? Baillie-Stewart was unlikely to have exclaimed 'Ach, nein!' Yet a German who could speak convincingly like a Wodehouse English aristocrat would be a phenomenon. Right from the start Lord Haw-Haw was a many-sided personality.

The Birth of Lord Haw-Haw

On the day that Lord Haw-Haw received his title, the apprentice news-reader, William Joyce, was given his first contract. From then on he took his regular turn, with the English-speaking Germans, on the news-readers' rota.

At this time the news in English from Germany dwelt largely on the rapid German advance through Poland. Comment was much concerned with pointing out to the British the futility of their gesture to the Poles and charging them with the responsibility for the war (the principal culprits influencing British policy were held to be the Jews, the democratic press, Winston Churchill, Leo Amery, Duff Cooper, Hore-Belisha and Stephen King-Hall). The French, the British listeners were reminded, were their traditional enemies, and the United States, they were warned, would stay neutral. Much effort was also employed to substantiate a German charge that the British liner *Athenia*, torpedoed on September 4th by a U-boat while outward-bound for New York carrying American citizens among the passengers, had actually been sunk by a bomb placed on board at Winston Churchill's orders in the hope of impairing German-American relations. Britain was repeatedly accused of infringements of Dutch neutrality by sending Royal Air Force planes across Holland on leaflet raids over Germany. The existence of a state of war between Britain and Germany was frequently deplored and various personalities (Countess von Zeppelin, an Englishwoman married to a German, was one) were brought to the microphone to appeal for Anglo-German friendship. The British and French Governments were identified with capitalism and British workers reminded that Germany was a National Socialist state.

The first co-ordinated and the most persistent single campaign to undermine the confidence of the British in their Government opened during the evening of September 28th with a statement from Hamburg: 'We have an important communication for listeners. Where is the *Ark Royal*? It was hit in a German attack on September 26th at 3 p.m. There was a terrific explosion. Where is the *Ark Royal*? Britain, ask your Admiralty.' The announcement was repeated twice that evening in the broadcasts to Britain and included in all the overseas bulletins in English. The next night it was taken up again by the usual German stations and by Warsaw, now operated by the Germans.

The Birth of Lord Haw-Haw

'No responsible British or foreign journalist has been invited to inspect the *Ark Royal*. Where is the *Ark Royal*?' The Propaganda Ministry having great faith in the value of repetition, the accusation that the British Admiralty was suppressing news of the loss of this aircraft carrier was reiterated for many months. At the time I supposed that the campaign was started as a German Naval Intelligence operation to force the British Admiralty to make a possibly revealing statement, but the programme staff appears to have regarded it as no more than another morale-breaking effort. The ship had not been sunk, and the British authorities maintained their silence.

In Britain estimates of the effect of German broadcasts differed widely. A Conservative Member of Parliament, Mr. Baxter, spoke for those who were worried about them when, on September 21st, he told the House of Commons that 'more should be done by the BBC for we are losing the radio war badly.' Mass-circulation newspapers were, however, taking a light-hearted view of foreign propaganda broadcasts. 'I earnestly ask all of you who are able to listen to broadcasts from Germany to this country to do so,' wrote the *Daily Mirror* columnist Cassandra on September 25th in a paragraph emphasizing their entertainment value.

Cassandra made no reference to Lord Haw-Haw, that nickname not having yet been adopted by other papers. Charles Graves, in the *Daily Mail*, even tried to destroy the impression of the broadcaster as a character like Bertie Wooster. 'Many of you must have heard this particular German announcer and perhaps formed your own impression of him. Some people suggest that he is a monocled ass, like one of P. G. Wodehouse's titled creations. This I regard as an insult both to P. G. Wodehouse and the peerage.' Graves, quoting Ward Price as concurring, was 'willing to have a small bet that he is a fat elderly Shakespearian actor, probably deported from England and until war broke out a professor of elocution at some small German institute', and he thought he sounded as though his name were 'Uriah Harbottle, or something like that'.

Jonah Barrington, striving patriotically in his *Express* column to nullify German propaganda, remained unchallenged in the invention of comic names for broadcasters. Winnie of Warsaw he renamed Winnie the Whopper, and, besides Lord Haw-Haw (who was being accorded the monopoly of broadcasting from Germany), he was now making play with two characters called Uncle Boo-Hoo and Mopey. In his column of October 2nd Barrington recorded with satisfaction that Lord Donegal had introduced, with acknowledgments to him, these personalities into his *Sunday Dispatch* feature. 'Good,' Barrington commented, adding in the true British 'let 'em all come' tradition: 'The more people who tune in to the foreign radio impropaganda experts, the greater the joy and laughter.'

But Winnie the Whopper, Uncle Boo-Hoo and Mopey never achieved an existence of their own. Lord Haw-Haw, however, leapt vigorously into a career which took him far beyond the column where he was born. A myth immensely more powerful than that of the Angels of Mons (a writer's unwitting creation) and the Russians with snow on their boots was in the process of evolution.

Donegal attempted to identify Lord Haw-Haw. During his inquiries he came upon someone who suggested the missing founder of the National Socialist League as a likely suspect. Obtaining Macnab's address, he wired that he wished to meet him about something important.

Macnab, now a volunteer ambulance driver, had no radio set, and his only experience of an English-language broadcast from Germany had been during an evening at the home of a friend whose wife was Polish. The hostess tuned in to hear a broadcaster from Germany whose voice she liked; the voice was unknown to Macnab and he found it displeasing—'like a stage lord'. He did not, of course, know that Joyce had started to work for Reichsrundfunk.

When Macnab and Donegal met, Donegal produced an article he had written for the next issue of the *Sunday Dispatch*, and said he wanted to know whether the broadcaster who was the subject of the article was William Joyce. Macnab replied that he was willing to listen to a broadcast in his company, that he would undertake to tell him no lies, but that he would not guarantee to tell him anything at all.

Donegal accepted this reservation. All he wanted, he said, was a yes or no to his question: 'Is this man now broadcasting William Joyce?'

They went into the next room, where there was an unearthed

short-wave set. Behind the deafening noise of the static Macnab recognized the voice of his friend whom he had last seen on Victoria Station. He did not need to comment.

'That's not the man I'm talking about,' Donegal remarked. Then he asked whether Macnab could come to his country house and listen in better conditions.

When they listened on the next day reception was good, and they heard a broadcast by the man whose voice had appealed to the Polish woman.

Donegal said: 'You see what I mean about calling him Haw-Haw, on account of the affected way he talks?'

'Yes,' Macnab agreed, 'it's a good name.'

'Is that Joyce?' Donegal asked.

Macnab could answer truthfully: 'Quite certainly not. There is no resemblance at all.'

Chapter 12

HONEST INJUN!

The recently-recruited news-reader spoke a clear and obviously native English, and on 3rd October 1939 the BBC monitors recorded their judgement on him.

'There is a new announcer on these stations who speaks perfect English, but with a much less ironical tone than the other English announcer.'

While he was being entered, anonymously and with this approving note, in the BBC's records, a character named Wilhelm Fröhlich was being added to the nominal roll of Reichsrundfunk. Joyce had no wish to conceal his identity but he was required, like all the foreign employees of the German radio, to adopt an alias for use if required. As a joke he translated what he claimed was the Joyces' ancestral name, Joyeux, into Fröhlich. So far as his employers were concerned, that was his official name.

It was not used consistently, however. To the German Ministry of Labour he was William Joyce and on October 4th he signed his employment book, just issued to him, in his own name. Every employed person in Germany had such a document containing personal details of the holder, his qualifications and a record of his employment. The entries in Joyce's stated that he had been born in Galway on 24th April 1906, and that his nationality was 'Great Britain'. His special qualification was entered as English, and his 'sporting qualifications' as swimming, riding and boxing. The claim to these accomplishments must have been made in the spirit of wartime applicants for Army commissions, who knew that they could pretend to be proficient in any manly sport without the risk of having their skill tested.

Now that his appointment was confirmed he was allowed to

apply for naturalization, Hitler having issued an order permitting aliens to be granted German nationality where desirable. In deciding on an alien's application the first consideration was not his ultimate safety but whether he would require to have access to classified material. It seems odd to the British way of thinking that Joyce was taken on in a position of trust without security clearance but there was in fact no procedure requiring the vetting of foreign staff. Certain German officials were unhappy about him, his devotion to the National Socialist régime seeming too intense to them to be true. Officers in the Abwehr (the military Intelligence service) suspected that he was a British agent, and Admiral Canaris, their head, was thought to share this view. But with nothing more to go on than the feeling that Joyce was an improbable phenomenon, they refrained from crossing swords with the Propaganda Ministry. The only interrogation was occasioned by Joyce's volunteering the information that he had made a false declaration to obtain a British passport. The incorrect place of birth had already been copied from his passport into his employment book, but while applying for German naturalization he decided to put the record of his birth straight at last, so he entered it as New York.

He thus provided German civil servants with the kind of problem every bureaucrat hates, one not covered by rules or precedents. Gestapo officials questioned him for a long time before accepting his explanation. That nearly a year was to elapse before he received his certificate of citizenship was probably not, however, caused by the authorities' suspicions but by the dilatoriness of the departments handling the application.

The war was now a month old and Joyce had been employed as a news-reader for three weeks. In the months and years to come many curious stories were to be told of what listeners had heard him say on the German radio. One of the most remarkable concerned the first month of the war and was not given publicity until Joyce's trial. In a trial the court has to hear evidence of the events with which it is dealing, even though those may be public knowledge, and the prosecution accordingly produced a witness to say that while stationed at Folkestone between 3rd September and 10th December 1939 he had heard Joyce broadcasting. He was a detective inspector who, having been present at Joyce's meetings before the war, claimed to be familiar with his voice, and he deposed that between the start of the war and early October he had heard Joyce's voice on the radio announcing that Folkestone and Dover had been destroyed. Joyce's counsel suggested that the witness must have been mistaken and observed that, no bomb of any description having been dropped on the country, it would have been a fantastic statement. The prosecution countered this objection by arguing that although the report would have sounded fantastic to residents in the area, it would not have done so to British soldiers and other people abroad. Commentators have since generally accepted that Joyce made a bad blunder right at the beginning of his career by putting out an obviously false piece of news.

It is, of course, naïve to think that any broadcaster on a state radio system can go to the microphone and say just anything he likes. If Joyce made this statement, it must have been one prepared by the Propaganda Ministry. The witness was unable to give the full text of the announcement or to say on what station and exactly when he heard it, but he was not to be shaken by the defence. The BBC was already at that time maintaining an extensive monitoring service, but no one seems to have asked it for confirmation. Wanting the text I have searched the BBC's records for this period, but I could not find the report in any of Reichsrundfunk's bulletins, whether directed to Britain or overseas. Nor did they contain news even remotely of that type. It is a pity that the BBC monitors, that most attentive listener, Jonah Barrington, and all the news-avid public were apparently tuned to other stations at that moment, because such a preposterous claim would, if reported, have provided all the columnists who were making so merry at the expense of Dr. Goebbels with the most riotously funny story of the war, and its skilful exploitation by the British Ministry of Information could have forced the German Propaganda Ministry to even more transparently ridiculous assertions. Any news service trying to put over the story of such a heavy blow at Britain could have been called on to explain why the operation had not deserved mention in the German High Command's communiqués and why the bald statement of the destruction of two towns was not followed up in subsequent bulletins by descriptions of the damage, estimates of the casualties and gloatings about the effect on the population's morale.

Honest Injun!

I should remark here that if the court had rejected this evidence, Joyce's fate would have been unchanged, as the production of his employment book would have been sufficient proof that he had broadcast for the enemy.

The situation in Berlin was, for those living there, fairly encouraging. Warsaw had surrendered on September 27th and the Berlin State Opera had reopened on the same day. Flags flew on October 6th to celebrate final victory over Poland and Hitler made a speech at the Kroll Opera. The cinemas had afternoon showings of war films, including pictures of the West Wall; the scenes of the irresistible attack in the east and the powerful fortifications in the west suggested that German might was unchallengeable. A sign of returning normality was the restarting of internal air lines. The bars were open and well stocked, and the imperfect black-out enabled the Joyces to find their way to and from Haffners, where Joyce sat in the evenings and talked to the habitués, who thought that because he was a foreigner employed in the radio he must be well-informed.

He was not as knowledgeable as his audience supposed. He still had no radio set and the only newspapers he saw were German. How accurate the bulletins he broadcast were he could not judge, but he was troubled about their presentation. With material sometimes being put into his hand while he was at the microphone, he had to be wary that he did not embark on a sentence containing some expression likely to cause incredulous laughter among English-speaking listeners. The occasion when he had to depart from a script to avoid telling the radio audience that a torpedo 'struck in the machines and kettles of the boat' was only one of many such occurrences.

Inquiries he made revealed that news scripts were produced in the Propaganda Ministry by an English Department headed by a former railway engineer who was conceited about his English and whose qualification as an authority was his authorship of a book on Nelson.

Joyce was not slow to criticize the English contrived by the Germans in the Propaganda Ministry and he proposed that the Ministry should employ his wife to correct radio scripts. She would do this, he suggested, without pay, because his salary sufficed for their needs. The Ministry, after some delay, accepted his suggestion that Margaret should be taken on but insisted on engaging her as a salaried writer of women's features, because there was no establishment post for an editor of scriptwriters' English and the civil service rules prohibited unpaid work. Provided she produced a few talks, gathered on visits to social institutions, she could devote her time to correcting other people's work.

An even greater annoyance to Joyce was the ten-minute topical talks which Reichsrundfunk had started on September 18th. Joyce thought the scripts ineffectual—he was critical of almost everybody's speeches (he excepted those of Goebbels), and was convinced that only he could make an impression on the British public. Determined to become a commentator, he wrote a talk. The text went the rounds of the Propaganda Ministry for three weeks before returning mutilated and hopelessly out of date. With no access to newspapers, monitoring and research material, he realized that he was handicapped. Refusing to be deterred he looked out for non-topical subjects. In the BBC's monitoring records Joyce's gradual penetration of the position occupied by Baillie-Stewart and his staff can be traced. Phrases about true nationalism and true Socialism, obviously emanating from Joyce, began to appear in the talks.

Ineffective though they seemed to Joyce, the commentaries were widely listened to in Britain, and not everyone found them as laughable as the newspapers insisted they were. Two visitors were having tea with David Lloyd George one autumn afternoon in 1939 when he interrupted the conversation to switch on the radio. The former prime minister listened attentively to Hamburg, and once he remarked: 'The Government ought to take notice of every word this man says.'

The broadcasts were popularly thought to reveal an uncanny knowledge of what was going on in Britain—although they had contained nothing to justify this reputation—and speculation on the identity of the speakers (or speaker) was intense. At first it seemed as though there would be no mystery. As early as October 4th the *Daily Telegraph* reported that people who had known Baillie-Stewart as a lieutenant in the Seaforth Highlanders had recognized his voice. Two days later the same paper said that British Intelligence officers believed they had identified another British announcer, said to be 'a former official of a political party in England who left for Germany shortly before the war'.

Honest Injun!

The puzzle of two of the broadcasters had been speedily solved. They were very different characters, one an ex-army officer and one a political propagandist. How did all the subsequent confusion then come about? Less than a fortnight later the two clearly-marked trails had inexplicably become fused.

'A special correspondent' in the *Daily Mirror* of October 17th disclosed that: 'Special Branch officers of Scotland Yard are building up evidence that the supercilious Englishman who broadcasts anti-British propaganda every day from a German short-wave station formerly held high rank in the British Fascist movement.' Police officers who had attended Fascist meetings, acquaintances of his Blackshirt days, and 'a woman who used to know him well' were all convinced that they had identified the speaker, whose 'polished manners at the microphone are very different from the violence which his wife used to suffer'.

Having now merged two suspects into one, the report concluded by nearly eliminating one of them. Scotland Yard was quoted as not being satisfied that Baillie-Stewart was 'one of the British broadcasters from Berlin'.

Whatever suspicions may have existed, no one in authority was yet willing to commit himself. Charles Graves, as he recorded in the *Daily Mail* of October 24th, 'took the trouble yesterday to call up the various offices in Whitehall as well as the BBC' and the result was that 'official circles have no official knowledge of the identity of anyone broadcasting in English from Germany'.

Scotland Yard might refer to the 'broadcasters' but the plural went unnoticed by those who, following Barrington's injunction, were ensuring that the joy and laughter increased. The Western Brothers, a pair of comedians who some years earlier had made a hit with 'The Old School Tie', now produced a song about Uncle Boo-Hoo of Moscow and Lord Haw-Haw of Zeesen which one of them over-optimistically described as their biggest number since that success. Another entertainer, Michael Moore, who according to Barrington was 'British radio's most brilliant impersonator', began a Haw-Haw act with Paddy Browne—'slim, snappy, wisecracking copper-brunette'—playing Winnie the Whopper, the act being introduced at a police smoking concert at the Piccadilly Hotel before doing a round of camp concerts in Britain 'just so that our troops can have a really good laugh'.

Honest Injun!

Giving this information in 'a fan letter to Dr. Goebbels', Barrington asked the German propaganda minister to 'take a look at their picture. Haw-Haw, you will observe, is pleading (as usual): "Rehly, you British, it isn't done—it isn't manlah. . . ." '

That was how Haw-Haw was supposed to talk, and the stage had been reached when no one was going to be persuaded differently. The public and the entertainers were agreed that they were listening to one man who had a superior manner and a very affected voice. The theme of the aristocratic traitor aroused such an immense public response that the jeering appeared to be directed as much at the traditional British upper classes as at an unknown traitor in Germany. Nobody was interested in a homely traitor with a name like Uriah Harbottle; the hated broadcaster had to have a high-class accent. The implications of this insistence seemed to have been perceived by the *Daily Telegraph*, which amended the nickname to Lord Hee-Haw and obstinately stuck to this title long after the name Haw-Haw had become firmly established in the columns of the *Daily Express*'s contemporaries. Letter-writers to the *Daily Mirror* ('Haw-Haw gives even an old woman like me a good laugh, as I take all his talks the other way round') and *The Times* ('Much of "Lord Haw-Haw's" nightly talks is the cause of ribald mirth in countless homes, but occasionally one detects a subtler shaft whose effect might well have unfortunate results unless immediately answered') began to use the name, which soon spread from the correspondence to the news columns.

Richly comic though the broadcasts were generally held to be, the idea grew that they ought not to be free of British radio comment. A *Daily Mirror* reader thought the BBC should broadcast on the same wavelength 'one of our radio comedians to assist Lord Haw-Haw with a few quips'; with the same idea in mind, but a different approach, a reader of *The Times* could imagine 'a well-informed and witty group of young university dons being able to formulate a suitable reply which would easily overcome any advantage that the enemy had gained'. This correspondent suspected that the Germans, far from being stupid, were subtle—'. . . the general public are just beginning to realize how clever the wireless propaganda happens to be. Obviously the German intention was to employ a pioneer who by his particular attributes should command the greatest publicity in this country and then in turn to replace him by someone much more instructive of the spirit of Germany.'

Whether to reply to the broadcasts or to ignore them officially was not such a straightforward question as alarmed members of the public thought; but with a large part of the population giving each other their version of what Haw-Haw had said the night before, the time had clearly come for an assessment of the size of Reichsrundfunk's audience. This was undertaken, at the request of the Ministry of Information, by the BBC, which had techniques of assessing the extent of its own audiences. A representative sample produced estimates that of the whole population over sixteen years of age, there were approximately six million people listening every day or nearly every day, eighteen million occasional listeners and eleven million non-listeners. These figures compared with twenty-three million regular listeners to the BBC news and ten million occasional listeners.

The report summed up the attraction of the broadcasts in these terms: 'The blackout, the novelty of hearing the enemy, the desire to hear both sides, the insatiable appetite for news and the desire to be in the swim have all played their part in building up Hamburg's audience and in holding it. The entertainment value of the broadcasts, their concentration on undeniable evils in this country, their news sense, their presentation, and the publicity they have received in this country, together with the momentum of the habit of listening to them, have all contributed towards their establishment as a familiar feature of the social landscape. All types of person are to be found among Hamburg's public but men are greater listeners than women and people under 50 years of age are greater listeners than people over 50.'

Listeners to the German broadcasts were, on the average, more politically conscious than the average non-listener, the report revealed. They took up a critical attitude to the conduct of public affairs, but there was little evidence that they would not have held those views in almost as great a measure if Hamburg had never broadcast in English.

Audience research being impossible for the German propaganda authorities, they had to rely on the British press, from which they concluded that they were doing quite well. Why, in this situation, should they have paid attention to the criticisms of one news-reader? It is not surprising that Joyce had to batter away at officialdom to get himself recognized as the most gifted propagandist in their service.

Life in Berlin, as the novelty wore off and the year drew to an end, lost some of its amenities. Food and accommodation became increasingly difficult problems. The Joyces had simplified their catering by eating in restaurants on travellers' ration coupons, which were convenient because they were valid for any period and could be saved up, but a lot of people had the same idea. An order appeared restricting the use of such coupons to persons in transit. When Margaret, unaware of the new regulation, was refused a further supply at the food office, she was incapable of following the official's explanation, and her husband had to present himself there to discover what was wrong. In reply to his question whether travellers' coupons could be issued on an authority from Reichsrundfunk he was asked to produce his identity card, so he showed his British passport. Having examined it, the official said politely but firmly: 'I am sorry, but even though you are British you will have to have the same coupons as other citizens.'

In December Mrs. Eckersley, as desperate for marks as the Joyces had been, joined Reichsrundfunk as a continuity announcer.

Difficulty in getting home after night shifts caused Joyce to look for a room nearer the Rundfunkhaus, and he found one in Steifensandstrasse. The landlady, a Viennese named Maria Chalupa, took an immediate liking to him. He was amused by her and promptly translated Chalupa as 'the sloop', which later became her nickname. In her eagerness to show him the room she pushed the door open without knocking, causing a good-looking young woman in a dressing-gown to leap behind the door. The room was small, with only a single bed (Maria pointed out that it was quite a wide one), and Joyce's request for a daily bath was met with the firm refusal: 'No, it's not done.' He took the lodging reluctantly because of its position but the change was a mistake. Soon after the Joyces moved in the central heating broke down. Not realizing how cold the Berlin winter could yet become, they endured the depressing chill of their room as best they could. Sometimes, when in the mood, they enjoyed listening to instalments of Maria's life story, the main pivot of which was a love affair with a Hungarian noble who had left her the flat and a small income, but at other times she caused them to long for a place where they could be alone.

Even sitting in Haffners Joyce felt pessimistic. The loss of the *Graf Spee* seemed to him a serious blow for the Germans, but it was not so much individual setbacks which worried him as the general defeatism.

He and his wife, missing their families and friends, found Christmas Eve particularly gloomy. Unaware that this was the one evening in the year when German restaurants close early, they declined the Haffner family's invitation to dinner and booked a table at the Kaiserhof Hotel. The atmosphere there was, to their surprise, anything but festive, the only two waiters on duty being obviously anxious to get rid of the diners so that they themselves could go home. Leaving early, the Joyces called on Frau Dr. Maja Gath, a Reichsrundfunk translator, for a drink, and then went to the office.

Here presents for the staff had been laid out. Although the gifts were impersonal and clearly despatched to names on a distribution list, Joyce cheered up considerably to see two parcels addressed to him. The first he opened contained a box of large cigars with the compliments of Dr. Goebbels, and the second held even larger cigars and conveyed the compliments of Reichsmarschall Hermann Göring.

The Christmas Eve English language programme, which Joyce was fortunate in not having to read, included a dreadful example of the kind of script produced by Germans who imagined they knew colloquial English. It came after the news (which was mostly about a visit of General von Brauchitsch to the Western front) and it was the story of a German First World War soldier who, dying in a British hospital, said to the nurse: 'Don't cry. This is the last war between Britain and Germany.' After reminding British listeners that the non-fulfilment of this prophecy was not Germany's fault, the narrator said: 'I know that what I am going to say may revolt some of you.' Had he known why it would revolt his audience he might have changed the script. He went pathetically on: 'But, Honest Injun, have you ever tried to rely on clear sober thinking rather than on sentimental prejudices? Just try for a while and think about the prophecy of the German boy. There is still a chance.'

On Christmas Day one of the evening news bulletins was read

by Joyce. News was thin and the contents rather contrived. There was a Tass paragraph ironically asking why the Allied press did not publish the number of miles the Allies had proceeded beyond the Siegfried Line and suggesting it was because the advance could not be measured in miles or yards but only in inches; a United States protest against the extension of the British blockade had not yet been answered; the Argentine Foreign Office had objected to the violation of her rights by belligerents, and the Prague News Agency had issued a statement that 'In our eyes the victory of the Reich is a vital necessity to us because we wish the co-existence of the two nations to bring us valuable results.' Talks in English followed by Walter Neusel, the boxer, and Roderick Menzel. Joyce was joined by his wife as he left the studio. They then met other members of the foreign-language services in the huts where they were accommodated behind the radio building and thankfully drank several schnaps. Christmas greetings came for Joyce from another quarter. A German in Hamburg, whom he had met in England, had recognized his voice, and telephoned him that evening.

After Christmas snow fell, the room in the Steifensandstrasse became so cold as to be uninhabitable, and they moved again, this time to two rooms in the Amtsgerichtsplatz owned by the cook at Haffners, who needed tenants because her ex-actor husband drank and contributed little to the household income. The rooms were warmed by so-called Berlin stoves, white briquette-burning edifices which reached to the ceiling and were, for the inexperienced, difficult to light.

The blackout had now become more effective and Margaret feared the dark streets, especially after an incident she witnessed when a girl walking a few yards ahead of her was suddenly pulled, screaming and struggling, into a car which had overtaken her and stopped. Horrified, Margaret stood still while the car door slammed as the car accelerated.

She ran home, told her husband, and suggested that they should both go to the police. Not hitherto a man to keep his mouth shut, Joyce had now learnt something about life in a totalitarian state and he thought they had better not, in case it turned out that the police themselves were the kidnappers.

One night he himself saw something. No one else saw it, but Joyce did not dismiss it as an hallucination, the product of a tired and worried brain. He recognized it as a flash of precognition.

In bright moonlight he was walking along the broad Kaiserdamm. Anyone passing might have taken him for a workman trudging home, because he wore an Arbeitermütze, a dark blue cap with a shiny peak and of rather nautical cut, which he had bought because he was losing his hair and the weather was too cold for him to go hatless. It demonstrated, too, his proletarian sympathies.

Suddenly he stopped and caught his breath. For a few seconds the solid buildings, intensely black in the moonlight, dissolved into jagged ruins.

Chapter 13

THEY SPOKE WITH ONE VOICE

The British claim to be able to tell a great deal about a man from his accent was scarcely sustained by the public speculation about the Haw-Haw voice. Moreover, people argued without suspecting that they were not all discussing the same person.

Who was Professor Lloyd James talking about when he described the accent as a 'bogus veneer'? The speaker's German, he added, judged by his pronunciation of the names of German newspapers, was 'not worth twopence', and the man was unlikely to have been educated at a university, although he might have been at a public school. The professor concluded: 'Actually I believe the man's accent to be northern, most likely Scottish.'

Harold Hobson, writing to *The Times* to observe that 'that ineffable voice of his, by Cholmondeley-Plantagenet out of Christ Church, has an irresistible fascination', was promptly attacked by Rose Macaulay, who asked what 'the curious popular legend about Lord Haw-Haw's voice being aristocratic, upper class, "haw-haw", and so forth' was based on. 'Lord Haw-Haw speaks excellent English,' Miss Macaulay wrote, 'but surely not "Cholmondeley-Plantagenet out of Christ Church". He seems to have a slight provincial accent (Manchester?) and to commit such solecisms as accenting the second syllable of "comment". I should not call it "public school" English. Do any listeners really think it is, or is the legend merely derived from music-hall parodies, composed and sung by those who are not experts in the niceties of accent themselves?'

Lady Cynthia Colville also resisted the popular view, and had 'never doubted but that Lord Haw-Haw's education in the English tongue has been conditioned by residence oversea. I am never quite sure what an Oxford accent is like, but I am entirely

132

sure that it is not his. His "wah" for "war" is as transatlantic as his nasal intonation, and I should place Chicago high among the probable influences that have produced his now famous, but hardly golden, voice.'

Rosita Forbes, writing in the *Sunday Dispatch* of 7th January 1940, under the title 'Lord Haw-Haw as I Know Him', 'conclusively identified' the speaker as 'Rolf Hoffman, Director of Publicity at the Brown House, the original Munich headquarters of the Nazis'. On the same day a no less authoritative announcement was made by the *Empire News* that Baillie-Stewart was living in Brussels and that he was 'not one of the band of Nazi broadcasters which includes "Lord Haw-Haw" '.

Despite the definitive identification by Miss Forbes, speculation continued. A day later the *News Chronicle* mentioned a rumour that Haw-Haw was Eduard Dietze, 'Glasgow-born Nazi, whose mother was Scottish and father German'. This was at least on the target, as Dietze was in fact a member of the team. The *Evening News* also scored by guessing Roderick Menzel, another component part of the Haw-Haw personality.

One journalist, Geoffrey Edwards of the *News Chronicle*, seemed actually to have taken the trouble to listen with an open mind to different bulletins; he observed that 'the title is rather loosely applied to any German who happens to broadcast in English.' Nobody took any notice.

Lord Haw-Haw had come to stay for the duration of the war. His rise to fame was celebrated at a Foyle Luncheon on 18th January 1940 when the Western Brothers gave their impression of him and (to quote *The Times*) 'Mr. Jonah Barrington, radio critic of the *Daily Express*, then made a modest speech on "the birth of Lord Haw-Haw", for it was he who gave him that apt name and encouraged his progress from "a hack Nazi announcer to a national clown and an international buffoon", whose name and activities are now mentioned in *The Times* and by the BBC, have a show to themselves at the Holborn Empire, and are incorporated in a biography by Mr. Barrington himself, copies of which could be obtained at the luncheon signed by the author. "Heil, Haw-Haw," concluded Mr. Barrington, "and long may he continue to keep us in fits of healthy British laughter." '

A few sourly refrained from joining in the hilarity. One was Hannen Swaffer, who said that the name Lord Haw-Haw was stupid. He was supported by Raymond Burns in a letter published by the *World's Press News* on 2nd February 1940: 'Was ever such a fatuous label given prominence in Fleet Street? Moreover, historians of this country may well have something to say about the mistake that has been made, by reason of extravagant publicity for this dreary name, in directing national attention to the only potentially dangerous system of enemy propaganda against this country's morale.'

Surprisingly, considering all the boosting they were getting, the Haw-Haw broadcasts now began to lose some of their audience. According to the BBC researchers, the peak was reached between 25th January and 1st February 1940 when 26·5 per cent of a representative sample answered 'Yes' to the question: 'Did you happen to hear any news in English from Germany yesterday?' By the end of February the proportion, although still substantial, had dropped to 16·9 per cent. Were the German programmes perhaps not up to what British newspaper readers had been led to expect?

Nobody, unfortunately, produced estimates of the audience for stories told by the British to each other about what Haw-Haw was understood to have said.

Chapter 14

THE SECRET STATIONS

The radio war was intensified by the setting up on both sides of so-called 'secret' stations, operated on their own soil but professing to be run by a fifth column in enemy country.

An example of a successful German one was La Voix de la Paix, a radio service put out by the Propaganda Ministry under the guise of an illicit station operated by French patriots in France. Conveying the impression that it spoke for a large underground organization of Frenchmen anxious for the safety, well-being and future of their country, it played up grievances and fears and sought to undermine the nation's will to resist. Its ultimate purpose was realized when the German Army invaded France. Integrated with the military operations, the station warned the population that the enemy forces were advancing at greater speed and in stronger force than the French Government admitted, advised the inhabitants of some districts to ignore official instructions and flee to others, and campaigned to create such panic that refugees swarming along the roads would hinder French troop movements and cause a breakdown of civil order and the supply services. The German High Command thought it had played its rôle effectively and, after the armistice, officially thanked the Propaganda Ministry and Reichsrundfunk staffs for their support.

Early in 1940, while inactivity and silence still prevailed on the frontiers, La Voix de la Paix was only in the preliminary stage of its operation, and plans were being made, in a heavily-guarded villa adjoining the Rundfunkhaus, to give the British public the benefit of a similar service. A department was formed called Büro Concordia and its organization assigned to Dr. Erich Hetzler, who had introduced Joyce to Walter Kamm. The Foreign

Minister had prevented Hetzler from serving with an anti-aircraft unit, and in January he had been transferred to Reichsrundfunk as assistant to the Foreign Section Director, his first job being to look after the foreign journalists, mainly Americans, who were still working in Berlin.

To produce radio programmes sounding as though they were British in origin posed a formidable staffing problem. The English speakers already being used in the Haw-Haw team could not broadcast both from Germany and from an under-cover location in Britain, so others would have to be found, and the demand for English scripts would greatly increase. Hetzler realized that the type of material put out in the overt services to Britain would not do; the men running a clandestine station must talk colloquial English and make local references. The problem of the scripts was easier to solve than was that of the speakers.

After pledging him to secrecy, Hetzler explained the project to Joyce. The first development, he told him, was to be a programme designed to persuade the British that they had been misled about National Socialism and that they were fighting the wrong enemy. This was a continuation of what Joyce had been saying for years, and he jumped at the idea. He liked it even more when Hetzler explained that the two of them would confer every morning on the choice of subjects and that Joyce could then give them his own treatment; there would be no delay such as occurred when scripts made their way from desk to desk in the Propaganda Ministry, censorship would be reduced to a minimum, and the talks would still be topical when broadcast. Joyce felt that with this relative freedom his spirit could expand, as it had when he ceased to be an official of Mosley's British Union and became the leader of his own National Socialist League. He was so enthusiastic that he undertook to write the whole programme himself.

Thanking him, Hetzler observed that his salary would, of course, be increased.

Joyce's answer was: 'I don't want any extra money. I get my salary and that's enough for me.' He remained adamant in his refusal, and all Hetzler could ever get him to accept was an occasional bonus for holiday expenses.

From now on, Joyce, in addition to his growing work for the 'Germany Calling' programmes, was to produce about nine-tenths of all the material used by the secret stations. Considered as bulk, this was the major work he performed for the Germans, and it might—if the war had developed differently—have been the most dangerous. He was ultimately condemned to the maximum penalty for his activities as an overt news-reader and commentator and the court was unaware of his vast output of scripts for Büro Concordia. A subsequent non-legal assessment of Joyce might conclude that there is a greater degree of culpability in talking subversion in the character of a patriotic British citizen on his native soil than there is in speaking openly from enemy territory as the official voice of the enemy.

Joyce, however, had no misgivings about the rightness of his conduct. He maintained that he was a British patriot doing his duty by warning the British that even if they won the war they would lose it, a task that could best be performed by his being fully committed to the Nazi cause, and when complimented on his work he was accustomed to reply: 'I am not doing anything more than a German worker who does his duty.' That he was capable of such reasoning is the measure of his anti-Semitic obsession and his remoteness from reality.

The problem of speakers for the secret stations was never adequately solved. In its early days Büro Concordia had to make its choice from among a very few native English speakers who, for one reason or other, happened to find themselves in Germany.

The first programme, and the most ambitious, was started in the latter part of February 1940 and put out under the name of the New British Broadcasting Station for half an hour each evening on short wave from Gumbinnen in East Prussia. The organization was not pampered. The entire administration was done by Hetzler and one secretary, working first in a hut attached to the Rundfunkhaus and then in an office under the press boxes at the Olympia Stadium. A less dedicated collaborator than Joyce would have complained about the poverty of the material available for his scripts. The principal British papers arrived a day late, which limited their usefulness for topical talks. They were supplemented by *The Economist*, the *New Statesman and Nation* and *Punch*. Suitable research facilities hardly existed. Radio monitoring ought to have provided topical material, but this was carried out by four organizations, none of them much good to Büro Concordia. The Reichsrundfunk monitors seemed to see their function as gathering news favourable to Germany and praising Hitler; the Forschungsamt (Research Office), headed by Göring, was chiefly interested in military affairs; the Propaganda Ministry to some extent duplicated the work of the Reichsrundfunk service; and the German Foreign Office's monitoring department maintained a superior attitude to the others. Ultimately, Concordia started its own service, directed by Frau von Petersdorf, a skater who had been prevented by the outbreak of war from returning to the United States, and this disregarded all foreign broadcasts except those dealing with the internal conditions of the target country.

A typically unreasonable restriction also handicapped this and all the other secret stations. While posing as the radio voice of organizations of French and British patriots, their staffs were never allowed to throw themselves so whole-heartedly into their rôle that they criticized the Führer or even the Reich. In their references to the enemy the clandestine stations were markedly discreet.

Directives for all the radio services were issued following Dr. Goebbels's daily meetings. Hetzler's superior, Dr. Rasken, attended them and then conveyed general instructions to Hetzler, Dietze, or whoever was duty editor. It was then time for Joyce to call at Concordia's office. He always arrived punctually, stood erect in the doorway—making the most of his height—and, heels together, bowed slightly. With the editor he studied the directives and, surrounded by the previous day's British papers and the monitoring reports, they planned the programme. What had caused the various interests represented in the Propaganda Ministry to decide on a particular policy did not concern them at their level; their task was to present the officially-approved views to the listeners.

The themes for the day noted, Joyce took a formal leave and walked smartly back to his office where, for an hour, he dictated fluently, very much as though he were addressing a meeting impromptu and had to keep going. Observers estimated that he did as much in that hour as any other two scriptwriters in a day. He went home to lunch, slept for a while, and returned to the office to check the material he had dictated that morning. With growing frequency he now also wrote and recorded the evening commentary, and he often typed the text himself before going to dinner. In the evening he went back once more, sub-edited or wrote more copy, and took his turn at the microphone in reading the news.

Even allowing that heavily slanted material which follows a uniform pattern requires much less thought and drafting than does a reasoned argument, his output was, in quantity, impressive. The standard, as judged from Berlin, was high; he could invariably enliven his constant theme with topical allusions and hammer home his arguments with a typically German emphasis —qualities apt to arouse interest in English listeners without carrying conviction. His German employers could not be expected to see that what they liked in his work was what made it sound alien to the audience, just as they could not detect his inability to write in a character other than his own. When they now realized that they had a versatile scriptwriter of enormous stamina, and one who never grumbled at being exploited, they piled more and more work on him.

The German Foreign Office—although it had (like its British counterpart) refused to take him on—enlisted his services too, and as a result he wrote his only book.

Chapter 15

TWILIGHT OVER ENGLAND

Joyce's own justification of what he did appeared in a curious work called *Twilight over England*. In commissioning it the German Foreign Office had in mind a propaganda publication suitable for circulation in neutral countries, especially the United States, and British territories such as India where disaffection already existed. For writing it Joyce was paid the handsome fee of 10,000 Reichsmarks (about £500).

That German propagandists wanted to exploit a politician who had, out of pure conviction, forsaken England for Germany, is understandable, and Joyce was not the man to reject such a chance; but in undertaking the assignment he accepted what was for him a severe handicap. Because of the German-Russian agreement of that time, he was not allowed to attack Communism and the Soviet Union. Another condition was that the typescript had to be circulated for clearance to various government departments. Inexperienced as a civil servant, and temperamentally unsuited as one, he found this inevitable requirement maddening.

Nevertheless, he embarked on the project in his usual uninhibited fashion. To him the author's ante-start agonies were unknown. With the assistance of a secretary named Vera he wrote the book (which came to 168 printed pages) in three weeks. Delivered by him without revision, it was a characteristic production, fluent, bitter and scolding, unplanned and untidy, with quotations and examples scattered through it as they occurred to him, blows struck in passing at the objects of his numerous minor prejudices, oracular predictions of doom and flippant sneers ('Hope springs eternal in the Jewish, even as in the human breast').

What form the Foreign Office had thought the book would

take I do not know. What it got was a personal statement by Joyce addressed primarily—none of the officials who cleared the text appears to have noticed this—to the British public, which was to have no opportunity of reading it. Nowhere did he turn for more than a few sentences to his intended audience in the United States, the English-reading populations of neutral countries or the Indians. Before him as he furiously worked he seemed to see not even the wartime British radio audience but the little groups at London street corners in 1938; in places he used the present tense as though the war had never started and nothing had changed in England since he left it. The clever-sounding remarks of the professional agitator filling out his time and giving himself an appearance of sophistication in the eyes of unlettered bystanders remained unpruned, as in the opening to the second chapter: 'The reader may have innocently hoped at the close of the last chapter, that the historical discussion had come to an end. In this life, the innocent are often maltreated and the hopeful disappointed.'

Possibly the German bureaucrats were impressed by the historical opening, as being in their own tradition of thesis-writing. Joyce set out 'to show how England's historical development contributed to the fateful and fatal action which her Government took on 3rd September 1939'. That day was the anniversary of Oliver Cromwell's birth and death. The Puritans 'had drunk all too deeply of Jewish philosophy. They were not content to read the Old Testament. They called themselves by such names as "Hew-Agag-In-Pieces-Before-The-Lord". Ben Jonson was hardly exaggerating when he called his Puritans Tribulation Wholesome and Zeal-in-the-Land. Certainly the materialism of the Jews, as exposed in the Old Testament, had bitten deeply into their souls: for with all their psalms and all their hymns, they soon began to make money hand over fist.'

The Manchester School, which emerged in 'the final struggle to eliminate everything that did not reek of materialism', was Jewish-influenced too. 'Tenth-rate philosophical hacks were bought and assembled with instructions to invent a science of economics and justify the abominations which the craw-thumping Radical plutocrats were each day practising on the masses of the people. The doctrines of this so-called school were very simple. The great and eternal verity of economics was announced in the golden words: "Buy in the cheapest market and sell in the dearest". This commandment being devotedly accepted, every other grace necessary to salvation would follow of its own accord. Hallelujah! How Jewish it all sounds.'

Puritans and Jews now having been exposed, statesmen he wanted to hit particularly hard were associated with one or the other. Stanley Baldwin was 'the pompous hardware monger from Ipswich, always trying to ape the ways of a country gentleman, with a canting Puritan whine in his voice'; Winston Churchill was 'the first Honorary Jew in the world' (but the term 'honorary', Joyce added, was not to be interpreted in its financial sense); Neville Chamberlain, under the influence of Jews, broke the agreement he had made with Hitler at Munich.

Chamberlain's declaration of war was unconstitutional, according to Joyce's interpretation of the British constitution, because governments held mandates only to execute the policy they had submitted to the electorate. Thus Joyce thought (and he was not alone in advocating the referendum system) that the British people ought to have been consulted on the declaration of war in 1914, the Treaty of Versailles, the return to the gold standard, the general strike, Baldwin's Indian policy, the abdication of King Edward VIII, and the attitude to the Abyssinian War. 'The system of Government in Britain today deserves one description only: it is a plutocratic oligarchy, materialist in philosophy, Jewish in purpose, and tyrannous in effect.'

His contempt for the British political parties was stated as though the reader were as familiar with them as his pre-war audiences had been. The 'poor Conservative Party wandered about from pillar to post, never quite knowing what it was trying to conserve'. The full force of his oratory was turned upon the Liberals: 'These Uriah Heaps [*sic*], these Victorian Pharisees, whited sepulchres, dead men's bones, talked glibly about the Parliament of Man and the Federation of the World, because their interest lay not in the building of an Empire but in the acquisition of a larger area for their financial depredations.' The Labour Party's 'endocrine glands were poisoned by Liberal politics, Marxist materialism, and the crazy doctrines of Rousseau and the French Revolution' and its Members of Parliament corrupted by sherry and champagne, 'forthcoming Duchesses', stock exchange tips, the Order of the British Empire and Freemasonry, failing to see that while being won over they were being laughed at. 'A tame revolutionary in the drawing room is something to amuse the County, when it comes up to Town and has been there long enough to get bored with the Night Clubs. Also the entertainment of freaks by the great shows how far tolerance can go in the beautiful system of democracy. Indeed some of those bored ladies who can create no sensation by talking about sexual perversion can often raise an eyebrow by producing some "wild man" who, poor devil, thinks that by taking thought, he can add a cubit to the stature of the working classes.' Old public school men, 'who found the competition a little too close in the Conservative Party', were able to make a career in the Labour Party, so that 'the young plutocrat' about to enter politics at least considered supporting Socialism. The Labour Party had taken over from the Liberals the function of providing a fictitious opposition, and the Government, appreciating this service, paid the Leader of the Opposition £2,000 a year 'for pretending to obstruct the conduct of its business'.

Any Indian readers the book secured would have learnt that democracy was not for them. 'If democracy has proved such a curse to Europe, there can be no justification for inflicting it upon the unsuspecting Indians.' India had been mapped out as a field for Jewish exploitation and, when the Jews saw that the conscience even of a British parliament might revolt against conditions in India, they needed some government less closely connected with Westminster and were confident that they could 'bribe any Indian Government into amenability'. The Indian nationalist who blamed England for everything failed to see that he and the English themselves were the victims of the same evil forces. Jewry was opposed to 'real imperialism' because a real empire would strive for autarchy, which was contrary to the interests of Jewish finance. Until 1933 the Jews had hated the idea of the British Empire, but after 1933 they saw the possibility of using its strength against National Socialist Germany. 'Examine every exhibition of Imperial flag-wagging since 1933, and a chorus of Jews will be observed dancing in the foreground.'

A passage on the League of Nations provided an example of Joyce's habit of hitting out, in an irrelevant parenthesis, at whatever happened to flit across his thoughts. The League, with its 'Secretariat of 600 Jews', was a Jewish imposture accepted by

Gentiles. 'Just as in Freudian psychology, Jazz and Surrealism, the Jew loves to see the poor Goy making a thorough ass of himself, crawling downstairs on all fours as it were, with top-hat on head and a piece of soap in his mouth, so there was something delightful to the Jewish mind in all the gabble that went on, all the mummery, and the thousand possibilities of shady intrigue that arose every day.'

In most of his pronouncements Joyce regarded the guilt of the Jews as self-evident; he required, for example, no more proof that a business was anti-social than the appearance of Jewish names in the list of shareholders. *Twilight over England* was an exception; in it he set out his considered indictment of Jews. In typical style he let himself go with accusations against Jews as fire-raisers, white slave traffickers, slave-driving employers and infiltrators of the British ruling class; but then, abandoning oratory, he enumerated his reasons for regarding them as inevitably a hostile force. Here are what he saw as the Jewish tendencies justifying his obsessional anti-Semitism.

'1. An incapacity to avoid forming a state within a state.

'2. Complete inability to view their Gentile hosts as possessing equal rights with their own.

'3. Predetermined specialization in all those processes which bring high profit. Hence, in capitalism, almost exclusive preoccupation with finance, distribution, and exchange as distinct from productive industry. Professional work undertaken either for profit or for the sake of social advancement.

'4. A natural tendency to utilize social and economic advancement for the purpose of gaining political power.

'5. An unholy dread of nationalism as a factor which would draw attention to their racial nature and expose their operations.

'6. The deliberate debasement of the standards of culture in the land of their sojourn.

'7. The elimination by competition of the Aryan who merely wants to get enough for himself and not more than anybody else.'

After this, for him, colourless passage, Joyce the prophet took over again with a prediction that 'sooner or later, the most influential Jew on earth will have no more influence on the course of Aryan affairs than a jelly-fish upon the time of sunrise. What

144

the English people do not see today, they will learn by bitter experience: the German people have seen the truth already. When twilight falls on the field of battle, it is the twilight of the Kingdom of Judah on earth. They have tempted God—these Jews—for the last time.'

His action in leaving England for Germany he justified in a sentence which anticipated the statement made after his arrest: 'If an Englishman cannot fight in his own streets against the domination of international finance, it were better for him to go elsewhere and impede by every means in his power the victory of his Government: for the victory of such a Government would be an everlasting defeat of his race: it would put an end to all prospects for ever of social justice and economic reform.' It followed that he saw England's salvation as lying in her defeat, after which the English would 'have the chance, so long denied them, of using their genius and their character in the building of that new world to which Adolf Hitler has shown the way. In these days it may be presumptuous to express either hopes or beliefs: yet I will venture so much. I hope and believe, that when the flames of war have been traversed, the ordinary people of England will know their soul again and will seek, in National-Socialism, to advance along the way of human progress in friendship with their brothers of German blood. That this hope and this belief shall not prove vain there are two guarantees, for me sufficient; the greatness of Adolf Hitler and the Greater Glory of Almighty God.'

Neville Chamberlain was still prime minister when the book was written. Joyce showed realism in attacking Winston Churchill as the major British statesman, but in one of the more extravagant passages, after quoting with approval a book called *Famine in England* by Viscount Lymington and condemning Winston Churchill for opposing protection for agriculture, he wrote: 'Before the Governor of a British prison accompanies Mr. Churchill on that last cheerless walk on a cold grey morning just before eight, it is to be hoped that the Chaplain will intone these passages from *Famine in England*, interlarded, of course, with suitable scriptural texts.'

His thoughts often turned to hanging. The preface, too, contained a reference to execution after Joyce had, whether challengingly or flippantly, confessed himself guilty of high treason. 'The preface is usually that part of a book which can most safely be omitted. It usually represents that efflorescent manifestation of egotism which an author, after working hard, cannot spare either himself or his readers. More often than not the readers spare themselves. When, however, the writer is a daily perpetrator of high treason, his introductory remarks may command from the English public that kind of awful veneration with which £5,000 confessions are perused in the Sunday newspapers, quite frequently after the narrator has taken his last leap in the dark.'

After he had delivered the manuscript he was time and again driven into a state of fury by the conferences over policy which, among other alterations, struck out a passage about money-lenders for fear of giving offence to Subra Chandra Bose, who was living in Berlin as the leader of the so-called Indian freedom fighters; by pedantic officials' dissection of every sentence (which perhaps accounts for the Germanic use of capital letters for nouns in some passages); by the changes in meaning introduced into the German translation. Added to the ban on anti-Communist and anti-Soviet propaganda, this niggling contributed to his growing feeling that the Germans were unworthy of National Socialism.

Yet in the preface he claimed: 'That I have been permitted to write freely what I would is due to that respect for freedom of honest expression which I have found everywhere in Germany since my arrival.' The impudent dishonesty of this passage shows Joyce at his facetious worst. The snigger is almost audible.

Intended to be his justification, *Twilight over England* painfully reveals Joyce's inability to rise to a subject. His First World War predecessor in the Old Bailey dock, Sir Roger Casement, would have availed himself of such an opportunity (as he used his chance to address the court) to make a dignified, rational and literate statement, moving even those who lacked sympathy with his cause. Joyce might have tried to produce an argument appropriate to the magnitude of his action in supporting the enemy, to give the world a glimpse into the mind of a man motivated by powerful convictions and emotions, even, perhaps, to ensure a place for himself in history as the author of an anti-Semitic classic. The policy restriction imposed on him by the German authorities would not have prevented him from doing this. What stopped him were his own limitations.

Finally cleared, the typescript was put into the hands of an elderly Italian named Santoro, owner of a Berlin publishing house called Internationaler Verlag, for production.

Chapter 16

A SMASH HIT

William Shirer, the Berlin representative of an American radio network, noted in his *Berlin Diary* on 4th March 1940 that when in the German radio headquarters he could 'hear Lord Haw-Haw attacking his typewriter with gusto or shouting in his nasal voice against "that plutocrat Chamberlain".'

Was this man with the broken nose the same radio commentator discussed by *Life* in its issue of 22nd April 1940? 'On this new psychological front, first blood now goes to Germany, which, like other belligerents, hires renegades and traitors to undermine their countrymen's morale. A smash hit is a mysterious nightly voice on the Hamburg wave length, the radio favorite star of 50% of all English listeners. "Lord Haw Haw of Zeesen" has an impeccable Oxford accent, cloaks his news and opinions with clever humor that Englishmen find irresistible.'

Employing as they were three main news-readers and several commentators, the German propaganda men were puzzled by the identity of this speaker who was getting such a good press. They had nobody to tell them that Joyce had nothing like an Oxford accent and that Baillie-Stewart's talks were not remarkable for their clever humour. But they realized that foreign journalists were creating for them a valuable radio personality, and they were not long in deciding to exploit this gift. By this time it was plain to them that William Joyce, alias Wilhelm Fröhlich, was not only a resourceful and tireless producer of scripts but a man of marked individuality, whose ambition it was to become the English Voice of Germany. Joyce, who detested the type of character envisaged by Jonah Barrington, was none the less mischievously delighted to play the rôle of the now notorious peer. By May the German radio, without comment and in a deadpan manner, was announcing talks by Lord Haw-Haw. The policy of preserving the anonymity of foreign speakers was, however, still observed.

Life had accorded Germany the lead in the radio war. Its estimate that Haw-Haw was heard by 50 per cent of English listeners did not accord with the BBC's calculation based on its sample, which between March 31st and April 6th showed a proportion of 15·7 per cent; but the interest in what the German radio said was not confined to those who actually heard the broadcasts. There was the secondary audience of those who listened to the remarkable accounts of what people claimed to have heard Haw-Haw say. In their campaign to arouse anxiety and encourage belief in German strength, the German propagandists were greatly helped by the mere existence of their broadcasts, irrespective of the size of the audience. The credulity of the British public seemed almost boundless; stories quoting Haw-Haw as the source found unquestioning acceptance.

Interest spread beyond the United Kingdom. No listener research was undertaken in Southern Ireland, but it would be a reasonable guess that the proportion of listeners was not less than that on the other side of the Irish Sea. Those Irish who enjoyed the anti-British jibes for a time, until England stood in acute danger and the Germans had once more demonstrated their lack of respect for the rights of small nations, were unaware of Joyce's views on Irish independence. Poor short-wave reception and the lack of short-wave sets limited the overseas audience, but the press in the United States and the British dominions reported the various Haw-Haw phenomena. The audience in Australia and New Zealand was negligible. Programmes were beamed to Canada but most Canadians knew the subject-matter of the broadcasts only from what they read in the papers; nevertheless, some Haw-Haw rumours circulated. Little impact was made in South Africa, although their anti-Semitic tone won the broadcasts some following.

With Germany apparently winning the war, all the German propagandists had to do was to keep up the pressure. It was not surprising that they seemed to be doing better than their British counterparts. Yet the German authorities never felt confident enough to abandon jamming or drop the penalties for listening to the enemy on the radio. Despite all the risks of listening, the names of the principal BBC speakers became household words, even though whispered ones, in Germany. The German security organizations did not underestimate British psychological warfare.

Joyce, as ignorant as any member of the public about the German High Command's intentions, was startled and depressed by the German Army's invasion of Denmark and Norway on April 9th. When this breakout was followed on May 10th by the invasion of Holland, Belgium and Luxembourg, he saw that the pattern of the previous war was being ominously repeated. His hopes of a quiet, face-saving settlement between Britain and Germany faded that evening, when Neville Chamberlain resigned and Winston Churchill, the object of Joyce's most vicious invective, became Prime Minister.

It happened that on that day, in Britain, the last poll was taken of the audience for German broadcasts. No significant rise was recorded and the decline had continued; the sample showed 13·3 per cent now listening. This was only half the proportion recorded in February, yet the result seems to have been received with limited satisfaction. Now, with Britain in danger of attack, concern about the effect of German propaganda began to grow. Yielding to demands that the enemy's talks should be answered, the BBC started postscripts after the news. Public opinion was not unanimous about the wisdom of noticing enemy propaganda. People who thought the effect would be only to increase interest were supported by the manager of the East Riding Relay Service, who reported that 'invariably after postscripts we are inundated with requests for Haw-Haw broadcasts, which we are not allowed to give.'

In May thousands of enemy aliens were interned under the Royal Prerogative and Mosley and his principal associates were detained under Regulation 18b. Sir John Anderson, the Home Secretary, told the House of Commons at the time: 'A certain body which is well known to be anti-Semitic and pro-Nazi has given instructions to its members that it is to turn itself into a rumour-monger and a channel for verbal propaganda.' It seems to have been hoped that segregating many of the former members of the British Union would diminish the flood of rumours, but there was no noticeable diminution. Mr. Mander, a Liberal Member, urged the Home Secretary to have a look at the British

Council for Christian Settlement in Europe because of its secretary, John Beckett, 'who was associated as co-worker before the war with Mr. William Joyce, better known as Lord Haw-Haw'. Although no official announcement of Haw-Haw's identity had been made, Joyce was now widely assumed to be the speaker.

Another attempt to combat defeatist talk was initiated, in the weeks following the Dunkirk evacuation, by Duff Cooper, the Minister of Information, who proposed that patriots should constitute themselves 'the silent column' and report gossips. Cooper's Snoopers, as the eavesdropping patriots were promptly named, were unpopular, and a few weeks later the Prime Minister disowned them.

The appeal of the New British Broadcasting Station to an imaginary anti-war movement became more urgent. Italy had declared war on Britain and France and the Germans had entered Paris when, on June 15th, Joyce produced a script demanding, in his rôle as an under-cover British patriot, 'the resignation of the Government and its forces. Whatever disturbances may take place in consequence of our revolt, they will be utterly negligible in comparison with the bloodshed, slaughter and devastation that we should be saving our country by so acting.'

German radio correspondents were rushed from Berlin to Paris to witness the signing of the armistice at Compiègne, and jubilant messages poured back to the Rundfunkhaus, swamping the reports of Churchill's 'This was their finest hour' speech.

Contempt and scorn, the Propaganda Ministry's recipe for dealing with British statesmen, were used by Joyce on June 20th in attacking, through the New British Broadcasting Station, one of his favourite targets. The style is so obviously Joyce's that it is surprising that his superiors did not fear that an examination of the scripts put out by the NBBS and by Hamburg would reveal their common source. Joyce wrote: 'There came over the loudspeaker last night a noise which, apparently, proceeded from the vocal chords of that strange being, Duff Cooper. It was a remarkable example of pure hysteria. . . . According to this amazing creature it will be easier to protect ourselves now because we are going to be helping the French to defend our outposts. This brilliant logic leaves us feeling a little weak.'

From the same 'station' he offered advice to the Local Defence Volunteers (the forerunners of the Home Guard), based on an assertion that accidental shootings had been hushed up by the British Government. As civilians the volunteers were 'lacking in the proper control and knowledge of arms that we should expect from soldiers'. He suggested that they should not shoot to kill but merely to disable. 'If your marksmanship is so bad that you cannot make this distinction, resign from the force, or else insist upon taking a musketry course.' The officers were incompetent too and volunteers should 'report without any hesitation to the competent military authority any instances of foolish or unsatisfactory conduct on the part of those who give you orders'.

Reichsrundfunk's overt foreign services were conveying a similar impression of hysterical disintegration in Britain. Using the device of quoting a neutral source, on this occasion Geneva, they were repeating a story that Churchill had ordered the arrest of the Duke of Windsor for protesting about the conduct of the British Expeditionary Force.

Raid warnings sounded and anti-aircraft guns were heard in Berlin that night. The capital was undamaged, yet this British hint of their reply introduced a faint but jarring note into the German news bulletins of the following day, June 22nd. Joyce was on duty as a news-reader when the German High Command reported the capture of St. Malo and Lorient, and the taking of over 200,000 prisoners, 260 aircraft and enormous quantities of war material. Billingham in England had been attacked; British air attacks over Holland had been beaten off with a loss to the British of 25 aircraft; 42,686 tons of shipping had been sunk by a single U-boat. Only the last two paragraphs dealing with military operations spoilt the success story; they admitted that enemy aircraft had penetrated to North and West Germany and had for the first time attacked the area round Berlin.

A later communiqué timed 1850 reported the signing of the armistice with France, to come into operation in about six hours' time after the Italian Government had notified the German High Command of the conclusion of the armistice agreement between France and Italy.

Reichsrundfunk's foreign services stood by to tell the world that the war in the west was over. Joyce read an announcement hastily drafted by Dietze: 'At precisely 1.35 a.m. German summer time, in a very few minutes, hostilities with France will cease, in accordance with the stipulation of the

armistice agreements with Germany and Italy. A special broadcast will begin at 1.30 to mark with due solemnity the termina-
tion of the war in the west.'

A celebration, with champagne, was held by the foreign
broadcasters. Toasts were drunk and Joyce addressed the speaker
of the French Service: 'We realize that it must be a difficult time
for you, but we wish your brave country well.' The Frenchman
made a speech and burst into tears.

The German High Command's final report on the operations
in France ended: 'After this most mighty victory in German
history over the opponent of the Greater German Reich recognized as the world's strongest land power, which fought both
skilfully and bravely, there are no Allies left. Only one enemy
remains: England!'

Chapter 17

JOKE OVER

Life was not alone in thinking that Lord Haw-Haw had been transformed 'from a figure of fun into a matter for concern'. Rumours which, if true, would have revealed that the enemy had the most detailed and topical knowledge of what was going on in British towns and factories, attained such currency (even being published in some newspapers as fact) that the British Ministry of Information issued a statement pointing out that if the Germans possessed secret channels for obtaining such information they would be scarcely likely to advertise their facilities, and that they had not shown awareness in advance of such important events as the arrival of the Canadians in England, the departure of the *Queen Elizabeth* or the occupation of Iceland. The Ministry added that press correspondents could telephone information issued for publication in the morning newspapers of the next day to neutral countries and that this news would arrive in Berlin, thus perhaps giving an unsuspecting listener the impression that the Germans had mysteriously obtained this item many hours before it became known in England.

The Germans were supposed to be so self-confident that they even disclosed their bombing plans. So widespread was the belief that Haw-Haw had announced that certain areas, and even individual buildings which he had named, were to be bombed on specific dates, that the Ministry of Information had to put out a further statement. 'It cannot be too often repeated that Haw-Haw has made no such threats.'

Official refutations of these rumours were reinforced by newspapers, including, with characteristic vigour, the *Daily Mirror*, whose columnist, Bill Greig, thought that in six months Lord

Haw-Haw had graduated from 'England's biggest joke' to 'a danger to the nation'.

His conclusion was based on readers' letters, which provided astonishing evidence of the myths arising from the existence of the German English-language broadcasts.

Above all, there were the clocks. Lord Haw-Haw was supposed to be uncannily well informed about British clocks. A resident of Banstead was reported to have heard Haw-Haw say: 'We know all about Banstead, even that the clock is a quarter of an hour slow today.' The man who heard this remark went to look at the clock, which was in fact a quarter of an hour slow. A reader who had been on a walking tour through rural Sussex had heard a similar rumour about the public clocks in every village through which he had passed. It was the same in London and other towns. The clock at East Ham had not escaped Haw-Haw's attention. In Cambridge he had been heard to remark: 'Don't bother about your new Guildhall clock. We shall put that right for you.' In Wolverhampton 'a clock there stopped one night at 8.55 p.m., and it was reported that at 9.15 p.m. Bremen broadcast the fact.' In Gosport everyone knew that Haw-Haw had stated, correctly, that the town hall clock was two minutes slow.

Haw-Haw's inside information on factories had impressed many readers. He regretted that when a certain munitions factory was blown up the occurrence would break up the pontoon school in the canteen. At Ipswich it was believed that he had said that 'the girls will slide down the banisters more quickly when we blow up the gasometer.' The reader sending this information commented: 'He must be telling the truth because the girls at the factory do slide down the banisters and there is a gasometer nearby.' A drop in production had been caused at a munitions factory in the Midlands employing five thousand workers by a story that Haw-Haw had threatened that the factory would be bombed in a few days and had proved his local knowledge by the remark: 'Don't trouble to finish the new paint shed, you won't need it.' At Oxford the whole town knew the date when the Germans were going to bomb the Morris and the Pressed Steel works.

No target was thought by the British public to be too insignificant for the Luftwaffe's attention. Haw-Haw had said, for example, that Orpington High Street needed widening. He had commented: 'Don't worry, we'll do that for you' and had added that the bakery on the arterial road was a good landmark for German bombers. Similarly, the residents of Portsmouth were supposed to have been assured that there was no need to take up the old tramlines in Commercial Road, as the bombers would do it for them. The reader reporting this story wrote: 'I dare not mention the effect this had.'

A doctor at a hospital receiving British wounded was reproved for having remarked to a party of visiting press men: 'This place has a reputation already—Lord Haw-Haw mentioned it over the radio the other day.' Asked how he knew, he replied: 'Well, I forget who told me for the moment . . . but he really did. . . .'

Troop movements were an obvious subject for such rumours. The wife of a company sergeant-major at Paignton was in tears when met by a *Daily Mirror* reader because Haw-Haw had said that a local territorial battalion was leaving Paignton for Devonport *en route* for Egypt and had voiced the threat: 'It is reasonably certain that German U-boats will see that not one of the men arrives at his destination.' A sailor's wife fainted on being told that Haw-Haw had reported the sinking of a British cruiser on which her husband was serving. 'For her that day was all bitter tragedy—till evening brought her husband home on leave.'

Two prosecutions were reported in June of persons relaying rumours. The first in the country was that of a civil servant at Mansfield who pleaded guilty to 'making a statement which he knew to be false in a material particular, contrary to the Emergency Powers (Defence) General Regulations, 1939, and amendments made thereto'. The alleged quotation from a Haw-Haw broadcast which he had passed on concerned the occupation of local schools and, had his story been correct, between the authorities' decision about the schools and the broadcast from Hamburg there would have been an interval of only one hour forty minutes. He admitted that he himself had originated this rumour after overhearing people passing his garden talking about the schools. At Birmingham a sub-contractor was fined for telling his employees that Haw-Haw had broadcast an account of a fire before the news became generally known in England.

Blaming the dissemination of rumours on to 'Hitler's fifth column in this country', the *Daily Mirror* suggested that 'If his broadcasts were jammed it would be impossible for Nazi slaves in this country to start such rumours and equally impossible for scatter-brained Britons to spread them.' As the Government did not respond, the paper took action on its own by forming the Anti Haw-Haw League of Loyal Britons who promised not to listen to German broadcasts or even any mention of the name Haw-Haw and to try to stop the spread of any harmful rumour. Members signed a form beneath this threat: 'And may Heaven help the rumour-mongers I meet.' As a reminder of his pledge not to listen, the member was to cut from the paper and stick on his radio set the notice: 'This set is Anti Haw-Haw. It hears no evil, speaks no evil.'

Four days later the *Daily Mirror* reported that membership totalled 'many thousands'. Bulk registrations came from anti-aircraft batteries (five gunners promised to 'take the necessary action' against any of their number who lapsed), searchlight stations, A.R.P. posts, hospital staffs, theatrical companies, and naval and merchant vessels (although sailors discovered that the notices would not adhere to bakelite sets.) A Lewisham street had become one hundred per cent anti Haw-Haw. The adherence of Lady Vansittart and May, Countess of Limerick, was announced. So was that of the proprietor of an Islington café who, as shown in a photograph, exhibited just below a Pepsi-cola advertisement a chalked notice: 'Don't go home and listen to that traitor Lord Haw-Haw. Ignore the B——.'

The Haw-Haw joke, the *Daily Mirror* decided, was over. 'Haw-Haw used to be a joke. Not much of a joke, but good enough for some apparently. These dolts went on boosting him as if he was Arthur Askey.'

On 26th July 1940 the Anti Haw-Haw League of Loyal Britons was wound up ('Murdered', as the eye-catching headline curiously expressed it), having, the paper explained, done its job of calling attention to the fifth-column danger.

What the League had actually done was to expose the non-sense that the country was rocking with laughter about the German broadcasts. But to attribute the stories to a fifth column was to concede the New British Broadcasting Station's claim that there existed in Britain an organized anti-war opposition. The myths arose in the circumstances which inevitably give rise to rumour; tense and anxious people tend to supplement a lack of information by their imagination. Under the threat of that time, they created the image of a diabolical enemy possessing super-normal powers. Even if a few mischievous Fascists had spread fictitious accounts of Haw-Haw statements, people in their normal minds would have rejected the preposterous suggestion that dissident citizens everywhere in Britain were collaborating to radio coded messages to Bremen about clocks, paint sheds, bakeries, tramlines and pontoon schools, and that the Germans were maintaining an intricate and costly organization to decode, write up and broadcast this material back to England within a few minutes. To run its network, the German Intelligence service would have needed to equip its agents, yet no one claimed to have seen truck-loads of short-wave apparatus and piles of code-books being delivered, nor did anyone try to explain how the busy short-wave radio traffic, the briefings and the reports, were being handled between Britain and Germany.

The Haw-Haw legend took root in the most unlikely places. After the war, in a report on the reaction to the broadcasts in one of the dominions, a government office innocently retailed a typical Haw-Haw rumour as though it were fact.

And the legend lives on to this day. Mention Haw-Haw in any gathering and out come the stories of what people heard, as they will insist, with their own ears. Joyce was a man who is remembered for what he did not say.

Chapter 18

NO PASSPORTS FOR SPIES

Three more secret 'British' stations were planned. Dr. Hesse, Head of the English Department in the Foreign Office, also suggested a republican station. Joyce strongly opposed any attack on the British Crown and, although he did not work at a policy-making level, the idea was dropped. The new stations were to be more specialized in their appeal than was the New British Broadcasting Station. One was to address disgruntled workers, another to appeal to the religious-minded, and the third to be the voice of Scotland.

An urgent need of new staff arose. To sustain the pretence that they were operating on British soil, Concordia's stations would need more native voices for the character parts of angry citizens, revolutionary workers, earnest Christians and separatist Caledonians. No further discoveries were likely among civilians, but it was thought that candidates might be found in prisoner-of-war camps where, German interrogators had reported, former British Union members had arrived.

Joyce, the mainstay of the NBBS and the expert on Britain, was briefed to visit a camp at Thorn in the Wartegau, interview selected men, and invite suitable ones to join a radio service operating to promote agreement between Germany and Britain and end the war. The material inducements were that volunteers were to be moved to Berlin, where they would be accommodated in a house, allowed to wear civilian clothes and paid a salary. No pressure was to be applied—a common-sense provision because while forced labour may be usefully employed in gangs on manual work, a script written by a sullen man under armed guard and read by a resentful speaker was unlikely to make good radio. Joyce had seen hardly anything of Germany outside

Berlin, so he welcomed the trip. Enjoying his unusual excursion, he found the area round the camp quite romantic and the camp itself 'rather nice'. His inability to imagine himself in somebody else's place was at times very pronounced.

Precautions taken by the camp command to guard his identity were in vain; he had interviewed only very few prisoners when he heard one run past the window shouting: 'I've just been talking to Lord Haw-Haw!'

Eight men, selected for their willingness and their different types of voice, arrived in Berlin. Joyce was far from satisfied with his haul, because he judged only one to be a convinced Fascist and none to be very promising as radio men, but they were a nucleus. He made no more recruiting trips. The staff was augmented from various sources and eventually included such dissimilar characters as William Humphrey Griffiths (a guardsman with a rough workman's voice, who at his trial claimed that Joyce had threatened his life), Leonard Banning (a teacher, a former British Union member and a one-time Conservative Party organizer), Cyril Charles Hoskins (a quiet, bookish young man who stipulated that he should not be employed in any anti-British propaganda), Walter Purdy (a former British Union member, taken prisoner while serving as a junior engineer in the Royal Navy; after the war he claimed to have made two attempts to kill Joyce), a thin blond young man named Winter (passed on by German Intelligence as having been helpful in Africa), and John Lingshaw, alias James (a civilian who joined after the German occupation of the Channel Isles and worked as a monitor). Feminine voices were supplied by the widow of a South African lost in a torpedoed ship, and a woman rescued from a sinking ship while travelling to join her husband in Burma.

Joyce's brief outing to Thorn seemed to him like a holiday because he allowed himself so little free time. His day off provided his main recreation, when he liked to have lunch or dinner with his wife at the Press Club and walk in the Grunewald. When in a good mood he would talk gaily, invent games, and address her by a variety of nicknames, some of them affectionately teasing—Mother Sheep was a favourite, he insisting that her laugh (which he wrote as 'Yp-baa') was like the noise made by a sheep calling its young—and others, such as Freja, romantic. When they felt lonely and homesick for England, he steered the conversation away from their situation. An important day, 2nd July 1940, when his British passport expired, passed without his mentioning it. If he did not then realize the significance of the date, it was to be impressed upon him later. So long as the passport was valid he could have claimed whatever the Swedish Government as the Protecting Power found itself able to do for him; it might have been as little as getting him a Red Cross parcel or as much as securing his repatriation if he became incapacitated and of no military use to the other side. Apart from using it to get himself out of England, he had not asked for anything since arriving in Germany except advice about how to return home.

Although he was employing all his energy and talents in the service of the Germans, he determined that no German agent was going to be equipped with his passport. He was engaged in a conversation once when his wife was puzzled to see him take out his British passport, which he always carried as his identity document, and write in it. Afterwards she asked him what he had written and, still having a law-abiding respect for passports, was horrified to see several pages covered with his handwriting.

Laughing mischievously, like a boy who has shocked his elders, he said: 'When we get German nationality we shall have to surrender our passports to the German authorities, and they're going to find mine useless for any other purpose.' The German Intelligence Service, he had learned, was keen to get hold of authentic British passports, so he had deliberately defaced his by writing addresses and telephone numbers in it.

He waved aside her doubts and added firmly: 'We'll make yours useless too before we give it up.'

On July 8th another secret station, Workers' Challenge, was heard on medium wave in Britain in a programme lasting about twenty minutes. Like its companion station (although the secret stations never referred to each other in broadcasts), it professed to be working somewhere in England; actually the programmes were put out by a portable transmitter moving about the Rhineland and later from Holland. The speakers purported to be tough factory workers (Guardsman Griffiths played a leading rôle) of Socialist views, and occasionally they used words never before heard on the radio in Britain. Unfortunately for the authenticity of Workers' Challenge, Joyce—for all his years of addressing open-air meetings in tough districts—had little idea how workers talked; like his Jews, they were comic paper or music hall characters, and they were obviously reading from scripts.

Hitler, addressing the Reichstag, now opened a new propaganda campaign against Britain in a speech whose theme was summed up in the sentence: 'I see no reason why this war should go on.' Following it on the same day, July 9th, Joyce wrote in a script for the New British Broadcasting Station: 'There is at this time a real possibility, I might almost say a probability, of a negotiated peace.'

The strains of 'Loch Lomond' preceded, on July 18th, an announcement, in a suitable accent, of another station: 'You are listening to Radio Caledonia, the voice of Scotland.' Ribbentrop, despite his time in London and ample opportunities to learn better, was convinced that the tyrannical English were holding down the other races in the British Isles by force and that these minorities were awaiting their chance of overthrowing their oppressors. This delusion was sufficiently widely shared for the Propaganda Ministry to suppose that a radio station advocating a separate peace between Scotland and Germany would arouse a response.

Inside Germany the propaganda line was that Germany was triumphant and unchallenged. On July 18th the German Army put on a victory parade through the Brandenburg Gate. Thousands got a half-day holiday and in the heat a lot of spectators fainted. It seemed, almost, as though peace had returned to Europe.

While the troops, their morale high, were marching rapidly in their parade formation through the avenue of swastika flags in Unter den Linden, Joyce was hard at work tapping out a script in which he impishly permitted himself some rude remarks about his old employer, Sir Oswald Mosley. That day Workers' Challenge called on the British proletariat to revolt. 'Here is Workers' Challenge calling all workers of Britain and Northern Ireland. Workers' Challenge against hunger and war! Churchill means hunger and war! Put him out and his gang of scabs with him! Every day they make new attacks on the rights of the working people! Sir Walter Citrine—Lord Citrine of Borstal—embezzles our union funds for the bosses. Then that bloated rat Bevin is armed with dictatorial powers to forbid all strikes. And then the bosses, seeing that the workers won't stand their bloody game any longer, are going to set up military courts all over the country. What for? Not to deal with a few hundred Fascists. Not by a long chalk. The Mosley gang is in the jug anyhow. And there's no difficulty in pulling in any of the old Blackshirts again. You don't set up military courts for that. They never dared say boo to a goose anyhow, except when they had the coppers in front of them. No, my friends, it's not the Mosley comedians that are making the Government set up military courts. These so-called courts, without any limits to powers, are aimed at you and me—the workers.'

The next day the German home radio broadcast its familiar fanfares and warnings to stand by for an occasion of exceptional importance. Announcements of an impending statement by the Führer were made in solemn tones in the foreign language services. Addressing the Reichstag, his speech being simultaneously interpreted into several languages, Hitler made a peace offer to Britain.

Immediate reaction was permitted to the New British Broadcasting Station. 'This is a day which will go down in history. Now, at the eleventh hour, when Churchill and his gang are urging us to pursue the war until London is in ashes, Hitler gives us another alternative. He offers us peace instead of annihilation.'

Writing for Workers' Challenge, Joyce was able to repeat the assertion he had made in *National Socialism Now* and at his open-air meetings that an understanding with Germany did not mean that Britain must go Nazi. 'The workers of Britain don't want to fight their fellow-workers of Germany. And if the Germans have a Nazi system, that's their look-out, not ours. If we make peace we're not going to have a Nazi system here. We're going to have a state of workers, run by and for the workers. . . . We know bloody well one reason why Churchill wants the war to go on. He's afraid that if he isn't kicked out by the Germans he'll be kicked out by us.'

As these stations were supposedly operated by Britons, they were not tied by the same official considerations as were the overt foreign services. Pending a clarification of the British attitude, the regular 'Germany Calling' commentaries were relatively restrained in tone and sounded as though they were drafted in the German Foreign Office. The Germans seem to have realized that Joyce was not the man for a diplomatic occasion. Whenever the situation required delicate handling, Joyce was kept in the background and other scriptwriters and voices took over. Now, for a few days, the British Government was to be given time to think.

But on July 23rd, after the British Foreign Secretary had officially made it plain that Britain was not going to respond to any peace offer, Joyce was let loose both as scriptwriter and speaker. Lord Halifax, he said, had spoken 'in the smug language of a sanctimonious churchwarden' and with 'snivelling hypocrisy'. He went on: 'Is he trying to qualify for the post of itinerant gospeller in the States when he returns there to avoid the consequences of the tragedy which he and his master Churchill are bringing on England? If the people of England silently allow these rulers to commit them to annihilation, then silence must be taken to signify consent. It is a pity! It is a thousand pities! It is a tragedy the Führer went out of his way to avoid. But if those who rule England and those who live in it care less for their country than the Führer has cared, force, which they regard as the sole arbitrator, must arbitrate.'

Concluding this talk, Joyce uttered a threat—not that a factory would be bombed or a high street widened but a vague prediction, capable of all sorts of interpretations, that England's ruin was imminent if her rulers remained intransigent. 'And that is the end of England,' he declared, 'not within a few years but within a few days to come.' The Haw-Haw broadcasts were not more specific than that.

Similar threats were uttered by him in a review of Britain's conduct of the war on August 2nd. By now the British monitors had sufficient evidence to identify Joyce conclusively as one of the Reichsrundfunk commentators and they noted this talk as delivered by him. He opened on a solemn note of reproach. 'There are times when it is unchivalrous to disparage an opponent, and there are times when it is definitely unwise, but it is not possible to view otherwise than with contempt the conceptions of fighting that Britain has shown in this war. Her behaviour is all the more surprising since she had established, and certainly not without justification, a reputation for the military virtues of courage and rugged strength.' Britain had failed to give practical help to Poland, had been driven out of Norway, and had been unable to prevent Holland and Belgium being overrun 'after the most extensive preparations for their participation in the war had been made'. Of Dunkirk he said that 'What the politicians regarded, or professed to regard, as a triumph, the soldiers regarded as a bloody defeat from which they were extremely fortunate to escape alive.' Britain had let down France, but after the collapse of the French 'the heroic might of the British lion suddenly showed itself at Oran. That inspired military genius, Winston Churchill, discovered that it was easier to bomb French ships, especially when they were not under steam, than to save the Weygand line.' Britain, already suffering heavy losses, was expecting invasion, and the answer of 'Churchill the genius' was to destroy German Red Cross planes and bomb German civilians. Now came the threat. 'It is unnecessary to say that a terrible retribution will come to the people who tolerate as their Prime Minister the cowardly murderer who issues these instructions. Sufficient warnings have already been given. Bombs will speak for themselves.'

It was typical of Joyce's work as an author and scriptwriter that he could not stop when he had got to the end. He had to shout after his opponent, make an insulting gesture, fling a stone. This talk, as usual, had a paragraph tacked on to it, revealing Joyce's fear that he had not made his point, his concern that listeners might not have grasped that he had been criticizing Winston Churchill. 'The same ineffectual, idiotic, petty attitude which has characterized Britain's whole conduct of the war marks the amazing training schemes for civilians upon which Churchill smiles with benign approval. Suicides' academies have apparently been set up all over Britain. The headmasters are cunning blackguards, who teach the inmates how to make bombs at the modest cost of two shillings each, how to poison water supplies by throwing dead dogs into streams, and how to kill sentries noiselessly from behind. So bombs at two shillings a time, home-made in accordance with Lesson 7, are to be used against the German Stukas. Truly the Lord has afflicted these people with blindness.' England would be as weak in defending herself as she was in defending her allies, he concluded. 'The people of England will curse themselves for having preferred ruin from Churchill to peace from Hitler.'

During discussions at Reichsrundfunk about talks presentation,

Joyce always argued forcibly that the British must not be
threatened. He had, of course, to follow the Propaganda Ministry's line, but so had his superior, Dietze, the Glasgow-born
German radio journalist, and the commentaries by the two men
made an interesting contrast. Dietze sounded like a reasonable
man; if the Propaganda Ministry had intended to be persuasive,
he should have been the main commentator. Joyce, by the way,
disliked Dietze, denying that he was a Nazi at all; if Joyce's
judgment was correct, it goes some way to explaining why Dietze
sounded more sensible to English ears. It seems that despite his
appreciation of how his audience would react, Joyce simply
could not help himself. His nature did not allow him to be persuasive; he had to scoff, scold and reproach, whether he was
speaking as the voice of Germany or writing scripts as an en-
lightened patriot for NBBS or as a worker who had seen through
it all for Workers' Challenge. For all his identification of himself
with the proletariat, he was not the popular orator; he was the
odd character who appears on the edge of a crowd under a garish
banner inscribed FLEE FROM THE WRATH TO COME, attracting
an awestruck minority who have abandoned other hope of salvation.

Joyce's attitude fitted in well with that of the Propaganda
Ministry. By now the psychological warfare against Britain had
developed into a steady barrage. News and commentaries were
its mainstays, and it was able to induce even unwilling listeners
to tune in by announcing the names and home addresses of
British prisoners of war. Supplementary to these offerings were
parodies of popular songs ('We're going to hang out our washing
on the Siegfried Line' was a gift to German parodists), sketches,
monologues and magazine items. In all of these the British were
caricatured as stupid, snobbish, obstinate, cowardly, contemptible and pitiable; this was a tactless way to address people if
they were to be persuaded that their best interest lay in making
peace with an enemy government holding these opinions of them.
The sketches and monologues were usually so absurd, P. G.
Wodehouse's novels having apparently been taken as reliable
guides to English conversation, manners, customs and social
divisions, that the laugh was on the German authors instead of
on the listeners; yet they were only conveying in a comically
grotesque way what was being said in the rest of the programmes,

which were designed to weaken, demoralize and panic. The Nazis' propaganda, like their armed forces, employed the Blitzkrieg technique.

This summing up does less than justice to some of the individual performances of the German broadcasters to Britain, who now and again showed ingenuity and humour, and it is not meant to deny that Joyce had a gift for taking an all-round look at the day's news and turning out, at remarkable speed, a commentary clearly spelling out the Propaganda Ministry's message for the day. But everybody was involved in the Blitzkrieg method, which necessitated constant assertions that something nasty was going to happen to the enemy very soon. Over a short period this plan may work, but when even the most nervous listener noticed that he was still alive, still eating, and that his Prime Minister had not after all fled to Canada, the Goebbels organization was faced with the choice of changing its policy or pulling even more hideous faces.

Concordia's next station, first heard early in August, showed a faint realization that another approach might pay. Introduced by the music of a harmonium and operating for a quarter of an hour daily on short wave, the new station was pacifist in sentiment and spoke for a non-existent body called The Christian Peace Movement. It at least tried, in a feeble sort of way, to take its listeners along with it instead of shouting abuse at them, but it is doubtful whether there was much heart behind this venture, and as its signal was weak it could have been received by few listeners.

The New British Broadcasting Station, with support from Workers' Challenge, remained the main instrument in this section of the invasion preparations and pursued the old threatening policy. The German High Command was interested in the NBBS, or was prepared to be when the occasion arose, but if the station was actually briefed by the military authorities the programme staff were unaware of it and they knew no more about secret weapons and invasion plans than any other government officials not in the confidence of the General Staff. When, as they did, they spoke mysteriously of new weapons, chatted knowingly about favourable invasion tides, or predicted where the German forces would land, their talks were aimed simply at creating apprehension among the British public.

Now and again a few lines in a British newspaper gave Concordia a hint that it had an audience. Duplicated extracts from its broadcasts were left in cinemas, and a man was charged with sticking inside a telephone box a label giving the NBBS wavelength. It was not much for a station claiming to speak for an organized fifth column, but the NBBS was intended to grow in importance as the attack on Britain developed. On August 14th it was able to be first with the news that parachutists wearing British uniform or civilian clothing and efficiently equipped with up-to-date maps and plans had landed near Birmingham, Manchester and Glasgow and were being concealed by fifth columnists. At that time the British public firmly believed that the invasion of Holland had been preceded by drops of parachutists disguised as nuns, and the Germans were not wrong in thinking the British susceptible to parachutist scares. The story was spoilt when British newspapers revealed the following day that although parachutes had been found they had been unmanned, as there were no traces of men making their way from the cornfields and other places where they were supposed to have come down. Undeterred, the NBBS ran the news for a few days, expressing alarm at this undermining of 'our defences'. A much bigger story for the British press was the bombing of Croydon Airport on August 15th.

Without his knowledge, Joyce's name was put on a list of civilians who were to be taken to England in the event of a successful invasion. When he was informed Joyce answered that he would of course go, as he was sure the German occupation administration would, without proper advisers, make serious mistakes through their ignorance of the British character, but he did not, he said, want any prominent position for himself. He hoped to stay in the background as an adviser. What he felt at the prospect of returning to England and meeting his family and friends he did not say. He was far from confident that if ever he went back it would be in the wake of victorious German forces.

Although nearly a year had gone by since, expecting to become at once a German citizen, he had left London, he was still without naturalization. Somewhere his application was, he supposed, still making its way from tray to tray. Then he learned from a small, anxious-looking man who called at 84 Kantstrasse and introduced himself (improbably, Joyce thought) as a Gestapo official, that apart from a few minor formalities his naturalization had been accepted. The caller produced the papers, checked the entries for William and Margaret Joyce, and announced that they would be notified when the certificate was ready for collection.

In case he should not have time to do so when the notice came, Joyce copied from his passport into a notebook such addresses and telephone numbers as he wished to keep.

Chapter 19

FAUST TO MEPHISTOPHELES

The first air-raid casualties in Berlin, ten killed and twenty-nine injured, occurred on the night of August 28th. Both Joyce and Shirer were in the Rundfunkhaus when the warning sounded. Shirer wrote in his diary: 'Lord Haw-Haw, I notice, is the only other person around here except the very plucky girl secretaries who does not rush to the shelter after the siren sounds. I have avoided him for a year, but have been thinking lately it might be wise to get acquainted with the traitor. In the air-raids he has shown guts.'

After his shift Joyce went to see the damage. In the street behind his lodging a house had been cut clean out of the block by a direct hit. Glass, rubble, bedding and splintered furniture lay scattered over the pavement and roadway and dazed survivors stood about, unable to grasp what had happened. Joyce stood for some time taking in the scene, profoundly moved at the distress of the bereaved and homeless, before he made his way back to 84 Kantstrasse, where he could talk of nothing but what he had just witnessed.

For the New British Broadcasting Station he was writing scripts conveying rising anger and a sense of urgency. Now he could indulge his fantasy of himself as a revolutionary leader. In the first person, as the head of the fifth column in Britain, he was urging his followers to violence against the Prime Minister and members of the Government. Writing of the NBBS policy towards the end of August, Peter Fleming comments: 'From then on the scripts seem almost to foam at the mouth and there is what can only be described as a *personal* note of malice in the daily exhortations to "go forward gloriously in a campaign of frank terrorism for the good of Britain".'

Faust to Mephistopheles

The appeals to the British to turn on their Government were indeed personal. They were the words of William Joyce, furious that the nation he had tried to serve had rejected everything he stood for. The frustrated patriot was threatening Britain with a Götterdämmerung.

In Berlin, on September 4th, Hitler told a cheering and laughing crowd that the British were asking: 'Why doesn't he come?' His wildly applauded reply was: 'Calm yourselves. He is coming!' The NBBS, which had now been playing on the imminent invasion theme for over a month, became even shriller with warnings that the order to invade might be given at any hour.

On September 7th, when the Luftwaffe launched its massive Blitz on London, the domestic and external services of Reichsrundfunk were telling their listeners that Britain had lost the first year of the war. The attack on the capital apparently took the German radio staffs by surprise, as some of the talks were not as topical as they might have been. Bremen, addressing British listeners (the talk was not by Joyce), was telling them that they had made a bad bargain in exchanging fifty United States destroyers for the lease of bases. 'The deal was covered with beautiful words about the community of ideals, but you know as well as anybody else does that these 99-year leases mean that Britain has given up valuable possessions for good.' Later on, much satisfaction was expressed at news that Parliament had adjourned for two hours the day before because of an air-raid warning. Zeesen put out a talk on the 'Refujew' problem in England.

Joyce, too, had written his NBBS scripts before the significance of that day's raid was known. He was addressing his fifth columnists. 'As the only connexion between the headquarters and the member is ether, it is impossible for the Government to stamp out the movement. I cannot supervise all your work personally. I issue instructions to you and you must follow my advice in detail.' He explained what he meant. 'For instance, if I tell you to advertise a station and indicate some ways of doing this, you must think out others. One collaborator has installed a radio set in his air-raid shelter and tunes in to NBBS during raids, so other families who share the shelter can hear our transmissions.' He went on to promise special broadcasts if the BBC stations went off the air during raids. 'We have numerous representatives with news agencies and if anything important happens we will always tell you, even if the BBC switches off.'

In the evening the NBBS news, warning listeners that no help would come from the United States, confided to its followers that American journalists had been instructed by their Government to minimize air-raid damage in Britain to keep down pressure to bring the United States into the war. The following commentary professed to answer fifth columnists who were uneasy about 'the movement's' hostility to Jewish shopkeepers. 'As a result of our campaign of "War on the Warmongers", a number of Jewish shops have been attacked. One group of collaborators pointed out that many of these Jews are totally unconnected with their competitors in high finance and asks if our campaign against those responsible for the war is to degenerate into mere anti-Semitism. While thoroughly appreciating the misfortune of the Jews who must suffer for the sins of other members of their race, we must emphasize that they are a united race and that Jewish propaganda played an all-too-important part in this country in the months prior to the declaration of war.' The programme (like Joyce's street-corner meetings) closed down with the playing of the British National Anthem.

Workers' Challenge exulted over the two-hour adjournment of Parliament—'Well, workers, Mr. Bleeding Churchill made a nice fool of himself in the House of Commons yesterday'—and staged a pub discussion, with music in the background, between two disaffected workers who addressed each other as 'mate'. Radio Caledonia demanded a separate peace between Scotland and Germany.

The next day, reporting the raids, Hamburg and Bremen contrasted the bombing of docks by the Germans with the destruction of civilian areas by the R.A.F., and—not for the first or last time—announced that the Royal Family was preparing to leave for Canada and that the Prime Minister and Cabinet were considering moving to America. Two days later Joyce, in his NBBS script, called upon his collaborators for 'one last great effort to bring about peace' and on September 11th pressed them to leave London, asserting that the Germans had a secret explosive immensely more damaging than anything known in the past. 'Make no mistake about it,' the script urged. 'Invasion is what is facing us.' At the end came a slogan: 'Remember, it's better to live for England than to die for Churchill.' Workers' Challenge, using non-BBC vocabulary, announced that the London docks would be out of action for years to come.

The 'Germany Calling' programmes were now employing the Hilversum transmitter and reception in England was strong. These commentaries, like those of the secret stations, were going all out to terrify. In a long talk, not by Joyce, the R.A.F. was accused of shooting Luftwaffe crews who had taken to inflatable rafts and warned that 'The day of reckoning will come!' Lord Haw-Haw was telling the British that there would be reprisals for the 'crimes perpetrated against non-combatants in Berlin, Hamburg and other German cities'. Some people had been saying, he remarked: 'An eye for an eye and a tooth for a tooth'. Then came one of his generalized threats: 'For every microscopic part of enamel England rubs off a German tooth, England will lose a complete set of her own.'

The Grand Mufti was interviewed for Arab reaction to the blows against England. Later, listeners were advised to stand by for messages from British prisoners of war, and to be ready to notify relatives in their vicinity.

The pre-invasion psychological attack may be said to have reached its height that night. Suddenly new directives went out from the Propaganda Ministry and the New British Broadcasting Station became coy about predicting the arrival any hour of German forces on British soil. 'Even if invasion does not come for some time', Joyce had to convey to his ghostly army of collaborators on September 13th, 'the air raids will make life impossible.'

His mother and father were among the non-combatants who suffered in the raids he represented to be the Luftwaffe's reprisals. During an attack in September their house in Dulwich was almost completely destroyed, but they survived.

Joyce's other propaganda onslaught on Britain, *Twilight over England*, was published in mid-September in an English edition of 100,000 copies. These were distributed in British prisoner-of-war camps (unfortunately no record was made of the reactions) and in neutral countries. No copies seem to have found their way to England during the war. Translations also appeared. The Swedish version was advertised in the Stockholm paper, *Afton*

Bladet, illustrated with a picture of the author looking upwards with a slight smile and captioned 'William Joyce (Lord Haw-Haw)', evidence of Haw-Haw's international fame and the value attached by the German propagandists to the title.

One of his author's copies Joyce presented to Dietze with the inscription in his handwriting: 'With the best respects of Faust to Mephistopheles.'

Another copy he handed to the secretary who, without grasping what the book was about, had given him some clerical assistance. In this he wrote: 'To Vera—who won't understand it but who may get a few cigarettes for it later.' If this was a prediction of the cigarette economy of post-war Germany, it ranks as one of Joyce's more remarkable intuitions.

Later William Shirer became another recipient. At about one o'clock in the morning on September 26th the American radio correspondent found himself in the Rundfunkhaus air-raid shelter in company with William and Margaret Joyce, and he was able to fulfil his intention of getting to know 'the traitor'. Usually the Joyces avoided going to the shelter but that night, instead of the 'all clear' sounding after a short while, the noise of guns had grown louder and the building had trembled.

Knowing that her husband would be late, Margaret Joyce had fetched him a bottle of schnaps, which she now had with her. They invited Shirer to share it, and the three found their way from the shelter into an unfrequented tunnel, where the bottle was opened. 'Haw-Haw can drink as straight as any man, and, if you can get over your initial revulsion at his being a traitor, you find him an amusing and even intelligent fellow,' Shirer noted in his diary.

Tiring at last of this retreat, they went upstairs to Joyce's office where they sat talking in the dark while watching the flashes from the anti-aircraft guns. Joyce was quite willing to talk about treason. He argued that he was no more a traitor than were the British and Americans who had become naturalized in the Soviet Union or the Germans who renounced their nationality after 1848 and fled to the United States. As he talked he said 'we' and 'us'; in reply to a question by Shirer about what he meant when he used these words, he replied: 'We Germans, of course.'

What Shirer could not know was that Joyce had a letter in his pocket, received only on the previous day, notifying him that his naturalization papers were ready and that he was to call for them at a police station. After Joyce had gone off duty and breakfasted, he was going to collect them and become officially a German citizen.

Joyce has frequently been described as undersized. To Shirer he appeared 'a heavily built man of about five feet nine inches, with Irish eyes that twinkle' and speaking a fair German. From the conversation he was able to diagnose two complexes, 'a titanic hatred for Jews and an equally titanic one for capitalists'. This is how he summed up Joyce's belief in National Socialism: 'Strange as it may seem, he thinks the Nazi movement is a proletarian one which will free the world from the bonds of the "plutocratic capitalists". He sees himself primarily as a liberator of the working class.'

Shirer, who must have noticed in this conversation that Joyce had nothing like an aristocratic voice, produced what probably appeared the only reasonable explanation of the inappropriate nickname by which the British had come to know him. 'On the radio this hard-fisted, scar-faced young Fascist rabble-rouser sounds like a decadent old English blue-blood aristocrat of the type familiar on our stage.'

Joyce made Shirer a present of his book after Shirer had given him a recently-published novel called *The Death of Lord Haw Haw* by Brett Rutledge (a pseudonym used by Elliott Paul, a prolific author and for several years Paris correspondent for American newspapers). This book, which caused Joyce a good deal of amusement, was a nice example of the American predilection of anticipating in fiction what has not yet been accomplished in fact. It paid Haw-Haw (but not Joyce) the compliment of calling him 'No. 1 Personality of World War No. 2'. The blurb, although not claiming that the work was other than fiction, hinted at an important 'but'. 'Brett Rutledge's *The Death of Lord Haw Haw* is straight fiction, but the author, obviously, is in possession of certain facts that have never been disclosed by the official news agencies.'

Rutledge certainly knew, or guessed, one thing ahead of other people, and that was that William Joyce was American born, but he dismissed Joyce, 'a party with a square head, shifty eyes, protruding ears and a scar from the right-hand corner of his sullen mouth to a point not far from his right ear', as a possible

Haw-Haw because, as 'a low and surly fellow' with 'an evil countenance indicating sexual abnormality of the aggressive type so common among Fascists everywhere', he did not qualify as a master propagandist. None the less, this Joyce had one quite aristocratic blot on his past—'it was hinted that while in school he had cheated at cards.' His scar was interesting, 'for it was exactly the mark certain American gangsters used to brand for life recalcitrant members who had squealed. On the other hand, it might have been inflicted with a saber, in a student duel at Heidelberg.'

Joyce's second wife was described as 'a ballet dancer who performed a lamentable vaudeville act'. This story about Margaret Joyce had already appeared in American newspapers and probably had its origin in an old photograph taken at a dancing class.

Perhaps, as the book was published as long ago as 1940, it is not unfair to reveal the author's surprise, which is that the Germans encouraged the idea that Joyce was Haw-Haw in order to shield the real Haw-Haw, 'an elegant Briton' named James McNeal O'Brien.

After the raid, and their talk with Shirer, Joyce and his wife went home in the early morning light. A few hours later Joyce left home carrying two passports in his pocket, his own, defaced by his scribbled notes, and his wife's, from which he had torn the front page. He handed them in at a police station and received a document certifying that William and Margaret Joyce had been naturalized as 'citizens of Prussia'.

Over a year too late, he had been admitted by the Third Reich to citizenship. In that year, so he and the other radio commentators were saying, Germany had as good as won the war. Yet far from being jubilant at the success of the cause he had backed, he was a disillusioned man. His faith in National Socialism and Hitler's essential rightness never wavered but from a distant view of the Führer that year he suspected that he was badly overstrained and suffering from paralysis agitans, while as for the Germans generally, he saw them as defeatists and muddlers, enmeshed in a crazy bureaucracy, strangers to common sense, unworthy of the ideals of National Socialism, and behaving almost as though they were trying to lose the war. Apart from

Hitler, the only member of the Government he admired was Goebbels, but he thought the Propaganda Minister had failed to recruit a competent staff for his ministry. His private name for Ribbentrop was Ribbentripe, he cordially disliked Dr. Hesse and he had a low opinion of most of the English-speaking staff.

It is this disappointment which accounts for what would otherwise seem a very odd omission in Joyce's career—his failure to become, officially, a Nazi. He could have joined the National Socialist German Workers' Party (as it was called), but he refrained because he saw what had happened to the movement. Everywhere the governmental machine was cluttered up with Party stalwarts who, although first-rate at shouting 'Sieg Heil!' at rallies, were disastrous liabilities as civil servants. 'When a leader of a Party comes to power', he said, 'he ought to shoot his old comrades.' Hitler had, of course, shot some of them but, Joyce professed to think, not nearly enough. Yet the man who suffered nightmares about shootings had really no desire to see anyone shot; the broadcaster who seemed to gloat over the prospect of destruction was upset at the sight of wrecked houses and homeless people. He could not admit to himself that he was witnessing the squalid fulfilment of his political ideal; he simply concluded that whatever disgusted him was a departure from the principles of National Socialism.

He began to think—and perhaps to hope—that he would not survive the war. The idea was implanted by a police officer, who warned him that there were reasons for suspecting that an attempt on his life might be made. For a while policemen took turns of duty in front of his flat, he was discreetly supervised on his way to and from the Rundfunkhaus, and he was given a pistol with permission to carry it.

At the end of October he and his wife had one of their rare holidays, four days in Dresden. There the only reminder of the war was the closed art gallery, the pictures having been removed to safety. Opera and concert audiences were unworried and wearing their best clothes. As they strolled through the town in golden autumn sunshine Joyce talked entertainingly, made his familiar teasing jokes, was kind and even-tempered. Margaret knew that it cost him an effort to behave like this, that he was determined not to spoil her enjoyment.

Only on the last day did he reveal his melancholy. For a long time he stood in the hotel entrance, taking in the view. Then he said to his wife: 'A beautiful place! But I shall never come back.'

On the night of their return the R.A.F. made a prolonged raid on Berlin.

Chapter 20

A LETTER TO JOYCE

Anna Wolkoff, a naturalized British subject, daughter of a former admiral in the Imperial Russian Navy, was tried at the Old Bailey in November 1940 for offences against the Defence Regulations, including an attempt to send a coded letter to Joyce. I write 'including' because she was also involved with Tyler Kent, a cipher clerk in the United States London Embassy, who took copies of secret messages; that part of her case is outside the scope of this book. As a member of the anti-Semitic Right Club, and an admirer of Joyce, she continued her campaign after the war had started, putting up at night such posters as this: 'Your New Year's resolution. We appeal to the working men and women of Great Britain to purchase the new Defence Bonds and Savings Certificates thus keeping the War going as long as possible. Your willing self-sacrifice and support will enable the War profiteers to make bigger and better profits and at the same time save their wealth from being conscripted.' She was the kind of person Joyce professed to be addressing in his New British Broadcasting Station scripts.

She came to be in the dock on this charge because she had trustingly handed to a woman a coded letter addressed to Herr W. B. Joyce, Rundfunkhaus, Berlin, thinking that this person would arrange to have it sent to Germany in the Rumanian diplomatic bag. The woman, however, handed it to her employers, the British security service. It was decoded, copied, and then forwarded as though it had not been intercepted.

The message contained advice to Joyce about the 'Germany Calling' broadcasts. 'Talks effect splendid but news bulletins less so. Palestine good but I.R.A. etc. defeats object. Stick to plutocracy. Avoid King.' She reported on reception and then proceeded: 'Here Krieghetze only among Blimps. Workers fed up. Wives more so. Troops not keen. Anti-Semitism spreading like flame everywhere—all classes. Note refujews in so-called Pioneer Corps guaranteed in writing to be sent into firing line. Churchill not popular—keep on at him as Baruch tool and war-theatre-extender, sacrificer Gallipoli, etc. Stress his conceit and repeated failures with expense lives and prestige.'

The original message ended: 'Butter ration doubled because poor can't buy—admitted by *Telegraph*—bacon same. Cost living steeply mounting. Shopkeepers suffering. Suits P.E.P. Regret must state Meg's Tuesday talks unpopular with women. Advice alter radically or drop. God bless and salute all leaguers and C.B. Acknowledge this by Carlyle reference radio not Thurs. or Sun. Reply same channel same cipher.'

Having handed it over, she asked for it back and added a request for a rebroadcast of a talk in the German domestic service about a Freemasons' meeting with this further advice: 'It is now very important that we hear more about the Jews and Freemasons. P.J.'

The initials 'P.J.' stood for 'Perish Judah'. P.E.P. meant Political and Economic Planning, a research body regarded in Joyce's circle as part of the international Jewish plot. Meg, whose talks she criticized, was Margaret Joyce, and the C.B. to whom she sent God's blessing was Christian Bauer.

Joyce had little or no need of suggestions for his talks, and the message was a rather thin one to risk a long term of imprisonment for. Part of Anna Wolkoff's defence was that she had not written the letter herself but had received it from a man to whom she was introduced by a naval officer friend. Without having seen all the evidence, it is impossible to know whether anyone else might have been involved, but it seems odd that the letter was addressed to W. B. Joyce when she was unlikely to know that he had a second Christian name and that she, not being an intimate of the Joyce family, referred to Margaret as Meg.

The letter was not delivered to Joyce, although he was informed of its receipt by the German censorship. He may have been instructed to acknowledge it 'by Carlyle reference'. At the trial there was a suggestion that he, or somebody, had done so, because a few days after the letter should (it was said) have reached Berlin the New British Broadcasting Station broadcast a talk attacking French culture which included the passage: 'We thank the French for nothing. Where is their Shakespeare? Who is their Carlyle?' Joyce could well have written these sentences anyway, but it certainly looks like more than a coincidence that he did so. Strangely, the sender of the message addressed Joyce in his Haw-Haw capacity, yet the acknowledgement came through the NBBS. Did Anna Wolkoff therefore know that Joyce was writing the NBBS scripts, and if so, how? Did the German authorities who retained the letter respond in code through the same channel (the Rumanian diplomatic bag) or did they (as would seem probable) not think it worth while to use this route to acquire such low-level information?

In sentencing Anna Wolkoff, on November 7th, to ten years' imprisonment, the judge called Joyce a traitor. His words were: 'You, a Russian subject who in 1935 became a naturalized British subject, at a time when this country was fighting for her very life and existence sent a document to a traitor who broadcasts from Germany for the purpose of weakening the war effort of this country.'

The judge was Mr. Justice Tucker, who four years later was to try Joyce at the Old Bailey.

Mentioned in Parliament, at the Central Criminal Court, and in thousands of conversations daily, the almost unknown agitator had now become, to the British, the man they hated most. Hitler, Göring and Goebbels were remote cartoon figures; Haw-Haw spoke to the British in their homes. Although the German radio presented only some talks as by Haw-Haw, the public still attributed them all, the lead-in announcements and the news bulletins as well, to this super-broadcaster. Simple people appear to have become persuaded that Joyce was actually running the war on the German side. According to Hannen Swaffer, writing in the *Daily Herald* while the Luftwaffe was still making its nightly raids on London, the wife of a former Mayor of Shoreditch was 'sometimes blamed for the constant blitzing of Shoreditch'. It was she who had become involved in an altercation with Joyce after he had, during the London County Council election in 1937, stuck a Fascist poster on her wall. A typical Haw-Haw rumour had become current in the neighbourhood that he had described the street where she lived as 'a street full of prostitutes' and threatened it with reprisals. 'Well,' Swaffer concluded, 'that Shoreditch street has been bombed many times and some of the residents think it is William Joyce's revenge.' Joyce had indeed become a figure of superstitious awe if it could be supposed that he was able to give orders to the German Air Force and employ it in costly operations simply to pay off a personal score.

BBC honorary local correspondents, inquiring whether there was at this time more listening to enemy broadcasts in English, seem to have encountered a reluctance to admit to listening. Some listeners said they tuned in to supplement the British news, hoping, for example, to identify that 'town in the south-west' which had been raided. Others admitted switching on for entertainment and music when the reception of BBC programmes was unsatisfactory, and there were claims to derive entertainment from the news and political broadcasts. The correspondents found negligible evidence of listening to the New British Broadcasting Station. A minority view was recorded that 'The Workers' Challenge has a heavy following. . . . The novelty was in the language, but the feeling grows that a lot of his remarks are true.'

With German landings no longer supposed to be imminent, the secret stations had lost their pre-invasion function, but they were kept going to exploit discontent and create general uneasiness. German interest in them either slackened or they were thought to be set reliably on their course as—after a period of interference by the German Foreign Office—Concordia was left to run them unmolested. At one period the Foreign Office, anxious to get all external propaganda under its control, had succeeded in appointing censors. The first, a Dr. Rössel, who came from the editorial staff of a German textile periodical, was not politically minded, but having lived in London he felt himself entitled to delay scripts while he made alterations in spelling and punctuation, as though they were to be printed instead of broadcast. Protests from Concordia secured his removal, and he was succeeded by Professor Mahr, an Austrian historian, who had left his work in a Dublin museum and gone to Germany just before the outbreak of war. On moving into the Concordia office he produced an alarm clock from a pocket and opened a case containing, among a variety of objects, a pair of braces and an orange. The staff's fears that they might be in for a period of eccentric obstruction were unfounded. Professor Mahr read the scripts with polite interest and handed them back untouched. After he was withdrawn there was no replacement.

Writing for the secret stations was a heavy commitment for Joyce which his recruitment of British prisoners of war had done little to lighten. These men became an administrative problem rather than an editorial asset. Wearing civilian clothes, living in a four-roomed flat in Soorstrasse, near the radio headquarters, and receiving salaries (which they supplemented by black-marketing their British Red Cross parcels), they were enjoying what Joyce had promised them at Thorn. But what they most hoped for, which was freedom, they were denied. The German Army Command in Berlin refused to allow British prisoners of war, even though they were employed by the German radio, to move freely about the city. Sentries of the Funkschutz, a unit of S.S. men formed to guard radio premises, patrolled outside the flat (which also served as an office) and escorted the prisoners daily for an hour's recreational walk.

Not all of them worked. Their voices had sounded suitable to Joyce when he interviewed them, but some of the men from Thorn were found to be unable to write grammatically or to read a sentence aloud correctly. These hung about their quarters, moodily gazing out at the armed sentries, gossiping, grumbling and quarrelling, making it more difficult for the better-equipped to perform such modest tasks as could be set them. Without professional experience, the scriptwriters were slow and uncertain workers. They might have got along better if Concordia had been able to provide them with clerical assistance, but no female secretaries were permitted entry to the flat because of the feared effect of their presence on men cut off so long from normal life.

While adamant in denying them liberty, the German Army Command listened sympathetically to other representations. As a result, at regular intervals the prisoners' escorted recreational walks became more purposeful and a party accompanied by an S.S. man with a rifle marched raggedly to a brothel near the Zoo Station. This parade was not compulsory and there were always some, including Hoskins, who opted out.

Ultimately the more unsuitable recruits, and those who had second thoughts about what they were doing, returned to prisoner-of-war camps. The original eight from Thorn became reduced to three and later to two.

Finally, Hetzler's contention that men doing confidential work should be trusted to lead private lives was effective. Concordia's remaining staff lived during the later stages of the war as civilians.

Chapter 21

DIVORCE

Now a German citizen, Joyce was liable to military service. He registered on 12th February 1941, being put in a reserved category. The military pass issued to him was in his own name, his place and date of birth were stated correctly, and his nationality was given as 'German, formerly English'. He gave his religion as 'Gottgläubig' (a believer in God, this curious term being then used in the registration of Germans who were not members of any church). He was described as a radio speaker knowing English perfectly and German, and he entered his hobbies, as usual, as swimming, riding and boxing. In recording details of his parents he promoted his father to the profession of architect.

Michael Joyce, an unpretentious man, was content to be what he was. By his enterprise and ability he had done well for his family, and William had no need to be ashamed of him. If his father had failed him at all it was in not insisting that his American-born son should have a United States instead of a British passport. But he wanted no foreign passports in a loyal British family, and he did not live long enough to know that William had become a German. He died at East Dulwich just a week after his absent son registered for military service in Berlin. British papers announced his death and that was how William learned of it. According to some of the papers, the father was known to have been bitter about his son's activities.

The news arrived in Berlin while Joyce and his wife were moving out of their lodging at the Amtsgerichtsplatz. They had found it impossible to get fuel to heat the huge stove there, and they were miserably cold in the freezing Berlin winter. Their new flat at 29 Kastanien-Allee, Berlin-Charlottenburg, only ten minutes' walk from the Rundfunkhaus, was well-furnished, light and quiet, with plenty of space for all the books Joyce had acquired, and the landlady served breakfast and looked after the cleaning and heating. The street was lined with trees, which he liked to contemplate from the balcony. The Funk-Eck, at the other end of Kastanien-Allee, became one of Joyce's favourite bars.

A man dedicated to a cause is apt to be an inattentive husband. In his own way Joyce was devoted to his wife. From the moment he first saw her, when she interrupted his speech by arriving late, he had determined to marry her. When he proposed he had accepted her flippant remark that they could always undo their marriage if they wanted to, but it had never occurred to him that their partnership could come to breaking point. Childlike he tested her affection and loyalty by permitting himself outbursts of rage against her without ever suspecting that she could be hurt. At times he behaved as though she were there only to listen to his scornful comments on the Propaganda Ministry's directives and the defeatism of the Germans generally, to pour out a drink and hand him his cigarettes while he frowned over the sheet of paper in his typewriter. In the new and more comfortable flat, she hoped, he might relax a little, talk to her, and enjoy their brief leisure. But he came home preoccupied as before, his expression strained, ready at a chance remark from her to relieve his feelings by shouting.

Margaret took to staying on in her office in Kochstrasse after the usual hour, accepting colleagues' invitations to drinks and supper—anything to shorten the time at home with her husband. A good-looking young man named Nicky became her frequent companion. He was amusing and gallant, and he soon grew impatient of always meeting her in public. She avoided being alone with him.

One evening Joyce returned in a temper after one of his trying days of dictating pieces for Concordia in the morning, writing his commentary in the afternoon and delivering it in the evening while coping with what he regarded as the idiocies of the Propaganda Ministry. He raved at her in the irrational way he had the night they moved into their last lodging in London.

Shaking with emotion, she left the room and telephoned to Nicky that she would meet him at his flat.

When she made a habit of coming home even later Joyce, surrounded by papers and cigarette smoke, a bottle of schnaps within reach, scarcely seemed to notice. At other times he stormed at her, but now she was better able to keep calm.

Her frank nature would not allow her for long to remain silent about the new situation. One evening, without any opening manœuvres, she found herself telling him where she was spending her evenings.

He was astonished and incredulous. She had to repeat what she had said. He began to talk incoherently but, strangely enough, he did not explode in anger. Gently, trying to understand, he implored her to help him to grasp what it all meant. The talk went on all night, with the same questions coming up again and again.

'How could you after all we have been to each other?'

'What made you?'

'Didn't you mean anything of what you said?'

'Is he better than I am?'

The following morning he went to work as usual, got through his tasks without betraying his emotional distress, gave his commentary, and arrived back at midnight to restart the discussion from the beginning. Margaret needed sleep badly but Joyce talked through the night until they could throw open the blackout curtains and let in the daylight. Again he went to the Rundfunkhaus and pursued his routine. At night he was back, his face drawn, requiring no sleep, only needing to think aloud. He did not want her to stay. She did not want to stay either, she replied. But he did not want her to go. He seemed to be searching for a reason which would explain her conduct and excuse it, but his talk went in a circle, and on the fourth day, with three sleepless nights and the incessant sound of his voice behind her, she left to lodge with a woman friend until she had decided what to do.

Fearing that unless Margaret was removed to a place where she could enjoy some tranquillity she would break down, the friend suggested that she should go away for a while. Joyce agreed, possibly because it would remove her from his rival's presence. The place chosen for her recuperation was an 800-acre estate near Danzig where the friend's sister-in-law lived. Before Margaret left Joyce told her that while he was prepared to care for her welfare, he would never take her back.

Divorce

The overcrowded train had no dining car. The other passengers, foreseeing that, had brought their food. Margaret was faint and hungry when, long after its scheduled time, the train reached Danzig. The last local train to her destination had gone, so she carried her luggage out of the station and looked in vain for a bus or taxi. No public transport was running. Uniformed men swarmed everywhere, the mass occasionally parting as army trucks nosed their way through. Hardly able to lift her cases, she stumbled across the road to an hotel.

As she entered she noticed the receptionist's expression of surprise. Civilians, and especially women, were rare visitors; nobody arrived there in those days without official warrants for accommodation. She shook her head almost before Margaret had begun to speak, telling her that every hotel in the town was full. All the girl could do was to let her telephone her waiting hostess to explain her delay in arriving.

With no idea where to eat and sleep, Margaret grasped her luggage and, numb with misery, simply walked. The black-out was less effective than in Berlin and it was apparent that she was in a main street. She put her luggage down and stood still, watching the thousands of soldiers milling past.

Three of the passing soldiers stopped, eyeing her with friendly curiosity. One asked if he and his two companions could help her. Confusedly thanking them, she stammered in her foreigner's primitive German that she did not know where to go. The man, still trying to be helpful, asked who she was. If he was surprised at the reply that she was English, he politely concealed it. Feeling impelled to explain her presence in politically-important Danzig, she told them that she had come from Berlin, where her husband was a radio speaker.

Military towns are dull places and the soldiers brightened at this unusual encounter. Lord Haw-Haw's reputation among Germans for releasing news still banned to the home radio had reached them. With zest they debated among themselves how they could help her. She could only follow when they picked up her cases and motioned to her to accompany them.

The house where they halted looked very old. In answer to their knocking a poor-looking elderly woman appeared and stared in puzzlement at the unexpected group. Smiling and ingratiating, the soldiers appealed to her to give their companion accommodation. Margaret could not follow their rapid talk, but she heard the name 'Haw-Haw' being used as though it were a password. Her lined face relaxed into a smile, the woman pulled the door back, and the soldiers stood aside to let Margaret in.

There was a spare bed in the grand-daughter's small room. The woman pointed to it and Margaret nodded, trying to convey her gratitude in the movement.

The soldiers waited downstairs to take her to a small Bierlokal, packed with noisy uniformed men drinking and eating. The atmosphere was in striking contrast to the brooding gloom of Berlin.

After a night's sleep she felt sufficiently recovered to do some sightseeing in Danzig before taking another train. At the small country station she stepped out into another, more spacious world. Healthy-looking and unworried, her host carried her luggage to a trap. The horse took them along a country road at an easy trot, through thriving fields worked by Polish labourers. These farm workers were plentiful; formerly they had come seasonally but now they had to take a job for a fixed time.

The farmhouse was large, comfortable and ugly. The meals were large too, and blacked-out Berlin seemed very remote.

After supper on the first evening her hosts wanted to know what was happening in Berlin and what people there thought of the war situation. Margaret had to search for words. Becoming impatient, the man interrupted with an urgent question.

'When is the war with Russia going to start?'

The Propaganda Ministry's strict directives that no offence was to be caused the Soviet Union had set up such inhibitions in German radio circles that Margaret was taken aback. Nobody in Berlin had dared to mention a war with Russia, yet here, obviously, it was thought to be inevitable. Her answer was that the departments she knew had concerned themselves almost exclusively with news from the west.

She had in mind that an early peace, to be brought about by a proletarian revolution, strikes or prayers (according to the programme the listener happened to be hearing), was still the theme of the psychological warfare against Britain. On April 1st the Christian Peace Movement station recalled that 'Last time it was four and a half years of misery before that crime was brought to an end. And bearing in mind how much it cost, the question is this: are we going to let this war drag on equally long? Or are we going to listen to the dictates of common sense and Christianity and make peace now?' On the same day Workers' Challenge was delivering a similar message in different terms. The Minister referred to in this passage was Lord Woolton, the Minister of Food. 'But when it comes to seeing the Minister, we ask what on earth is the use of seeing him unless you are determined to kick his backside and sling him out? His mind is made up. His policy is settled. It's all cut and dried. . . . Now a deputation of tough workers who went to see him and beat him up would be quite a different matter. It would produce a great sensation. It would have a high propaganda value. There would, of course, be some police court cases, but they could be knocked on the head by large strikes, which the Government wouldn't dare to face. And if old Woolton had to go to hospital for a fortnight, he'd be as much use to us there as anywhere else.'

In her farmhouse Margaret discovered that the Haw-Haw broadcasts could be received on her hosts' radio set. A routine quickly became established; she listened to the news in English and to her husband's talks and tried to translate the sense of them for her news-hungry companions.

On April 3rd the news ran its course and called for little inter-preting, as her companions were only mildly interested in the propaganda campaign against Yugoslavia and Greece, indicating that an attack on those two countries was imminent. The com-mentary by Lord Haw-Haw was announced. Suddenly Margaret, startled, forgot to translate. Instead of the usual reference to the German High Command's communiqué, Haw-Haw was saying that he had never wished to be anonymous and that he had at last been given permission to reveal who he was. Speaking with even more than his customary deliberation, he said:

'I, William Joyce, left England because I would not fight for Jewry against Adolf Hitler and National Socialism. I left Eng-land because I thought that victory which would preserve exist-ing conditions would be more damaging to Britain than defeat.'

For the British public the announcement came a year too late and it rated no more than a few lines in the newspapers, but it allowed Joyce to address his audience under his own name. The nickname was too valuable a trademark to drop, however, and from then on the announcement ran: 'William Joyce, otherwise known as Lord Haw-Haw.'

As Margaret translated the statement she was reflecting that he had had an additional reason for coming to Germany—the desire not to be parted from her.

A few days later a neighbour, granted a small petrol ration for official business and having to go to Danzig, took Margaret and her hostess for the ride. On the way the car pulled out to overtake a column of marching men. Black-uniformed guards, their rifles slung, were at the rear. Ahead were men in what appeared to be prison garb. Shaven heads were turned, expressionless faces looked at them, as the car went by.

An exclamation of distaste came from her hostess. 'Oh, don't look out of the car! They stare so!'

But who were they? Margaret wanted to know. This was a sight not seen in Berlin streets.

They came from a concentration camp in the neighbourhood, the other woman replied curtly, making it plain that she did not want to talk about them.

Joyce did not meet his wife at the station on her return to Berlin. She went to a room provided by another woman friend. Aware, as she was, of looking well, she suspected when she saw him the next day that he was affronted by her restored appearance. His manner was formal, reserved and weary. After politely inquiring about her health, he became sternly practical. During her absence he had seen the man who was, as he insisted on thinking, the cause of the trouble, and forbidden him to meet her. She was to take no steps to see him, and so that she could more easily avoid him Joyce had arranged for her to be transferred from the Soorstrasse office, the scene of the unfortunate encounter, to one in Hetzler's department, where she could work on archives, produce scripts, and be under his observation. She was on her own now but he had ensured that she would not starve.

Although parted domestically, they remained united on the radio. When she gave her talks—the criticisms in Anna Wolkoff's message were not unmerited; they were stilted little pieces—she was announced as Lady Haw-Haw.

The German propagandists were now wrestling with American Lease-Lend, and were once again handicapped by their ministry's policy of going all-out on a short-term campaign. Eight months previously the war had been as good as over; the contemptible British, fighting to the last Pole or Frenchman, would never do any fighting themselves. Their pride and obstinacy having prevented them from coming to a sensible agreement with Germany, they were to be invaded; the Führer had given his promise, in jocular terms conveying that the operation would be easy, that the German forces would arrive. No German soldier landed, but the U-boats and the Luftwaffe were knocking Britain out of the war. Yet the war was still on. Now the British, who had been confidently warned that they would get nothing out of the Americans, were being told that anything they did receive would be a bad bargain for them and a good one for the Jewish-American financiers and their handful of British hangers-on; addressing the Americans, the German radio was emphatic that they would lose every cent they spent in backing the crafty British.

Then Goebbels and his staff were set an unprecedented problem through the arrival by parachute in Scotland during the night of 10th–11th May 1941 of Rudolf Hess, the Deputy-Führer. A cautious pause was followed, in the English-language service, by a carefully-worded and obviously ministerial comment, suggesting that Hess had really thought he could do something for peace but that he had been under great strain and that his mental condition had been causing concern for some time. The matter was too delicate for the Haw-Haw treatment. Joyce was probably glad to be relieved of making a comment, because the incident had upset him badly.

Not until May 14th was the typical Joyce style heard, and then not in the overt 'Germany Calling' service but on the New British Broadcasting Station wavelength. Joyce in his script shrugged the affair off, using the familiar platform speaker's technique of starting as though he were going to comment, edging away from the subject with a joke and working round to an attack on accustomed targets. In this passage he managed to switch the main attention to Churchill.

'We had no intention of entering into any discussion upon the arrival in peculiar circumstances of Rudolf Hess in Scotland, but since he has created far more interest than the Loch Ness Monster and since we believe this interest to be disproportionate to the event, we feel constrained to make some comment on what has become a matter of public opinion.' He went on to suggest that Hess should be offered a seat in the House of Commons as an Independent Conservative Invasion member. 'Whether he is sane or insane is of no importance in this connexion for he would be working with men like Winston Churchill whose mental condition has long been open to doubt . . . Hess is with us but victory is as far off as ever. If we could, however, persuade Churchill to undertake a flight to Germany, there might be some cause for public rejoicing.'

An observer of the psychological war might have noted that Britain had now gone over to the offensive. The 'V' for victory campaign directed to the occupied countries was worrying the German forces. The German Propaganda Ministry tried to hit back with a 'P' campaign. On January 21st the New British Broadcasting Station, pretending that the idea had been taken up on a big scale in Britain, urged its listeners to carry on.

'Most of you know of the letter P campaign. You have probably seen this letter written in your locality. The idea is very simple. It is to keep peace in the public mind. War is widely advertised and we think peace should have publicity too. . . . So keep on with this idea. It is small but it is directed towards a great and noble end.' Workers' Challenge on the same day, dismissing British trade union leaders as 'swine' and 'skunks', issued this message: 'Organize strikes on a mass scale, withdraw your labour from industry and the war must stop within 48 hours.'

While peace was thus being urged on the British, German troops were already moving to open the attack on Russia.

Although he had dreaded a two-front war, Joyce took the shock of the news fairly calmly. To his excited landlady, the habitués at the Funk-Eck, and everyone else who thought he must be well-informed, he said that the outcome would be all right so long as America did not enter the war. Certainly as a propagandist he would now be able to bring out of stock his invective against the Jewish-Bolsheviks, the Russians as enemies having automatically become Jews again, but his new freedom was not immediately apparent. In his Haw-Haw commentary he either did not know what to say or had been told to mark time; all he produced was a colourless rehash of Hitler's proclamation.

Bremen's statement, not by Joyce, had a Foreign Office ring. 'Germany's experience in her relations with Moscow during the last few years confirms the political and moral impossibility of maintaining normal and reliable political relations with the men who govern Russia at the present day.'

Workers' Challenge was uncertain in its comment. It might have taken the line that Britain's strained resources were now to be depleted even more to help the Soviet Union, but it predicted that Britain would send nothing to Russia. Aid had been promised to 'practically every bloody country in Europe and what did we give?' The answer was a colloquial coarse one.

The new turn in the war caused a flurry in Büro Concordia, which had been extending rapidly and coping with difficult foreigners. Setting up an Indian station had created problems which were then further complicated by the staff's fear of air-raids and their consequent transfer to Holland. Barely had a clandestine station for Yugoslavia begun working than one had to be started for Russia. The speakers and scriptwriters were of a very different type from those in the English-language department. Mostly captured Russian officers, they were so temperamental that they needed a special administrative officer; the post was filled more or less successfully by a Russian-born woman refugee. The policy adviser was a German Communist, a former deputy-minister of forestry in the Soviet Union, who had defected. The station's line was that the Soviet Government was not genuinely Communist; all real Communists were called upon to oppose it.

In July a Member of Parliament elicited a renewed assurance from the Government that British broadcasters in enemy employ would be brought to justice and the information that these broadcasts were being recorded. Just then Joyce's thoughts were much occupied with another kind of legal case; he was taking steps to divorce his wife.

His pre-divorce conduct was scarcely less odd than had been his proposal of marriage. Still angry with her, he none the less insisted on seeing his wife on their day off, for lunch or dinner or both, but he would not meet her at the Press Club at Leipziger Platz or introduce her to the new friends he had met during her absence.

The preparations needed discretion, because in the ministries and the radio organization divorce was semi-officially frowned on, both Hitler and Goebbels being known to disapprove of it. The lawyers were accordingly instructed to make the grounds as mild as they could. Doing their best, they first presented the case so that it looked scarcely more than a slight disagreement between the parties, but they were advised that without stronger reasons the suit might not go through. One of Joyce's acquaintances, who worked in the SS head office, gave a helping hand behind the scenes and was thought to have tipped off the judge. The lawyers did some redrafting.

In the case as it was ultimately presented on 12th August 1941, Joyce sued on the grounds of infidelity. His lawyer told the court that the wife, despite warnings, had gone out a great deal and come home very late, sometimes not arriving back until nearly two in the morning.

Margaret cross-petitioned, alleging cruelty. Instead of making the reproaches which would have been justified, her lawyer urged, her husband had abused her immoderately, saying that he had lost all respect for her and despised her.

Number 35a Zivilkammer looked strange to the petitioners, being simply a room bearing no resemblance to a court, and the judge reminded them of a nonconformist minister. They were relieved to see that only eight people, including the two lawyers, were listening.

After the lawyers had spoken, Margaret, whose thoughts had been wandering, heard a question addressed to her. Not understanding, she shook her head vaguely. At this the judge irritably snapped at her lawyer that she must be made to understand. Her lawyer managed to convey to her that she was required to say whether she wanted alimony. This had been the subject of a brief passage between herself and her husband before the case opened when he, stern and tense, had warned her that if she put in for alimony or costs he would make the whole affair known regardless of consequences. She had not intended to make such a claim, and now she replied that she had a job and was able to maintain herself.

Neither party contested the other's charges. The court accepted that the marriage had broken up and that no reconciliation was likely. The divorce was granted, the parties to pay their own costs.

Divorce

Appearing reserved and self-composed, they left the court accompanied by their two lawyers. With an appropriate gap between them, they walked through the corridors of the Land-gericht to the entrance. They were only just outside when they halted and turned slowly to face each other. To the lawyers' amazement the couple who, a few minutes earlier, had been declared irrevocably parted, burst into tears and rushed into each other's arms.

To separate at that moment was unthinkable. When they had regained a measure of composure, they asked each other where they were going. The lawyers, witnessing this confirmation of the widespread view that the English are incalculable, took them-selves off, leaving their clients clinging to each other. It was mid-day, so Joyce invited his ex-wife to a meal at the Kaiserhof.

After lunch they rose to part but, finding themselves on the verge of tears, postponed the final moment. By the evening they still had not said good-bye, so they dined together.

In the late evening Joyce dejectedly returned to the flat in Kastanien-Allee and Margaret to her refuge with her married woman-friend in Bülowstrasse.

Chapter 22

THE YELLOW STAR

Two of his early influences, his Jesuit education and his upbringing by a mother of Northern Irish Protestant origin, were
brought to the surface by Joyce's divorce. Though he needed his
wife's company he made it plain, when they met, that he regarded
her as a fallen woman and he himself as magnanimous in talking
to her. For Joyce the divorce had been a necessary gesture to
express his profound shock and disapproval; Margaret had had
to flee because of his intolerable behaviour. After the battering
they had given each other's nerves they might have been expected
to part thankfully. Yet it did not occur to Margaret to refuse
Joyce's imperious demands for meetings; it was not in her nature
to bear resentment and she had a humility which came from
being frank with herself. They could not live with or without
each other, and no final break was possible, if only because each
felt responsible for the other's presence in Berlin.

During one of their encounters—it was on 1st September 1941
—they were out walking. Joyce was being demonstratively kind.
Preoccupied, Nicky having been warned of a possible transfer
from Berlin, Margaret was saying little.

Towards them, at a sedate pace, as if taking the air in some
peaceful spa, came an elderly man. Passers-by stared at him. He
appeared not to notice.

Joyce stopped talking. Something about the man was drawing
everybody's attention, but he continued to approach unhurriedly,
a dignified procession of one.

What was arousing the public interest became apparent. On
his black suit was a splash of colour, a yellow star. For the first
time Joyce was seeing a Jew wearing the badge ordered by the
Nazi Government as a degradation.

The branded Jew and the passionate anti-Semite passed within a yard of each other. The Jew saw nobody. But Joyce was acutely aware of him and deeply disturbed at this sudden confrontation with a fellow human suffering such a humiliation. His jibes, denial to Jews of ordinary humanity, insistence that no exceptions could be made for 'harmless' Jews, were temporarily inappropriate. Again he was upset at having seen the unpleasant materialization of his ideals.

It would be easy to conclude that he was insincere either in his anti-Semitism or his feelings of outrage at witnessing persecution, but it would be a false judgement. He was not a monster who wanted to drive living prisoners to a gas chamber, but a man possessed by ideas and taken aback when theory became reality. Attracted to military life and the concept of empire, he disliked army officers and pukka sahibs when he met them. His Jews, capitalists, aristocrats, diplomats, trade union leaders and workers were actors in his private puppet theatre, expected to conform to the stage conventions he had established and speak the artificial text he had written. When in real life they disregarded his rules he was upset or he exploded in incredulous anger. The Jew he saw that day ought to have been a Fagin-type character instead of appearing, disconcertingly, as a gentle, likeable old man who brought out Joyce's basic kindliness.

More effort was now ordered by the Propaganda Ministry to persuade Americans that their aid to Britain was wasted. Reichsrundfunk accordingly offered the Haw-Haw talks to the Columbia and other networks for rebroadcasting. Whether the offer was a piece of effrontery or made under the impression that the attention devoted to Haw-Haw in the American press had created a public demand to hear him is not clear; probably it was not plain in the minds of the originators of the proposal. The refusal prompted the German radio organization to indulge in an elaborate trick.

On October 4th, in the short-wave service for the United States, the German announcer said that Lord Haw-Haw had been banned from the air, without explaining why or by whom. The following commentary was not by Joyce, nor was his voice heard the next evening. Press speculation arose, Haw-Haw being such an established character by now that the war would hardly have been the same without him. The joke was carried on for four days and then Haw-Haw was heard declaring mischievously that it was the American networks which had banned him by refusing his talks.

The third winter of the war which the German Propaganda Ministry had declared virtually over in the summer of 1940 was approaching. Joyce kept up his output with its confident tone although in his private and public life he saw little reason for hope. His rival, Nicky, had left Berlin, to Joyce's satisfaction, but very soon he was back on leave and Margaret moved to a villa where Nicky and several acquaintances kept a *pied-à-terre*. Missing the meals and walks with his ex-wife, on his off days Joyce brooded, drank, or played chess with Subra Chandra Bose, the leader of the Indians in Berlin, who insisted on being addressed in public as 'Your Excellency'.

German advances in the east and the British shipping losses quoted in 'gross registered tons' (an expression the news-readers tended to dwell on) provided plenty of strong material for a commentator who was not called upon to examine how it was that Britain had remained in the war. One event—the torpedoing of the *Ark Royal* near Gibraltar in November 1941—could have been an occasion for jubilation but the lengthy propaganda campaign to convince the British public that it had been sunk in 1939 now boomeranged. The sinister question: 'Where is the *Ark Royal*?' had been asked so persistently that it had become almost a German station identification signal. Caught out by the British Admiralty's admission of its loss, Reichsrundfunk's commentators were forced to the lame comment that they had never said the aircraft carrier was sunk but had only asked where it was.

'Everything will be all right provided America doesn't enter the war,' Joyce had said, cheering up his colleagues, his public-house audiences and himself. His view had been widely shared, and the Japanese raid on Pearl Harbour caused much apprehension in Germany. Joyce took a grim pleasure in observing this reaction and assumed a studied nonchalance.

There were the initial successes for the Propaganda Ministry to gloat over. On December 10th the Germans led their foreign news bulletins with the sinking by the Japanese of the *Repulse* and the *Prince of Wales*, and a commentator assured English-speaking listeners that 'The United States cannot repair its fleet damaged at Pearl Harbour as its yards are full of damaged British warships.' Just as they had done with Britain, German propagandists were eliminating the United States at the start of the war. The radio talks showed evidence of some hasty rethinking inside the Goebbels organization. Hitherto British listeners had been told that United States help was negligible; now this assistance had to be presented as substantial enough for its withdrawal—because the Americans would need the material themselves—to be disastrous for Britain.

Broadcasting over a widespread network including Luxembourg and Breslau, Joyce opened by discussing the British declarations of war on Finland, Hungary and Rumania, contrasting these actions with past expressions of friendship for these countries and particularly with the British attitude to the Soviet-Finnish war of 1939 and 1940. Then he turned to an assessment of Britain's situation with the United States forced into war in the Pacific.

'And now for the results of Mr. Roosevelt's materialism. We have seen where they have landed him and Mr. Churchill at last. Just take a glance back. Can Britain hold her insecure position in the Far East any longer? Is she not in danger of being locked out? Is not America in danger of being forced to stick to that Monroe doctrine which has always been so ignored by Mr. Roosevelt? What about the Far Eastern lines of communication with the Soviet Union? What about the famous Burma Road, the lifeline of China? Does anyone think this backdoor can stay open long? These are just a few aspects. Another and more important aspect likely to be felt by England and the Soviet will be that the so-called arsenal of the democracies will in future need everything in the way of war materials and supplies for itself. America's fighting forces are, as it is, untrained and insufficient, and any hope of further help for England and her Bolshevik ally therefore goes by the board. The American navy has been doing just about all it can to damage Japan and Germany, yet the battle of the Atlantic has continued with disastrous effects for England. Now the Yankee navy finds itself compelled to fight the battle of the Pacific. Well, England has got her allies now: the losing Bolsheviks and the unprepared Yanks, who can no longer help her as they once did, or pretended to. In declaring war on another three European countries Britain struck a blow at her own chances. The new situation with regard to Japan has at once increased England's war liabilities, endangered her Eastern possessions, placed further burdens on her Navy, and cut off, or at any rate cut down, her vital supplies of food and munitions from America. The British people must now ask themselves the vital question: "Who will help us now?" '

Workers' Challenge foresaw Britain having to make sacrifices for her new allies. 'So we have all got to work a lot longer, first of all to supply ourselves, then perhaps to supply Russia, and then —who knows?—we may be forced to supply the United States as well.'

Germany and Italy declared war on the United States on December 11th. Events had moved so fast that commentators could hardly keep pace with them, and Joyce admitted as much in a Saturday evening survey entitled 'An Historic Week Behind Us'. When he had given his previous weekly review, he said, he had not known that 'in a matter of hours the whole setting of world affairs would be so radically changed'. His summing up, though based on Propaganda Ministry briefings, was typically Joyce at his most provocative. Of the Japanese onslaught he observed: 'The Japanese command has shown a splendid example of comprehensive modern strategy, and the troops have proved again that heroism for which the Japanese nation has been famed throughout the centuries. Roosevelt certainly wanted war with Japan, but it is very hard to believe that he wanted this kind of a war.' There was no doubt about the result. 'Germany, Italy and Japan as comrades in arms with the greatest military strength and the greatest resources in the world at their disposal fight on until victory is gained.' The German advance into Russia would slow down because of the winter but 'the magnificent victories won by Germany and her allies have rendered the defeat of Bolshevism and its complete extermination quite inevitable.' Britain was mentioned almost incidentally. 'Meanwhile, the British island is being attacked both by air and by sea. The German blockade is being enforced with unremitting vigour, and the Luftwaffe is continuing its systematic bombardment of objects of military importance in Britain.'

'Unremitting vigour' and 'systematic bombardment'—these expressions were not the language of the Blitzkrieg but of a long slogging war. The complete extermination of Bolshevism was inevitable but the talk admitted that the Russians would still be on their feet at the end of the winter. Perceptive Germans who stayed tuned in while their stations switched to the English-language broadcasts could have found Joyce's review discouraging. Their home service did its best to cheer them up, however, with an academic analysis of the performance of the American navy in the Spanish-American War.

Lady Haw-Haw also gave her weekly talk that evening. She had too candid a view of herself to be a good propagandist and probably her heart was not in the business then. Nicky's leave over, he had left, uncertain of his destination but suspecting that he was bound for a Baltic military headquarters. He had given her a forwarding address. Since then no letter from him had arrived in Berlin. At the villa his friends, also without news, grinned, shrugged their shoulders, and remarked that one could have a pretty gay time at some of these headquarters. Well, she came to think as her increasingly desperate letters evoked no response, his charm had enabled him to have a good time in Berlin and was no doubt proving equally effective wherever he was now.

She still worked where Joyce could, as he had planned, keep her under observation, and there was no hiding from him that she was unhappy and ill. He was miserable too. The flat was cleaned and his meals served by the landlady; materially he was well off. Audiences for his conversation were never lacking. There was always somebody to have a drink with him and play a game of chess. But he no longer looked forward to his days off. The long walks, the laughter at his fantasies, the shared memories, the pleasant lunches, the wifely admiration tempered by common sense—everything he had really enjoyed in Berlin lay in the past. In the late evenings he hung about the Rundfunkhaus rather than return to an empty flat. Covertly he now observed how she had lost her liveliness. But his pride was still smarting from her desertion, and for a while he nursed his resentment.

One morning she was not in her office. He called in later, to see whether she had arrived, and felt a sudden alarm at the sight of the unoccupied space. Even catching glimpses of her as, with a set expression and a curt nod, he had hurried by, had been an essential part of his daily routine. When at last he learned that she was ill he had to restrain an impulse to rush to her.

A tired and casual doctor called on her belatedly in response to her message. He was coping with five times as many patients as before the war, doing duty during air-raids, and growing accustomed to telling sick people that he could not prescribe for them because the necessary medicaments were unobtainable.

'Gastro-enteritis,' he said. 'Take carbon tablets.' Moving towards the door he paused to remark over his shoulder: 'If you can get them.'

The colleague who answered when Margaret telephoned the office was sympathetic but pessimistic about the availability of carbon tablets.

Finding excuses to visit that office much more frequently than usual, Joyce was given an account of what his former wife had said. Everybody within earshot joined in, relating cases of sick people they knew who had to do without treatment.

Joyce left with the determination that if there were carbon tablets anywhere in Berlin, he was going to find them. The thought had formed in his mind that he could win her back. His campaign would start with this unusual but highly practical evidence of his devotion.

Chapter 23

THE RED ROSE

In 1942 Büro Concordia still went on growing. To support Rommel the largest and most expensive secret station yet was set up, the German Propaganda Ministry having been advised of the tremendous effect of the spoken word in Arab countries. Arabs were scarce in Berlin and, with different ministries bidding for their services, very expensive. Free Arabia, as the new station was called, had to have them and to pay their price, and the result was thought to be convincing. An official Turkish bulletin quoted Free Arabia, accepting it for what it professed to be. The dashing Rommel became the symbol of a vigorous, audacious Third Reich. News poured into the Rundfunkhaus and the commentators made the best of things while Rommel's successes lasted.

Joyce scored two personal triumphs in that year: he won his wife back and he achieved his aim of becoming the chief commentator in the English Language Service.

He persuaded his wife to return by a Blitzkrieg, launched when she was ill and neglected. Having paid one visit, the doctor did not reappear. Her friends were working and nobody willingly undertook evening trips across Berlin in the black-out, with the possibility of being marooned in an air-raid shelter for hours. No letter came from Nicky.

After a restless night, she fell asleep during the day. When she woke she saw a cigar box on her bedside table. It contained carbon tablets, a red rose and a note from William.

Such old-world chivalry, from a man not given overmuch to graciousness, touched her. As Joyce had known she would, she telephoned him. Naturally enough, he said that he hoped soon to see her well again; they must meet and have a chat. She could not refuse.

He was good company, lively, amusing and gentle. They arranged another meeting and soon the old routine was re-established. After their solitude they enjoyed being together.

But Margaret, her memory of the strain of life at Kastanien-Allee still fresh, felt that events were again getting out of control. Imploringly she wrote to Nicky to answer, telling herself that if he did not she would know that he was determined to drop her. She waited, giving him ample time to reply, but in vain.

While she was in despair Joyce proposed that she should return to him. She went back to her room and wrote what she intended to be her farewell letter to Nicky, telling him of her hopelessness and of her decision to go back to her husband.

Joyce gave her no chance to change her mind. They must be married again, he resolved, as soon as it could be arranged.

Their second wedding was almost as discreet as their divorce. The ceremony took place at Berlin-Charlottenburg register office on 11th February 1942 and they returned to their flat.

Three days later a furious Nicky telephoned her, outraged at her lack of faith, injured by her assumption that he had been luxuriating in a staff job, protesting that he had been in the greatest danger and out of reach even of such comforts as the delivery of mail. The High Command's bulletins, taking a broad and reassuring view of the situation, devoted no space to minor and ugly engagements when the German troops did not sweep all before them. Partisans had cut off his group for weeks and would have exterminated them if relief had not arrived. There he had been, thinking of her, while she. . . . Words failed him at the faithlessness of women. His temper had not subsided by the time he returned to the eastern front, and he left without giving her his army post office address.

Joyce was appointed chief commentator in June. The contract, which came into force on July 3rd, gave him a salary of 1,200 Reichsmarks (roughly £60) a month (not extravagant considering all he was doing), a Christmas bonus, and the right to three months' notice. Baillie-Stewart, the original (and in accent the only) Lord Haw-Haw, had retreated to the Foreign Office.

It is surprising that Joyce had to wait so long for recognition. His employers seem to have realized at this time that they had been unappreciative, as they offered him special facilities for a holiday abroad. Given, by the Propaganda Ministry, the provisional choice of Norway, Turkey or Portugal, he selected Norway—a fortunate decision as it turned out to be the only country to which the Gestapo would let him go. He was flown to Oslo on a plane carrying occupation officials, Margaret travelled by train and ferry to meet him there, and they then went northwards to a requisitioned hotel reserved for the Gauleiter of Norway and his guests.

Food was plentiful in the hotel, in contrast to the situation outside. To Joyce's annoyance a young German was allocated to them as an interpreter, and possibly to keep an eye on them, but as the Joyces liked walking and their unwanted companion did not, he was easily persuaded to stay behind while they tramped the countryside.

One valley reminded Joyce of Connemara. They walked there several times, getting on visiting terms with an hospitable young farmer, to whom Joyce revealed his identity.

'You'll be hanged if they get you,' said the young man.

'I know,' replied Joyce. 'It doesn't matter.'

Over beer the host expounded his political views. He liked neither the Germans nor the English, and hoped for economic reunion with Sweden. Joyce pondered on this plan, without apparently being able to incorporate it in his own political scheme.

Breaking the return journey in Oslo, the couple met some Norwegian quislings. These shared Joyce's opinion that National Socialism had got into the wrong hands, and he concluded that they were the most sincere National Socialists he had met since leaving England.

A critic of Joyce's broadcasts appeared in Berlin in October. He was John Amery, the ne'er-do-well son of a distinguished British statesman. When France collapsed he had been living in the south. Associating himself with the Axis cause, he was now in Berlin to persuade Dr. Hesse to give him and other Englishmen a British radio hour in which they could speak uncensored. He urged that Baillie-Stewart's and Joyce's propaganda had been misdirected, being hostile when it should have tried to win the British over to an anti-Bolshevik crusade. All he got, apart from government hospitality, was a promise that his proposals would be examined and forwarded to the Propaganda Ministry. He attributed his rebuff to Joyce's influence. Joyce denied having any prejudice against Amery; all he had done, he said afterwards, was to warn Dietze that Amery was irresponsible and that his playboy past would nullify his propaganda.

To judge by such talks as he gave, Amery was unlikely to have been more persuasive than Joyce or to have successfully challenged Haw-Haw's supremacy, for what that was now worth. German broadcasting still had a British audience, but the Ministry of Information obviously thought its size would not justify a full-scale survey. Inquiries of over 1,000 BBC local honorary correspondents revealed that 85 per cent thought listening was 'very small' or 'fairly small', but only 4 per cent claimed that it was non-existent. The amount of listening may well have been underestimated, but the conclusion that there was no ground for concern was reasonable.

His press publicity in Britain having fallen off, Joyce had little audience reaction to encourage him, but occasionally he received fan letters from German listeners. One, directed to Lord Haw-Haw, Esq., Reichssender Berlin, from a Hamburg listener, he preserved, perhaps because of its curiosity interest. The writer addressed him as 'Your Lordship' and went on: 'Some time ago you cited a few sermons of the Archbishop of Canterbury, the ill-famed Dr. Lang. The sermons amazed me and in my Tagebuch I made the following notation about them: "When I heard of the sermons of the Archbishop of Canterbury, I came to the conclusions that there must be an 'ill-church' in the land of 'Church-ill.' "' The writer concluded by assuring Joyce that 'I am always enjoying your "views on the news." '

Joyce replied: 'Dear Sir,—Thank you very much for your encouraging and amusing letter. I appreciate your puns and thoroughly conform with your views.

'It is good to know that you enjoy my "views on the news".

'Heil Hitler!

'WILLIAM JOYCE
'(Lord Haw-Haw).'

A solemn note was struck for the celebrations on 30th January 1943 of Hitler's accession to power, when dedication to a mighty cause was the theme. The campaign on the eastern front was going badly. In his Haw-Haw talk that evening Joyce, unusually reflective, declared: 'If National Socialism had accomplished nothing more than what already lies behind it, it would rank as one of the mightiest manifestations in the history of the world.' He went on to admit that the German forces were suffering 'hard blows of fate' but, he added, these were nothing compared with what would happen if the barbaric hordes swept over Europe. He warned the Jewish leaders, who were exulting, that National Socialism would carry on the fight fanatically.

That rival crusader against the Bolsheviks, John Amery, now caused him some slight uneasiness by turning up in Berlin again; Joyce guessed that Hesse would have liked to employ this well-connected outcast. This time, however, Amery was recruiting a British anti-Bolshevik legion. A unit was formed and, after being bandied about by different authorities, ultimately became absorbed in the SS, by which time Amery's connexion with it was slight.

In early April the Propaganda Ministry had to do what it could with the Stalingrad defeat. Joyce's talk, despite a good start, again demonstrated his inability to rise to an occasion. 'It would be idle to deny', he began, 'that during the course of this past winter there did arise a crisis of grave magnitude upon the solution of which the survival of European culture and of all those values that we honour depended.' The lesson of experience had been learnt and 'in due course certain powerful and decisive facts will speak for themselves.' This was the kind of vague threat, committing nobody to anything but preceded by 'in due course' to suggest inevitability, which occurred time and again in his talks. Reasonably enough he made the point that on the eastern front there was a comparative lull and the Germans had, for the time being, stabilized their position. If he had stopped there the talk would have shown a certain dignity suited to a serious situation.

But then his demon took over. From a weighty subject Joyce turned to an article in the *News Chronicle*, a paper he incorrectly described as Jewish-owned. The military commentator was now transformed into the Speakers' Corner crank, oblivious to everything but his private nightmare while he intoned his clichés.

Stalingrad was a comparatively straightforward problem compared with the resignation of Mussolini on July 25th, when the Propaganda Ministry was caught completely off balance. The Allied landing in Sicily had been played down as not being the second front the Russians were demanding, the invading forces were said to be immobilized by transport losses and the Italians to be standing firm. Joyce, in his Haw-Haw capacity, had represented the operation as another Churchill misadventure: 'Churchill seems to have entertained some crazy notion that if only he could have delivered a blow on Italian territory Italy would collapse. It is evident already that the whole Italian nation is united as never before and inspired with the ardent determination to defend the fatherland.' While his recorded voice was actually saying, in his 'Views on the News': 'It seems highly improbable that any argument will induce Mussolini to strip Rome of its defences and give an undertaking that its railways should not be used for military purposes', Mussolini was already under arrest.

Embarrassed, the Propaganda Ministry embargoed the news for the time being. The first German reference to the Duce's resignation came in a transmission for Europe at 3.37 a.m. on July 26th. 'It is assumed that this change in the government is due to the condition of the health of the Duce, who has recently been ill.' The original announcement broadcast to the Italian people the previous night was then quoted, stressing that Italy would continue the war. This line was also followed in a broadcast in English from Calais.

Joyce's first comment was made in the character of the patriotic Briton speaking on the New British Broadcasting Station, who found the news 'very agreeable indeed', declared it represented a great triumph for Allied propaganda and diplomacy but warned British listeners not to expect the end of the war as, whatever the condition of Italy, Germany would fight on. The proletarian on Workers' Challenge asked: 'Will the next gang be any better?' and answered his own question: 'They seem to be soldiers, aristocrats and the like.' Two days later the NBBS grew cautious, advising listeners to hear the broadcasts in English from Rome before forming an opinion.

The 'Germany Calling' commentary by Dietze on July 28th was, as usual, fairly restrained; he said that it was 'too soon to pass final judgement'. But even Dietze had seldom been as restrained as all that. For once the Propaganda Ministry had been forced to admit its ignorance.

Speaking the following night, Joyce had to abandon his normal omniscience and pad his talk out with matter that was barely relevant. He followed Dietze by saying that 'there is no object for the present in discussing the internal developments in the Italian situation during the last week.' It is human to appreciate for the first time something which has just been lost, and perhaps he was innocently deceiving himself in claiming to be an old admirer of Mussolini. Anyway, he elaborated on his respect for the Duce, and talked to the requisite length by including a highly subjective reminiscence. 'When I joined the first Fascist movement in Britain on December 6, 1923, I saw that night in Battersea the mob violence, the broken heads and the broken bodies, the typical evidence of the disruption which Communism can bring into a nation, and while I heard the dismal wail of 'The Red Flag' intoned by the sub-men out for blood, I thought of Mussolini and of what he had been able to do for Italy. I was not pro-Italian, I was merely pro-human. There were many millions of people throughout the world at about that time who had the same thoughts, and when I look back on these twenty years I can only say that Mussolini has, in that period, become one of the greatest figures in history.'

Joyce was temperamentally unsuited to be an official. He would have liked to run the English Language Service as a one-man show, and to a surprising extent he managed (with some welcome assistance from British journalists) to establish himself so that he could make it sound like one; but what he never became reconciled to was that his present task was to project other people's policies. The lone agitator, which he by nature was, never has responsibility and accordingly is never in the wrong. Even when Germany was winning the war and he could put over an 'I told you so' attitude he had been unhappy about the Propaganda Ministry's policies; now that the Axis was running into trouble, he found himself in the unwelcome rôle of the official spokesman glossing over his government's reverses. Left to himself, he would have relieved his feelings by a few contemptuous remarks about Wops, who in his estimation were only a stage or so higher than Jews. Once he remarked in conversation: 'I can imagine no greater handicap upon any universal creed than that the Son of God should come upon earth as a Jew and His Church be left to the tender mercies of the Wops.'

Overtired, but never permitting himself to relax, he seemed to forget that his wife had so recently left him and now—the situation no longer requiring the cavalier with the rose treatment—he felt free to indulge his moods. Having no other outlet, he would shout at her as though she personified the Propaganda Ministry, von Ribbentrop, or whatever he was angry about at the time. His good-humoured phases were sometimes even more trying, because then he treated her with kindly condescension.

Again she became reluctant to go home. In case she suddenly needed a retreat, she rented a room. She did not occupy it but it provided an address, and from there she was able to write to Nicky, whose army address she had got from his friends. Now Nicky replied, and soon they were both writing as regularly as the vagaries of the military mails permitted.

In the summer she and her husband spent a week-end in a country cottage near Hamburg, at the invitation of the man who had telephoned Joyce during the Christmas of 1939. The host was anxious to learn what the famous radio commentator thought of the conduct of the war and Joyce, free of all the briefing and script-editing which went on in Berlin, expressed his opinions with some vigour. With this assurance that the visitor was a safe man to talk to, the host, at first cautiously and then with increasing candour, revealed his disquiet, even going so far as to suggest that Ribbentrop, the man who infallibly gave Hitler the wrong advice, should be murdered. Immured in the artificial world of the propagandists as he was, Joyce was taken aback by this proposal, especially as it appeared to be made seriously and he was informed that a good many other Germans were of the same way of thinking. He was not disposed to defend 'Ribbentripe' but neither was he, for all his incitements to violence in the NBBS scripts, the kind of man to be party to an assassination. Vehemently he argued that, disastrous though the Foreign Minister was, his violent removal, and the revelation of dissension within the Government (the Hess affair had been bad enough), might cause irreparable harm at this crucial stage of the war.

Joyce was back in Berlin before the catastrophic raid on Hamburg which, devastating whole districts, gave the Third Reich a terrible warning of what was to come. News of the unprecedented scale of this attack came on the direct line from Hamburg to Berlin, and soon the Berlin staff were interspersing their return messages with anxious inquiries about the safety of relatives. The Reichsrundfunk engineers took the hint and expedited the removal, already begun, of the short-wave station from Berlin to Königswusterhausen.

Somehow Büro Concordia fought off another threat in the form of a secret station to be run by Amery, who was in Berlin again having talks with Dr. Hesse. Later Amery said that Hesse offered him control of a 'secret' English-language radio station but 'the whole affair having to pass through the Propaganda Ministry and Joyce's friends I accepted it only to return it without its having, with me, effected a single transmission.'

The 'other man', whom Joyce had imagined banished for good, suddenly returned to Berlin. Margaret met Nicky again.

Joyce was absorbed in typing a talk when she walked into the flat and stood watching him. Slowly he looked up.

'I'm going,' she said, without any preliminaries.

This time he seemed scarcely surprised.

'Nicky?' he asked quietly.

'Yes.'

Bracing herself for the outburst of incredulous reproaches, she waited.

'Oh,' he said dully.

As she went out he turned again to his typewriter. The sound of tapping followed her as she left for the room she had rented but so far not occupied.

Joyce was now thirty-seven, an age when men begin to wonder whether youth has slipped by unnoticed. His hair was thinning. Physically he was not in good shape. For four years he had overworked, smoked and drunk too much and, when preoccupied, lived on odd snacks. He had refused to exploit his position by asking for better rations; the only privilege he had requested was a special allowance of cigarettes, because without a constant supply he could not work. He had, after a good deal of persuasion, bought himself a smartly-cut navy blue suit, but otherwise—apart from books—he had treated himself to little. Now, not surprisingly, he decided to have a bit of fun. There were plenty of girls looking for a bit of fun too.

Recovered from its recent shocks, the Propaganda Ministry was again taking a positive and optimistic line, and perhaps Joyce, in his determination not to be defeated by solitude, was in closer harmony with his employers than he had been lately. As Germany and Britain entered the fifth year of the war, he declared: 'German victory is certain. The final blow will be struck by Adolf Hitler.' A few days later Italy surrendered. On this occasion the news was expected, and the rapid succession of events which followed enabled the German radio commentators to sound victorious. German troops occupied Rome, Mussolini was liberated in a paratroop action of theatrical audacity, and on September 15th—with the Duce once again in control—the Axis was re-established. Everybody was heartened by this firm handling and the scripts practically wrote themselves.

In October Joyce had another trip, this time to Luxembourg, where he stayed at the Hotel Alfa with his current girl-friend. While there he recorded his 'Views on the News' as usual.

He had only just returned to Berlin when Margaret walked unexpectedly into his flat. Caught with 'the other woman', Joyce was hideously embarrassed, the would-be sophisticated radio commentator reverting to the prudish, guilt-ridden boy from Galway. The two women, by being calm and casual, helped him to regain an appearance of self-composure, but he was a long time getting over the shock of being involved in a scene where he had looked silly and been tongue-tied.

Air-raid warnings, noisy nights, the walk home to the sound of grit and dust crunching under the feet, were now the routine. When the sirens sounded on 22nd November 1943 the English-speaking staff, having a meal break, strolled back to the Rundfunkhaus. They were hardly there when a tremendous explosion rocked the building. Preparing for a transmission, Joyce rushed into the control room to check that the broadcast would go out, arriving in the middle of a row between an engineer and a superior who had ordered him to the shelter. Joyce joined in with his customary gusto and the three were shouting at each other when another bomb fell on the path along which the staff had come only a few minutes before. The men were swept apart by the blast as the suddenly windowless building filled with choking dust. The broadcast went out on time, but the bombs had been the closest yet.

John Amery was awarded a distinction for exceptional bravery in the raid of the following night. His presence was no longer disturbing to Joyce as the Propaganda Ministry had found a use for him. He was to return to France, there to tour the West Wall, and then go on to Belgium, Norway and Czechoslovakia, holding press conferences and giving radio interviews. His tone was shrill.

The handsome Nicky could not settle for long. Chafing at the restriction on his liberty to roam the town, he proved to be as bad-tempered as Joyce. Rows became frequent and so intense that the loudest air-raid could not interrupt them. One night he walked out and did not come back.

As 1944 opened, everybody knew that it would be the invasion year. The policy was to scoff at the possibility of a successful Allied landing in Europe. 'What British politician wants to hear of Poland today?' Haw-Haw demanded derisively, reminding British soldiers that they had been asked to die for an independent Poland. Now hundreds of thousands of British and American soldiers were 'to die for the Jewish policy of Stalin and Roosevelt'.

Whatever the end was going to be, it was fast approaching and Joyce wanted to tidy things up. It was no time for carefree fun with girl-friends when he was wondering whether the bomb he heard falling would demolish the house where his wife lived. If the warning sounded while she was at work he looked in at the shelter to assure himself that she was there, and after learning that Nicky had gone, he called at her lodging.

Following a heavy raid he went to the Rundfunkhaus shelter and said to her abruptly: 'You'll move back home. I'm sick of having to come to your place first to see if anything has happened. We can talk about Nicky after the war when there's time.'

When drunk on his thirty-eighth birthday he wrote in a notebook (he was much addicted to the composition of trite aphorisms): 'The beginning of true knowledge is certainly self-knowledge, but, in most cases, providentially, it is the end,' and signed himself 'Confucius W. Joyce aus Brooklyn'.

Chapter 24

'THE HANGING JUDGE'

For the benefit of its enemy listeners, Reichsrundfunk gave extensive coverage to the invasion. What purported to be running commentaries on the landings were given by speakers who described, against a background of battle noises, the invaders' heavy losses and made such comments as: 'I wouldn't care to be out there myself!'

Joyce produced three scripts on the first day. In his Haw-Haw rôle he put over the Propaganda Ministry's ingenious explanation —reserved for this occasion—of the German reverses in Russia and Italy. 'It is no longer necessary for me to observe that restraint which was until today requisite in discussing German withdrawals in Russia and Italy, for now their underlying cause is manifest.' The place and the time of the invasion, he said, 'could not be better from the German point of view' and he begged his listeners not to forget that 'this holocaust was organized at Stalin's request'.

As the British patriot on the New British Broadcasting Station the voice reading Joyce's script asked: 'Where is the Russian offensive? News of a fresh push by the Red Army is awaited with impatience in London.'

The proletarian, pursuing the vendetta against Churchill on Workers' Challenge, expressed in Joyce's words relief that 'our promise has at last been kept' but suggested to his fellow workers that 'as soon as Churchill shows the least sign of trying to double-cross our Russian allies then we've got to step in.'

Now the long-promised secret weapon to annihilate the enemy was produced; the first flying bomb landed in England during the night of 13th-14th June 1944. Neither on the British nor the

German population was the effect as great as had been anticipated. Both were assured, by the different German radio services, that the new missiles were being brought into use at the most strategically favourable moment, and that even more devastating weapons were on the way.

The 20th of July 1944 was one of those free days by which Joyce set such store, when he went for a walk with his wife and dined at the Press Club. While there they became aware of unusual animation among the members. The diners at neighbouring tables seemed as puzzled as they themselves, so they moved towards the entrance where, out of the rising volume of voices, they gathered that an attempt had been made on Hitler's life. The startled Joyce bounded to the door, determined to rush to the Rundfunkhaus and discover whether the story was fact or rumour.

He needed only to take the few steps to the entrance to have proof that something strange was going on. Soldiers with fixed bayonets ordered everybody back into the building. Beyond he could see soldiers standing about, looking awkward and obviously as mystified as the civilians.

Fuming, Joyce waited, overhearing conversations, putting questions to the usually well-informed, finding that nobody could add to the bare report. The moment the soldiers were withdrawn, press and radio men poured out of the club.

On the way back to the office Joyce dashed into his flat and collected his revolver. The Rundfunkhaus, however, was well guarded by troops (the usual SS guards were nowhere to be seen) manning machine-guns at the windows, no reinforcement by armed civilians was required, and Joyce had nothing to do but try to find out what had really happened.

The speakers on duty that day were cautious, confining themselves to Hitler's statement, translations of which were soon being circulated through the building. Because of the frenzied conversations and the general uproar, the Joyces did not leave until seven o'clock the next morning. They were so eager for news that sleep was impossible and they returned to the Press Club, where they joined several people for lunch.

Joyce was on edge and, as usual, contemptuous of the excitability of the Germans. In emergencies he tended to be aloof like the traditional Englishman among temperamental foreigners. He

scarcely joined in the hysterical talk. When his wife made what
he thought an indiscreet comment he kicked her under the table
and muttered in English: 'Shut up! You can't talk like that now!
They've gone nervy!'

The conspirators who had tried to kill Hitler were convenient
scapegoats when Haw-Haw had to do what he could with the
news that Paris had been liberated. They had, he said, kept part
of the army away from the fronts, but these troops were immediately being released for battle. Putting the situation in perspec-
tive, he observed that the Germans were now fighting on the
First World War battlefields, and their defeat could be taken for
granted only if Germany had exhausted her reserves. He admitted that he could understand the satisfaction of the Allied
propagandists but he reaffirmed his conviction that ultimate
victory would go to the Third Reich.

On the fifth anniversary of the outbreak of war decorations
were scattered around and one landed on Joyce. He was awarded
the Kriegsverdienstkreuz (War Merit Cross) 1st class, a civilian
award of the type allocated to government departments on a
ration basis, like those for which British civil servants queue up
for years and just as meaningless. Although it bore Hitler's signa-
ture it was not handed to him by the Führer whom, in fact, he
never met, but by a radio official. Joyce was not flattered.

Londoners heard a tremendous explosion on September 8th.
If Haw-Haw had been as well-informed as the British supposed
him to be, he could have told them where the new secret weapon,
V2, had landed, and got back at least part of the audience he had
lost. To avoid assisting the rocket launchers, the British Government maintained silence, and a statement was not made by the
Prime Minister until November 10th. The German home audience, who had been long promised a dramatic surprise, were
treated to imaginative accounts of the tremendous havoc caused
by the rockets. Those still willing to believe in Hitler's infalli-
bility wondered when the steady British bombing would slacken
and the invading forces brought to a halt by the collapse of the
home front behind them.

On September 15th Joyce's mother died at St. Mary's Hospital, Paddington, London. One of her last messages was: 'Tell
William I shall always be with him.' The news of her death, and
her last acknowledgement of his devotion to her, did not reach

him until eight months later, when it comforted him in the contemplation of his own approaching end.

His death was often in his thoughts, and sometimes he spoke of the different ways he could die. A British agent might murder him; he might fall fighting the Russians in the Berlin streets; he could easily be killed in an air-raid—the windows of the Rundfunkhaus had been blown in many times, walls had collapsed, and his office had been moved to an unused studio in a safer part of the building. Another way he might die he never mentioned now, except obliquely. In his studio office he kept a stock of drink and he playfully pretended that his room was a pub called 'At the Sign of the Hanging Judge'.

While von Rundstedt, in a manner reminiscent of the German Army's last great effort in 1918, was crashing forward in the Ardennes offensive, Joyce was being called up to the German equivalent of the British Home Guard, the Volkssturm. He had written many thousands of words making fun of Britain's part-time anti-invasion force but now he went, his spirits revived at the thought of doing military service, to register in the Bataillon-Wilhelmplatz, the special unit of Propaganda Ministry staff.

'Any previous military service?' the registration clerk asked.

'Yes. British Army,' Joyce answered. Boyishly he always hoped that the revelation that he had been an enemy alien would throw officials into consternation, but none ever reacted with as much as a raised eyebrow.

The clerk filled up a card with Joyce's correct name, place and date of birth, dated it Berlin, 21st December 1944, and handed it to a slightly disappointed Volkssturmmann Joyce.

A long time had passed since he had drilled on the square in Worcestershire and taken Certificate 'A' in the Officers Training Corps. The German rifle he found a heavy, clumsy weapon and his old inability to handle anything mechanical now made him so awkward that he came near to killing a fellow Volkssturmmann with an anti-tank weapon. He was the most awkward man in a very awkward squad of civilians.

In this desperate period of the war it would have seemed appropriate for the Propaganda Ministry to review its commitments. The pre-invasion secret stations were still working. What were they now supposed to achieve, and was it conceivable that a single listener believed that they were on British soil? Büro Concordia kept going, employing a hundred transmitters at its peak, as though the populations of enemy countries could still be stampeded. Other German-run English-speaking stations were at work, chattily telling British and American soldiers that their girl-friends' virtue was not proof against a long absence, cutting in on Allied forces' wavelengths—these had at least some relevance to the existing situation. But to enemy listeners abroad the Propaganda Ministry had nothing new to say. Even as viewed from Germany it was now unrealistic to suppose that a wedge of any size could be driven between Britain and the United States, yet the machine went on turning out material as though little had changed since 1940. Two talks put out in English on 23rd December 1944 are good examples of the policy of telling the British that they were being sold to the Americans and the Americans that they were doing the fighting for the British.

Speaking to Britain, Joyce said: 'What the dollar imperialists succeeded in acquiring during this war they will certainly not yield up to their British cousins after the cease-fire has sounded. The bases and other territorial acquisitions, the markets, the capital values and the commercial opportunities which the U.S.A. have gained, will be set off against the services, real or imaginary, rendered by Roosevelt to Churchill.' There followed a passage in which Joyce repeated yet again that Churchill was half American and on excellent terms with the American Jewish millionaire, Baruch, after which he reverted to those old destroyers. 'There was no occasion then for surprise when Mr. Churchill surrendered a colonial empire to Roosevelt in exchange for fifty-eight tubs, misnamed destroyers, or when he presented his American associates with investments and markets vital to Britain's future existence.'

About the same time Donald Day, the former *Chicago Tribune* correspondent, was telling North American listeners: 'Some day the British will have to fight. Until now they have got other nations to fight for them. A special species calls himself a Royal Crown Briton and thinks he is too good to fight. The Canadians and men of other dominions are tired of it. Everyone is fighting for Britain, and that is why today the U.S.A. is losing fifty Americans for every British casualty in France. You have only to look at the map of the Western front to see that the British sector is very small—and that it is manned by Canadians. Roosevelt's lend-lease plan is crazy, and Britain takes full advantage of it. Food and materials are sent to Britain free and she sells them to her people for cash.'

Donald Day might have expanded a little on that newly-discovered species, the Royal Crown Briton; he apparently thought the term so well known as to need no more than that brief explanation.

Joyce, in common with many of the staff, was now visibly suffering from strain. He never actually missed a studio booking, but he caused much anxiety by not appearing until the last moment to record his commentaries. Shivering in the Berlin winter, he faced the microphone wearing his hat, overcoat and muffler and, if there was a raid on when he finished, he hung about the underground studio, apologizing for getting in everybody's way. He still had enough spirit to joke occasionally with the girls on duty, but generally he seemed ill, nervous and perpetually exasperated.

When drunk he was subject to fits of hilarity, which were not always well-timed. One night, in a section of an air-raid shelter reserved for Press Club members, he set out to teach English songs to a French journalist. The resultant singing caused the appearance of a tall, dark, severe-looking air-raid warden, who peremptorily ordered the two men to stop.

Pugnaciously Joyce asked why he and his companion should not sing in their own air-raid shelter.

'Because', said the warden, 'you are annoying your fellow-citizens.'

Joyce snarled: 'Why? Are you all *that* frightened?'

'Leave the cellar at once!' shouted the warden. Joyce's reply was emphatic and very impolite, in his best Workers' Challenge manner.

The warden stepped forward and grabbed Joyce and an undignified scuffle ensued, in which Joyce received a cut lip and the warden a black eye. Before retreating the man warned Joyce that he would report the incident.

Hilarious and overwrought, Joyce found this threat funny and his laugh of ridicule sounded through the shelter.

His mirth at German absurdity was revived a few days later by his receiving an official document informing him that he was to be charged with an offence known as sub-treason. Having passed the paper about among his immediate associates, he took it to Dietze, expecting his superior to think it amusing too and to assure him that the officials bringing the charge would be put in their place. Joyce's grin died away, however, when he saw Dietze's expression.

'It's nothing to laugh at!' Dietze said sharply. 'Do you know that that warden was Freisler's personal chauffeur?' Freisler was the president of the dreaded People's Court.

Still Joyce, with his consciousness of being an important man, could not grasp that the prestige of the Reichsrundfunk and the Propaganda Ministry would not be able to save him from court proceedings.

'You must realize that you're in a serious position. It might take as much as the Propaganda Ministry can do to get you out of it,' Dietze added, annoyed at Joyce's nonchalance.

As a foreign radio speaker Joyce had lived a comparatively sheltered life and was ignorant of what to an ordinary German citizen were the daily facts of life. He was incredulous when handed a summons ordering him to appear for preliminary examination before a judge on a charge of sub-treason. Could this really happen to Lord Haw-Haw, the voice of the Third Reich?

It could, and he found himself in court having to give an account of his career as though he had never been heard of. He was even made to prove that he was a naturalized German citizen, and the court retained his naturalization certificate for inspection.

After the hearing he was unnaturally reticent, merely telling Dietze that he thought he had got on not too badly.

'Don't think a charge of sub-treason is disposed of as easily as all that,' his superior warned him.

Whether the Propaganda Ministry's wire-pulling could have affected the court was never put to the test, thanks to the United States Air Force. Flying Fortresses, in a daylight raid, caused enormous damage in the centre of Berlin. The law courts were hit and their records buried in the rubble. The charge sheet, the record of Joyce's interrogation, and his naturalization certificate were lost, and with them disappeared the chief prosecution witness, the stern-looking warden, who had been trapped in the cellar.

The Yalta conference opened in February. Previous meetings of enemy leaders to determine post-war policy had seemed like wish-fulfilment play-acting to those who believed that Hitler could not lose. This time many were prompted to make their own plans to survive the Nazi collapse.

'Have you and your husband got false papers?' a friendly official asked Margaret.

'No,' she answered. 'Do you think we ought to have them? Could we get them?'

'Certainly you ought to have them!' was the emphatic answer. 'And very soon!'

So everyone about them, all those men and women still loyally working, were planning to change their identities! That night she told her husband of the conversation.

Joyce could not look at the facts rationally. He flew into a temper, as he almost invariably did when the world and his fantasies clashed.

'Soldiers can't run away,' he shouted, 'so why should I?'

She remained silent. Although familiar, his violence still pained her. Now, she knew, he would be abusive, would talk himself into a state of utter irrationality.

'If you want to clear out, go!'

Still she said nothing. She knew—and he realized it, too—that now she would remain with him to the end, whatever it might be.

Now in his Götterdämmerung mood, Joyce raved about staying to the last in Berlin and fighting on the barricades until he had only two bullets left, one for his wife and the last for himself. He was still that romantic Galway boy, fixed in a nineteenth-century dream of martial glory.

But his higher sense, which on a moonlit night before a single bomb fell had shown him the black ruins of Berlin, had told him the truth all along. Stepping over twisted steel girders and fragments of walls, shuffling through the powdered brick, he looked about him and said: 'I can't bear to see the city dying. She is dying and will never be saved.'

Chapter 25

GOEBBELS TRIES TO SAVE JOYCE

With a shamefaced air, as though their listeners were watching, the Reichsrundfunk staff prepared to leave. No official admission had been made that Berlin was doomed. No orders implied that broadcasting might soon cease.

Toni Winkelnkemper, the foreign services director, instructed Hetzler to seek accommodation for Büro Concordia in Dresden. Gauleiter Mutschmann, ambitious for his city to become the headquarters of German radio, conducted his visitor over an available building, and was disappointed when Hetzler pointed out that parts of it were collapsing. Dresden was struck off the list of possible refuges.

Other departments had already been ordered to disperse. Dismantled teleprinters, typewriters and packing cases littered the entrance hall; their arms full of scripts, files and gramophone records, secretaries made their way to waiting cars and trucks. In abandoned offices plaster fell unheeded. Men Joyce had been accustomed to greet about the building and in the shelter were suddenly missing. Confidently opening a familiar door, he would see only a dust-covered chair and feel the draught from an unmended window. In the streets he would pause to watch soldiers digging a tank trap or dragging together the material for a barricade.

London evening papers did not arrive in Berlin, so he missed a paragraph in *The Star* of 8th March 1945 mentioning rumours that he might try to evade the law by claiming to be an Irish national and that he had recently been negotiating for the purchase of a house in Eire. Presumably these rumours arose from public anxiety that he should not escape, but Joyce had no money to buy a house in Ireland, even if he could have got there.

At the flat in Kastanien-Allee the subject of doing anything but stay in Berlin was taboo.

Early in March the Propaganda Ministry ordered the English Language Service to move to Apen, a small town between Bremen and the Dutch frontier, where it was to continue broadcasting. Volkssturmmann Joyce was stunned at the wrecking of another fantasy. He was not to fight and die in the heroic last stand in Berlin but was required to pack his clothes and papers and retreat westwards. Sullenly he joined the rest of the staff in getting together the equipment, including a dismantled teleprinter, which they had been told to take with them. He left behind some miscellaneous writings, accumulated over the years. These papers were still in his office when the Russians arrived.

With a lot of luggage, first-class tickets, and every kind of pass to intimidate obstructive authorities *en route*, a large party boarded one of the now infrequent and slow trains to the west, and after hours of crawling and stopping changed at Oldenburg. While Margaret left to find hot drinks for them, the others settled down stoically to guard the heap of cases and apparatus. To their surprise a train arrived almost immediately. Expecting it to wait a long time, they were loading their burdens into it in a leisurely manner when it started and they had to scramble in. Leaning from a window, Joyce made urgent, shouted inquiries of a railwayman below.

At the far end of the station Margaret, carrying drinks, helplessly watched them pass. 'You'll be all right! There's another!' Joyce yelled.

Quite a lot of cases, and several pieces of teleprinter, had now become her responsibility. Night fell before the next train arrived. In deep darkness, with unknown hands helping her, she got the luggage in and found a seat. Her fellow travellers were dim white faces, some sleeping, others talking in a dialect she could not follow.

Not daring to doze she sat stiffly. No gleam shone in the stations where they stopped. Passengers struggled out at places she had never heard of. She was on her feet as soon as a voice with an unfamiliar accent shouted: 'Apen!'

Sleeping forms around her came to life to hand down her burdens. A waiting group broke into shouts of welcome.

Work started the next day, the engineers already having installed a transmitter in the Bahnhofshotel, assembled teleprinters and made direct contact with Berlin.

The Joyces were billeted on a policeman's wife. Her husband was away in the army and, although not bitter or unpatriotic, she was tired of Hitler. Above the guests' bed hung youthful pictures of the Grand Duke and Duchess of Oldenburg. The lodgers could sleep undisturbed through the nights. When Joyce remarked to his landlady on the tranquillity she replied with a warning: 'If you go for a walk, keep away from the middle of the roads.'

Spring was beginning to show in the woods, the sky was clear, and Joyce, who had not enjoyed rural walks since visiting Miss Scrimgeour in Sussex, was tempted to dismiss what the landlady had said as the nervous talk of a woman who had not experienced air-raids. The exercise put him in a good humour, he was absorbed in his own conversation, when a deafening roar just behind their necks, as it seemed, drowned his words. Reacting before he knew what he was doing, he pushed his wife into a ditch and jumped after her. As their heads rose they saw for an instant the receding tail of a British fighter aircraft.

Across the quiet fields came a sound, just a distant vibration, so faint that it seemed to stop when they listened for it. One night, when the window was opened, it increased to a drumming noise and the old-fashioned ornaments rattled. They thought it came from the south-west. By the morning it had stopped.

On March 28th Margaret started back for Berlin on a trip organized for her by the administrative officer, who needed to send papers to Dietze and simultaneously give her the chance of fetching more of her possessions and replenishing her husband's cigarette stocks. She travelled as far as Bremen with an engineer sent to fetch accessories for the transmitter. They hung about all day in Oldenburg because no trains moved during the day. In the darkness of the Bremen train a Gestapo man with a torch perfunctorily looked at their papers and went off with a weary 'Heil Hitler'.

They alighted in the darkness when they heard shouts of 'Bremen', but lost each other in the crowd. Finding herself among several women, Margaret learned that the Hamburg train now left from the other end of the town. As they walked in a group, ignoring the air-raid sirens, they encountered a policeman waving a red lamp, and they feared he would order them to a shelter. Margaret fumbled in her bag for her duty pass, but he merely asked them politely to cross the road to avoid an un-exploded bomb. Another hour's walk took them to the station, where the train waited until the raid was over.

Berlin had been steadily battered since she left, the sky showed in unexpected places where a fortnight before buildings had stood, and untouched débris blocked the streets.

Büro Concordia finished its packing on Good Friday. Some of the staff had been allowed to leave earlier for various reasons; one of them, Winter, had acquired a yacht and he was determined not to let it out of his sight.

Hetzler had handed everybody three months' pay, arranged for a credit of 250,000 Reichsmarks (nominally about £12,500) in Helmstedt, and was glancing round his office for the last time, when all the Arabs appeared, clamouring that they had been given no money. The cashier's office being closed, they gathered around the only authoritative person they could see, holding out their hands and refusing to move as though he were a wealthy tourist during a slack season. He could escape only by sharing his three months' salary among them.

As their transport turned out of Masurenallee into Messedamm the staff glanced back for a final look at the Rundfunkhaus, where some of their fellows were still working in the dust-laden air. The cars put on speed and roared westward down the Avus and on to the Autobahn. Nobody knew that there was little between them and the American Army but pathetically young Hitler Youth parties wretchedly equipped with improvised anti-tank weapons. The countryside looked incredibly peaceful. No air-craft appeared and they heard no gunfire.

At Helmstedt they entered the hotel booked for them, to be greeted by the staff of the Indian secret station, returned from Holland and already highly unpopular in the town for causing a milk shortage by outbidding the usual purchasers for available supplies.

Without delay the engineers assembled their equipment, the editorial staff got to work, and that evening the Oebisfelde trans-mitter put out the NBBS programme. Apart from some recordings and scripts in stock, the station now had to get along without its chief scriptwriter.

On March 31st Margaret, having collected her more portable possessions, dined for the last time at the Press Club, and left to take the Hamburg train, due to depart when conditions permitted from a small station in north Berlin—the usual terminus, Anhalterbahnhof, being out of action. While she was waiting on a bench an army major opened a conversation; he was obviously puzzled by her foreign accent but he was too polite to question her. This talk was interrupted by Dietze who had arrived to say good-bye and give her messages for the staff at Apen. Dietze spoke in English, sometimes dropping his voice, but by the time he had left the officer had guessed who she was and he took her under his care. On the journey he shared a bottle of home-made liqueur with her and, at Bremen, overruled a protesting military police sergeant and got her a place on a crowded army truck, which landed her at Huchting on Easter Sunday. There she sat all day in the station, her sustenance some sandwiches given her by a soldier in exchange for tobacco. In darkness the last passenger train to run on that line during the war crawled to Apen.

The little town was undamaged and peaceful. The radio staff, conscious of living on the edge of an abyss, were in nervously high spirits, and at the sight of the tobacco and drinks she had brought they stopped work and held an impromptu party.

A week went by during which Joyce, from this rural retreat, produced his commentaries. Occasionally a tremor passed over the countryside, the doors rattled faintly, the noise of an aircraft engine swelled and died away. On the railway nothing moved. Sometimes German tanks and trucks briefly disturbed the quiet. But for the clicking teleprinters the radio staff might have felt themselves isolated and forgotten.

But suddenly Goebbels, who had done nothing to expedite the naturalization of Joyce and his wife, remembered them. On April 7th the teleprinters spelt out a priority message from the Propaganda Ministry in Berlin.

'The Joyces are at all costs to be kept out of Allied hands.'

Chapter 26

HAW-HAW'S FAREWELL

The administrative officer at Apen, whose task it now was to transfer the Joyces to Hamburg as the first stage in saving them from capture, appealed to his district superiors, the authorities of the Weser-Ems-Gau, for a car and driver. After a good deal of trouble a car was supplied, but on the strict condition that it did not travel beyond the Gau boundary. Standing instructions were that transport was to remain within the administrative area, and even with enemy tanks approaching no German bureaucrat was willing to break a rule. Accordingly the driver had been ordered to leave his passengers in Bremen. It was the sort of situation which had so often caused Joyce to sneer at the German conduct of the war.

Accompanied by a young radio speaker who was being transferred to Hamburg because his home was there, they drove across the flat, rural countryside, passed through Oldenburg and took the road to Delmenhorst. Nobody spoke until the driver slowed down, jerked his head over his shoulder, and growled: 'Look behind you!'

Low on the horizon were long, thin trails of smoke, interspersed with denser clouds which rose, expanded and slowly dispersed.

'HKL,' remarked the driver, using the now familiar abbreviation for Hauptkampflinie, the main front line.

Joyce squeezed his wife's hand but said nothing. The driver drove fast along the empty road, but on rounding a corner just before Delmenhorst he braked sharply and swerved to avoid several stationary tanks which were thickly covered with budding branches. From the turrets grinning young men looked down at them, amused to see civilians on what would soon be a battlefield.

'Modern warfare,' Joyce observed. 'You spend most of your time waiting.'

The driver left them at Bremen station, where they sat in the sun on a low wall framing the entrance to an air-raid shelter until a train arrived. Running according to no schedule, it stopped frequently because whenever the train crew heard aircraft they shouted, at which everybody jumped out, dispersed and lay flat. This procedure was becoming tedious and the response growing perfunctory, when a succession of fighter aircraft flew low over the train. The passengers pressed themselves into the grass, not daring to look up until seconds after the last screaming engine had died away.

'If they had wanted us that would have been the end,' said a bored young soldier to Joyce as they climbed back into the train.

The short journey from Bremen to Hamburg took nine hours. A room had been booked for them at the Atlantic Hotel for the maximum permitted period of three days. Despite the terrible devastation of large areas of Hamburg, the view from the hotel across the Outer Alster looked surprisingly normal, there was running water in their room, and the beds were comfortable. No air-raid occurred that night. The next morning Joyce went to the radio headquarters. The administrative officer there booked accommodation for an indefinite period at the Vier Jahreszeiten, to which the Joyces were to transfer after they left the Atlantic Hotel, and Joyce received instructions how to continue his 'Germany Calling' broadcasts until Berlin ordered the next move.

In Berlin an audacious plan to save Joyce was being discussed. He and his wife were to be shipped by U-boat to the west coast of Southern Ireland. The neutral Irish, it was thought, could be relied on not to hand him over to the British. Sounded on this idea, Joyce said at once that he was willing to try, but he considered the scheme impracticable. The commentator who had so often dwelt on the invincibility of the German submarine fleet now felt compelled to tell his would-be saviours that he believed a U-boat's chances of dodging the British Navy and the Royal Air Force and reaching Ireland were very slight.

Air-raids were soon resumed. Like the other guests, the Joyces kept emergency luggage always with them so that they could rush to the shelter without delay. Their closest escape came on April 13th, the day Vienna fell, when Joyce had just opened a half-bottle of wine he had coaxed out of the head waiter. Explosions suddenly shook the Vier Jahreszeiten, although there had been no warning.

'This doesn't sound right!' Joyce shouted. 'Drink the wine up before it gets blown off the table!' As they put down their glasses the windows of their room fell in. With their emergency luggage they were dashing through the door when part of the wall collapsed. The stair windows had gone. Joyce pushed his wife into a corner and stood protecting her just as a bright yellow flash split the darkness. They stumbled into the cocktail bar, which was serving as a shelter, and found themselves surrounded by officers, including a bare-footed general in cap, gold-braided greatcoat, and pyjamas.

What decided the abandonment of the project to get him away by submarine Joyce never knew. The next order, sent to the Hamburg Gestapo, was that he was to be given a false identity document. This time Joyce indulged in no heroics, and he resignedly accepted the passport of a Wilhelm Hansen, a teacher born in Galway on 11th March 1906, resident in Hamburg, with the distinguishing mark of a scar on the right cheek. The photograph showed him as fuller in the face than he had been on acquiring his British passport twelve years before. The document was backdated to 3rd November 1944, to avoid its appearing suspiciously new. As a fugitive's equipment it was far from being a brilliant production, and Joyce had little faith that it would help him. Although he kept it in his pocket he took care to have with him his Wehrpass, made out in his real name, against the risk of being picked up and summarily dealt with as a deserter by the German military police. His wife, schooling herself to remember her new name, recited it so often that she found herself addressing other women as Frau Hansen.

On Joyce's birthday, April 24th, his 'Views on the News' went out as usual from Hamburg and Bremen. In the talk he cast Hitler and Goebbels as barricade heroes in Berlin, a rôle that he had claimed for himself. 'The Führer has given the ultimate proof of his good faith, of his devotion to the cause of the West, by taking the great and momentous decision that henceforth what forces Germany possesses shall be concentrated on the imperative task of defending not only Germany but also Europe against the onslaughts of the Red Army and the infamous power of destruction it represents. The Führer has taken his post in Berlin, side by side with the Commissioner for the Defence of the Capital, Dr. Goebbels, and he is directing the fanatical resistance of the tough and valiant Berliners in the fight for every street corner, every heap of ruins, every cobblestone in that city, greater than ever in the invincible majesty of its ruins.' His position, he reminded his audience, had not changed. 'Even at the height of this crisis, the greatest of our modern era, I am as convinced now as on the day when I arrived in Germany in August 1939 that there can be no security for Britain, nor safety, I would even say no hope, without an independent German Reich strong enough to prevent the Soviet monster from swallowing the West.' He concluded: 'Without Germany there cannot long be an England.'

That day came the news of Mussolini's death. Joyce, who had publicly praised but privately despised the Duce, was shocked. Mussolini, after all, had been the inspiration of the British Fascisti, in whose service he had first fought 'the Reds' and gained his still vivid scar; it was on the model of Mussolini's theoretical corporate state that he had drafted his plan for a National Socialist Britain. His birthday was made tolerable only by alcohol.

Drink could be had by those with good contacts. With everybody wondering how long it would be before British troops poured into Hamburg, storekeepers who had dutifully conserved their stocks and limited their allocations strictly according to the rules could now be persuaded that what was not consumed within the next week or so would be enjoyed by the enemy. A brief, end-of-the-world plenty obtained. Rumours of disaster circulated, such as that Goebbels and Hitler were dead. Nobody in Hamburg knew the truth. The teleprinters and telephone went on working, transmitting material from Berlin to be broadcast by Hamburg, and issuing orders.

On April 30th the propaganda staff was summoned to meet. Every possibility of what they might hear had been canvassed, and nothing could now surprise them. Many were more occupied with personal problems of how to get home, or where to go, or how to find their families, than they were with the collapse of the Third Reich. A Propaganda Ministry official gave them the news that their chief, Dr. Goebbels, and the Führer were dead. They were not told of Hitler's wedding to Eva Braun in the

Chancellery air-raid shelter; the official story, not yet released to the German public, was to be that the Führer had died in action. They were not interested in the appointment of Admiral Dönitz as Hitler's successor. This was the end and the meeting broke up.

Joyce was one of the first to go. 'My work is over,' he said. 'I shall now write my last talk.'

Others, including Margaret, were detailed to work on a programme to follow the announcement of Hitler's death over what remained of the German radio network. Before they had finished Joyce returned to give Grupe, the producer, a copy of his script. Had Grupe foreseen what was going to happen, he would have had the recording done straight away.

Everybody was now invited to what was called a snack. It was the final share-out, the radio staff's version of the scorched earth policy. The last tin, the last jar, the last bottle was produced. Such a display of food and drink had not been seen for years. People ate, drank toasts, talked and shouted with laughter, as though they were celebrating a victory.

Joyce, normally a heavy drinker, had throughout his radio career been helped by schnaps to turn out his unceasing flow of scripts. Often he had gone to the microphone having drunk rather more than a broadcaster safely can, but he had always got a grip on himself. He had never, while recording, been so far gone as he was now. Reeling away from the party he went to the studio. The technical staff were probably as drunk as he was, as they recorded the whole talk instead of stopping him. He read slowly, with long pauses, sometimes raising his voice almost to a shout, then dropping it until he was nearly inaudible. His usual mannerisms were exaggerated; Danzig was more than ever Dantsisch, and his American or northern English pronunciation of the long 'a' sounds was very marked. His title, Lord Haw-Haw, seemed even more grotesquely inappropriate. Sometimes, as if facing an audience, he banged the table in emphasis.

He spoke as the man whose warnings had gone unheeded, who had always hoped for an understanding between Britain and Germany, and who now could do no more. 'If it cannot be, then I can only say that the whole of my work has been in vain.' Of the British people he said: 'If they will not hear, if they are determined not to hear, then I can only say that the fate that will overcome them will be the fate they have merited. More I cannot say.' He made some effective points in his old manner when comparing the issues at the start of the war and the situation in 1945.

'How modest, how harmless does Germany's request for the return of Danzig seem in contrast to the immense acquisitions of the Soviet Union and the further ambitions of the Kremlin. Stalin is not content with Poland, Finland, the Baltic States, Rumania, Bulgaria, Hungary and Eastern Slovakia. He wants the whole of Central Europe, with Norway, Turkey and Persia thrown in. And if these territories fall to him, his lust for aggrandisement will only be stimulated still further. . . .

'Britain's victories are barren. They leave her poor and they leave her people hungry. They leave her bereft of the markets and the wealth that she possessed six years ago. But above all, they leave her with an immensely greater problem that she had then. We are nearing the end of one phase in Europe's history, but the next will be no happier. It will be grimmer, harder and perhaps bloodier. And now I ask you earnestly, can Britain survive? I am profoundly convinced that without German help she cannot.'

Enigmatically he remarked: 'You may not hear from me again for a few months.' He went on to admit sadly: 'Germany is, if you will, not any more a chief factor in Europe.' But at the end he made a gesture of defiance. 'Es lebe Deutschland!' His voice boomed into the microphone as he said that, and then died away as he concluded: 'Heil Hitler. And farewell.'

Now he had nothing to do but wait to learn whether the authorities in Berlin were still interested in trying to save him. He was a German citizen with a false passport, possessing little more than his clothes, a few books, a modest supply of cash which would soon become nearly worthless, and a pistol. He was tired out after five and a half years of frantic, dedicated work, troubled by pain from an ankle he had twisted in the Berlin blackout, and mourning a cause.

Büro Concordia went on working until the Americans arrived in Brunswick, so near to Helmstedt and Oebisfelde that they could overrun these districts within a few hours. The staff's only hope was to scatter. All the foreigners had German identity cards, to enable them to submerge themselves into the population, but some had thought of posing as foreign workers, of whom there were large numbers in Germany, slipping into Holland, and living there until wartime emotions had abated.

When the local Landrat was asked by Hetzler to supply identity cards of the kind carried by foreign workers, he reacted in the manner of all those well-drilled German officials who went on up to the collapse abiding by instructions, refusing to exceed their authority, checking the petty cash, demanding signatures for issued stores, and being awkward about scales of entitlement. It was unthinkable, he said, that he could issue such documents without authority from Berlin. A patient explanation that these aliens had been working for Germany for nearly five years and were now in imminent danger, a reminder that within a few hours or days the Reich Government and the Landrat himself would have lost control over what happened in Helmstedt, failed to move him.

Half expecting to hear the rattle of American tanks behind him, Hetzler hurried back to the hotel, assembled a party of the Funkschutz, and returned with them to the town hall. Confronted by armed SS men, the Landrat and his staff shrugged their shoulders and hung about while Hetzler made out Dutch workers' identity cards.

The staff assembled to receive their identity cards and salaries. Winter was there, still in possession of his yacht. James was accompanied by his German secretary, whom he had married, and their two children. The rest were burdened with as much of their acquisitions as they could transport. The Indians stood by themselves, keeping their own counsel. Hetzler advised everyone to disperse and do the best they could for themselves.

Only the Indians were properly organized for the next move. With their business acumen which had enabled them to corner Helmstedt's milk supply, they had now succeeded in hiring a bus—a transaction which, at that time, required exceptional negotiating ability. They loaded their baggage, climbed in and departed eastwards, with the intention of meeting the Russians and representing themselves as anti-imperialists who had been fighting against Britain throughout the war.

A Pole named Kowalski was the last to broadcast for Concordia. Shortly afterwards technicians arrived from Berlin and put the Oebisfelde transmitter out of action. Hetzler made a bonfire in the hotel yard of all the discs, tapes, scripts and paper.

Haw-Haw's Farewell

Helmstedt was quiet and apparently deserted, the population fidgeting and waiting behind shuttered windows, when American tanks, trucks and jeeps drove through the town. Soldiers occupied the town hall, requisitioned accommodation, and posted notices warning civilians to keep off the streets except between 9 a.m. and 2 p.m. Soon small parties of Russians and Poles, released from prison camps, were wandering about.

Early the next morning Hetzler, defying the curfew, set out by bicycle for Wernigerode to join his family. He was accompanied by a man who had the same destination. Unmolested they rode through the unnaturally silent countryside.

Chapter 27

RUSSIAN ROULETTE

Goebbels was dead but there were still officials to fulfil his orders. Commanded to keep Joyce out of Allied hands, they produced the only plan which might give him a chance to escape. He was to be sent to neutral Sweden. Joyce and his wife were ordered to stand by on the night of April 30th for a car to take them to Flensburg. From there they would be passed on to Copenhagen, and then shipped across the narrow sea.

Surrounded by their luggage they waited, hour after hour. They were despairing of getting away that night when, at three in the morning, an SS man strode into the hotel and asked for them. They left immediately, shivering in the night air, and did not stop until the driver pulled up before the Flensburg town hall. Hot-eyed from their sleepless night, they were received by a harassed but friendly Burgomaster, who directed them to the Police President as the official who would provide a car for their further journey and currency for their use outside Germany.

The Police President was sympathetic but unhelpful. He had received no instructions to issue currency, he said, and even if ordered to supply a car he could not do so as he had none at his disposal. Joyce had had little if any hope of escape, but he became irritated at this early breakdown of the plan, went to the Reichsbank, and after a lot of haggling persuaded the manager to sell him fifty-two Danish kroner. He had wanted Swedish money too but the official was adamant about that. The driver who had brought them from Hamburg received permission to take them to Aabenraa. There he handed them over to the SS Town Commandant. They had accomplished the first stage of their escape; they were on Danish soil.

For the Town Commandant they were simply one more worry.

He was obsessed with anxiety about his wife in Berlin, and although the Joyces were sure they had never met her, he several times asked whether by chance they had news of her. He had an impossible problem on his hands, he told them, caused by the arrival there of shiploads of destitute refugees from West Prussia and Danzig. Joyce had to interrupt to remind him that they had an urgent problem too, and were under instructions from Berlin to get to Copenhagen as soon as they could.

The Commandant promised to do his best. As he had no spare transport, however, all he could undertake was to accommodate them in the town until a car came through on the way to Copenhagen. If it had seats to spare he would put them on it.

Expecting to be summoned to the Commandant's office at any moment, they waited all the next day, imagining the Hauptkampf-linie advancing remorselessly northwards, alert whenever they heard a motor vehicle pass. Another precious day went by. If Berlin's plan had worked, and cars been supplied, they should by now have arrived in Copenhagen and might even have crossed to Sweden. The time dragged intolerably on the third day, with Joyce speculating on the reasons for the lack of German Army transport heading for Copenhagen.

On the fourth day a message came that they were to present themselves at the Commandant's office at once. Assuming that within a few minutes they would be speeding out of Aabenraa, they hurried. The Commandant's message was brief.

'I have heard from Copenhagen that you are on no account to go there.'

While they had been waiting, a British force had landed in Denmark ahead of them, and the backdoor to Sweden was closed. They were hopelessly trapped.

Obviously on the verge of a breakdown, the Commandant looked at them helplessly.

'Do you want to stay here?' he asked. 'If you do you will probably be interned.'

Fear of internment had driven Joyce from England in 1939 and, if he had had the right currency for railway tickets, would have caused him to return from Berlin to London. At the sound of the word internment he reacted instantaneously.

'I'm going back to Germany! I'm not going to be arrested by these damned Danes!'

There was no certainty that he would be able to cross the border. Danish Communists were rumoured to have seized the frontier post and to be turning back all civilians. The only hope was to travel with a military party, and for this purpose Joyce was given the cap and greatcoat of an infantry major and his wife the cap and coat of a woman signals auxiliary. Two military identity cards with photographs bearing no resemblance to them were thrust into their hands. As he emerged from the office Joyce was saluted by some German privates, but their salutes died away and they stared as they saw Joyce's blue civilian trousers and the hem of Margaret's green skirt. The incident was not a good omen; the fugitives were going to need a bit of luck to get past any hostile controls.

There was no lack of transport going to Germany, and they were given seats in a car driven by a man in Luftwaffe uniform. Wisely he decided not to try to bully his way past the armed steel-helmeted civilians at the border, but to be discreet. He slowed down as a man raised a hand. 'Now it's coming,' he said.

Approaching, the frontier guard slung his rifle over his shoulder to free his hands to take the passes, and in doing so knocked his steel helmet over his eyes. He pushed his helmet back over his forehead, settled his rifle in a less awkward position, and then put out his hand. The driver and his service companion showed him their documents. Then he turned to the Joyces. It was a tense moment. If he had compared the photographs with their faces, and ordered them out of the car, they would have been exposed at once by the civilian clothes under their coats. A search of Joyce would have produced his passport in the name of Wilhelm Hansen and his Wehrpass in his correct name. The man gave the passes a perfunctory glance, did not even look at the couple, and waved the car on.

Entering Germany was like coming home. At the Flensburg control post a German naval officer, after exchanging a few words with the driver, opened the rear door, put his head in the car, and bawled cheerfully: 'Ach! Familie Haw-Haw!' With a loud laugh he wished them good luck.

Driving into Flensburg, the driver asked his civilian passengers what they wanted to do now. Each crisis in Joyce's life had found him without any firm plan and now he was, as usual, undecided.

He and his wife might have tried to lose their identities among the hordes of homeless people drifting about the country. Even in the post-war chaos this would not have been particularly easy; the Hansen passport might have got him through low-level controls, but no German who encountered him for more than a few minutes would have taken him for a fellow-countryman, and Margaret was plainly nothing but English. His other handicaps were formidable. With his ugly scar he was literally a marked man; even in a country where men had duelling scars on the cheek he stood out, because no student would have acquired a wound like that. His voice had been heard at some time by most British soldiers. Still, if he had not given way to apathy he could have tried, and he would have needed only to escape capture for a year or so for his fate to have been different.

As the car nosed its way through the crowded streets (the Flensburg population had doubled in a year) Joyce said he supposed they had better return to the Police President's office. They removed their military coats and caps, the driver set them down and, with his companion, unloaded their luggage. The Joyces staggered into the building with their burdens, but were intercepted just inside by a policeman, who told them that as the Police President was holding a reception, uninvited visitors would have to wait until the next day to see him.

The car had left and they stood surrounded by cases and bundles. The policeman turned away to attend to more important duties. Suddenly the building was filling up with uniformed men. The Joyces could not have left had they tried. SS officers formed a line on each side of a door. Everybody remained motionless in an expectant silence until the black-uniformed ranks stiffened, hands flew up in a salute, and Heinrich Himmler, the SS leader, strode smiling and saluting between them. The SS officers turned and followed him into a hall where some of the surviving leaders of the disintegrating Third Reich were meeting for the last time.

Joyce and his wife, neither of whom had seen Himmler before, struggled away as the throng in the entrance dispersed. The only other person they had met in the town was the friendly Burgomaster, and for want of any other idea they went to him. As they expected, he proved useless. Talking rapidly and nervously, he confessed that he was no longer in control and could not even find them a room. He did not know how much longer he would be nominally in office.

With their last hope of assistance gone, they dragged their luggage through the streets, fearful that it would be stolen if they put it down for a moment. All they could do now was to go through the motions of finding accommodation, so they made for the Bahnhofshotel. They were near it when Joyce bounded forward and grasped the hand of a large, grey-faced, unhappy-looking SS officer. Surprised, Margaret hung back, watching the two men greet each other and walk slowly together into the building.

Accompanying this fortunately-met acquaintance, Joyce said to the reception clerk: 'Herr Staatssekretär wants me to stay here to be near him. I presume you have room.'

SS uniforms were still dreaded, an under-secretary continued to enjoy prestige, and hotel rooms were even then kept vacant in case an important arrival needed one.

'Yes, sir, of course,' responded the clerk, reaching for the key to room 17.

Joyce returned to the entrance and beckoned his wife. They were conducted to a comfortable, well-furnished room. This sudden turn in their fortunes was almost too much for them to grasp. Margaret flung herself on the bed and lay silent. Joyce contemplated the room, the luggage and the closed door, and was grateful for this refuge. His apathy left him, and several times he said: 'Everything will be all right.'

In the morning they breakfasted in the hotel and then, having nothing to do, went for a walk. Cut off from their past, having no foreseeable future, they tramped about as they had done in Berlin in 1939, waiting for what would happen. Joyce was not going to run away or commit suicide. His hopeful mood of the previous evening had faded, but he was tranquil, a spectator, looking pitifully down at the refugee-crowded decks of the ships tied up in the harbour, as though his plight were not immensely worse.

They were tired from walking, congratulating themselves on having somewhere to rest, when they returned to the hotel. Being convinced that their luck would last a little while, they were dismayed when the reception clerk, giving Joyce the key, said that he was afraid he would have to cause them some inconvenience, adding: 'I must ask you to give up your room.'

For once Joyce was speechless as in imagination he saw them once again in the street with their luggage.

'But only for one night,' the clerk hastened to assure him. He had no idea of the significance for the two guests of the explanation he now gave them. 'You see, the first two floors have been requisitioned for some British officers on their way to Denmark. But only for tonight. Tomorrow they will have gone and you can come back.'

That was how Haw-Haw personally experienced the German capitulation. He was deprived of his hotel room.

Showing no emotion he asked, as might any guest, whether the clerk could offer anything else. Surprisingly, he could. He would allocate them a bed in an air-raid shelter. It was dry and clean, he said, and would not be uncomfortable for one night. They went to look at the place by daylight, so that they could find it in the dark (nobody had lifted the black-out regulations) and were welcomed by a pleasant nurse who pointed out where they were to sleep.

In the hotel dining-room that evening there was an air of tension, just as there had been when they breakfasted in the small Berlin hotel nearly six years previously. While eating the meal conjured up by the cook, they were awaiting a broadcast by Admiral Dönitz, Hitler's successor. They had been without news for some while, but the Admiral told them nothing they could not have assumed from the fact that rooms upstairs were reserved for British officers.

The next day, May 7th, General Jodl signed the capitulation, but the official end of hostilities was unnoticed in the town. In the morning the hotel clerk greeted Herr and Frau Hansen, the friends of an under-secretary, and handed over the room key. The guests of the previous night had arrived and departed unseen by them.

Lacking any other plan they decided to keep room 17 until turned out. Joyce refused to hide and he even invited capture by inventing a game he called Russian roulette. Played between himself and any group of British soldiers he and his wife happened to pass while tramping about the town, it was nerve-racking enough to deserve the title. He called out a greeting to them in English and if they failed, as they invariably did, to recognize his voice, he had won that round. When in this euphoric state he talked gaily, teased his wife and acted as though enjoying a lark. Swinging to another mood, he plodded on silently, apparently unseeing and unhearing.

He paid his last bill at the Bahnhofshotel on May 11th. With service the charge was 5.83 Reichsmarks, and the clerk meticulously added 10 pfennigs tax. The whole hotel had been requisitioned and there was no hope of moving back. They spent an uneasy night in the shelter, with hundreds of other homeless people, and went for a walk early in the morning.

During one of their aimless excursions Joyce paused before a signpost pointing to Wassersleben. The name had lodged in his memory, as had that of the Hotel Continental when Mrs. Eckersley casually mentioned it in 1939. For a while he could not recall where he had heard it, until he remembered a conversation with a radio speaker in Berlin, who had said that he intended to flee there with his girl-friend.

They might as well walk there as anywhere else, Joyce said. Even if they failed to find their former colleague, they might look for a lodging, the place presumably being less overcrowded than Flensburg.

Cautious inquiries in the village revealed that the Nazi administration had not yet been superseded, so Joyce went to the municipal office, learned that an Englishman and his wife were registered in the district, and procured the address.

Their acquaintance, having reached Wassersleben in the first wave of the evacuation rush, had been fortunate enough to find an attic in a villa. This he and his companion were willing to share with the new arrivals, but he suggested that before deciding they should call on an old English widow living in the adjoining hamlet of Kupfermühle with her two daughters and the Dutch fiancé of one of them. Wearily but hopefully Joyce and his wife set off again.

The widow spoke a mixture of English and German which at times Joyce could barely follow, but he gathered that she had married a German waiter in England before 1914, waited for him during his internment and accompanied him to Germany in 1919. She took a liking to the Hansens and turned the young Dutchman out of his room so that they could have a place to themselves. They fetched their possessions from Flensburg and settled down to wait.

Kupfermühle, among idyllically peaceful woods, seemed forgotten. Joyce wandered about in the sunshine, or lay on the ground looking at the budding birch trees, more tranquil than at any time since his wife had known him. Such shopping as was possible could be done in the village, so they seldom went far. Once they ventured into Flensburg, to find that the swarms of people were even denser. British soldiers still walked about in compact little gangs. Joyce tried an occasional game of his Russian roulette, but the parties went by with scarcely a glance.

A few British soldiers appeared in Kupfermühle, members of a small military post. The 'no fraternization' rule was in force and, bored and lonely, they strolled about looking curiously at the inhabitants. Somehow they discovered that there were residents who understood English living in the same house as the widow's two pretty daughters. After dark they took to dropping in with small gifts of chocolate, tea, cigarettes and other luxuries. One presented Margaret with a *Daily Mirror*.

Their cigarettes glowing in the darkness, the khaki-clad young men sat in the widow's living-room, plying the girls with chocolate and talking in English to the supposed Herr and Frau Hansen. One night the party included a politically-minded soldier who was delighted to encounter a fellow-spirit in the scar-faced man with the fluent English. Readily carried away in conversation, Joyce was soon holding the floor with an impromptu edition of his views on the news. He spoke naturally, with no attempt to disguise his voice, yet nobody suspected who he was. For his anonymity Joyce could thank his numerous parodists, who had implanted in the public mind an impression of a voice which bore scarcely any resemblance to his. For the soldiers to have realized that they were listening to Lord Haw-Haw he would have had to pronounce Germany as Jairmany, lingering absurdly on the first syllable, and snarl like a music hall comedian in a skit on Victorian melodrama. It seemed that his game of Russian roulette was not so dangerous after all.

The original Lord Haw-Haw got as far as Altaussee in Austria before he was captured. One of his first statements was a claim to this coveted title. Baillie-Stewart was still nursing a grievance against the usurper Joyce whom, according to the *Daily Telegraph* of 21st May 1945, he described as 'a thug of the first order'.

Hetzler had reached Wernigerode unmolested and joined his wife and children, who were staying with relatives. Two days later the house was requisitioned, and he moved with his family to a summer house in the woods. There he stayed in bed suffering from an abscess in the ear, until arrested by American soldiers. Uncomprehending, his children laughed with pleasure to see him being given a ride in a jeep. He was delivered to an internment camp, where he was soon joined by Hoskins and James.

The Indians, who had so ably organized their getaway in a hired bus, reached a Russian unit and introduced themselves as anti-imperialists. The Red Army soldiers, however, were interested only in the bus, which they promptly seized. Ignoring the occupants' frenziedly-expressed pro-Soviet sentiments, they arrested them and returned them to the British.

Monday was shopping day in Kupfermühle, when the shops opened briefly, sold their small stock of rations, and closed again. The Joyces accordingly walked into the village on May 28th; they were lucky, because bacon was on sale. On the way back they sauntered through the woods to gather sticks for the stove.

Joyce, who had been unusually even-tempered for some time, was feeling irritable. He had no immediate cause for annoyance but, although he had not shown it, he was badly overwrought. He started a quarrel about nothing, lost his temper, shouted and then relapsed into a sulky silence.

It was Margaret's turn that afternoon to wash up the household crockery. She was busy doing this when Joyce walked into the kitchen and said abruptly: 'I'm sorry about this morning. Come for a walk.'

The washing-up rota had been arranged with the widow and the two girls, and Margaret could not leave the work unfinished. She told her husband that she was not yet ready. Too impatient to wait, he named a place in the woods where she would be able to find him. Limping slightly, because his ankle was paining him, he walked out of the house and she heard his footsteps die away along the road.

Shortly after setting out he changed his mind about his route, went through Wassersleben, and climbed a hill to a point which gave a fine view of the harbour. He had been there several times with his wife. Contemplating the view, he seems to have fallen into a trance-like state. 'With the utmost earnestness,' to use his own words, he 'prayed for help and guidance'. That sudden calmness which gives relief during periods of acute anxiety descended on him. 'I felt that my prayers would be answered,' he later wrote.

Margaret was delayed in following her husband. As she was about to leave the house, the landlady's son arrived, hoping to see Herr Hansen. He gave Margaret his message, which was that he had just been warned that so much Danish currency was circulating that it was losing its value. As he knew that Herr Hansen had a few kroner, he wanted to tell him urgently.

When at last she got away, Margaret hurried to the place where Joyce had said he would be. She waited, grew uneasy, and called. As she had once done when lost in the Berlin Grunewald, she even imitated a sheep bleating. This private joke died away in the silence of the woods. She turned homewards.

Joyce came to himself, realized that his wife would be expecting to find him in another part of the woods, took a final look at the harbour, and walked off in the direction of his original destination. Beneath the trees the ground was uneven. A painful twinge in his ankle made him decide to make for the road instead of going straight through the woods.

This change of direction brought him within sight of two men in the uniform of British army officers. He could have altered his course to avoid them. They were gathering wood and would not have been interested in a weary-looking, underfed man who meekly turned aside to avoid an encounter. But Joyce kept on.

He never explained what was in his thoughts in those few fateful minutes, if indeed he was ever able to analyse his mood. The calmness following his prayers may have lulled his awareness of danger. He may have felt drawn by goodwill to these two men, and even by a sense of kinship; he had been furious with the British for what he thought of as their folly, but he had never hated them, and although he had included himself in the phrase 'we Germans' this identification had been a superficial debating point to give his activities a legal and moral justification; emotionally he had felt towards the Germans a superiority which is supposed to be typically British and he had not attempted to assume the personality of the Wilhelm Hansen whose passport he carried. Unconsciously he may have been tempted to give himself up. His life's work, as he saw it, had been in vain, and he

was now a fugitive in hourly danger of discovery; he had not
believed in the efforts to save him and he could have been wanting to get his ordeal over. Or the sight of the khaki uniforms may
simply have prompted the mischievous and irresponsible side of
his personality to play another round of Russian roulette; it had,
after all, proved in many tests to be a harmless game and its
results could have forced him to the reassuring, even if humiliating conclusion that nobody was likely to recognize his voice.

Caution had not entirely deserted him. He could not resist
speaking to the two men, but he spoke in French. Captain
Alexander Adrian Lickorish, of the Reconnaissance Regiment,
and Lieutenant Perry, an interpreter, straightened their backs
and looked at him. Joyce repeated his friendly advice in English.
'Here are a few more pieces.' Then he continued walking towards the road.

Lickorish had a sharper ear than the many soldiers who had
recently heard that voice; to him the stranger's tone sounded
familiar. In his perilous game Joyce had spun the magazine once
too often. But the British captain could not have been quite sure,
because before acting he discussed his suspicion with his companion. They followed and overtook the limping man (Joyce's
version of what happened was that they came after him in a
jeep; the vehicle was not mentioned in the condensed account of
the incident given at his trial). Perry accosted him with the
question: 'You wouldn't happen to be William Joyce, would
you?'

The conditioned response at that time of any European when
his identity was questioned was to produce an official document.
Joyce put his hand in his pocket to take out his German passport. Thinking that he was reaching for a weapon, Perry fired his
revolver, a bullet entering Joyce's right thigh and passing through
his left thigh, causing four wounds. Joyce fell to the ground.
According to Lickorish, as he did so he cried: 'My name is Fritz
Hansen.' Even under the stress of that moment a man named
William was unlikely to have converted his *nom de guerre* of
Wilhelm into Fritz (the diminutive of Friedrich), so Lickorish's
hearing or recollection may have been at fault. Anyway, Joyce
had failed by a few seconds to make audible his claim to be a
harmless German teacher.

It may seem slightly impulsive of Perry to have fired quite so promptly at a civilian who was outnumbered but it must be remembered that the war was scarcely over, the occupying forces did not know what danger lurked among the population, and the suspect was Haw-Haw, the super-enemy who became tolerable only by the pretence that he was a joke, whose agents were so ubiquitous that they could keep every public clock in Great Britain under constant supervision, who accurately predicted not only British troop movements but even the minor postings of civil servants, who knew in advance the targets of the German bomber force and commanded it to act according to his whims. The British public would not have been surprised if, in that Flensburg wood, Haw-Haw had carried in his pocket a secret weapon capable of annihilating an armoured brigade.

For years after the warning he had received Joyce had anticipated that someone would shoot him. When it happened, there was a certain grim justice in its being done by a German Jewish refugee. The lieutenant's name was not really Perry; foreign members of the British forces serving against the Germans had been officially encouraged to discard, either permanently or temporarily, obviously Jewish names. Some months were to pass before Joyce learned how Fate had granted Jewry its revenge.

As it was, Joyce was unarmed. Lickorish immediately made sure of that. While searching him he found Wilhelm Hansen's passport and William Joyce's Wehrpass. The fabulous Haw-Haw who, Goebbels had ordered, was to be saved from the Allies at all costs, had by his own impulsiveness fallen into the hands of two men who were only looking for firewood.

Lickorish treated the wound. Not long afterwards Joyce and his documents were handed over to the guard commander at the frontier post.

'The boys are early tonight,' Margaret Joyce remarked, as military boots crunched the gravel outside. A loud bang on the door startled her—'the boys' had always entered quietly for their evening of forbidden fraternization. The door flew open.

'Does a Mrs. Joyce live here?' An English voice sounded through the house.

'I am Mrs. Joyce.' She advanced to face a lieutenant, who was supported by ten soldiers, two Bren gun carriers and a lorry.

'Your husband has been arrested,' he told her, adding that he was going to arrest her and everyone in the house.

All the occupants, including the old woman who spoke her individual Anglo-German dialect, were ordered into the lorry and driven to the frontier post. There, under guard, they waited outside.

Margaret was in the state of shock caused by disaster, and she was unaware of how long they waited. She took a grip on herself when a door was flung open and soldiers emerged carrying her husband on a stretcher. He looked very pale and his face was sunken because he was without his false teeth. As the party passed slowly before her, he looked up and waved.

Summoning her wits to help him, she shouted desperately: 'Erin go braa!' The message 'Ireland for ever' was intended to suggest to him that he should claim to be Irish. He gave no sign of hearing.

The women were taken into the building to be searched by a Danish female customs officer and then driven in the lorry to the police headquarters at Flensburg, where the Joyces had been received on the first stage of their intended journey to Copenhagen.

At ten o'clock Margaret was sent for by a weary-looking but very polite British officer.

'Will you tell me truthfully', he asked, 'whether those people in the house knew whom they were sheltering?'

She answered, truthfully, that they had not. Her fellow-prisoners were promptly released and driven home.

Margaret was kept in a cell in the police headquarters. During the night several groups of British officers, including a padre, came in simply to look at her.

Next morning the commanding officer sent her to Kupfer-mühle to pack a bag for herself and one for her husband. The room the Joyces had occupied had been ransacked. Their two typewriters had gone. Somewhere in the luggage had been Joyce's revolver, and that was never officially found. The land-lady had lost her entire stock of spirits and food. The dark suit made for Joyce in Berlin, bought on the special clothing coupons allowed him as a foreign journalist, was still there, and Margaret packed it. The costume presented to her by an aunt in 1936 had also been left, and this she put on.

Russian Roulette

Only sparse facts were issued to the press about Joyce's arrest. 'Lord Hush-Hush—Why?' asked the *Daily Express*, which had first published the original title. The correspondents did their best on the little to hand. Joyce had talked throughout his seven-hour ambulance journey. To the British soldiers—some shouting 'Jairmany calling!'—who had crowded round the ambulance, he had said, 'in those sneering tones we know so well' (to quote one version): 'One doesn't look into other people's windows!' and (to take another): 'In civilized countries wounded men are not peep-shows!' Three Irish nurses were reported to be annoyed at having to look after him, and British and Allied wounded in the hospital to have expressed their disgust at having such a neighbour. Joyce was 'making a great fuss about his wound, and pretends he is in great pain'.

Reporters could not bring themselves to concede that he might be legally married. Margaret was variously referred to as 'his alleged wife' and 'the woman who claims to be his wife'. One writer, who described her as 'prinking' her hair, was impressed by her turnout; not knowing that her costume was nine years old, he commented that it would have caused women to turn round and admire her had she walked down Regent Street.

Journalists had been busy in England too, Joyce's sister being quoted in the *Daily Mirror* as complaining: 'His name only drags me down. I've already lost a job through him,' and his mother-in-law, affirming that she still loved her daughter, as remarking: 'We didn't have a wireless set, or, perhaps, we might have learnt where she was, from her traitor husband's broadcasts.'

Guarded by soldiers, some embarrassed, some indifferent and some affable, Margaret was detained for a week at Second Army headquarters in the villa in Lüneburg where Himmler had committed suicide. Her request for her copy of Shakespeare—she needed something to read—received extensive publicity.

The military authorities assured her that her husband was not seriously wounded and passed her a message from him. Far from complaining, Joyce was tranquil and appreciative of his treatment as he entered on the most remarkable phase of his career.

Chapter 28

'GOD BLESS OLD ENGLAND'

From the moment that his identity was discovered Joyce was frank and co-operative, concealing nothing relevant. No searching interrogations were required to break him and no investigator could make a valid claim to Joyce as 'his' case. Joyce behaved as though grateful that the British authorities were at last going to listen to him, and his one concern (apart from diverting any blame from his wife) was to expound his attitude clearly.

When he dictated his first formal statement to Captain William James Scardon of the Intelligence Corps in the military hospital at Lüneburg on May 31st he obviously had no thought of the line the defence would take at his trial. He began by justifying his pre-war claims to be British instead of denying that he could be subject to British law. He related the circumstances of his birth, said he believed his father had lost his American citizenship through failing to renew it, claimed that the Joyce family had generally counted as British subjects both in Ireland and England, and explained that he had acquired German nationality in 1940.

His motives he set out with the fluency of a commentator who had formulated them many times. He had attempted 'to bring about a reconciliation or at least an understanding between the two countries'. In the later stages of the war, with Russian power growing, he 'became certain that Britain, even though gaining a military triumph over the Germans, would in that event be confronted with a situation far more dangerous and complicated than that which existed in August 1939; and thus until the very last moment I clung to my hope of an Anglo-German understanding, although I could see that the prospects thereof were small'. He concluded: 'I know that I have been denounced as a traitor and I resent the accusation as I conceive myself to have been guilty of no underhand or deceitful act against Britain, although I am also able to understand the resentment that my broadcasts have in many quarters aroused. Whatever opinion may be formed at the present time with regard to my conduct, I submit that the final judgement cannot be properly passed until it is seen whether Britain can win the peace. Finally I should like to stress the fact that in coming to Germany and in working for the German radio system my wife was powerfully influenced by me. She protests to the contrary but I am sure that, if I had not taken this step, she would not have taken it either.'

From Lüneburg he was moved to the military detention barracks in Brussels, to which he paid a compliment. In a letter to his wife he summed up his time there: 'Main disadvantages were lack of sunlight and exercise and having to sleep—or lie—on a board without mattress or pillow. No good with four wounds. But the food was very good and plentiful, whilst the N.C.O.s, though they sounded demented, were efficient, just and conscientious. As a glass-house, the place was A.1.'

He was detained in Brussels from June 10th to June 16th to give Parliament time to pass the Treason Act 1945[1] which simplified the archaic procedure in treason trials and made it the same as for murder. The Act was passed on June 15th and on the following day, escorted by Lieutenant-Colonel Leonard Burt (later Commander Leonard Burt of the Scotland Yard Special Branch) and a military party, Joyce was flown to England.

During the flight (Burt recorded in *Commander Burt of Scotland Yard*), a guard having passed him an autograph book, he wrote: 'We are about to pass over the white chalk cliffs—England's bulwark. It is a sacred moment in my life—and I can only say whatever my fate may be—God bless Old England on the lee.' This is surely one of the most remarkable entries ever made in an autograph book, but Joyce would have seen nothing odd in it. As sentimental as any English exile about the white cliffs, he was convinced that he had acted in his adopted country's best interests; it was the measure of his distance from British thinking that he believed that a lot of people would see his point of view even if they did not share it. As he said, he knew that his

[1] For a comment on this Act see J. W. Hall: *Trial of William Joyce*, pp. 12 to 15.

broadcasts had aroused 'resentment', and he knew all about the Haw-Haw jokes, but he never realized that he had become, for the British, the most hated personality of the war.

When he landed in England the first step in his long legal ordeal was his arrest by Chief Inspector Frank Bridges. At Bow Street police station he was formally charged under the Treason Act of 1351. All he said was: 'I have heard and taken cognisance. Today I shall not add anything to the statement I have made to the military authorities.'

Haw-Haw's presence in London caused great public excitement and a lot of people, most of whom failed to get into the police court when the case came up at Bow Street on June 18th, were so curious to see him that they endured a lengthy wait in a queue. Press photographers even crowded tenement windows behind the court building in the hope of taking a picture of him exercising in the yard. Those who gained admission were rewarded by seeing a typical Joyce military-style entry, but they were disappointed by his appearance and surprised that he looked so short. Surrounded by uniformed men selected for their height, defendants seldom dominate the court scene, and no one remarks on this. But spectators were incapable of judging Joyce physically by normal standards. To measure up to the amount of fuss that had been made about him, he would have had to be eight feet tall and of terrifying aspect.

The proceedings were brief and routine. Chief Inspector Bridges told the Court that the charge was high treason and announced that the case for the Crown would not be opened that day. Everybody strained to hear the prisoner say 'No, sir,' three times after being asked by the magistrate, Sir Bernard Watson, whether he was legally represented, wanted to question the witness, or objected to a remand until June 25th. Joyce then said he would like to apply for legal aid, and the hearing concluded.

In the hospital of Brixton Prison, where he was being treated both for his wound and for a scalp infection, he was visited the next day by his brother Quentin and his friend John Macnab, both of whom he had last seen at Victoria Station in 1939. He was delighted and talked cheerfully about himself—he could now walk without sticks, he was greatly satisfied with his medical treatment, and the prison officers were fair and decent.

He had learnt of his mother's death only six weeks before, and he pressed Quentin for details. After hearing the news of his brothers and sister he asked about Miss Scrimgeour's welfare. In response to messages of good will from her and from other old acquaintances, he said: 'Tell them that I shall fight as I have never fought before.'

His chief worry was that he had no news of his wife and he supposed that she was still on the Continent. The visitors promised to try to find out where she was and Joyce asked them to ensure that, whatever happened, she should not be left unprovided for or unassisted.

Visiting Joyce again on June 21st, Macnab found him looking rather better, cheered by several letters he had received, and relieved that he now knew where his wife was and could write to her.

Before Joyce's next appearance in court the disconcerting rumour spread that he was not a British subject. It looked as though the infinitely cunning Haw-Haw might get away with it, because if he was not British he could not commit high treason. A queue formed four hours before the court was due to open.

The legal skirmish during this hearing showed that the rumour was well-founded. Joyce pleaded not guilty to the charges of committing treason by broadcasting for the enemy and by becoming naturalized in an enemy state. For the Crown Mr. L. A. Byrne, Senior Prosecuting Counsel to the Treasury (later Mr. Justice Byrne), made it plain that if Joyce were an alien the prosecution would contend that in some circumstances aliens owed allegiance to the Crown. Mr. C. B. V. Head, a solicitor assigned to defend Joyce, refused to accept that an alien abroad could commit treason and he told the court that his client was not a British subject.

It was clear that the case might call for a legal decision of great importance. Joyce, for all his expressed determination to fight, would have been prepared to write himself off, but now he sniffed the complex and subtle arguments that lay ahead, and he listened with the appreciation of a man who knew a good dispute when he encountered one. Once during the evidence he laughed; that was when his Kriegsverdienstkreuz, the decoration he had been given, was absurdly called an Iron Cross.

Sir Bernard Watson committed him to the July session at the Old Bailey, but as the defence needed more time to gather

253

evidence about his nationality the trial was postponed until September.

While awaiting the Old Bailey hearing, Joyce began a series of letters to his wife and friends which he continued until the last morning of his life. His earlier letters to Margaret, whom he addressed by various nicknames—Meg, Meb, Mae, Mary, Margaret Mary, Freja, Mother-Sheep, Little Ape Face, die Olle, Ol—dealt mostly with her well-being. Trying to assure her that he was in good spirits and his normal self, he sometimes used comic spellings and a mixture of English and German words, or the flippant style of his New British Broadcasting Station scripts. In his reflections on his capture, which had involved him in what he mildly called 'unpleasantness', he treated the episode, and his guards' precautions to prevent him committing suicide, as a joke: 'Some slight ill-feeling seems to have arisen because I was unsporting enough to behave like the fox that, instead of running for its life, sat on a fence and smoked a cigarette. Also I refused to be impressed by threats as to my future, and, to crown all, I made no attempt to commit suicide, but laughed at the idea. Dammit all, Sir, after such Nazi caddishness on my part, it is no wonder that poor Meg had an uneven reception. Like yourself, I cannot understand really why "authorities" are so ready to attribute suicidal motives to prisoners who have not the least intention of breaking Trade Union conventions. However, it is probably the exceptions that justify the rules! . . .'

He apologized repeatedly for the position he had put her in, and when she protested against his taking all the blame, he wrote: 'It is I who must ask forgiveness for ditching you through my rashness. But I honestly think it was so written by the Finger of Providence.'

The man who had dreaded internment responded to the orderliness of prison life. It seems to have provided him with something of what he had hoped to find in a military environment and a National Socialist state. 'One thing I like about prison here is the pleasant sense of being in an organization which functions perfectly at every point. It is a mental tonic. Despite my grey hairs, I still, like you, dear, have some capacity for adaptation, which, however, reminds me uneasily of the chameleon that was placed on the Mackenzie tartan and, after a moment, burst! But that is what the mathematicians call "the limiting case". It doesn't

happen in real life: and except for my heartfelt concern for you,
I am quite happy. I am keeping down the fat with exercise, which
includes voluntary window-cleaning!'

He brooded over his ill temper, being prompted to do so by a
book from the prison library: 'I have just read Cronin's "Hatter's
Castle". Do you know it? It is the sordid epic of a Lowland
megalomaniac domestic bully—well told, if a trifle prolix in parts.
It could be a classic: and it should be studied by all bad-tempered
and conceited husbands. Might be a Set Book for the Marriage
Exam of the future Social Order! Anyhow, it has deepened my
repentance: and you know that I am not often influenced by
books!'

Occasionally he gave superficial views on the news. On July
18th he wrote: 'At present Stalin, Truman and Churchill are
meeting in Potsdam. Many issues—including the future of Germany and Turkey. I think the answer will be a lemon.' He had
been out of England for several years and his slang was outdated.
He doubted whether the atomic bombs dropped on Japan had
been as powerful as was reported. 'I think (of course, I would!)
that you exaggerate the horrors of Honourable Atomic Bomb. I
am unregenerate and believe that the second (Nagasaki) annihi-
lated only one square mile.' He blamed the German High Command (OKW) and the Foreign Office (Auswärtiges Amt) for
letting Quisling down. 'He seems to have been badly served by
some of his OKW friends and, of course, by the Auswärtiges
Amt of Ever Evil Memory! They were bound to preserve the
most incriminating documents!'

His own voice having been much discussed, he in turn deplored British soldiers' accents. 'I heard young Tommies from
the Midlands and North who had laid aside their own honest
dialects and were resorting to a scarcely human articulation . . .
these poor people could hardly understand me, either, tho' I
thought my English clear if nothing else. So now I have concluded that even from the linguistic point of view I am obsolete.'

He wrote affectionately to Miss Scrimgeour. 'I hope to see you
years and *years* before you die. We must not be presumptuous:
but I do not think it presumptuous to hope confidently that God
will grant your prayer and those of my other friends.' Miss
Scrimgeour assured him that she had not changed her views. He
replied that he had done enough to warn the British of impending

dangers but they were stupid. 'Yes—it passes my own comprehension how any civilized people can prefer Bolshevism to National-Socialism. But, of course, it is useless to think of the people as being intelligent.'

Reflecting on his situation, he once recalled ruefully how even the Germans had accused him of sub-treason. 'I ain't nobody's darling, except yours!' he told his wife.

His solicitor assembled a team of experienced lawyers; Mr. G. O. Slade, K.C., was to lead it, assisted by Mr. Derek Curtis-Bennett, K.C., with their junior, Mr. James Burge. Pleased and impressed though he was, Joyce viewed his prospects soberly. He anticipated that the decision at the Old Bailey would go against him; he thought he stood a slight chance with the appeal, but his real hopes, such as they were, rested with the Lords. Gently, in a letter written on 11th September, he tried to prepare his wife for the first setback. 'I had my final conference with Head yesterday, and, he told me, Slade is so satisfied with the case that, if necessary, he will take it to the Lords. But I hope and expect that it will not be necessary to go so high in order to secure the administration of the law.'

Chapter 29

SOMETHING IN THE CITY

An observer who recalled the days of Haw-Haw, the Great
National Joke, might have reflected that there was an astonishing
turn-out at the Old Bailey on 17th September 1945 for the trial
of a harmless clown. The laughter, which had always had a nervous edge to it, had died away at the sight of the Army returning
from Dunkirk. Joyce, rather than the remote figures tried at
Nuremberg, had come to personify the enemy. That was why
the journalists, distinguished writers and radio commentators
crowded the court, overflowing into the space usually available
for spectators. The tension of the trial was felt far beyond the
court room because, as anyone who was in London at the time
will recall, the public was anxious about British justice, not from
fear that a man could be condemned unfairly but through concern that he might be found not to have broken the law, when
they would be robbed of their revenge.

The prisoner, as he looked calmly about him at the wigged
and gowned barristers, the aldermen and sheriffs, the police, the
red-tabbed Military Intelligence officers, and the men and
women who would be reporting his every change of expression,
rated his chances lower than did many lawyers. Since his
appearances at Bow Street he had put on weight, his complexion
had cleared, and his hair—although still short—had grown. To
honour the occasion he was smartly dressed in the Berlin-made
suit, with a shirt and tie of the same colour. When he said:
'Not guilty' after the clerk of the court had read the charges he
spoke the only words he was to utter during those three days;
some spectators thought he smiled slightly while doing so. After
that he had nothing to do but listen, make notes, stand up and sit

down when the two prison officers accompanying him indicated that he should.

The proceedings in the Joyce case were, for the most part, not about his actions but about what he was. Everybody knew what he had done; if anyone had, unaccountably, any doubts about the prisoner's activities, Joyce's frank statement made shortly after his arrest would have cleared them up; the problem for the court was whether he came in the category of persons who could commit treachery against the British Crown.

The Act under which he was charged dates from 1351; it was originally written in Norman French and unpunctuated; half the time in the famous trial for treason of Sir Roger Casement in 1916 was occupied with arguments about its ambiguities, the defence contending that it covered the crime of adhering to the Crown's enemies only within the realm, whereas Casement was being tried for what he, an Irishman and a British subject, had done in Germany in attempting to raise an anti-British Irish force. This point was settled when the court held that the law covered adherence, by a person owing allegiance, both within and without the realm. Casement, in a letter from prison to a friend, reflected on lawyers. 'They are a race apart—and as for their Cokes and Blackstones (what is Coke but an emasculated Blackstone?) and Flemings, God deliver me, I say, from such antiquaries as these to hang a man's life upon a comma, and throttle him with a semi-colon.' A similar thought might have occurred to Joyce as he waited to know whether the Act could be stretched to cover the activities of himself, an alien, in a foreign country.

All the complications and subtleties, the intricate legal cross-talk, too long and technical for this narrative, can be studied in the published accounts of the trial, one edited by J. W. Hall and the other by C. E. Bechhofer-Roberts. In non-legal language, Joyce was charged with high treason on two counts of having broadcast for the enemy and on one count of purporting to become on 26th September 1940 a naturalized German subject. The two charges of broadcasting propaganda were the same except that one covered the period from 18th September 1939 (the date of his contract with the German radio) until the day of his capture and one from the date of his radio contract until the expiration of his British passport.

The counts were framed in this way because of the doubt about his nationality. If he were proved not to be a British subject, the two dealing with his naturalization and his broadcasting throughout the war would be dropped (as they were) and the prosecution would then maintain that the court had jurisdiction and that he had owed allegiance to the Crown so long as his British passport was valid. A further indictment, which was not read, charged him with an offence under the Treachery Act of 1940, which covers acts by 'any person' and not only by British subjects performed within the United Kingdom with intent to assist the enemy; the judge stopped its being read because, as he explained at a later stage of the trial, he thought it better to deal with one thing at a time. How the Treachery Act would have applied to Joyce, unless the sound of his radio voice constituted an act within the United Kingdom, is not clear.

When a case has received such publicity that the members of the jury are likely to have already formed an opinion about it, they are customarily enjoined to dismiss from their minds what they know and to disregard any feelings they may have. In the Joyce case not only the judge but presumably everyone in court except the prisoner's friends had at some time spoken of the prisoner as a traitor, or had at least thought of him as one, and many would have felt the strongest personal resentment at his activities. The Attorney-General, Sir Hartley Shawcross, K.C., M.P., particularly emphasized the jury's duty on this occasion, reminding them that they were sworn to try the prisoner according to law and on the evidence alone, remarking that 'in the pages of history it will count for nothing what happens to William Joyce in the course of this trial', that Joyce would leave no mark upon those pages but it would count for a great deal that those concerned in the trial comported themselves in accordance with the best traditions of English law.

Sir Hartley argued that Joyce's passport 'placed him under the protection of the British Crown, it clothed him with the status of a British subject, and it required from him the duty of faithfulness and allegiance to the British Crown in return'. He then reminded the court that even during time of war the holder of a British passport in an enemy country can derive some benefit from his passport, in that he is entitled to the rights which belligerents accord each other's subjects and he can call upon the neutral protecting power for assistance. In a phrase that has been much quoted, Sir Hartley said that Joyce had 'so to speak, enveloped himself in the Union Jack, secured for himself the greatest protection that he could secure'.

Joyce listened to the Attorney-General's speech with growing respect. Hitherto he had not had a high opinion of Sir Hartley, whom he had been accustomed to refer to as Hotcross, but now he recognized the skill (without accepting the validity of the arguments) with which the case against him had been opened.

Prosecution witnesses were called to produce documents showing his persistent assertions that he was British. Out of the past came the words of a schoolboy anxious to join the Officers Training Corps, when Joyce had to listen to his expressions of desire to serve the Crown just as, twenty-nine years before, Casement had had to hear his letter to Sir Edward Grey, the Foreign Secretary, conveying his loyal gratitude to the King for his knighthood.

The only evidence by a witness who claimed to have heard Joyce broadcasting in the period while his British passport was valid was that given by the detective inspector who asserted that in the first month of the war he had heard a voice which he recognized as Joyce's saying that Dover and Folkestone had been destroyed, and that he had heard him on other occasions. Slade challenged this identification of Joyce's voice, but the witness insisted that he could not have been mistaken.

Slade then submitted that there was no case to go to the jury, as the prosecution had not even made a *prima facie* case that the prisoner was or ever had been British, but the judge was unwilling at that stage to ignore the claims of Joyce and his father to be British. He ruled that there was some evidence to support the proposition that the accused was British, so Mr. Slade began his speech for the defence, on which he was still engaged when the court adjourned for the day.

While Joyce was being taken back to prison, a conversation was proceeding in the Crown Counsel's room at the court between Sir Hartley Shawcross and Professor J. H. Morgan, an eminent constitutional lawyer who had been one of the defence team at the Casement trial. A fortnight before Joyce's trial came on Sir Hartley had written to Morgan asking for his comments on this difficult case. Now, at the close of the first day, he asked: 'Have we any chance?'

Something in the City

Morgan replied: 'No, I don't think you have—not unless the judge is prepared to make new law.'[1]

That evening some people were said to be offering odds of 6–4 that Joyce would be acquitted.

After supper Joyce started a letter to his wife. He wrote in the knowledge that the letter would take some days to reach her and that she would therefore know the result before she received it.

'And now, my darling, I have just returned from my business trip to the City. For these few days, dear, you would have been able to say that your husband was "something in the City". Of course, by the time you get this, the trial will be over and I shall either be awaiting the Appeal hearing, or else studying the alternative attack which success would bring. From experience, I know that it is misleading to judge a trial by the first day, which, *ipso facto*, belongs to the Prosecution. Nor shall I be disappointed if the case has to go to a higher Court. As you know, dear, I have always emphasized that possibility. Anyhow, the fray is joined. Crown had completed its statement of case and evidence before 3 p.m. Old Hot-Cross Buns, at whom I have been inclined to jest, is certainly very able. . . . This morning, we had plenty of blast; but I did not notice any "Volltreffer" [direct hit]. Obviously, the case will depend, in its final stages, on Law. More I won't say, at the moment, but, as soon after the close of proceedings as I can, I shall give you full impressions. By the way, the "Treachery Act 1940" did not emerge today at all, but I suspect it to be lurking round the corner.'

At two o'clock the following morning a girl private in the A.T.S. sat down in the doorway of the Old Bailey. Four hours later she stood up, the first in the queue now forming for the second day's hearing. She and nineteen others were the only members of the public for whom there were places.

Six years before, on that day, Joyce had signed his contract with Reichsrundfunk. He had too much to think about now to recall the anniversary. Before the court assembled he was seen in the cell below the dock by his two defending counsel. Discussing his prospects they remarked, according to him, that they had been threatened with assassination if they got him off.

[1] See article: 'Two Cases of Treason' by R. Barry O'Brien in the *Daily Telegraph*, 9th August 1957.

Something in the City

'Surely it would be more appropriate, in that case, to assassinate the Attorney-General!' Joyce commented.

The defence's first task, to prove that the accused was an American national, involved not only submitting documents relating to Michael and Gertrude Joyce and their son William but producing witnesses to swear that the man in the dock was the William Joyce to whom some of the documents referred. The prisoner himself was not called to give evidence on this subject because, as Slade put it, 'he cannot possibly give you any evidence of when or where he was born' and 'still less can he give you any evidence of when his father was naturalized.' Frank Holland, who had married Joyce's mother's girlhood friend and often visited the Joyce family in New York, appeared, now a deaf old man. Having become an American citizen on Michael Joyce's advice, he had, on his return to England, been irritated that the police made him comply with the regulations governing aliens and, unlike Michael Joyce, he had regained his British nationality. He identified William Joyce and smiled at him as he did so. He and the other defence witnesses were not questioned by the Attorney-General who, in reply to the judge, said that he would not press the point of Joyce's nationality.

'Very well, Mr. Attorney,' the judge said. 'I think everybody must agree that the evidence which has been tendered is really overwhelming.'

That was the end of count 1, which charged Joyce with broadcasting throughout the war from the day of his contract with the German radio, and of count 2, dealing with his naturalization in Germany. The defence had won an important point; Joyce was established as an alien, but the crucial legal ruling of whether he had owed allegiance to the Crown had yet to come. He did not permit his hopes to rise.

The sparkling display of mental agility and legal erudition fascinated him as lawyers argued over previous judgments (Perkin Warbeck's case in 1500, Calvin's case in 1608, Aeneas Macdonald's case in 1747, the case of a Turkish subject born in Palestine who landed in Britain with a British passport and who in 1940 was held to be an alien, and about thirty-five other cases) and—to Joyce's particular scorn, as will be seen from references in his correspondence to all the judges meeting in a pub—about a resolution by all the judges assembled in 1707 at the command of

Queen Anne covering the position of aliens who settled in England under the protection of the Crown and then, leaving their families and effects in this country, returned to their native land and there, during a war, adhered to the King's enemies.

Occasionally, as counsel picked up volumes from the heaps about them, found their references and read complex passages, Joyce scribbled a note, but in doing so he was thinking of the Appeal and not of the present hearing. He returned to prison convinced that on the following day he was to hear the sentence of death pronounced on himself.

Evening newspapers, with reports that the judge had ruled that there was no case to go to the jury on the first two charges, were on sale in the streets before the court rose. Some people appear to have misunderstood what had happened as, according to the *Daily Mail* of the next morning: 'A crowd of angry people gathered outside the door of the Old Bailey yesterday following a rumour that William Joyce, otherwise "Lord Haw-Haw," had been acquitted and would walk out of the court at any moment a free man.'

Joyce finished the long letter to his wife which he had begun the previous evening. In it he tried to make her smile, and to reassure her about his well-being he penned one of his striking tributes to the British prison administration.

'When Slade said: "and that baby, William Joyce, was the prisoner in the dock—" some of my Scotland Yard and M.I. patrons were hard taxed to restrain their smiles. And I had to keep a face no more crooked than usual.' (Joyce's memory was confused; Frank Holland was examined by Mr. Curtis-Bennett.)

'The staff responsible for taking me to Court and looking after me while I am there are most chivalrous and are showing me every possible consideration consistent with their duty, and, to put it simply, are splendid. The Senior Medical Officer is also looking after me. When I returned here, I had nearly a litre of the most exquisite chocolate-koko waiting for me. I don't want to dwell unduly on the excellencies of this 'tution, but really, tho' I am not British and tho' all my views remain unchanged, I much doubt if any other people in the world would, in like circs, treat me so well.'

Later he wrote another letter commenting on 'the day's

festivities'. 'Let me say that tho' tomorrow may bring a conviction, I am confident now that the ultimate result will be in my favour. The indictment for High Treason contained 3 counts—or specifications, 2 of them based on the assumption that I was British. These two counts have been officially demolished, and it is now finally established that never at any time have I been a British subject. That *we* knew but the point was to convince others. So much has been achieved. As to the 3rd count, involving law re. passports, I will say nothing yet, since the subject is still being argued. But be of good cheer, my dear, and remember my references week after week to the Higher Courts. You can guess what a responsibility rests on one judge in a case like this, and as I know little about My Lord, I had better refrain from predictions. . . . The general public will probably be deeply disappointed with the clean dryness of the case—absence of rodent revelations, etc: but I can honestly say that I should not like to have missed the brilliant and intensive legal battle which began to rage shortly before lunch, when the evidence for the defence closed. . . .

'The calm, sensible, realistic attitude which you show in your letters when you discuss future possibilities, has been and is my greatest help and relief in our somewhat complicated situation. Our faith has been tested, and it may be even more sorely tried in coming weeks: let it emerge, in the end, triumphant and vindicated, to give us a new purpose in life.'

When the third day of the trial opened the Attorney-General asked leave, which the judge granted, to amend counts 1 and 2 to make it clear to the jury that they had been drafted on the assumption that Joyce was of British nationality. On count 3 the judge gave his ruling after lunch. He announced that he would direct the jury that on 24th August 1939, when the passport was issued, the prisoner 'beyond a shadow of doubt' owed allegiance to the Crown, and that nothing had happened during the material time to end that allegiance.

This was, in effect, the end of the story of Joyce's British passport. Obtained 'for holiday touring', on a false claim to be British, it had settled his fate.

The trial was not yet over. Slade was left with little enough to attack, but he made a gallant last-ditch effort by reminding the jury (who were sworn to consider only the evidence given in court) that the sole evidence put before them of Joyce's broadcasting between 24th August 1939 and 2nd July 1940 was that by the detective inspector, and he suggested that this witness could have been mistaken. The evidence of the German employment book, Slade urged, was that it was the intention of the Germans to employ Joyce for broadcasting, and the jury was not concerned with intentions.

As the judge acknowledged in his summing-up, the defence counsel had put his finger on a weak point in the prosecution's evidence, but the judge observed that the jury were entitled to take into account the evidence of the employment book and Joyce's own statement. Had Slade put Joyce in the witness box to deny having made that particular broadcast, Joyce could have been examined by the prosecution and asked about other broadcasts which he would not have denied. The two defence counsel had done, as Joyce recognized, everything they could, but after the judge's ruling on Joyce's legal position as the holder of a British passport, all that the jury now had to consider was whether the prisoner had assisted the King's enemies.

The judge directed the jury to return a verdict of not guilty on counts 1 and 2. Concerning his ruling on count 3, he said: 'I may be wrong; if I am I can be corrected'—a reference to the Appeal which was certain to be made.

The jury took only twenty-three minutes to arrive at their verdict. They found the prisoner not guilty on the first and second counts and guilty on the third.

Joyce stood stiffly to attention as the clerk of the court said: 'Prisoner at the bar, you stand convicted of high treason. Have you anything to say why the court should not give you judgment according to law?'

For a moment it seemed as though Joyce was about to speak, but he said nothing. He looked fixedly at the judge, now wearing the black cap, determined to stare him out.

The judge read the formal sentence: 'William Joyce, the sentence of the court upon you is, that you be taken from this place to a lawful prison and thence to a place of execution, and that you be there hanged by the neck until you be dead; and that your body be afterwards buried within the precincts of the prison in which you shall have been confined before your execution. And may the Lord have mercy on your soul.'

The chaplain said: 'Amen.'

Joyce bowed deeply, turned sharply and walked as smartly from the dock as he had entered it.

For his wife he set down, in the course of three letters written during the following fortnight, his feelings on being sentenced to death.

Mentioning press reports, about which he had learned from visitors and his wife's letters (he was not allowed newspapers), he wrote: 'It is true that I snapped noiselessly when the Clerk of Arraigns asked me if I had anything to say as to why sentence of Death should not be passed upon me: but that was only because he did not allow me an instant in which to make my intended formal reply to the effect that I was leaving the case in the hands of my counsel. I thought of interrupting the judge and demanding my undoubted right to make a reply: but my contempt for the judgment, combined with a somewhat belated respect for my own dignity, kept me silent.'

He was also discussing press and radio reports when he commented: 'I *might* have created a sensation, not by wilting but by some aggressive demonstration. But through my head on that day there kept running Marvell's lines: "He nothing common did or mean, Upon that memorable scene", and so the conclusion was quite decorous. Some papers, I am told, have stated that my expression was contemptuous: it probably was. But whether I bore myself becomingly is, after all, for others to judge: but I do believe that I did nothing to shame me in the eyes of my lady: and I am therefore content.'

His customary flippancy of language did not desert him even when he reflected on the judge's black cap. 'It gave me no small degree of satisfaction in the dock at the Old Bailey to see that His Lordship, complete with vampire chapeau, after once meeting my eyes, read his precious sentence into his desk. Ah! My dear, those were a proud few minutes in my life: and I think that you and I owe it as a duty to our many friends to set the highest example of stoic dignity: it is wonderful, indeed, that you, as the woman of my choice, should in this respect, be entirely at one with me.'

By the way he dwelt on his silence, and by later assertions that if tried at Nuremberg he would have addressed the court, Joyce seems to have regretted missing his last opportunity of speaking in public. What would he have said? Would he have raised the real and important issue of what a man should do in an ideological war if he finds himself on the side to which he is opposed? To do that he would have had to condone the position of Germans who had fought against Hitler. The issue of conscience had already been raised by Casement from the dock in a statement of a dignity which would have been foreign to Joyce's manner. 'When this statute was passed, in 1351, what was the state of men's minds on the question of a far higher allegiance—that of man to God and His Kingdom?' Casement asked. 'The law of that day did not permit a man to forsake his church or deny his God save with his life. The "heretic" then had the same doom as the "traitor". Today a man may forswear God and His heavenly Kingdom without fear or penalty, all earlier statutes having gone the way of Nero's Edicts against the Christians, but that Constitutional phantom, "The King", can still dig up from the dungeons and torture chambers of the Dark Ages a law that takes a man's life and limb for an exercise of conscience.'

Joyce, more likely, would have tried to add simply another anti-Semitic statement to those he had already made. His silence maintained the dignity he had preserved throughout his trial.

He had to bear the public's full fury at the Haw-Haw team's broadcasts which, now that the trial was over, the newspapers could express.

On the day following the sentence *The Times* commented in its second leader: 'Having been indicted in this country he was—and remains—entitled to the full benefits of the impartial processes of the law courts; but the verdict of the jury on the facts will be received with public approval.' The fact that Joyce was technically an alien, the comment proceeded, 'cannot in any degree lessen in retrospect the detestation and contempt which his conduct provoked.'

The *Daily Telegraph* wrote under the heading 'Strict Justice'. 'The case will make legal history as establishing for the first time certain conditions under which an alien may be condemned for treason, and it may possibly suggest to Parliament the desirability of legislation further qualifying the duties and liabilities of persons holding British passports. . . . Why he should have elected to requite in this detestable manner the country whose hospitality he had enjoyed for many years and whose protection he sought at the passport office is still something of a mystery, and is not much elucidated by the diffuse statement which he made after his arrest and which was read out in court. His conduct, as described in evidence, betrays not a single redeeming feature, and no verdict has ever been more in accordance with the evidence.'

'Never was punishment so richly deserved,' wrote the *Daily Mail*. 'Of all the creatures who served the Hitler gang none was so detested as this man, who sought to weaken the resolution of the British people in face of a mortal enemy. . . . It matters not to the ordinary man whether he could claim American or German citizenship. He betrayed the country that sheltered him.'

As a convicted prisoner he was moved from Brixton Prison to Wormwood Scrubs. According to the *Daily Mail* of September 21st, people living round the prison could see the light in the condemned cell. 'And these people get a great kick from looking. It is a great satisfaction to them to know that under this light sits William Joyce, the man whose voice they so often heard jeering and taunting over the German radio during the dark days of the London blitz.'

Chapter 30

'THEY HAVE ME TAPED'

Lodged in Wormwood Scrubs while the condemned cell at Wandsworth was being prepared, Joyce immediately resumed his correspondence. He tried to allay his wife's anxiety about his condition and to prepare her for the dismissal of his Appeal. 'Now, sweetheart, no worry! My only concern in the whole melodrama was the fear that you would be shocked and disappointed. Hope you were not. To epitomize the trial as dispassionately and charitably as possible, I would say that My Lord was not the man to bear the onus of settling legal issues of that magnitude: and for similar reasons, I am quite prepared to see the case go to the Lords who, I think, would not hesitate to set their judgment against any extraneous factor: and you will have noticed that Tucker took for granted reference to Higher Courts. Do not think that I am unworthily trying to cheer you up: if you had heard Slade's splendid argument in Court, you would be most hopeful. Distinguished lawyers present were laying 50 to 1 on an acquittal: but I was not.'

On September 27th he reported to her that he had signed his Appeal forms 'and thus performed the single act whereby, at this stage, I can help myself. I have also, however, been making to Head several suggestions on law—quite academic, of course, nothing to do with evidence—which, merely as an O. Bailey observer, I think to be pertinent.'

He assured her that he was still treated with kindness and was not without conversation. 'When I arrived here I was asked "Religion" and I truthfully replied that I did not belong to any Xtian denomination: but the C. of E. padre here, who has seen me several times, is a splendid man. I had thought of asking for the R.C. padre, but was told that to get him, I should have to notify formally "change of religion": and the chaplain I have met is such a decent fellow that I should be sorry to lose him. . . . We have interesting discussions on philosophy, philology, etc., and thus, I am not getting rusty. I would stress the fact that I am being well-treated and that my existence here is anything but tedious. There is never a dull moment! I miss the newspapers, of course, but can reconcile myself to this absence.'

One item of news indicated that he was now accorded the privileges of a condemned prisoner. On September 24th he wrote: 'I hate to tell you, but must: today I had some really good beer! 'twas my first 'cohol since May. Of course, it cannot be equated to wine or Schnapps: but, none the less, I enjoyed it. The chaplain continues to spend much time with me: and, really, I am fortunate to have the company of such a good, intelligent man: he is a captain, M.B.E., B.Sc., and no pedant.'

His views on German concentration camps were written in reply to a letter from his wife who had seen reports of a trial of concentration camp staff. 'Now that I have no newspapers, I cannot follow the trial, but was not in any case particularly desirous of so doing. Assuming, however, that at least a proportion of the allegations is well-founded, the main factors which I would consider are these. 1) It was certainly not the best type of man who sought employment as a KZ official, but probably the worst. . . . 2) Most of the inmates were probably of an order not only unknown, but unconceived in the British imagination. 3) We have seen the Germans really trying to organize in a struggle "Um sein oder nicht sein", or, as Churchill would say: "for dear life". But if we picture them organizing merely to keep a hostile political or criminal substratum alive, in the teeth of the enemy's bombing campaign we can, perhaps, by induction, reach the idea of something which, if not exactly Belsen, would nevertheless not be Brixton. I see that, according to one allegation, altho' there was no food in Belsen, there was plenty in a Wehrmacht institution nearby. Now the British seem to think that this food could simply have been moved to Belsen. *We* know that before this end could have been attained, several plots against the Führer and perhaps even a minor civil war would have been needed: but that is something which the Briton would have no hesitation in disbelieving. Nor will the defendants ever be able to explain why the food could not have been moved. Then imagine a [word missing] dealing with incipient typhus, aided by a doctor who wrote articles for the "12 Uhr Blatt" on the thesis that smoking makes women sterile or that it is fatal to drink water after eating fruit. My dear, Germany is always a Wonderland but sometimes—alas! a Blunderland.'

Although Joyce was here writing for an audience of only one (if we except the prison and military authorities who would have had to read and pass the letter), the explanation is a good example of the agitator's technique which he used with such facility. First, as he did, for example, when commenting on the flight of Rudolf Hess to Britain, he gives a shrug, implying that he is expressing his views on a minor matter only because some exaggerated fuss has been made about it. Then he makes the point that concentration camp staffs were of poor quality; obviously this was largely true but he assumes falsely (he may not have known otherwise) that they were all volunteers. He then uses the known fact that concentration camps contained a proportion of criminals to slip in a supposition that most of the inmates were 'probably' criminals of an unspeakable type and hardly, in an emergency, worth saving. From here he moves to a criticism of German bureaucracy and alleged inability to improvise, traits which are not in themselves venal and about which he is rather patronizing, and then he gives the impression that he could have foretold that, given certain circumstances, this situation would arise. He follows this with an extravagant jeer at German thesis writers, and rounds the passage off with a phrase that would raise a laugh at an excited public meeting. The subject has not been faced at all but he is apparently satisfied that he has disposed of it. He was not, of course, unique in explaining away uncomfortable facts. British Left-wingers have been no less adept in excusing the more disagreeable aspects of Russian policy.

On September 28th he was moved from Wormwood Scrubs to Wandsworth Prison, where he became Number 3229. He reported the change to his wife: 'As you will notice from the superscription, I am no longer Wormwood Will—but Wandsworth William. The alliterative effect is preserved. I was moved here this morning at short notice. Why I cannot tell you, but it is not my business to inquire into such questions. The main facts are that here too I have comfortable quarters, am well fed, and am being very well treated. Indeed, I prefer these lodgings to Wormwood, good as it was, but am extremely sorry to have lost my excellent chaplain, Captain Mervyn-Davies, whose society I should greatly enjoy in any circumstances. However, in comparison with my separation from you, dear—I need hardly complete the sentence. But it was an experience to meet such a splendid parson. To my delighted relief I have been enabled to continue my correspondence with you forthwith and I have no doubt that your letters "en route" will reach me here in due course. Moreover, altho' nothing can be taken for granted, I expect to be staying here "for the duration". Last evening I read the grounds of Appeal, which seemed to me to be very well formulated; there will, I think, be much heavy argument: and, whilst having quite an open mind as to the Court of Appeal, we must not be surprised or perturbed if the case ultimately goes to the Lords. Not that I have any doubts but that the law is on my side: but, as I have hinted before, there *may* be a judicial tendency to throw the responsibility onto the highest quarters: and then again, there may not. I am truly sorry that you should be subjected, on my account, to this added strain of long waiting.'

On October 2nd he wrote to Macnab. First he inquired about his friend's health, as he customarily did, before discussing his own situation. He permitted himself in this letter a stronger note of resignation than when writing, at that stage, to his wife.

'I know that if it is God's will that I should survive my present danger, I shall be far better for my experiences since last May. Indeed, without them, I should be regrettably poor. I have the feeling, founded or unfounded, that every minute of experience in these months has had its value and that nothing has been left to chance. If, then, God wills that I should indeed survive, then so I shall. If He does not, then it would be hideous presumption on my part to wish to stay.

'I am satisfied beyond doubt that nothing can long separate Margaret and myself; and the friendship, the loyalty, the support, the aid which I have received give me to think that if I were to vanish, it would not be without some trace, however humble.

'But, my dear John, I see no grounds at present for a valedictory attitude. On the contrary, I have confidence in our case, and am sure that, in law, I am right. If the law be properly interpreted, the O.B. conviction will be quashed. In the dock, I had to think, with an inward laugh, of Dryden's lines:

'They Have Me Taped'

*"What weight of ancient witness can prevail
When private judgement holds the public scale?"*

'But it would be ungenerous to assume that "All the judges of King George VI" are going to meet in a pub and settle the case in advance! What a charming image!

'But, in sober reality, it might well have been expected that such an issue would have to be defined on a plane higher than that of the municipal posse of London City; more I need hardly say.'

He wrote to his wife on the same day, beginning with a reference to his studies in psychology under Professor Aveling. 'First I should explain that Aveling's school of psychology is known as Personalism. The real founder on the philosophical side was Aveling, tho' the psychological method and name were due to Stern of Hamburg. Then Spearman, Burt, and, to some extent, McDougall were drawn into it. The Personalists make the greatest use of Gestalt (Köhler and Koffka), but insist that a Gestalt is no democracy, and stress that, on the higher levels, the super-relation of the Gestalt relations has *personal* attributes—or, to be clearer, that in such activities as willing and knowing there is something transcendental (i.e. "hinausreichend"). Thus the human organism is not merely the sum of its parts, but an entity over and above them. Naturally, the thesis cannot be properly expressed in a short letter: but the root of the matter can be found in Lange's discovery that the rate of human metabolism can be altered by acts of willing. The doctrine relates not only to the omnipotence and omniscience of God, but, also, in a different context, to personal survival, which I shall discuss another time. Vulgarly expressed, Personalism throws the main emphasis onto the psycho-physical nature of the personality. It seems to me the only tenable theory of psychology: but I don't think that the Freudians and Behaviourists have ever understood it.'

The 'gallant little Doctor' in the next passage was, of course, Goebbels, who committed suicide with all his family. 'In my opinion, the greatest hero of the Götterdämmerung was the gallant little Doctor. And if recreants who want to exculpate themselves by denouncing me link my name with his, they pay me a greater compliment than they imagine, poor things! . . . I wonder what our surviving friends in Germany think: at least those fools who thought I was a spy ought now to be convinced

273

that there was one case in which they were wrong. Or are they relying on the Higher Courts to prove their thesis right?'

To old Miss Scrimgeour he was the William Joyce she had always known, combative and confident. 'One day, I hope, it will be recognized that, whether or not I aided the King's enemies (who made them?) I was no enemy to Britain: but I had no intention of offering any apology or excuse for my conduct, which history will surely vindicate. . . . As the days go by, it will become more and more obvious that the policy which I defended was the right one. The discovery may come too late: but, at any rate, events seem to be moving rapidly already. I feel no satisfaction but cannot quite restrain my contempt for those who would hang me for treason. Had I robbed the public and impeded the war-effort by profiteering on munitions, a peerage would now be within my reach if I were willing to buy it.'

Joyce liked the Wandsworth padre. 'He is a very *good* man,' he wrote to his wife, 'and, again to my surprise, I find that we have much in common.' He continued to reassure her about his welfare. 'Have no concern about my personal comfort. It would be impossible for me to write too highly of my conditions, which are better than in any prison yet. The food here is excellent. I have plenty of books, some German, and I have been amusing myself by reading Shakespeare in Dutch. We have much chess: and in the evenings I generally have a mug of beer and a good smoke as I discuss philosophy, psychology, telepathy and kindred topics with the chaplain, a very charming man, who gives me the pleasure of his company very often. . . . Once again I must pay my tribute to the excellence of the care which I receive in this prison: it is a great pity that the general public does not know what splendid people the prison officials are. Really, prison is the only place apart from my Jesuit school where I have seen any attempt to apply psychology consistently and sensibly.'

The suggestions which Joyce had made to the lawyers had, his brother Quentin told him, interested them, and he wrote to his wife: 'By the way, Q tells me that the lawyers have found my suggestions interesting and useful. I dared to hope that they might. Possibly I have more time than they in which to consider some of the legal issues involved in my case. At any rate, the old jelly-bag [brain] has been feebly vibrating, I hope to some purpose.'

He was gratified to learn, during a visit from his brother and Macnab, that a Catholic priest was to say mass for him, but he made it plain in a letter to his wife that he was firm in his intention not to return to the Catholic Church. 'They seem to be in contact with a number of Catholic priests, one of whom publicly announced that a Mass which he was celebrating was being said on my behalf. I must say that, although I am a stray son, the "Alma Mater" is rallying in a manner which surprises me, *and* without any regard to my doctrinal beliefs. It is better so. I should not like it to be thought that I was rushing back into the pen merely because the wolves were becoming a trifle too intimate. On the other hand, I do believe in the efficacy of honest, earnest prayer.'

In the same letter he continued his thoughts on human personality and survival after death. 'I think really that there is available no positive proof, altho' Oliver Lodge and William Browne, to mention only two scientists, have adduced evidence which could not be lightly rejected. I omit reference to the overwhelming consensus of religious teaching, which would be "begging the question". In my opinion, it is sufficient to reinforce faith and, what is more potent, intuition, by showing that the possibility exists. On physical death, there clearly occurs a change in the psycho-physical Gestalt. The body obviously becomes lifeless matter. Millions—trillions of its cells live on for some time: but the super-relation of the component electro-magnetic energy systems has gone. Whither? To assume that it has not changed into something else, but merely vanished without trace is not only bold, but very rash. Indeed, such a complete disintegration of an energy system might perhaps produce effects not unlike those of the Atomic Bomb. To me, it seems easier to suppose that, in some modified form, the Gestalt is perpetuated. What the reactions of the new pattern $\times$ to the old body $+$ might be, it is hard to say. Probably such activities as depended on the physical medium—e.g., memory—would be very weak. We do not know. Lodge and Browne thought otherwise: may be they were right.' He went on to 'stress the possibility that the body is a medium for the "Personality" but not an *indispensable* factor of its existence. Not for a moment do I suggest that the "Personality" would be the same with or without body: I only contend that, according to the canons of rigid science, it is impossible to prove that physical death is the end of personal existence.

When, of course, some of us enter the non-scientific territory of metapsychosis-transmigration—"Road to Yesterday" and such like, we know from intuitive experience that, in some way, we have lived before.'

Now he showed that curious trait, which appeared so often in his writing, of ending a quiet and reasonable exposition with a sudden eruption into clowning and violence. The letter went on: 'Personalism (I am glad my sketchy explanation was of use) certainly puts Ye Olde Tin Hat on Behaviourism. As to the stinking Freud, I never could discover that he had any system: what does not exist cannot be confuted: the only antidote to him is mental and physical cleanliness—Karbolik! He never advanced an argument—only a series of phallic myths. Just a quack whose merchandise had an enormous appeal to the repressed . . . but a very dangerous quack.'

In this letter he also made a brief reference to his trial. 'And now I learn for the first time that it was Mr. Justice 'Ucker who tried the Wolkoff case, and that, in the course of the proceedings, he described me as a "traitor". But we are not making this significant fact a ground of appeal. So to do would be psychologically wrong: and, in any case, success would only mean a retrial at the O.B., whereas we prefer to get to grips with the Law. It is, none the less, reassuring to find that old 'Ucker did not approach the trial in a state of what might be called, for lack of a better phrase, "mental virginity".'

On October 27th the Governor informed him that his Appeal was to be heard on October 30th and that he was to be in court. Joyce wrote to his wife repeating his view that he would lose the Appeal and that the case would go to the Lords.

The Court of Criminal Appeal consisted of the Lord Chief Justice (Lord Caldecote), Mr. Justice Humphreys and Mr. Justice Lynskey.

Joyce returned from the first day's hearing, and, starting a letter at the first opportunity, apologized to his wife for writing under pressure as 'my daily routine is deranged by these jaunts to town'. The court, he wrote, 'unless I am totally mistaken, will dismiss the Appeal as soon as it can. Of course, I may be and should like to be wrong: but my eyes and ears have deceived me if the Bench has not made up its mind already.' The proceedings on the following day, during which he listened admiringly to

Slade, confirmed his view that the Appeal would fail, but he thought that the judges needed to find a formula. 'What probably worries the present Bench is the difficulty of framing a judgment which the Lords would not upset.' On the final day, knowing that he would now have to wait some days before the judges made their decision known, he thought that 'the Bench is against us on everything but jurisdiction' and that if they were to allow the Appeal it would be on this point. Then, he warned his wife, the Treachery Act would be invoked.

On November 2nd he summed up the grounds of the Appeal and his assessment of how the case stood. '1. We claim there is no jurisdiction in this country to try an alien for acts committed outside the King's Dominions. Bench uncertain (?). 2. We claim that the allegiance which an alien may owe to the Crown terminates the instant he leaves British territory. Law *for* us, but Bench most truculent (!). 3. We claim that there is no evidence to show that the passport was ever used to claim protection or, indeed, at all. 4. We claim that nobody can acquire the legal *right* to protection by misrepresenting his nationality. On points 3 and 4, their Lords seem to have decided, offhand, against us, altho' in the Lords, these arguments should be of major importance. All the legal authorities are on our side: but, as I have said, our opponents are relying on the resolution passed by "all the judges of Queen Anne" when they went into a corrupt huddle with the Attorney-General of the day, just before some alien who had left his wife and effects in England was found guilty of treason for adhering to the King's enemies abroad. We say that, in passing their resolution when not actually sitting in judgement on a particular case, they were usurping the function of Parliament, which alone has the right to alter the law.'

Although he must have been under great strain during the Appeal, he denied that he was affected by it. 'Let me tell you, darling, that so far from being tired by strain, I am now stronger than ever, troubled only by the plight of my dear Mother-Sheep! . . . And, after all, I am getting used to being a professional eater of "Henkermahlzeiten" [condemned men's last meals].' Despite this assurance, the letter was rather less detached than were some of his earlier surveys of his case. It contained remarks about the Lord Chief Justice and the Attorney-General of a kind which had characterized his Haw-Haw broadcasts.

'They Have Me Taped'

In a letter to Miss Scrimgeour on November 4th he expressed himself even more forcibly. 'If, by any chance, this Bench pronounces judgement for me, my troubles will not be by any means at an end. There will, in my opinion, be further litigation: and you may be sure that the Jewish interests in this country will make every conceivable effort to "liquidate" me.'

He wrote copiously to his wife, sometimes indulging in jokes. 'First I must disappoint you by admitting that there are no arrows on my suit, altho' much tape in lieu of buttons. They have me taped!' And sometimes he reflected on the recent past. 'How many people realize that the propaganda war was decided before ever hostilities began? For foreign affairs, the Reich had but one eye, and that eye was Ribbontripe. . . . And what a strange irony that the German people should have become the pioneers of National Socialism. Much as I love the "Heimat", I think it was a pity. For the poor dears were about as amenable to the real N.-S. spirit as would have been the Chinese—with the difference that the Germans loved their comforts more.' Repeatedly he thanked Margaret for her support. 'No words can express my gratitude to you for your bearing—not that I am at all surprised by it: but still, we all know that there is a difference between having courage and being able to apply it at the right time.'

On November 7th he learned that his Appeal had been dismissed. 'Well, I have just returned from the C.C.A., the result being as we expected. That I feel for you, dear, with all my heart, goes without saying: for I suppose that even though intellectually you did faithfully accept my advice that we must be prepared for an adverse decision, you probably did cherish the hope that, perhaps by some chance, my pessimism might be unjustified. Nor would I blame you, dear. So many people who heard and read the proceedings expected that the Appeal would be allowed: but neither my legal advisers nor I were deceived for a moment.' He thought the judgment contained 'a number of holes'. His argument, which he developed at some length, was that he had not travelled to Germany with the intention of returning; that he had not used his passport to claim protection but had wound up his affairs in Britain and placed himself under the protection of the German Reich; and that an alien outside the jurisdiction of the Crown could not be held answerable for acts committed by him under another jurisdiction. These were, he observed, points more suited for the House of Lords than for the Court of Appeal.

Shortly after his Appeal was dismissed the Governor told him that the date of his execution had been fixed for November 23rd. Joyce's first reaction was that the Attorney-General must have refused the fiat for the case to go to the Lords, but he was assured that the fixing of the execution date was automatic and that the date would be cancelled if circumstances required it.

Chapter 31

BUSINESS AS USUAL

'I do not mind admitting that I am glad to be able to write that the "Fiat" has been granted,' wrote Joyce to his wife on November 17th. 'Hotcross signed it yesterday. . . . So we really can say: "Business as usual".' Then he apologized for failing 'to live up to that code of complete frankness on which I have always so emphatically insisted' because he had not told her of the Governor's notification of the execution date. He had hesitated because he was expecting the fiat to be granted and she might have had to wait several days after being told the date before she learned that there was to be an Appeal to the Lords.

He was upset by a week's gap in the receipt of letters from his wife, and he was writing to her expressing concern when the Governor entered. 'But—whoops . . . much excitement—the Governor has just been in to tell me that you are in England— and that you are coming to visit me—Ol! Ol! What joy!'

The visit took place the same day. When Margaret had left he was stricken with remorse that he had talked too much. 'Words cannot describe my joy at seeing my darling friend—my beloved wife again. It would be useless, at the present stage at least, to attempt to express my feelings. There was so much I wanted to say, there was so much I wanted to hear from you, dear: and I do hope you will forgive me for "taking the floor" as I did.'

She was lodged in Holloway Prison. He hastened to reassure her about British prisons—'unless I am much mistaken, you should be more comfortable in Holloway than in Brussels. Once you become familiar with the routine, you will probably find that all goes well. I know nothing about women's prisons: but if they compare with the men's, you will share my admiration for the Service.' He had 'thought it proper to ask the Governor to convey to the Home Office my gratitude for its action in enabling me to see you. He agreed to do so.'

On November 23rd, the day originally fixed for his execution, he remarked in a letter that 'there is a certain humour in being alive after the time appointed for one's execution, ni'? Of course, it is not a novel experience, but is still a trifle uncommon. Let us, however, stop "talking shop".'

British subjects who had assisted the Germans were now being tried, but on lesser charges than treason. Some, he was astonished to learn, had even been granted bail. He remarked on the disparity between the treatment of these and of himself, an alien. 'Had I been a British soldier, joined the Waffen SS and broadcast for the RRG [the German radio corporation], my life would not be at stake. However, I'm not grumbling at that. I should scorn to purchase indulgence with such currency: but from what we might call the Euclidean point of view—"Things which are equal to the same thing are equal to one another", the disparity is at least noteworthy.'

John Amery, however, was charged with high treason, and the news that he had pleaded guilty to all eight counts, and been sentenced to death in a trial lasting only eight minutes, came to Joyce as a 'bombshell'. He declined to comment at once except to say that 'whatever we may have said about the fellow in the past, he seems to have acted with courage on this occasion.' Having reflected on the news, he observed: 'In the face of such a tragedy, we cannot be petty,' and he added: 'I suppose he will petition the Home Secretary and I wish him luck. Certainly, on the showing of the *prima facie* case, his conduct was no more treasonable than that of the court-martial defendants who have not been condemned to death.'

Joyce retracted nothing of his original statement, and he advised his wife not to amend hers. 'Morally, if not legally, it is highly pertinent that we firmly believed ourselves to be serving the best ultimate interests of the British people—a fact which was appreciated and respected by the best of our German chiefs. And it was always our thesis that German and British interests were, in the final analysis, not only compatible but mutually complementary.'

He made frequent reference to the support he was receiving both from friends and from people unknown to him. Macnab and Quentin were raising a fund to defray the costs of preparing copies of the record of the trial for the Lords Appeal and other expenses above those covered by the grant of legal aid to Joyce. A couple 'living on the Plimsoll line in Kensington, seeking to preserve the bygone decencies', had sent a cheque for £50, and a small Suffolk farmer contributed ten shillings 'for a very brave gentleman'. 'I feel overwhelmed by the generosity of my friends and these tributes from complete strangers,' Joyce wrote. 'I am *really* embarrassed.'

The details of the setting of the Appeal hearing he learned from an *Evening News* shown to him by his brother through the glass of the prison visiting box. He communicated what he remembered of it to his wife. 'I am supposed to sit in the Diplomatic Box, which as I am an alien, is the right place for me: and, it is said, I am to eat in the Queen's Robing Room! It does not say that the cellars will be unlocked. Then, continues the screed, it is ironical that Joyce, who raved against Parliamentary institutions, should have had to resort to this Appeal! But really—I thought it was the House of Commons that I attacked! . . . Only about a dozen people unconnected with the Appeal will be present, amongst them a special friend (John?) and my brother. Q showed me his Pass—a grandiose document with Lion and Unicorn, to be returned to the Lord Chamberlain's Office. He is to enter through the Norman Porch! So with you in Warwick Castle [Holloway Prison] and me in the Queen's Robing Room, it will be a historic week.'

The hearing of the Appeal in the House of Lords began on December 10th, the members of the court being Lord Jowitt (the Lord Chancellor), and Lords Macmillan, Wright, Porter and Simonds.

Mr. Slade argued that local allegiance was due from an alien only while he was within the King's dominions, that the protection which drew allegiance meant the protection afforded by the laws of this country, that it meant the right to protection and not that which might be enjoyed by a person who had obtained a passport by fraud, that the courts had no right to try an alien for a crime committed abroad, that there was no evidence that Joyce's passport afforded him any protection or that he had ever sought such protection. To this last contention Joyce's counsel added that if there was any evidence that Joyce had availed himself of the protection of his passport, or intended to, that was a matter for the jury and the judge had failed to direct them on it.

In the diplomatic box Joyce could not be seen by the press representatives, but several lords appeared in the chamber and Members of Parliament, not allowed to enter, clustered round the entrance. They stared at Joyce and he at them. Never an habitually smart dresser himself, he was struck by the shabbiness of the M.P.s, whose standard, he thought, 'resembles my average'. He was well looked after, except in the matter of drinks. 'The luncheon was very good: but—alas!—alcohol was "verboten".'

The scene on the second day was much the same, except that the M.P.s were called away for a division. He identified several of the onlookers, including a Jewish peer whom he described as 'a horrid piece of work'. 'Luncheon—rabbit and tart—was again very good.'

He warned his wife that he did not care for the way things were going. 'I think that a majority of their Lorps have the desire to find against me if suitable formulas can be found, but that the C.C.A. formulas are not considered good enough! The possibility of success is not precluded by anything that has happened today: and perhaps I am unduly sceptical: but, of course, twice bitten three times shy.'

On the third day, when the Court sat only in the morning, the Attorney-General finished his case. Joyce was now, in his correspondence, retreating from his position that the Law Lords were essentially different from the judges in the lower courts. Two, he believed, were hostile, and he thought the final decision would depend on the Lord Chancellor, whom he found himself unable to assess. On this day, however, for no reason which he could trace, Joyce experienced that sudden hopefulness which comes to people in a desperate situation. Having warned his wife to be 'prepared for either event', he added: 'I have a strong feeling that, whatever happens, there is going to be some good event, and that you and I will soon be together again. This is no counsel of optimism: and it is a view which seems at variance with the facts: but still, it must have a cause, if not a reason.'

He did not dwell on this mood, but almost immediately reverted to his sober realism, after mentioning Macnab's optimism. 'I should think, on the whole, that I am, in the matter of the Lords, more pessimistic than the average. Were it not for the composition of the Court, I should be more confident of success: but 'tis useless to chew the rag in this fashion: tho' not Liberals, we must "wait and see". You will be glad to know, however, that after surveying my Parliamentary surroundings, I am more satisfied than ever that I did right. The sight of the Lords and Commons today reminds me of a parade of G-Sender rejects. [G-Sender is an abbreviation for Geheim-Sender—secret transmitter. He was comparing the members of the two houses with the British prisoners of war who were rejected for work on Concordia's clandestine stations.] Of course, appearances are often misleading: but it is weird to look upon victors whose air is what might be expected of the vanquished. Duncan Sandys took his usual place today and old Lascelles was there for a while. Yesterday, a beer baron crowded up to the edge of my box and all but examined me with a magnifying glass. Was he afraid of losing a potential customer, I wonder? Hotcross today was good, but, of course, much helped by W. and M. [Lords Wright and Macmillan.] I almost wrote M. and B.'

Of the final day he reported: 'Today was the most "dramatic" of the hearing. Slade did *very* well this morning in replying to Hotcross. He finished at 1 p.m., and then the L/C said: "The House will adjourn till 3 o'clock." So then I thought: "Ha! 'Tis signed, sealed, and now only has to be delivered." Our retiring room overlooks the Thames and Lambeth Bridge. It was a wonderful afternoon—crimson sun on the water, mist, leafless trees, a picture which stirred my heart with memories of the Heimat. We played nap till nearly three, and then arose from our becoroneted chairs. I thought of the Wilhelmplatz and, looking at the arches, felt that perhaps I had a little more Norman blood than some of the peers whom I have seen during the last few days. Through a laneway of Commoner ghouls, we marched into the House, where a number of noble ghouls had assembled in joyous anticipation of the Kill. I bowed to the L/C who gravely acknowledged and who then called on Counsel to stand. He curtly said: "We require a little more time to consider this case and shall give judgment on Tuesday morning at 10.30." The *continuere omnes ora intentique tenebant* attitude of the assembly dissolved into a ripple of surprise, and the ghouls picked themselves up and slunk out of the House like schoolboys "creeping unwillingly to school". Of course, I don't class all present as ghouls: I was

referring not to those who attended *durchaus* [throughout] but
to the "last-nighters", those, who in the days when peers hunted
foxes, instead of less reputable animals, would have said that
they meant to be "in at the kill".'

The following day he looked back on his experience, reflecting
that the two principal documents in his case—his passport and
the resolution of all the judges of Queen Anne—were missing.
(The original manuscript of the judges' resolution was, in Slade's
words, 'apparently non-existent'. Counsel quoted it from Foster's
Crown Law.) Special Branch police had, he had learnt, been
waiting in some strength outside the Chamber when the court
reassembled at three o'clock. 'To say that the Special Branch feet
are flat is a slander. They are not. They are inquiring, patient,
almost wistful. They see what the mere eyes miss. And I am sure
that they often initiate action instead of just obeying orders.'

Prison rules which forbid a condemned prisoner the use of a
knife were applied while he was in the House of Lords. 'Perhaps
the funniest experience in the Lords was that I had to eat my
lunch with spoon and fork—knives being forbidden by regulations. The saddest was that the House offered to open its cellars,
and regulations again inflicted upon me that "most unkindest cut
of all". Still, the offer was something. And my custodians most
chivalrously confined themselves to H_2O.' His smart appearance,
commented on in a broadcast report, was due to the prison staff.
'My custodians have seen to it that I should appear "well-
groomed"! Clothes beautifully pressed, etc.'

His wife had told him of her treatment in Holloway. 'I am so
glad that you are in such good hands', he wrote, 'and personally
very grateful to those who are caring for you. Now you probably
understand why I have written so enthusiastically of the English
prison system and character.'

The Governor informed him, on the day before the judges
were due to state their decision, that he was not to attend the
House of Lords to hear the judgment. Joyce found this 'a
peculiar piece of news' and he speculated on its meaning. 'I
suppose that the police do not want me to be there. In the event
of an unfavourable decision, the trip would be useless; and should
the result be otherwise,[1] well, it might, in their opinion, be easier

[1] The Cabinet had discussed a proposal that if Joyce were acquitted he
should be interned in Germany while his position was considered.

to spirit me away from here than from the H. of Lr. I draw no inference, of one kind or another, from the news. I was allowed to attend the C.C.A. judgment, and it did me no good: so let us hope for better luck this time. I should actually have liked to hear the judgment, whatever it may be: but still, I am not too disappointed. Frankly, I think that with all these crime waves, the police want to save themselves trouble. But I know that Q and John will be surprised to discover that I am missing. So will the Press! But the disappointment of the journalists will not cause me any lack of sleep.'

Chapter 32

CLOSE OF PLAY

When the judges assembled in the House of Lords at 10.30 on the morning of December 18th there was an unusually large gathering of peers to hear Haw-Haw's fate. The proceedings were brief. The Lord Chancellor and Lords Macmillan, Wright and Simmonds announced their agreement that the Appeal should be dismissed. Their reasons, the Lord Chancellor said, would be given at a later date. Lord Porter would have allowed the Appeal because, although he agreed that Joyce's renewal of his passport on 24th August 1939 was evidence from which the jury might have inferred that he retained it to the day, 18th September 1939, when he was proved to have first adhered to the King's enemies, and might therefore have inferred that he continued to owe allegiance to the Crown up to that date, 'the question whether he did so retain it was never left to the jury, but they were directed as a matter of law that his duty of allegiance was extended to the later date.'

The subject of this distinguished gathering, sitting in his buttonless grey prison suit in Wandsworth Prison, was feeling the suspense. He had expected to hear the result very soon after it was delivered, but the morning dragged on, the midday meal was served, and still the Governor did not come. Early in the afternoon he began his daily letter to his wife.

'It is now approximately 14.00 hrs. and I have been expecting ever since 11.00 to hear the Lords' decision. I suppose that I shall be told nothing till a copy of the judgement arrives, presumably by courier. Well, I do not mind admitting that I am curious to know the result. If it is unfavourable, I can meet it in the right spirit: if it is good, so much the better! But I shall be glad when the suspense is over. I am wondering if I shall be allowed to have any visitors this afternoon: for perhaps they might not be permitted to see me till the Great Document has arrived. I suppose that by this time, the news has been imparted to you, dear: and I sincerely hope that it did not prove too much for you. . . .'

At this point the two prison officers in attendance sprang to their feet as they heard the familiar sounds heralding the Governor's arrival. Joyce stood up.

A few minutes later he calmly resumed his letter-writing. 'Well—the Governor has just told me that my Appeal has been dismissed. So that is that! At long last, the suspense is over, and except for your dear sake, I am pleased. For it was, in itself, an indignity to sue and plead before my enemies, to observe their pretence at "fair play", not serving to mask their determination to liquidate me. Now, quite naturally, at this harsh moment, all my thoughts go out to you, dear: and I curse myself for not having allowed you to go your way in 1941. I needed you absolutely: that is my excuse, not my justification. But now—alas!—there is nothing I have to offer you, except my non-material being for all time. . . . Please do not take what I write amiss. I know your feelings—as I know my very own: but death would be the simplest matter in the world if it did not leave you in such a predicament. Today's tidings have in no way weakened my faith in God: and if it be His Will that I should go, I trust that He will provide for you whilst you are here and later join us together in every way.'

That afternoon he was allowed visitors as usual. When Quentin and Macnab called, Joyce's main concern was for his wife, and he asked them to do their utmost for her. His message to his friends was: 'Ihr habt doch gesiegt.' (You won, nevertheless.)

Later his solicitor, Head, called, and gave him a full account of the morning's proceedings. Joyce was furious that the judges who had rejected his Appeal had postponed giving their reasons; he had already calculated the probable date of his execution and he guessed that he would never learn the grounds for the dismissal. He thought it curious that Lord Porter was able to state at once why he would have allowed the Appeal, and supposed that the other judges needed time to present their case plausibly. He made a will, leaving the little he had to his wife, and named Quentin as his executor.

His visitors departed, he concluded his letter to his wife. 'And now, about what happened on the hill overlooking Flensburg Bay just before my capture, it is curious that John [Macnab] should have said that everything in my life since August '39 has fitted into a pattern. That I know and that I still feel. Why it should be decreed to end thus, it is beyond my wisdom to fathom: but, of course, the limits to our knowledge are strait. I can only say honestly that I do believe that this, your terrible ordeal, is destined: but that is no consolation to you. May God give you the strength to bear this cross. That is a prayer which, I feel, will not be denied. . . . My own beloved—do, I beg, forgive me for having spoilt your life. You know that it was fated to happen. That is my excuse. But now, at least, I can show, I hope, that you gave yourself to a man—and not to a craven weakling.'

The London evening papers agreed with the majority verdict, but they published, to Joyce's satisfaction when he learned of it, a statement by Macnab that Joyce had no apologies to make. Next morning *The Times* gave a bare account of the proceedings without comment. The *Manchester Guardian* devoted an editorial to the case, explaining the issue which had arisen from Joyce's possession of a British passport, and commenting: 'One can say that this document, which he ought never to have possessed, has been—unless the Law Lords judge differently—the deciding factor in Joyce's sentence. One could wish that he had been condemned on something more solid than a falsehood, even if it was one of his own making. At the same time, leaving the sphere of law for that of common opinion, here was a man who chose to leave us at the outbreak of war to do all he could from enemy soil to sap our resolution when it was being tested most. It would have seemed extraordinary to the majority here, and still more so to our allies on the Continent, if this man had escaped. Yet one may still wonder whether the death sentence is appropriate. Joyce—and Amery, for the cases have much in common—held strongly certain opinions which were once shared by many who walk untouched among us. He carried his opinions, which he never hid, to their logical conclusions. We detest those opinions and may feel that he ought to be restrained from ever again advancing them, which would be a worse penalty for a man like him than death. Even in these days of violence killing men is not the way to root out false opinions.'

For the first time in his life Joyce found himself thinking well of the *Manchester Guardian*. The article held, he wrote, 'quite correctly, that death would be a lesser punishment for me than to make it impossible, by life imprisonment, for me to advocate them [his views] in the future.' He continued: 'Nobody would expect the *Guardian* to go the whole hog: but what I like is the rather chivalrous recognition of the fact that I have stood by my beliefs. For this alone, I must retract the many unkind remarks that I have made about the paper. After all, it is something that one great daily should implicitly admit my sincerity: not that I HAVE to care much—for human opinions contrasted with conscience: but still I do appreciate chivalry when I see it.'

The trial of Walter Purdy, whom Joyce had recruited for Concordia, was now proceeding. Purdy claimed that he had made two attempts to assassinate Joyce. Although writing only two days after his Appeal had been dismissed, Joyce made a typical joke. 'This is an occasion for Henker [Hangman] Pierpoint (also from Lancashire, I think) to write a letter to the *Daily Herald*, defending honest trade union principles. . . . Anyhow, if his assassination statement were true, it would give him common ground with the gang which has determined my liquidation.'

After his wife's visit on December 20th he wrote: 'Well, darling, you were superb—as I knew you would be. How proud of you I am, I cannot very well say. But you gave me a feeling of exaltation which will be with me to the end.' He began to worry that the authorities might have decided that this was to be his last sight of her. The following morning he handed to the Governor a petition asking that she should be allowed to remain in London until after his execution. Before the petition had left the prison, however, the Governor received a message that Joyce's request had already been granted. 'The Governor has just informed me', Joyce wrote, 'that it is not proposed to send you back to Brussels until after close of play.'[1]

The Governor also brought another piece of information, which Joyce conveyed to his wife in these terms: 'And the dear, sweet, nice Sheriffs, bless their little stars, have fixed January 3rd as the Festive Day. That is about the time I had calculated. I shall survive my *Annus Mirabilis*: and that was one of my sekret ambitions! But it does not seem as if I should learn the

[1] After the execution Margaret Joyce was interned in Germany, while her status was debated. She died in London in 1972, having regained her British nationality.

reasons for their Lorps. decision. Curiouser and curiouser—but, to me, not very disturbing. For the reasons are bound to be irrelevant. Sorry to have to announce the date, beloved, but I thought it best to tell you as soon as I could.'

The flippant style of this letter was adopted to spare his wife's feelings. He was likewise concerned not to hurt Macnab, who would have liked him to re-enter the Catholic Church. Perceiving that a remark of his had been misunderstood, Joyce wrote to Macnab on December 23rd: 'Few know better than you, my dear John, how I can hedge if I want: but this is no occasion for hedging. It is with real personal sorrow, then, that I must admit my inability to resume communion with the great and holy Church of which you are a member. I deliberately use the phrase "resume communion",—because the word "reconciliation" might posit an attitude on my part which does not exist. It might, for example, suggest that I had been engaged in some sort of latent quarrel with the Church which is not the case. What I meant to convey on the 18th, when by verbal clumsiness I conveyed a wrong impression, was that I had become convinced of the Divinity of Christ, in which, for many years, I did not believe. I am sorry, John, that I aroused false hopes. From the private Communion which I receive here I derive great comfort; but I receive it without being bound by dogma.

'Your analysis of Formal Assent as the first step towards Ardent Faith is clear and sound. But I can only believe what I believe: and having only about 10 days in which to live, I would not give my formal assent to anything in which I did not fully believe. My differences with your doctrines are too numerous to examine individually: but I think, dear friend, that the crux of our failure to agree lies in the fact that you regard membership of the Roman Catholic Church as being necessary to salvation, whilst I do not. That nobody can be saved outside of the Church is a proposition which I would always reject: and if it be untrue, there is no need for me to resume Communion with the Church. Did I feel spiritually lonely, did I doubt the essential verities, had I no personal and intuitive experience of God, then indeed, my case would be parlous: but I feel quite otherwise. To me, God is the supreme reality: and He cannot be made more real by human interpretations of His nature. You will know that I am neither obdurate nor curt when I say that my faith is complete and that I do not experience the need for any spiritual strengthening. All honour to you and to your holy, majestic, age-old church: but the fact of my standing on the threshold of death cannot make the least difference to my attitude to religion. Nor would you expect it to do so. I beg you to believe that I, too, have devoted much thought to spiritual problems and that if I am satisfied to be as I am, it is not because I have been too immersed in the welter of mundane controversy to be capable of taking my bearings from time to time. On the other hand, I thank you, John, sincerely, for making an effort which you held to be imperative and which, as my dearest friend, you felt bound to make. I only regret that I cannot respond as you would naturally wish.'

On Christmas Eve he wrote to his wife, avoiding the word Christmas, as he had years before when corresponding with Macnab. 'My beloved wife, dearest cousin—*Dominus tecum et cum spirituo tuo*! I had said that I would conspire to pretend that the Weihnachten were not with us: and, in the main, I will try to adhere to that resolution—hard though such adherence may be. And this morning, I must admit, I have had poignant feelings, for reasons which I need not mention. I must, however, thank you with all my heart and soul for the inexpressible happiness that you have given me at Christtide after Christtide. It may seem churlish: but now I do so wish that we had spent all our Weihnachten in Germany alone. Our Weihnachten were wonderful: but I could have made them better. . . . When you have recovered from the sickening shock, you will begin to rejoice at all that was good and beautiful in our mortal time together here. . . . I tactfully hinted to John this afternoon that I would not take out a false passport to travel to Heaven, tho' to him I did not put it so frivolously.' He then, after mentioning the deaths of Spearman ('A great thinker. No wonder he jumped out of a window!') and Aveling, discussed survival after death. '. . . being of their school, and having also studied Gestalt, I have not the slightest doubt about the survival of electro-magnetic systems probably so organized as to be impervious to such things as blast. In fact, the conformation of the Alster did not alter for more than a few seconds when those bombs dropped into it. It is probably a question of another medium. I think, moreover, that, when functioning as scientists, men like Oliver Lodge and William Browne would not allow themselves to be deceived by false evidence. And, then, intuition, *déjà vu*, "historic conscious-ness", the testimony of the ages, apart from Christian teaching, all build up an inductive case which calls for acceptance. And when one considers the omnipotent, omniscient Super-Relation of all Relations as endowed with superior will and consciousness, the only tenable theory, unless we argue that *intelligence* and *will increase* as the organism gets lower, it surely seems to be no strain on the imagination to hold the doctrine of survival.'

Unexpectedly, his wife now arrived. He finished the letter afterwards.

'Cheers! More cheers! Darling, you have been to see me! How grand—am Heiligen Abend! The visit was a happy surprise. For-give me if I left much unsaid, but I did not realize the "Sitzung" [meeting] would be limited to half an hour. I suppose now that better facilities are, thank God, available, the visits may be shorter. Anyhow, it was just splendid of the authorities to let you come on Holy Eve, when, I should imagine, the prison staff problem is most knotty. . . . My darling Meb, I don't think that I am equipped to write a directory of life for you or anybody else: but I will certainly set down some ideas, which I will let you have in a few days' time.'

On Christmas Day, reflecting on predestination, he wrote to his wife that through all the months of hoping he had had a feel-ing 'of predestined inevitability—as though each trial was im-material and I must go on without deviation to some appointed end—an end which would mean anything but annihilation. I did not want to give way to this feeling. Otherwise, I should have had to say with Longfellow:[1] "The sunset of life lends me mysti-cal Lore And coming events cast their shadows before". But, strong as the reasons for hope were, I wondered why every stick and stone of Flensburg, Wassersleben and Kupfermühle were so preternaturally clear to me—not only after my arrest, as might be intelligible, but before it as well. Noyes[2] conveys a faint suggestion of the experience in his "Look thy last on all things lovely every hour". But to follow that maxim unwittingly when death seems removed is new. You know that I rarely have eidetic

---

[1] He was thinking of Thomas Campbell's lines in 'Lociel's Warning':

> *'Tis the sunset of life gives me mystical lore*
> *And coming events cast their shadows before.*

[2] His memory failed him here, too. The author was Walter de la Mare.

imagery: but the pictures of that stretch of Baltic shore have been startlingly vivid.' He went on to write of places in Galway, the scenes of his boyhood, to which he had hoped to take his wife, and where, looking out towards the Aran Islands, he had first 'gained that glimpse, mysteriously, of the Infinite, which is now so near to me', and he commented 'What a saga my life would make! And now, in these last days, I am nearest to my boyhood again. . . . I know my faults and am sorry that I have made others, you in particular, suffer for them. At least, I am painfully aware of my own former smallness in personal dealings. "Nymph, in thy orisons, Be all my sins remembered". It is of transcendental consolation to me to see that you are adjusting yourself to our temporary and partial separation, which is the bitterest test that could be laid upon us.'

Margaret was brought to see him during the evening of Boxing Day. By the following morning he was fearing that he had been flippant and had perhaps hurt her by his 'gallows humour'. 'I ask to be forgiven for my somewhat crude "Galgenhumor"; but it is not quite unintentional. Too much of it would probably be as intolerable as you found my jesting amidst a hail of bombs. But often, by looking at the unpleasant squarely and laughing at it, we deprive it of certain not very desirable characteristics with which tradition has invested it. The death which a man suffers by one sudden means or another is usually infinitely more comfortable for him than his birth was for his mother. And if that death be, as in my case, honourable, why then, there is no need to think of it with awe: but I shall try to refrain from 6-wheeled jokes in bad taste—which is another matter.'

Then he set himself to write 'a directory of life' for which his wife had asked him, although, as he protested again, he thought himself ill-equipped to do so.

'At a venture, from all the guides, directions, formulas and dispensations, the 10 Commandments and the Koran excepted, I would say I recommend the very hackneyed passage in *Hamlet*, Act I, Scene 3, when Polonius begins: "There, my blessing with thee!/And these few precepts in thy memory/Look thou character". When I re-read it, I think it very cunning indeed. In comparison, these few crude suggestions that I uncouthly and most incompletely set down are not likely to draw much admiration. But here goes.

'1. Life has a purpose or it is nonsense. For many it is nonsense: but for you it is purposive: and your first duty is to serve, as best you can, the Omnipotent Omniscient Deity—the Super-Relation of all Relations.

'2. Self-deception is the commonest and the most dastardly sin of all.

'3. All humans are fallible and the best imperfect. Find another's coefficients of deception, self-deception, and unreliability: estimate your own: and then a practicable basis of social relationship with the other exists.

'4. Coition is a commonplace, not an achievement: a personable woman has no need to be proud of inducing a male creature to lie with her, after lying to her. In sex, the aristocracy of selection is sound, the democracy of promiscuity rotten.

'5. Do not seek to win the admiration of others. Deserve it: and if they fail to give it, mark them down as fools.

'6. A personable, and—*a fortiori*—a beautiful woman must realize that the greatest pleasure she can give to many of her female acquaintances is to fall into misfortune. If they can contribute to her distress, so much the better. When they see her broken, they will flatter themselves on their wisdom and expect thanks if they stop to pick up the pieces.

'7. Punctuality is a form of troth-keeping. To be late is to be either rude or inefficient. We live in Time: let time then be honoured as a prime function of consciousness.

'8. Good works are the sole justification for existence.

'9. Most people judge by the superficial. Reserve is, then, a good protective mechanism. Never be as familiar as you could be if you wanted.

'10. Never give offence unintentionally.

'11. Attainment breeds not satisfaction but desire.

'12. Have little respect for learning. What one man can acquire of it is too little to be admired. Character is, in any case, more important than intellect.

'13. The border between moderation and excess is the locus of the greatest sensuous pleasure.

'14. A lie is more honest than equivocation.

'15. Know your motives surely before you act. Once a motive is firmly adopted, it may twist reason and sentiment to suit itself. Indeed, the motive is the most primitive and powerful factor in the human being. It cannot be *too* closely examined before it takes root. Later may be too late.

'16. Keep worthy company—else you waste yourself. Leave the shallow to the shallow and the niddering to the niddering. Keep thine eye on the Sword in the Roof-Tree.'

He added a footnote. 'Perhaps, darling, I shall think of a few more "maxims" within the next few days: but if this issue has made you "satt" you need not regard them as having been written. I cannot pretend, in these present circumstances, to lay down a code of living: I can only give you some of the thoughts which, cheap and ordinary as they may be, come into my mind. Darling, it is wonderful that you are allowed to visit me daily, and I cannot say how deeply grateful I am to the prison authorities. The haunting dread of my days in Brixton was that I should never see you again. The cables had been badly torn, and letters alone could not quite mend them. But now, bitter as our temporary separation will be, bitter beyond all words—it will be possible for us to salute each other as if I were going to the Reichssportfeld [Concordia's office] and we were to meet for lunch in the Club to begin a Free Day that would last for ever.'

On the same day he thanked Macnab for his 'splendid letter of Xmas Feast'.

'You were quite right', he wrote, 'to examine my [religious] position. Indeed, you could not, in conscience, neglect so to do: for it might have been that some discrepancy did exist between my attitude and my inward inclination. In that case, were there anybody in the world to whom I should have responded, it would have been to you. But since no such lack of perfect correlation exists, you can, having done your duty, feel that I shall go in gratitude for an act of the truest friendship which, though it has not produced the result which you would most have wished (i.e. to die fortified by the sacraments of the Catholic Church), has nevertheless contributed to the peace of my last days and has further strengthened me by evoking some salutary meditation. Moreover, I feel the benefit of the many prayers which my Catholic friends and well-wishers have been saying for me: and I know that, apart from all formal and doctrinal differences, the good God answers, in His own way, the supplications of those who in humility and sincerity call upon Him. . . .

'I do recognize what a special responsibility, in the circumstances, rests upon me: but I feel quite able to bear it. You are quite right in saying that I have had an accession of spiritual power beyond, yes, far beyond, my natural resources. Since it has not been acquired through any merit of my own, it must have come from prayer. Nobody knows better than I what gross faults I have: but to be able to recognize them for what they are is to have learnt something. . . . Though this life of mine is to cease, I am far from thinking that my work will be ended with its cessation. Into the mysteries Beyond, I may not yet peer: but the intuition is strong within me that there is a definite Divine purpose in this pattern of events, and this purpose does not confine itself to the bestowal of greater happiness on unworthy me. Hardly that! . . . Tell all my friends with whom you communicate that I am happy and that, so long as they can keep me in their hearts, they need not mourn my loss: for I shall be more with them than I could be when I was in Germany.

'That we can together write at the end of this chapter *Ad maiorem Dei gloriam* is a decent ending.

'And, for the rest,

"*Anon he rose[1] and twitched his mantle blue;*
Tomorrow to fresh woods and pastures new." '

One of his visitors was an old acquaintance, the Reverend Father Marshall-Keene, who asked him if, although not a Catholic, he would wish a blessing. Joyce knelt, made the sign of the Cross, and received the blessing with great devoutness. He also gladly agreed that mass should be arranged so as to support him at the last moment.

On the next day, in his letter to his wife, he brooded on the warnings he thought he had experienced of his destiny and he apologized for his outbursts on their first night at Eardley Crescent and during their last days at Kupfermühle. He recalled, too, their visit to Ryde just after the Munich crisis, when he talked excitedly the whole night. 'It was, in those hours, as if some shadowy foreknowledge were given to me, causing a convulsion of what you rightly call "burning of energy". I knew that all I had and more was required of me: and I suppose I was in an emotional state arising out of "knowledge" hidden from the

---

[1] A misquotation—*At last he rose* . . .

conscious mind. My fear on each occasion was that you would be physically torn from me: but far stronger was the feeling that we should never be spiritually separated. And the hill—our hill—over Flensburg harbour provides the final clue. Remember—in our finite way, we know the elements of electro-magnetics: but, obviously, there is much we cannot know.'

To Miss Scrimgeour, in a letter written on December 28th, he was the self-confident man with a mission, the enemy of the Jews.

'It is always good to hear from you, and particularly good to feel that you are constantly with me in the spirit during these last days of a life which I feel not to have been in vain.

'I trust, like you, that the works of my hand will flourish by my death; and I know that there are many who will keep my memory alive. The prayers which you and others have been saying for me have been and are a great source of strength to me: and I can tell you that I am completely at peace in my mind, fully resigned to God's will, and proud of having stood by my ideals to the last. I would certainly not change places either with my liquidators, or with those who have recanted. It is precisely for my ideals that I am to be killed. It is the force of ideals that the Hebrew masters of this country fear; almost everything else can be purchased by their money: and, as with the Third Reich, what they cannot buy, they seek to destroy: but I do entertain the hope that, before the very last second, the British public will awaken and save themselves. They have not much time now.'

He returned to his premonitions in a letter to his wife on December 30th.

'And do you mind my strange Kaiserdamm premonition which sounded so silly when I uttered it? You recall how, at certain periods, I felt that I was being prepared for some great task. Well, again now, I have the same feeling, only stronger than ever—not at this time a mere feeling, but a certainty. Let that cheer you, my darling, and let it strengthen you for the last but not the hardest part of this—the ordeal that I was fated to thrust upon you.'

In the same letter he referred to his self-possession at their meetings, and his determination to maintain this at her final visit. 'When, in days to come, dear, you look back upon these sessions, try not to think of me as stiff, callous, academically precise, and generally unemotional. It has been necessary and will be particularly necessary at our last interview to "keep the ears straight". It is not only a matter of honour and dignity, but it is logical in view of what we so firmly believe. But I admit to you now, dear girl, that there have been times when the sheer emotion of my love for you has nearly overcome all else. Not now, but later, I want you to reflect that beneath the crust was a yearning tenderness. It was perhaps a long time before you found out that I could be soft-hearted: and, in that respect, you know me far better than anybody else ever has done.'

On the last day of 1945 his wife arrived in the morning. 'Your visit this morning was a pleasant surprise,' he wrote, 'and the authorities were very considerate to arrange the time so as to avoid the worst fog conditions. D'ye know, I quite forgot that it was New Year's Eve, and accordingly failed to say "Prost"— which, as you know, simply means "may it prosper!" Maybe the omission of a conventional salutation was just as well. I did say "Hals- und Beinbruch",[1] however! But honestly, darling heart, I do wish and pray that 1946, badly as it begins, will do something to restore your happiness. We have worked very hard to lay a new foundation, and I believe that we have succeeded—though, of course, it is only a foundation.'

He made a reference to Hitler. 'At so late an hour as this, I will spare comments which would be doubly ungenerous because the Old Man did not know what he was doing: but never in myth, story or history have I read such a tragedy.'

Support for him, he had been told, had been expressed in an unexpected quarter. 'I hear that the Anarchist newspaper *Freedom* has come out with an article very strongly in my favour. Well, well, you never know, my dear, as I used to say platitudinously. But you don't really—at least I don't. Sorry I've lapsed into nonsense: but Anarchist support *has* almost disturbed my complacency.'

He concluded his 1945 correspondence with the note that 'it is the end of my fateful year, and I take a sort of mischievous pride in having seen it through. For that reason, I felt quite pleased when the Lords deferred their judgment: and, by the way, that reminds me that the L/C has still not given his "reasons". *Quel ramp!*'

---

[1] A good luck greeting, grim in Joyce's circumstances: 'May you break your neck and your leg.'

Close of Play

On New Year's Day he wrote the last letter which his wife would receive from him while he was alive.

'And may the New Year see you advance from strength to strength. I think it will. Every day you look more beautiful. And that is a great credit to you under the recent strain. But, as I have always said, breeding tells: and tell it will in the future, however rotten the world may be at present. As I move nearer to the Edge of Beyond, my confidence in the final victory increases. How it will be achieved, I know not: but I never felt less inclined to pessimism, tho' Europe and this country will probably have to suffer terribly before the vindication of our ideals. . . . But the most wonderful news you tell me is that you feel a spiritual peace. So do I, dear. And, as you very rightly observe, such a gift of grace could only come from without. Neither of us could have generated it from within. Nothing can buy it and no purely human source can confer it. I am glad that my remarks on electro-magnetism were of some use. Of course, I know that you would have liked much more: but it is hard in little letters of this kind to expound a scientific doctrine which, nearly, comprehends the whole universe. But be sure that the testimony of the Ages counts for more than the pompous burblings of the half-boiled atheists from Voltaire to the late Victorian scientists, the inadequacy of whose materialistic theories now stands revealed for all to see. . . . Forgive the shortness of this letter: but tomorrow I shall write more. Tonight I want to compose my thoughts finally: the atmosphere of peace is strong upon me: and I know that all is ready for this transition.'

Visitors besides his wife found that they left Joyce with a sense of peace. Macnab expressed the feeling in these words. 'In his last days, although in perfectly good health, his actual body seemed spiritualized, and without what you would call pallor, his flesh seemed to have a quasi-transparent quality. Being with him gave a sense of inward peace, like being in a quiet church.'

Some of his former teachers at Birkbeck College, who remembered their likeable, hardworking, although strange student, sent a message to the Governor of Wandsworth Prison on the eve of the execution. They did not condone Joyce's later activities, they wrote, but they recalled him as they had known him and if it were within the rules they would like the Governor to tell him that they wished him well.

While awaiting those who were to visit him for the last time,
Joyce sent a note to Miss Scrimgeour 'just to wish you all the best
until we meet again' and thanking her for her and her brother's
friendship which 'did so much to contribute to my happiness
during my stay on earth.'

He then began a letter to his wife, whom he was not expecting
until the afternoon.

'I never asked you if you wanted to receive posthumous letters:
the question was too delicate, even for me: but I assumed your
wish. For I think you are sufficiently strong now to overcome the
grief of this blow, and that your faith will triumph over tears. For
my part, I want to write as long as I can and then mend the
snapped cable in an eternal way.'

Here he broke off, because his wife had arrived. They had both
anticipated that the visit would take place later in the day, and
they felt the time was too early for their parting. When she had
gone he continued his letter in a smaller, neater hand.

'Oh! My dear! Your visit. With no words can I express my
feelings about it: I want the "children" to be able to take leave of
me, of course, as they will this afternoon: but now I am anxious
to die. I want to die as soon as possible, because then I shall be
nearer to you. With the last glimpse of you, my earthly life really
finished. With you, dear, it is otherwise, because you are destined to stay for a time and will have me with you to help: I am
more confident than ever that we shall be together: but, after I
have seen the "children"—the lag-end will be of no use to me
except in one way—that I can still write some lines to you. Let me
tell you, though that, *spiritually*, an unearthly joy came upon
me in the last instants of the visit. And you will know exactly why.
You would not blame me for being impatient now to go Beyond.
Still, despite my impatience, I shall be glad to talk this evening to
my kind, good chaplain, who has done so much for me and who
will give me Communion tomorrow morning. There will be a
great chorus of prayer as I pass beyond.

'And now please do thank, on my behalf, your authorities, particularly the Deputy-Governor and your officer for the care they
have taken of you. I should like them to know how sincere my
gratitude is, even if they do not want it.'

In an emotional and eloquent passage he told her of his love
and the restraint he had had to exercise that morning to 'keep the

ears straight'. 'On the nature of life and death,' he continued, 'I advise you to read the Gospel of John repeatedly—with, of course, our insight. To me it has recently been a revelation. It has contributed much to my understanding. Try it. I need hardly say that I have no fear of dying: for there will be no "death".'

The letter, in two instalments, covered eight pages of prison writing paper. It was personal except for two brief and defiant references to his case. 'Well, I have done my best by my old chief,' he reflected in an allusion to Dr. Goebbels, and he remarked of his seven-month ordeal: 'As I look back on all that period, I see that I am the object of the most flagrant hoax in the history of "British Justice". Well, so be it. I am all the prouder!'

Joyce had seldom been able to resist writing a provocative and defiant last paragraph, even though to do so might spoil the effect of a different impression he had just created, and now he drafted the final postscript to his life. He had missed the chance of addressing the court from the Old Bailey dock, but he was going to achieve the equivalent of a speech from the gallows. With it he gained the satisfaction of having, so far as he was concerned, the last word. When members of his family visited him that afternoon he handed to Quentin his parting message for publication.

'In death, as in this life, I defy the Jews who caused this last war: and I defy the power of Darkness which they represent. I warn the British people against the aggressive Imperialism of the Sowjet Union.

'May Britain be great once again; and, in the hour of the greatest danger to the West, may the standard of the Hakenkreuz be raised from the dust, crowned with the historic words "Ihr habt doch gesiegt". I am proud to die for my ideals; and I am sorry for the sons of Britain who have died without knowing why.'

At dusk Joyce looked through the tiny window at the dark branches of the tree which was all he could see of the outside world. He was calm. His stormy marriage was ending in the closest understanding with his remarkably courageous wife. In the last terrible months he had achieved a triumphant adjustment to his circumstances, being self-controlled, courteous and appreciative. He, and his wife, had won the liking and respect of prison and other officials. Now, concentrating his thoughts in trying to send her a telepathic message, he had the one worry that he did not know what would happen to her.

Close of Play

The morning of January 3rd was cold, but a crowd of about 300, some of whom had travelled a long way, collected outside the prison for the morbid thrill of reading the notice that the execution had been carried out.

After receiving Holy Communion and praying with the prison chaplain, Joyce composed his last letter to his wife. He entered his number, 3229, and his name, 'Joyce. W.', in the spaces at the top, and the date in the left-hand top corner. His writing was larger and more ragged than usual, but still controlled and legible. He addressed her by one of the many pet names he had for her and at the end he described himself as 'at the last roll-call', a Volkssturmmann, in which capacity he had hoped to die defending Berlin.

'Beloved Freja,—In this last hour of my earthly life, I confirm all my vows to you and promise never to leave you.

'I have just received Holy Communion and we prayed for you. This morning the spirit of St. Pauli is strong upon me. I will not write much more. The letter which you left yesterday was the most marvellous I have ever received. Just before my last escort comes, as it soon will, I shall send you a message of love by my tree.'

He then quoted the message he had given his brother for publication, and added: 'I gladly and proudly give the example which my old chief demands. "Wir haben doch gesiegt!"

'I salute you, Freja, as your lover for ever.

'Sieg Heil! Sieg Heil! Sieg Heil!

'Your Will.

'Beim letzten Appel, Volkssturmmann der Bataillon-Wilhelm-platz.'

Underneath he wrote, in brackets, the call—'Yp-Baa!'—of their private sheep game, the sign of infinity, the words 'with *all* my kisses', and the time, underlined—8.36.

With twenty-four minutes to go before his execution, he wrote to Macnab.

'Beloved John,—I have now so far moved away from all earthly things that the remaining minutes of my life seem like tenants who have not paid their rent.

'Thank you for the David and Jonathan reference. Thank you for your devotion to me, and above all for your prayers.

'More I will not write, save to say that when we meet again, we shall regret nothing that has happened now.

'God bless you and Catherine,

'With all my love, in Christ, William.'

While he was still writing, mass was already being said for him by the Very Reverend Father Johnson (who had known Joyce before the war as the friend of his parishioner, Macnab) at Our Lady of Dolours in Fulham Road, London, by the Reverend Father Marshall-Keene at the Catholic Church in Crowthorne, Berkshire, and at the chapel he had attended as a Catholic schoolboy in Galway. The start of the mass had been timed so that the supreme moment, the Consecration, should coincide with the moment of his death, being preceded by the memento for the living and immediately followed by the memento for the dead.

By midday Londoners were reading Joyce's message in the *Evening Standard*. The BBC broadcast it in its news bulletins—the last script for radio that Joyce wrote.

Chapter 33

THE POPULAR HAW-HAW SHOW

The 'Germany Calling' team and the Concordia English-speaking staff consisted of German nationals (who were not subject to British law), British subjects (who were), and one man whose position was a legal puzzle. All performed similar actions yet the penalties the non-Germans suffered ranged from death to a few months' imprisonment. It was the odd man who was made the victim of a highly legalistic approach, while fellow broadcasters were—doubtless for sensible and humane reasons—reprieved or tried on non-capital charges. The disparity between Joyce's death sentence and Baillie-Stewart's punishment of five years' imprisonment[1] gave rise to an ingenious and picturesque story, as fantastic as any of the Haw-Haw rumours, that the ex-officer was a British agent who was given credibility by a fake trial in 1933 and planted in Germany in 1937 to win the Nazis' confidence, which assignment he brilliantly carried out by becoming a radio speaker so that he could interpolate code messages into broadcasts to Britain. Joyce's execution, the explanation went, was the secret service's revenge on him for ousting their agent from his post.

A great deal of legal effort went into hanging Joyce. Lord Jowitt, the Lord Chancellor, described the issue raised by the case as 'a question of far-reaching importance' when, on 1st February 1946 he gave his and his three fellow judges' reasons (none of which would have been unfamiliar to Joyce) for rejecting the Appeal. Many hours of subtle and finely-balanced legal argument were required to establish that the accused was subject to British jurisdiction and guilty of high treason. One does not condone Joyce's actions by questioning whether his life ought to

[1] See Brian Inglis: *West Briton* (pp. 192–4)

305

have depended on what final words were spoken in this closely-reasoned debate. That the British public would have been angrily uncomprehending if Joyce had not been executed is possibly true but is irrelevant to the legal issue; we do not allow prisoners to be lynched by angry mobs.

A brave man with likeable qualities which he revealed only to those (including prison officers) who came to know him well, Joyce as a public speaker belonged to a not uncommon type of agitator who derives a sense of unassailable superiority from a belief that he has diagnosed the basic evil of society and knows the one remedy for it. His pride in his logical pursuit of his anti-Semitic objective was such that he uncomplainingly accepted the position he found himself in on arrest, did not deny his motives or try to shift blame on to anybody else, never protested that he had only a beginner's minor position in the German broadcasting organization when the Haw-Haw character came to be established, and was content to be regarded as the personification of the multi-voiced Reichsrundfunk English language service. Neither he nor anyone else questioned whether William Joyce and Lord Haw-Haw were identical.

When the German Propaganda Ministry began broadcasting in English it planned a department of news-readers, commentators, scriptwriters, continuity announcers and other staff whose spoken output was subject to the policy directives, editorial control and censorship which are particularly strict in totalitarian countries but exist in some degree in all radio organizations, whether during war or peace. Nobody conceived the audacious idea of pretending that the entire show was run by a mysterious aristocratic-sounding Englishman possessing an inside knowledge of the German High Command's intentions and a super-normal faculty for knowing the smallest details of what was happening in Britain at any particular moment. One can imagine that if some psychological warfare genius had put up the plan even Goebbels, who was not averse to excursions into fantasy, would have dismissed it as impracticable. Yet, without the Germans and their foreign staff doing anything towards it their programmes were given a personality—an invaluable asset in radio—and widely advertised as too funny to be missed. Lord Haw-Haw, who was not found amusing for long, acquired an existence quite apart from that of Baillie-Stewart, Joyce or any other of the

Reichsrundfunk speakers, becoming the focus of superstitious fears and a source to which the most extravagant rumours could be convincingly attributed. The actual scripts broadcast from Hamburg and Bremen were disagreeable enough to listeners in Britain, but what caused the greatest worry and fury (as the letters to the *Daily Mirror* clearly showed) were the unfounded rumours about the omniscient Haw-Haw's references to clocks, tramlines, lunch-hour pontoon schools, hospitals, munition works, naval and military troop movements, and bomb targets. Whatever Joyce was guilty of it was not this subtle form of sabotage—all he knew about the fabulous radio peer he learned from the British and American press—but with his unlucky gift for assuming the wrong label he wrapped himself in the robes of Lord Haw-Haw, thus ensuring that he would die while fellow broadcasters lived.

Let us get Joyce and Haw-Haw into proportion. Intelligent, well-educated, dedicated, hardworking, fluent and sharp-tongued, Joyce was well-equipped as a Fascist propagandist, but as a morale-shaker he was not in the class of Haw-Haw. The defence was put to some trouble to establish Joyce's nationality; Haw-Haw's need cause us none. Lord Haw-Haw was made in Britain.

BIBLIOGRAPHY

Edward MacLysaght: *Irish Families*. Hodges Figgis, Dublin.

Rev. Caesar Otway: *A Tour in Connaught* (1839). William Curry, Dublin.

Richard Bennett: *The Black and Tans*. Edward Hulton.

The Loadstone: Michaelmas Term 1925; Spring Term 1927. Birkbeck College.

The Review of English Studies, Vol. 4 (1928); Vol. 5 (1929). Sidgwick & Jackson.

Oswald Mosley: *The Greater Britain* (1932, revised 1934). British Union of Fascists.

A. K. Chesterton: *Oswald Mosley: Portrait of a Leader* (1936). Action Press.

W. A. Rudlin: *The Growth of Fascism in Great Britain* (1935). Allen & Unwin.

Frederic Mullally: *Fascism Inside England* (1946). Claude Morris.

Colin Cross: *The Fascists in Britain*. Barrie & Rockliff.

William Joyce: *National Socialism Now* (1937). National Socialist League.

William Joyce: *Twilight over England* (1940). Internationaler Verlag, Berlin.

Cecil Roberts: *And so to America*. Hodder & Stoughton.

Brett Rutledge: *The Death of Lord Haw Haw* (1940). Random House.

William Shirer: *Berlin Diary*. Hamish Hamilton.

Peter Fleming: *Invasion 1940* (1957). Rupert Hart-Davis.

Earl Jowitt: *Some were Spies*. Hodder & Stoughton.

Lindley Fraser: *Propaganda*. Oxford University Press.

Leonard Burt: *Commander Burt of Scotland Yard*. Heinemann.

Brian Inglis: *West Briton*. Faber & Faber.

Bibliography

J. W. Hall: *Trial of William Joyce* (Notable British Trials Series). William Hodge.

C. E. Bechhofer-Roberts: *The Trial of William Joyce* (The Old Bailey Trial Series). Jarrolds.

H. Montgomery Hyde: *Trial of Sir Roger Casement* (Notable British Trials Series). William Hodge.

Helmut K. J. Ridder: *Der Fall William Joyce* (1952). J. C. B. Mohr (Paul Siebeck), Tübingen.

Sir John Barry: *Treason, Passports and the Ideal of Fair Trial.* Address delivered at Cornell University, USA, in April 1955, reprinted in *Res Judicatae*, Journal of the Law Students' Society of Victoria, Australia, June 1956.

INDEX

Index

Index

Index

Index